# MASTERS OF DEATH

# MASTERS —OF— DEATH

## OLIVIE BLAKE

**TOR**

TOR PUB

MASTERS OF DEATH

Copyright © 2018 by Alexene Farol Follmuth

Interior illustrations by Little Chmura

Endpaper illustrations by Paula Toriacio (polarts)

A Tor Book
Published by Tom Doherty Associates / Tor Publishing Group
120 Broadway
New York, NY 10271

www.tor-forge.com

Tor® is a registered trademark of Macmillan Publishing Group, LLC.

The Library of Congress Cataloging-in-Publication Data is available
upon request.

ISBN 978-1-250-89246-1 (hardcover)
ISBN 978-1-250-90289-4 (signed edition)
ISBN 978-1-250-90978-7 (international, sold outside
the U.S., subject to rights availability)
ISBN 978-1-250-88488-6 (ebook)

Our books may be purchased in bulk for promotional, educational, or business use.
Please contact your local bookseller or the Macmillan Corporate and Premium
Sales Department at 1-800-221-7945, extension 5442, or by email at
MacmillanSpecialMarkets@macmillan.com.

First Tor Edition: 2023

Printed in the United States of America

0  9  8  7  6  5  4  3  2  1

*For Garrett, an alleged mortal without whom my existence would be bleak;*
*For my mother, who assured me that this book is not blasphemy;*
*And for you, for being here, when so many Otherworlds are calling.*

# CONTENTS

# MASTERS OF DEATH

# PRELUDE

Even after centuries of practice, it never grew less unsettling when it happened this way—sloppily. Gorily. Murder had never been his favorite method of disposal.

"What's this?" he asked impatiently, staring down at the bloodied mess on the floor.

"Oh good," remarked a figure concealed by shadows, a familiar glint of malice appearing from the darkness of the room. "You're here. Finally, I might add."

Worrying. Very worrying.

"This," he remarked in lieu of jumping to hysterical conclusions, "is quite an escalation. Are you responsible for this?"

"Depends on how you look at it, doesn't it?" replied the figure, with the faint suggestion of a shrug. "You could very well be *responsible,* couldn't you? If that's the verbiage you're going with."

Sequentially speaking that wasn't untrue, and he supposed he had played fast and loose with the literal.

Still—"I'm not the one holding the knife," he placidly observed.

"Fair enough." An arm sluiced through shadow as the figure tossed the blade, still gruesomely slick, onto the floor between them. "Though that doesn't really matter, does it? Now that we have you here, I mean."

That flickering, primeval sense of concern flared again, unhelpfully. Best to stick to the assets, like what was or wasn't true. "*Have* me? I assure you," he said, "you don't *have* me."

"Well, then," a second figure suggested, stepping pointedly into the light. "Try to escape."

No.

No, no, no.

This was all wrong. Very wrong.

"But *you're* not—?"

"But I am," the second figure confirmed, nodding once.

"But surely the two of you aren't—?"

"Oh, only by necessity, of course," the first figure said, another beam of motion splitting the shadows as the two figures exchanged a complicit nod. The effect of it was uncanny, as if shared between two separate planes of existence.

The prick of danger—of the past catching up with him at last—finally set in.

"Don't worry, you'll understand soon," the first figure assured him.

Two thoughts flashed epiphanically before him like a promise fulfilled: A face. A memory.

No, three thoughts. The dizzying lightness of being irrevocably fucked.

No, four thoughts. "Is this supposed to be a game?"

In unison—like a slithering ouroboros, darkness consuming light—the two figures laughed.

"Everything's a game if you play it right," the second figure said.

"But strictly speaking, this is no longer a game," said the first figure. "Now it's a war."

And then everything went dark.

# I

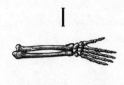

## TALES OF OLD

Hello, children. It's time for Death.

Oh, you didn't think I spoke? I do. I'm fantastically verbose, and transcendently literate, and quite frankly, I'm disappointed you would think otherwise. I've seen all the greats, you know, and learned from them—taken bits and pieces here and there—and everything that humanity has known, I have known, too. In fact, I'm responsible for most of history's adoration—nothing defines a career quite like an untimely visit from me. You'd think I'd be more widely beloved for my part in humanity's reverence, but again, you'd be mistaken. I'm rather an unpopular party guest.

Popularity aside, though, I have to confess that humanity's fixation with me is astonishing. Flattering, to be sure, but alarming, and relentless, and generally diabolical, and if it did not manifest so often in spectacular failure I would make more of an effort to combat it—but, as it is, people spend the duration of their time on earth trying to skirt me only to end up chasing me instead.

The funny thing is how simple it all actually is. Do you know what it really takes to make someone immortal? Rid them of fear. If they no longer fear pain, they no longer fear death, and before long they fear nothing, and in their minds they live eternal—but I'm told my philosophizing does little to ease the mind.

Not many who meet me are given the privilege to tell about it. There are some exceptions, of course, yourself included—though this is an anomaly. In general, as your kind would have it, there are two things a person can be: human (and thus, susceptible to the pitfalls of my profession), or deity (and thus, a thorn in my side).

This is, however, not entirely accurate, as there are actually *three* things a person can be, as far as I'm concerned.

There are those I can take (the mortals);

Those I *can't* take (the immortals);

And those who cheat (everyone else).

Let me explain.

The job is fairly straightforward. In essence, I'm like a bike messenger without a bicycle. There's a time and a place for pickup and delivery, but the route I take to get there is deliciously up to me. (I suppose I could employ a bicycle if I wanted, and I certainly have in the past, but let's not dip our toes into the swampy details of my variants of execution quite yet, shall we?)

First of all, it is important to grasp that there is such a thing as to be not dead, but not alive; an in-between. (Requisite terminology takes countless incarnations, all of which may vary as widely from culture to culture as do colors of eyes and hair and skin, but the term *un*-dead seems to serve as an acceptable catchall.) These are the cheaters, the ones with shoddy timing, who cling to life so ferociously that I—by some sliver of an initial flaw that widens like the birth of the universe itself to a gaping, logic-defying chasm of supernatural mutation—simply commune with them. I exist beside them, but I can neither aid nor destroy them.

In truth, I find they often destroy themselves; but that story, like many others, is not the story at hand.

Before you say anything, I should be certain we're both clear that this is not a vanity project. Are we in agreement? This is not my story. This is *a* story, and a worthy one, but it doesn't belong to me.

For one thing, you should know that this all starts with another story entirely, and one that people tell about me. It's stupid (and quite frankly libelous), but it's important—so here it is, with as little disdain as I can manage.

Once upon a time, there was a couple in poor health, cursed by poverty, who were fool enough to have a child. Now, knowing that neither husband nor wife had much time on earth left to spare—and rather than simply enjoy it—whatever enjoyment is to be taken from mortality, that is—I've never been totally clear on the details—the husband took the baby from his ailing wife's arms and began to travel the nearby path through the woods, searching for someone who might care for his child.

A boy, by the way. A total snot of one, too, but we'll get to that later.

After walking several miles, the man encountered an angel. He thought at first to ask her to care for his child, but upon remembering that she, as a messenger of God, condoned the poverty with which the poor man and his wife had been stricken, he ultimately declined.

Then he encountered a reaper, a foot soldier of Lucifer, and considered it again, but found himself discouraged by the knowledge that the devil might lead his son astray—

(—which he most certainly *would have*, by the way, and he'd have laughed doing it. Frankly, I could go on at length about God, too, but I won't, as it's quite rude to gossip.)

(Where was I?)

(Ah, yes.)

(Me.)

So then the man found me, or so the stories say. That's actually not at all what happened, and it also makes it sound like I have the sort of freedom with which to wander about *being* found, which I don't have and don't appreciate. In reality, the situation was this: The man was dying, so for obvious reasons and no paternal motivations, there I was, unexpectedly burdened with a baby. They say the man asked me to be the child's godfather; more accurately, he gargled up some incoherent nonsense (dehydration, it's murder on the vocal cords) and then, before I knew it, I was holding a baby, and when I went to take it back home (as any responsible courier would do), the mother had died, too.

Okay, again, I was there to take her, but let's not get caught up in semantics.

This is the story mortals tell about a man who was the godson of Death, who they say eventually learned my secrets and came to control me, and who still walks the earth today, eternally youthful, as he keeps Death close at his side, a golden lasso tied around my neck with which to prevent me, cunningly and valiantly, from taking ownership of his soul.

Which is *so* very rude, and I'm still deeply unhappy with Fox for not putting a stop to it ("never complain, never explain" he chants to me in the voice of someone I presume to be the queen). Fond as I am of him, he does chronically suffer from a touch of motherfucker—a general loucheness, or rakery, if you will—so I suppose I'll just have all of eternity to deal with it.

And anyway, this is my *point*, isn't it? That this isn't my story—not at all, really.

It's Fox's story. I just happen to be the one who raised him.

Why did I name him Fox? Well, I'm slightly out of touch with popular culture, but I've always liked a good fairy tale, and out of all the things he might have been (like dutiful or attentive, or polite or principled or even the slightest bit punctual), like an idiot I merely wanted him to be clever. Foxes are clever, after all, and he had the tiniest nose; and so he was Fox, and just as clever as I'd hoped, though not nearly as industrious as I ought to have requested. He's spent the last two hundred years or so doing . . . well, again, that's not my story, so I'll not go into detail, but suffice it to say Fox is . . .

Well, he's a mortal, put it that way. And not one I would recommend as a friend, or a counselor, or a lover, or basically anything of consequence unless you wish to rob a bank, or commit a heist.

I love him, but he's a right little shit, and unfortunately, this is the story of how he bested me.

The *real* story.

Unfortunately.

# II

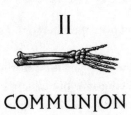

# COMMUNION

The sign outside the little rented space on Damen Street reads, simply, MEDIUM. The building is old, but the street is trustworthy and near the Blue Line stop, meaning that although this is an odd part of town, it's safe enough to travel freely, and finicky mothers mostly worry about imaginary dangers, like tattoos and the ghosts of old Ukrainians. The street is populated with taco stands and trendy doughnuts (yes, *doughnuts*) and thrift shops, all which contain old eighties fringe and leather boots; and then, scarcely noticeable amid the others, there is a building above one such shop, and if you took the time to look up at its peeling, black-framed windows, you would see the sign.

**MEDIUM.**

The label on the building's buzzer system is peeling slightly from use, but the intercom works well enough, and were you to buzz the unit marked D'MORA, you would likely hear his voice, oddly soothing, as it stretches through the air between you.

"Hello?" he'd say. "This is Fox."

"Hello," you'd reply, or perhaps "good afternoon," were you in a mood to be both friendly and cognizant of Time's relentless clutches; and then you'd pause, as many do.

"I'm looking to commune with the dead," you would eventually confess.

And you wouldn't see it, but upstairs, Fox D'Mora would smile a rather cutting smile, and then he would adjust the tarnished silver signet ring on his right pinky, coughing delicately to clear the mirth from his throat.

"Excellent," he'd say over the intercom, and then he'd promptly buzz you up.

Fox D'Mora isn't the only spiritual medium in Bucktown, and certainly not in all of Chicago, but he is the best one, largely because he is a master of disguise. You, apprehensive—as no doubt you are—might enter the unit from which he provides his services expecting to see dusty curtains, flickering tapered candles, perhaps even a glowing crystal ball; but Fox has none of those things, and thus, upon entering the mediumship of a strange man with a strange name and even stranger reputation, you might feel something you'd eventually come to realize is *relief.*

Because what Fox *does* have, surprisingly enough, is a state-of-the-art kitchen, and cold brew on tap, and being quite the genial host, he'd likely offer you a glass before leading you to an empty seat in his living room, whereupon he would gracefully place himself across from you, peering at you through unreadable hazel eyes. (Gray around the edges, amber in the center, a sunburst through a hazy wash of sepia. Reminiscent of pressed leaves in autumn, love letters rounding at the corners, other such things of the past.)

"Okay," Fox would begin. "So. Who is it?"

If you still had doubts before coming here, they would likely have begun to dissipate by now. For one thing, Fox is quite well-dressed, though not *so* well-dressed as to arouse suspicion. His hands, in particular—expressive, and in constant service to hospitality, pulling out chairs and fetching drinks, adjusting the blinds to your liking—are welcoming, the nails trimmed and clean. His watch is old and slightly battered, but it has a rather nice leather band and looks like it might have been worth something, once. You might consider it an heirloom.

Continuing your perusal of the man before you—*this* man, with such an odd name, and such an incongruous image, who can (so they say) so easily bridge worlds—you would notice that Fox himself, tall and lean but not *too* tall, nor *too* lean, sports a recently trimmed head of dark waves worn fashionably parted to one side, and that in general, he is given to smiling.

Fox is a man who smiles, and undoubtedly, this would relax you.

When he asks with whom you've come to speak, you might say your grandmother or your father, or perhaps you are even less fortunate and have lost someone very close to you too soon, like your husband or your child. Fox, hearing this, would gladly sympathize. He would sympathize with a softened look in his sepia-toned eyes, a gentle curving of his mouth, and you would feel that he understands you.

And he does, really. Fox has lost many people in his life and has felt the sting of it sharply enough; and anyway, perhaps it wouldn't matter to you in the moment that Fox D'Mora has not grown close to another human being in the last two hundred years or so, because whoever he is, and whomever his loyalty belongs to, he sympathizes so deeply, so humanly with your loss.

And more importantly, he is present, and he is here to help.

"Let me call him," Fox says—or her, or them, or whatever the identity may be of whomsoever it is that you have requested—and then his eyes close, and his hand slips ever so carefully to the silver signet ring adorning his right pinky finger.

"Now," he murmurs. "What would you like to say?"

The words, once buried in your soul, dance temptingly on your tongue.

You lean forward.

This is communion.

— Ω —

This particular instance of summoning belonged to an unremarkable day of an inauspicious week amid an unimpressive year, no thanks to the economy. The studio—or well-camouflaged den of iniquity, such as it was—was in its usual state of hastily obscured bachelordom (the take-out containers successfully masked with ambrosial Febreze, laundry sitting patiently for the third straight week below the bed, which was itself concealed cleverly behind two bookcases, one stolen, and a decorative tapestry currently unaccounted for by the Metropolitan Museum of Art) when Death materialized with an inaudible *pop* to stand beside Fox's covetable Eames chair, which was not stolen. (Having been purchased at an estate sale for which no other buyers had arrived, it was, however, a steal.)

Across from Fox's usual chair—his long legs crossed, right over left, in irritating service to Fox's sockless fetish and the loafers he had no doubt plundered from some unsuspecting professorial type—was the usual love seat; vintage, tufted upholstery, exquisitely selected, curated no doubt to set off the subtle undertones of green in Fox's eyes, because he was many things, vain occasionally among them, but never careless, never unintentional. Never dull.

And on the love seat, of course, was a woman. Very much to Fox's taste, which as far as Death could tell began and ended with a pulse. Well, that wasn't entirely true—the odds of an undead paramour given Fox's proclivities were low, but never zero. So perhaps instead it was the element of wrongdoing that was so unmissably Fox upon Death's arrival to the scene.

"Well," Death sighed, surveying the placement of his godson, the woman on his godson's love seat, and the hovering spirit lowing mournfully between them. One glance was all it took to determine the whole thing to be—what was the word? Dickery. "I see it's more of the same."

"Hush," Fox sighed under his breath, cracking one eye to smile cheekily, as one might do to a favorite spinster aunt. "Is he here, then?"

"Yes, yes," Death muttered, tutting softly as he inspected the supplicant on Fox's sofa (pretty, certainly, very pretty for those who enjoyed such things, and of a variety that Death, certainly not an enjoyer, could only describe as *fusion*, like the sushi burritos from the truck nearby on which Fox so profligately overspent) before sparing a glance at the spirit still hovering between them. The supplicant, the woman, was frozen temporarily, unable to see or sense Death aside from a stray shiver, perhaps a tingle of déjà vu like a half-remembered dream, or the fleeting sense of having forgotten to turn off the oven. Always best, in Death's opinion, to remain politely outside the realm of observation. "Let me guess. This is her husband?"

"Fiancé," Fox corrected in a blandly guiltless tone. "He passed just before they could be wed."

"How fucking convenient," Death remarked with a sensation he often experienced but had not felt prior to Fox's guardianship. It was a mix of things. Not anger, exactly. More like disappointment.

"Papa," Fox warned, arching a brow in expectation. "What did we say about the cursing?"

Death lifted a hand, dutifully snapping the rubber band he wore on his wrist for the reward (if such a thing could be said) of Fox's indulgent smirk. "I still don't see why this is necessary," Death growled under his breath. "What does it matter what I say when nobody aside from you can hear me?"

"You're the one who insisted on a New Year's resolution," Fox reminded him with—for fuck's sake—a twinkle in his eye.

"I meant for that to inconvenience you, not me," said Death gruffly. "And when is the resolution supposed to end? It's been at least a century."

"Nonsense, you've just lost track of time," said Fox, who was almost certainly lying despite the essence of beatitude that graced the fine features of his face. "And anyway, all that cursing is bad for your health. Didn't you read that mindfulness book I gave you?"

Death, being a creature of near omniscience and mostly unquestioned venerability, surmised that he was being mocked, which was itself the branch of a more perennial suspicion that he'd erred somewhat critically during the formative years of his recalcitrant ward. In lieu of pressing the issue, however, Death turned again to the woman who sat curled in around herself on the love seat, waiting patiently for Fox to have called upon her Bradley.

"Well," Death sighed, "what does she want to know?"

In the same moment that Death was experiencing the usual blow of agonized fondness (and its eternal counterpart where it came to Fox—forbearing remorse), Fox was having two simultaneous thoughts. One was what could best be described as a lurid sort of daydream. The other, critically, was the faint recollection that he had yet to pay the electric bill. So he cleared his throat, leaning forward to address the woman who'd sought his counsel.

"Eva," he murmured, and at the sound of her name, that afternoon's supplicant looked up, blinking herself free of his godfather's usual chill. Fox, who had a very keen sense of when a client's love language was touch, offered his hands, summoning a smile when she placed hers delicately in his. "What would you like to tell Brad?"

"Bradley," Death corrected from Fox's right shoulder, smothering a yawn.

"Bradley," Fox dutifully amended, kicking himself as a moment of doubt flickered across Eva's face. "Apologies. I know he dislikes the diminutive."

The present tense was very purposeful, though Fox, of course, could not see Bradley where he hovered in the room. (The comparison would not have helped Fox's already troubling ego.)

"He does," Eva whispered, and blinked, moisture suddenly drawing to the corners of her eyes. "You can see him?"

"I can," Fox confirmed with a nod, glancing into a random distant corner of the flat. He ignored the rude gesture from his godfather in his periphery, presumably intended to indicate his showmanship was incorrect. "Band," murmured Fox before adding to Eva, "What would you like to say to Bradley?"

She bit her lip, considering it. (Death gave his wrist a perfunctory *thwap*, then flicked the back of Fox's head.)

"Tell him," she began at a murmur, and then swallowed, overcome by emotion in much the way supplicants usually were. Which, Fox reminded himself, was very much the purpose at hand, along with paying the electricity and come to think of it the Wi-Fi (his neighbors had recently changed their password; disappointingly, Death was not so helpful there), more so than the looks she'd been holding overlong. (His imagination, surely, except Fox's imagination was not so much overactive as it was aspirational. The difference, one might suppose, between an artist envisioning an underpainting and the more common sin of pure delusion.) "Tell him that I love him, and I miss him," said Eva to what Fox could have sworn was his mouth, "and that I hope everything is going well—"

"It isn't," Death cut in sharply, looking sour. "Bradley committed several different kinds of tax fraud and is currently floating around in the Styx. Oh," he added flippantly, "and he cheated on her." A pause. "Twice. Though, to be fair—and these are his words, not mine—he *was* torn up about it." The last bit Death delivered with a mostly straight face before adding privately to Fox, "Not torn enough to pull out, one assumes—"

"He misses you, too," Fox assured Eva, running his thumb comfortingly across her knuckles as she bowed her head, fighting tears. "He wishes you all the sweetness life has to offer—"

"Nope, wrong," Death said. "Relatedly, do mortals still gym, tan, laundry?"

"—not in those words, of course," Fox corrected smoothly when Eva looked up, a crease of confusion between her manicured brows. "But Bradley never did find the words to tell you how much he loved you," he added on a whim, increasingly certain her posture had shifted in quite a promising way, "and he's asked me to give you the poetry he always thought you deserved."

"Oh, for fuck's sake," Death muttered as Eva's full lips parted in earnest. The love seat was ever so slightly higher than the chair in which Fox presently sat, a shift in elevation that afforded a rousing sense of escalating stakes when Eva uncrossed her legs, leaning forward to close what little space remained between them.

"What else does he say?" Eva asked, fascinatingly breathless. (Fox's two thoughts had by then suffered a slight rearrangement of priorities. Passwords were guessable, and even if not, the internet was mostly the newest rendition of grand-scale collective shame.)

"What does who say? Bradley? Nothing," Death helpfully supplied. "He says 'Eva who'?"

"He says," Fox began, matching Eva inch for inch, "that you were the only woman who ever understood him. Who could read him with a look, and who could fill him with joy in the same breath, and who made of him someone of consequence—of worth," he murmured, squeezing lightly against her hands. "He says he would look into your eyes and know the value of his own soul, and that he is grateful to you for that; and he tells me that because you were in his life in his final moments, he can rest eternally in peace, knowing that you—" and here, a slight moistening of one poet's lips "—will go on to be . . . happy."

Eva's gaze softened, her pupils dilating slightly.

"Happy?" she echoed, her breath suspended.

"Happy," Fox repeated. "And he says that he knows you will go on to make someone else as happy as he was with you, and that although it's time for him to move on and find rest, he wishes you all the blessings of heaven and earth."

"Oh," Eva whispered, letting out a breath, as beside Fox, Death announced, "Oh, FUCK."

"Hush," Fox muttered out of the side of his mouth, flicking a glance admonishingly to where his godfather stood. "That's a rubber band for sure, Papa."

"Oh, fuck you," Death said with a theatrical snap of the band, and then another, presumably as a form of preemptive strike. "You're going to sleep with her now, aren't you?"

Fox, who did not believe in pointing out the obvious, ignored him, turning Eva's hands over in his to draw his fingers gently over the creases in her palm. "You know, you have such a beautiful heart line," he told her, tracing it as it ran across the top of her palm and danced off, disappearing between her fingers. "There's so much love you have yet to give, Eva."

"You think?" she asked him, and he smiled.

"I know," he said softly, and she gazed at him with wonder.

"Do you think that I was meant to find you?" she asked. She wore a beguiling perfume, something botanical but not too nauseating. A bit like a walk in the woods, branches snapping underfoot. The call of a bird on the wind somewhere, like the thrill of a promise kept.

"I genuinely hope," Death sniffed, breaking Fox's momentary reverie, "that she gives you a terrible Yelp review."

He doubted it. As a practitioner, even a fraudulent one, Fox had something of a satisfaction guarantee, though not always so mutually beneficial.

"I believe Bradley guided you to me," Fox confirmed for Eva, and Death let out a groan.

"I'm leaving," he announced. "Wear a condom, you twat."

"Band," Fox muttered to him, and Death gave a long-suffering scowl before once again giving Fox the finger, enigmatically (and with, quite frankly, the usual unnecessary theatrics) disappearing into time and space.

"Bradley's gone now," Fox offered comfortingly to Eva with a re-hearsed look of regret. "He's passed into the next stage of existence, but he's happy, and y—"

He broke off as Eva leaned forward, catching his lips with hers.

"Eva," he gasped, feigning breathless astonishment. "I mean—Miss—"

"Fox," she whimpered into his mouth, half-clambering onto his lap in a fit of epiphany, or possibly acceptance, akin to running the five stages of grief in one fell swoop. (Fox D'Mora, a credit to his vocation!) "This," Eva murmured, speaking between kisses as she slid his top buttons undone with an admirable dexterity, "this is—this has to mean something—"

"I'm—" Fox paused, glancing down as she ripped the remainder of his shirt from his torso "—quite sure it does," he continued, casting about for something that a moderately . . . What was the word? Moral, ethical, something implying a modicum of restraint? Memory, as ever, failed him—man would say, "but still, you're vulnerable, and you've suffered a loss, and so perhaps we shouldn't—"

"Oh, but we *should*," she very reasonably insisted, grinding her hips against his and tossing her head back as Fox, finding her argument logically sound, brought his mouth to the bit of skin beneath the parted neckline of her blouse. "Bradley, he—he would have wanted me to—"

There was a soft pop from somewhere over Fox's right shoulder.

"I forgot to mention," Death announced, and then promptly covered his eyes, making a face. "Oh, Fox. *Fox*."

"What?" Fox mumbled impatiently as Eva, effervescing with brilliance, shoved his hands under her skirt. "I'm busy, you know," he pointed out, gesturing to the grieving (albeit faultlessly sensible!) woman in his lap, and Death rolled his eyes.

"You know what? Never mind," Death told him. "I'm sure you'll find out soon enough."

"Find out what?" Fox asked, and then grunted incoherently as Eva's fingers (nimble! inventive! worthy of—and he could not stress this enough—great and profound celebration!) made their way to the clasp of his trousers. "Fuck, just—" Fox groaned. "Tell me later, Papa, would you?"

"Band," Death said with prodigious smuggery (begging the question of where, indeed, Fox had learned it) before disappearing, leaving Eva to slide between Fox's legs, positioning herself between Fox's parted knees.

"Shall we?" she asked, teasing her hand under the lip of his boxers.

Fox D'Mora, man of prizeworthy restraint and probable feminist hero, slithered down the chair's leather upholstery, hoisting her up to fit his shoulders snugly between the curves of her enviable thighs.

"One second," he whispered to the satin-softness of her skin, shifting to snap the rubber band on his left wrist (in service, of course, to the New Year's resolution some epochs ago that had bought him one or two alternative sins). "Okay," Fox permitted, nuzzling what he was delighted to find was silk, "*now* we shall."

And when, eventually, Eva What's-Her-Name's luxuriant heart line—and the rest of her palm—closed virtuosically around him, Fox closed his eyes with a sense of philanthropic satisfaction, reminding himself to give her a 10 percent discount for his services.

# III

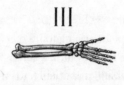

# MANAGEMENT

Viola Marek was a very normal person.

*Very* normal.

Almost aggressively normal, really, minus a few things here and there. One thing in particular, but there's no need to rush into that.

After all, you've only just met.

— Ω —

"I'm back," Vi called into the expanse of the Parker mansion's foyer. She set one of two cheery reusable bags (filled with exquisitely curated charcutier selections, a fresh rustic loaf from Streeterville's best Italian market, and whatever god-awful bubbly water was on sale at Whole Foods) onto the cool marble floor before reaching the tip of one finger toward the ornate mahogany banister. "Have you been behaving yourself?" she asked, satisfied to come away without a speck of dust.

"Never," replied Thomas Edward Parker IV, his voice echoing throughout the foyer from the nearest sitting room. "I'm insulted you'd even ask."

Vi, abandoning the second bag of groceries for the moment, poked her head into the parlor to see him sitting stiffly atop one of the parlor's Victorian chairs. The walls were an intoxicating Gilded Age shade of emerald, augmented by ribbons of Parisian satin prints. Light streamed in from the stained-glass window beside the hearth, touching the gleaming mahogany paneling with the tenderness of Adam's hand to God's and falling gently on the room's only occupant, crowning his equally glowing waves of immaculately styled hair.

"Tom," Vi lamented, shaking her head as she leaned against the doorframe. "Have you tried doing any of the things I suggested?"

"What? Reflecting on my life? Sure," he sniffed (an annoying but forgettable affectation) before rising to his feet and swatting gracelessly at a large, intricate vase that sat atop a sculpted Neoclassical column.

A perilous strike, or would have been had circumstances been different. As it was, Tom's hand passed through the crystal, and he scowled.

"Not like there's much damage I can actually cause," he said, pointedly flicking at it.

Vi, who'd been through worse than being unable to destroy a vase currently valued at three times the cost of her annual rent, concealed a sigh of irritation. Technically, Tom Parker was not the most difficult client she'd ever had to work with, as he did not have access to her phone or email and thus could not harangue her outside of work hours or try to send her memes. He was not technically a client at all, and in fact by some definitions he was also not even a person. He was, however, a problem.

Thus, any attempt at sarcasm, while undoubtedly more satisfying, would inevitably be futile.

"Don't be so hard on yourself," she reminded him, for perhaps the tenth time that week. "I'm sure you could cause quite a bit of damage if you put your mind to it, you know."

"You liberals," Tom muttered, letting out a frustrated sigh that resonated through the room, disturbing the static in the air. "You and your incurable optimism. Fucking unbearable."

(How sincere he was in needling her progressivism was unclear. It was her fault, probably, for goading him with her eat-the-rich T-shirts and her collection of bodice rippers she made a point of leaving behind; he had also been undesirably clear about his many reservations about estate taxes. Sartorially, though, he had no interest in hats, red or otherwise, so overall it was a wash. Regardless—)

"Yes," Vi reminded him, "we know."

"Honestly, how do you live with yourself?" Tom demanded, aiming a useless kick at a centuries-old tapestry as Vi, remembering her disinterest in the conversation, decided to simply leave, returning instead to the foyer for her buyer-luring bags of tasteful meats.

Tom, unfortunately, wafted after her on a breeze of recently updated air conditioning (exorbitant, absolutely *ungodly* to maintain, but who that could afford this house would not desire the decadence of a crisp, autumnal sixty-eight?) and malaise. "Waltzing around all day, making money off my family—all that *money*," Tom wailed in Vi's wake, throwing his hands up before walking through a wall to follow her into the kitchen. "TOTALLY WASTED—"

"How do I *live* with myself?" Vi echoed, arching a brow as she refreshed the white tulips (unseasonal, frankly obscene, by god this house was eating her budget alive, but what aside from white tulips whispered so sensually of both opulence and taste?) in the kitchen vase. "In my body," she reminded him, "fully alive."

Unwise, she knew, to indulge a sardonic comment at his expense, but fortunately (or rather, unfortunately), he did not appear to suffer the intended slight.

"Oh *please*," he scoffed instead. "Fully alive?"

She froze, bristling.

"Yes," she replied, turning to the fridge with an armful of La-Croix. From the mirrored surface of the brand-new state-of-the-art appliance she could see the signs that Tom had found the afternoon's source of entertainment, so she hastily reached for the door at a conspicuously selected angle, pulling it open to obscure the look of condescension she knew was imminent on his face.

"I've seen what you keep in your purse," he reminded her darkly. "The juice boxes are clever, I'll give you that, but don't think I haven't noticed that you don't *eat*. You've had how many open houses now?—and somehow never touched your precious cheese plates," he pointed out, swooping over to stand beside her as she began stock-piling cans into the fridge. "*And* you don't go into the room with my grandmother's rosary," he said with an air of impending victory, "*and* you never look at your reflection—"

"That," she cut in pointedly, "is because I hate my hair."

"Oh *bullshit*, Viola," he said, delighting in her discomfort. "If that wasn't obvious enough, there's still the fact that you're the only person who can see me," he concluded with a triumphant flourish. "Doesn't that seem like a bit of a warning sign to you?"

She arranged the sea of Pamplemousses neatly, aligning the labels with care.

"First of all," she informed him, having regained a momentary sense of control, "people see ghosts all the time. And maybe I'm, like, meaningful somehow. To your life, or to your death or something." She shrugged, pulling out the set of ceramic-handled Crate and Barrel cheese knives from the nearest drawer. They, of course, had been purchased for the intended sale, back when such purchases seemed sensible and not, for example, the void into which she would ultimately pour her life and sanity for three months overlong. "Have you considered that?"

"Have you considered that maybe you can see me because you, too, are fucking dead?" Tom countered in an irritated drawl, shifting to place his hands combatively on his hips. From that angle, the gaping of his shirt—white and neatly pressed, excepting the bloody mess at the center where the knife had gone in—gave her an unsolicited view of his chest, from which she promptly turned away, busying herself with a spread of luxuriant cheeses. "Riddle me *that*, Vi," Tom mocked, pursing his lips and waiting.

"I'm not dead. *You're* dead," she reminded him. "I, if anything, am undead. Big difference. And anyway," she continued, searching for a bit of honeycomb to place beside the brie, "I'm managing my condition."

"Managing your cond—" Tom broke off, staring at her. "Viola, you're a fucking vampire!"

She sighed.

"Only a little," she said. "Not in any of the important ways."

And it was true.

It was *true*.

— Ω —

"How's the ghost?" Vi's friend Isis Bernat had asked her that morning, joining her as they bullied their way down the tourist-infested Magnificent Mile. "Still a total asshat?"

"For the most part," Vi confirmed. Isis was a personal trainer, and since both of them worked fairly irregular hours, their friendship had blossomed mostly due to a surplus of free time. (Coincidentally, Isis was also a demon, and they'd met in a Creatures Anonymous meeting in Old Town; but these were near-insignificant details as far as Vi was concerned.)

"You want?" Isis asked, holding out a juice box, and Vi nodded, accepting it. She punctured a hole in the carton with a plastic straw and felt, for a moment, a leap in her stomach, thinking of other, more satisfying punctures; of *bites*, and—

"You're getting that look," Isis warned, and Vi shuddered, quickly bringing the tip of the straw between her lips.

"Sorry," she murmured. "I've been feeling a little off lately."

"You look a bit pale," Isis agreed, smirking, to which Vi rolled her eyes.

Isis, unlike Vi, appeared in many ways the picture of health— she was some sort of mix of tropical things, all tanned and glowing and cool, and leanly muscled in a way that suited her profession. Of course, Isis had been dealing with her condition much longer, give or take a few centuries, so she had been the one to teach Vi how to coexist in civilization.

"Juice box," Isis had offered the first time, handing her a waxy, palm-sized container with a disconcerting yellow smile on the label (Isis's design, as Vi would later learn). "People think it's a bit juvenile, I'll admit," Isis added before gesturing to the viscous red liquid making its ascent through the straw, "but if the only thing they're judging you for is high fructose corn syrup, I personally call that a win."

"Huh," Vi had said.

It had all been very new back then.

Viola Marek had been born very normal. Brown hair, brown eyes; pretty enough to be pleasing upon close inspection, but unremarkable enough not to draw attention in a crowd. She wasn't associated with any sort of spectrum (that she knew of), and she didn't have any particularly distracting qualities—no major pockmarks or missing limbs, no triggered psychoses; no noticeable beauty marks, either—and she was the only daughter of two very conventional academics: her father, a Hebrew Studies professor at UC Berkeley, and her mother, a professor of journalism at Columbia.

Sure, she was a child of divorce, but wasn't that the height of normalcy these days?

Vi had finished at the top of her class in school—but not too high—and she'd chosen a major that was neither unduly stressful nor requiring any particular sort of genius. Vi was defined by her diligence and her ability to keep her head down, and so when she rose to the top of her archaeology program and was sent (among half a dozen others) to a dig site in the Bondoc Peninsula of Luzon during the spring break of her senior year, she'd expected to do . . . well, much of the same.

What she hadn't expected had been the bite.

"Hello," the man had said; as normal a greeting as any. Her mother was Filipino (so was Vi, she supposed, though mostly her mother was from the suburbs of Las Vegas; not unlike the way Vi's grandfather whom she'd never met was from Warsaw, but her dad, who conversely she knew very well, was from Brooklyn) and Vi hadn't noticed whether he'd approached her first with English or Tagalog. Had he been pale? She hadn't noticed that, either. Then again, she hadn't known the undead frequented tropical climates. Let that be a lesson, really. You can never truly know a culture until you've been bitten by one of its myths.

"Hello," Vi replied in a normal effort at politeness, reaching up to shade her eyes from the sun and squinting at his silhouette. Later, she would learn after extensive research on vampires in Southeast Asia that her mistake had been not looking him in the eye; evidently if she had, she would have seen her reflection upside down, and that would have been warning enough to run.

Unfortunately, she hadn't, and she'd been alone, and though he'd seemed charming and friendly when he offered her water and food—things that seemed normal to accept at the time, owed in large part to Vi's mistaken assumption that he was part of her cohort's research team—he'd changed the instant the sun had gone down.

And when Vi woke up again, about a mile from her campsite, so had she.

"Good morning," the man had said, definitely in English that time, while conspicuously licking his fingers. When Vi had looked down, discovering a rather noticeable gash where her liver should be, she deduced herself to be the delicacy at hand. "We're to be wed, my love."

She remembered, then, flashes of the night before—of a man who had been a wild boar, and a tusked explanation for why she'd been so unsubtly gored.

She remembered pain, too, but didn't feel it. It seemed a sensation that no longer existed within the limitations of her reality, and instead she watched as her stomach repaired itself, the skin closing over as the sun rose anew.

"Oh," she said, blinking. "No, thanks."

He pursed his lips, displeased.

"Yes," he insisted. "Marriage."

"Why?" she asked him, and he shrugged.

"Lonely," he told her, and though it was a normal enough reason for a normal enough institution, she still hadn't been fully obliged to comply.

After striking him with a rock and struggling to wrap the gash across her stomach, Vi had taken off, stumbling back to her professor's campsite and finding herself quite unable to explain why as soon as the sun went down, she saw the world through different eyes.

Specifically, *cat* eyes.

The first time she'd looked down and seen paws where her hands should be, it had certainly been alarming; though the initial shock of new discoveries was by then approaching the point of expected. She prowled around, sleepless and utterly *starving*, and by the time the sun came up, she was exhausted.

She couldn't keep down food; meat smelled rancid, produce turned her stomach, and despite the signs, she hadn't realized just how bad things could be until her professor had accidentally cut himself while they were the last two in the taxi line to the airport. The smell of his blood—tangy and citrusy but also musky, and rich, and with a coppery hint of something that had brought an unexpected growl of longing to her throat—had been such a shock to her waning system that resistance was instantaneously futile. When his eyes met hers, wide with concern, she wished she'd thought to warn him to check whether his reflection had been upside down.

She was really very sorry about the way things had gone, though she'd be lying through her teeth if she said the whole thing hadn't been carnally satisfying. It had been a cruelly euphoric experience, really, and no human flavor—neither sweet nor savory, nor salty nor tangy, nor the distinctly Filipino knack for all of those at once—could ever compare to the taste of Professor Josh Barron's heart. It hadn't even required seasoning.

It's a generally accepted philosophy that there's no finishing college when one has eaten any portion of one's research advisor, so Vi hadn't bothered going back to Indiana. She was glad, though, that she'd chosen the Midwest for school. Despite her initial opposition, Vi found she now rejoiced in the slush of unseasonably precipitous snowfall, simply because it didn't look or feel or taste like where she'd been before. She shivered upon arrival, freezing, and she reveled in it, in the frigidity of *cold*; it made her feel something akin to alive, as it were, and thus, she'd been able to take certain steps to change her life.

Chicago was a natural choice. A bigger city provided a better means of camouflage, and Viola Marek found herself even more conveniently forgettable amid the millions who jostled by her every day. It wasn't particularly close to either her father or her mother, and she retained her human voice even in cat form, so apologetic messages of "sorry, can't come home just yet" or "sorry, too busy with work" were a simple enough matter. By then she'd already come to understand that so long as she paid both parents equal amounts of inattention, neither was especially fussed.

Lots of tenants owned cats, a very normal pet, so Vi bought a kennel and an elaborate scratching post, claiming she had an overactive tabby but in reality using it to give herself a boost to the window (with a purposefully broken latch) beside the fire escape of her Lakeview walk-up.

Vi got her salesman license in real estate, the best job she figured she could get with only three-quarters of a university degree, and established herself fairly quickly within the North Side circle of Chicago's most exceptional brokerages. It was a job that didn't require much collaboration, permitting her to keep her nights open, and that gave her a certain degree of freedom, so that the days that her eyes were more bloodshot than others, she might opt for phone calls rather than open houses.

She found the dilapidated building in Old Town when she was there making cold calls, sniffing out possible sales. Isis Bernat had been outside, smoking.

"Oof," Isis said, watching Vi scope out the building's eighteenth-century molding. "Been awhile since you've eaten?"

"Excuse me?" Vi asked, frowning.

"You look a little bloodless," Isis replied. An unsettling choice of words, which by the look on her face—an intensely knowing look, less a vocational matter like a doctor or detective and more like that of a headmaster, or a parent—must have been intentional.

"Something going on in there?" Vi asked, gesturing to the building from which Isis seemed to have emerged, and Isis shrugged, putting out her cigarette beneath the heel of her new-looking cross-trainers.

"Come see," she beckoned.

For whatever reason, Vi had obliged, following her up the narrow, creaking stairs (original floors! historical authenticity! for better or worse, the sale Vi wouldn't ultimately make was already forming) and watching her knock three times with a deliberate interval of pauses before a slot in the door suddenly opened.

"Who's that?" someone asked. A set of eyes behind the door, pale blue, appraised Vi from a distance.

Isis shrugged. "Vamp," she said, and Vi blinked, startled.

"Entrance granted," the voice confirmed, and then the door swung open, revealing a small, threadbare room with perhaps a dozen folding chairs arranged at the center and a makeshift station of beverages beside the door.

"Here," Isis said, reaching for a small paper cup patterned bucolically with sheep and pouring some of the punch into it. "Have some. You seriously look starved."

"Thanks," Vi said with confusion, though she accepted the cup. She swirled it around to watch garnet tears slip down the sides of the waxy interior, like a heady glass of Cabernet. "What's in it?"

"O negative," Isis replied. "Don't worry," she added quickly. "It's from a donor."

"Wh—"

"Drink," Isis said firmly, and pulled Vi's wrist to the circle of chairs in the center of the room, yanking her into a seat. "Ever been to one of these?"

"One of what?" Vi asked, and took a sip.

Not punch. *Definitely* not punch.

Delicious, though. She'd later learn that O negative was, in fact, her drink of choice.

"Meetings," Isis supplied. "There's not a lot of them. Well," she said, apparently reconsidering, "a couple in the South Loop, a few more up near Evanston. Maybe one or two in the Loop, but nobody really *lives* there, you know what I mean? You ever need a lunch fix, though." She shrugged. "That's your spot, man. The financiers get the best shit, you know? But they're hard to track down."

"Right," Vi permitted faintly, taking another sip.

"Better," Isis noted, glancing at Vi's complexion and nodding. "You look much better. You not getting enough to eat?"

For some reason, Vi didn't find it necessary to argue.

"I mostly go for mice," she explained, and Isis groaned.

"That's your problem," she said. "You need *humans*, you know? You can do it without killing anyone." She paused, reaching into her pocket for a piece of gum. "Unless you're good with the killing part," she qualified with a shrug, holding out the container. "Gum?"

"Sure," Vi said. "To the gum, I mean. Not murder."

"Hey, to each their own," Isis told her. "Personally, I find it messy. You kill people, you gotta keep moving, you know? I got clients to keep track of. Eternity to endure. Can't be moving around all the time." She waved a hand, gesticulating wildly as she spoke. "Plus, you ever had Lou Malnati's? Had it done *right*, I mean? Chicago Classic, well done. Fuck me," she groaned, tone bordering on sensual. "*Fuck.* Delicious."

"You eat pizza?" Vi asked with amusement as she sipped her "punch," and Isis shrugged.

"Not a vamp," she explained, gesturing to herself. "I can eat."

"But still, isn't it—"

"No veggies, though," Isis said, shuddering. "Makes the whole operation soggy."

"What?" Vi asked, confused again. "Oh, right. Pizza."

"Pizza," Isis breathed out happily. "Gotta treat yourself sometimes. Blood's of course necessary," she added, gesturing to Vi's cup. "But hey. I've got a diverse palate."

"What do you do?" Vi asked, since it felt like a normal question to ask under this or any circumstances, and Isis reached into her pocket a second time, pulling out a business card.

"Personal trainer," she said. "Pizza's a luxury," she clarified, gesturing to the beautifully defined tear-shaped muscle in her upper thigh for evidence. "But like I said, gotta treat yourself."

"And the smoking?" Vi prompted skeptically, eyeing the card. "EQUINOX," she read aloud, surprised. "IT'S NOT FITNESS, IT'S LIFE."

"Life," Isis echoed with a chuckle. "Isn't that hysterical? I fucking love it. And the smoking's just a bad habit. We all have our vices," she sighed, kicking her feet out and resting them in the center of the circle. "Mine just happen to be humanity and cigarettes."

"Gonna quit?" Vi asked, an attempt at being conversational and droll, and Isis turned, scrutinizing her.

"Was that a joke?" she asked.

Not a great one, but Vi had never been known to dazzle on a first impression. "Sort of."

Isis stared for another long moment.

"I like you," she finally declared, and lifted her feet as someone moved to pass. "You seem chill." She paused. "What was your stance on killing again?"

"Did it once," Vi admitted. "Felt bad."

"Remorse," Isis sighed, sympathetic. "A bitch of a human impulse."

"So you're not human at all, then?" Vi asked her, taking another sip of not-punch, and Isis shook her head.

"I think the generic term is *demon*, though that seems a bit unfair," she lamented. "I mean, hey, what happened to nature versus nurture, right?"

"I think that might be a different thing," Vi said slowly, but by then a man—or something that looked very convincingly like a man—had cleared his throat from the top of the circle, furthest from the door.

"Phones off," he implored. "Please."

"Yeah," Isis contributed. "We're creatures, not animals."

"Miss Bernat," the man sighed impatiently, and Isis smirked, leaning over to whisper in Vi's ear.

"Werewolf," Isis explained, gesturing to him. "Named Lupo. Thinks he's creative." She rolled her eyes. "Isn't."

"Mm," Vi agreed, as Lupo continued to speak.

"I see we have someone new among us," he announced, turning to look at Vi. "Would you like to introduce yourself?"

"Oh," Vi said, clearing her throat. "Um, sure. Hi, I'm—"

"Stand, please," Lupo invited briskly, and she rose to her feet, feeling inordinately silly as the eyes in the room all swiveled to face her.

"Hello," she said again, waving awkwardly. "I'm Viola—"

"Hi, Viola," the others droned in unison.

"—and I'm a—" She hesitated. "Well, um. I guess you could say I'm a—"

"Say it out loud," Isis whispered, grinning, which Vi ignored.

"I'm a vampire," she pronounced blandly.

She looked around, waiting for a reaction.

"If you're a vampire," one of the young men to the left of the circle said, "why aren't you at one of the night meetings?"

"Yeah," a woman added from Vi's right. "Isn't there some sort of cardinal rule about the sun?"

Isis scoffed loudly, crossing one ankle over the other in a theatrical show of disdain. "You're all uncultured swines," she informed the rest of the group. "If this isn't proof of inherent, *long-standing* European bias then frankly, I don't know what is."

"I'm not the Dracula kind of vampire," Vi agreed, nodding to Isis and resuming her address to her audience (without, of course, any mention of the novel's antisemitic roots, which she assumed they did not have time to cover). "I'm, um. An aswang, technically." Her pronunciation of the word still felt off despite her ample postmortem research, like reaching back two generations for someone else's tongue. "I was bitten in the Philippines."

There was an indistinguishable smattering of discord; something along the lines of muttered agreement, or even commiseration.

"Southeast Asia," Lupo lamented sympathetically, voicing what seemed to be the room's consensus and giving Vi a look she supposed was meant to be comforting. "A bit of a landmine to navigate, even for us."

His face was scarred, Vi noted, but kind.

Sort of puppy-looking, if she really thought about it.

"So," Isis pressed, giving the back of Vi's knee a nudge with her foot. "What brings you to this circle of degenerates?"

"I'm in real estate," Vi explained. "I was just looking at the building."

"Oh." Isis's expression soured as the others around the circle grunted conspiratorially in distaste. "Well," she said, her lips pressed thin. "We're not selling."

"Isis," Lupo sighed again, scrubbing at the shaggy bristles of his salty chestnut beard. "That's my line."

"Well, we aren't, are we?" Isis returned, and Vi, hearing an upsurge of combativeness in her tone, hurried to placate her.

"I was just looking," she clarified quickly. "I had no idea there was anything like . . . this," she admitted, for lack of a better word. "I've just been trying to get my bearings, you know—have a 'real job' and all that—"

"We all have real jobs," Isis informed her. "Lupo's a drug counselor."

"Had a bit of a problem with heroin for a while," he supplied in answer to Vi's look of surprise. "Helps to have a purpose."

"I work in computer programming," offered the man to their left, and Isis swiveled to face him.

"You're a hacker," she corrected, making a face. "And that click-bait shit you call a real job doesn't help anyone, you know. He's fae," she added, pivoting her torso to mutter over her shoulder to Vi. "Don't piss him off. He'll haunt your dreams and spoil your hard drive."

"Noted," Vi agreed.

"I'm in banking," contributed the woman on Vi's right. "I-Banking, specifically."

"Troll," Isis supplied, coughing it into her fist, and the woman pursed her lips.

"Bartender," another woman said, her voice tinged with a faint French accent. For a moment after she spoke, Vi was dazed; as if she'd been hit over the head and re-awoken, and the first thing she'd seen had been a pert set of rose-colored lips, deep blue eyes, a flash of perfect teeth—

"Siren," Isis interrupted, giving Vi another nudge and then crossing her arms over her chest. "Keep your distance, if you know what I mean."

"Oh, it's fine. I'm straight," Vi assured the siren, who grinned.

"Not for long," she murmured, tossing her blond hair over her shoulder as if Vi had thrown a gauntlet on the ground.

"The point is," Lupo ventured loudly, resuming his introduction, "it's very possible to carry on a normal life, Viola. In fact, we're all here to support each other," he added encouragingly, "so that we don't fall back on bad habits."

"Bad habits," Vi repeated slowly. "Like—?"

"Murder," the computer-hacking fae supplied. "And/or trickery that leads to blood-letting."

"Luring men to their deaths," the siren agreed, checking her teeth in a tiny pearlescent compact.

"Theft," the troll offered. "Also, hoarding. And I used to have an online gambling addiction," she said privately to Vi, "but I really think crypto is the future."

"Cheryl, we've talked about this," said Isis just before Lupo's timely interruption.

"We all have our individual impulses," he assured Vi. "But we do what we can to be there for each other. Most of us will outlive any humans who enter our lives," he added, looking slightly withered as he said it. "So it's important to have a community. A safety net."

"Something to keep us honest," Isis contributed wryly, and then glanced up, pinching Vi's elbow. "So, are you in?"

Vi blinked, considering it.

"Yeah," she said, surprised at how normal a group full of mythical creatures could be. "Yeah, I think I am."

— Ω —

"So," Isis had said a few weeks later, nodding to Vi as she approached their usual meeting spot outside the building in Old Town. Isis was standing on the corner with a half-drunk latte and a spontaneously purchased bag of crew socks while Vi, who'd been having one of those days where she was five minutes late to absolutely everything, hurried breathless from the direction of the lake. "What's new in the fast-paced world of residential real estate?" Isis prompted cheerily, toasting Vi with her Starbucks cup. "Is it a buyer's market? Have any new cheeses been added to your spread?"

Yes and yes, not that Isis was ever really asking. All her questions had an undertone of omniscient bonhomie. "Bad news," Vi said, huffing residually from her day of tiny crises. "I have a ghost problem."

"Bad news indeed," Isis replied, putting out her cigarette and gesturing for them to go inside. "Poltergeist?"

Vi frowned, thinking. "What defines a poltergeist?" she asked, and Isis, too, paused to consider it.

"Troublesome buggers," she ruled eventually. "Means *noisy ghost* in German."

"Well, he's certainly noisy," Vi sighed. "Incredibly mouthy."

"Ah," Isis said. "Unfinished business, then?"

"If he's got it, he doesn't know what it is," Vi muttered. "Says he doesn't know how he died, or who killed him, or why."

"Who is he?" Isis asked. "Anyone important?"

"Thomas Edward Parker the fourth," Vi answered, imitating his lofty East Coast boarding school affectations and leaning into the words *the fourth*. "He's haunting the new property I told you about—you know, the mansion? The Parker house over in Gold Coast."

"He's a Parker?" Isis looked stunned—no, worse, Vi realized. She looked *sympathetic*, and not to Vi, who was obviously more aggrieved than the ghost of a white male billionaire. ("Millionaire," as Tom would later correct her, "and leave your little wealth tax out of it.")

"Well," Isis said with a look of contemplation as they climbed the rickety staircase (less charming now, Vi thought), "the poor thing was fucked from birth, then. You know about the Parker curse, don't you?"

"I wouldn't call him a 'poor thing,' exactly," Vi grumbled, thinking of how Tom had very deliberately toyed with the electricity during that morning's inspection. Thanks to him the house had failed its various inspections three times, and the list of contractors who weren't glorified crooks was already short enough without adding *cool with the paranormal* to the list of qualifications. "And I don't think he's cursed. Are curses even real?" Vi asked thoughtfully, as they nodded to Lupo, each pouring themselves a small cup of punch. (B positive. Not her favorite, but still refreshing at times.)

"'Real'?" Isis echoed dubiously, giving Vi an admonishing look. "I'm surprised that phrase means anything to you anymore."

"It doesn't," Vi admitted, taking a sip and letting it soak gladly into her chapped lips. "But still, a girl can dream."

— Ω —

All of which was to say that Viola was doing very well, all things considered. Though that of course did nothing to obstruct her poltergeist's ongoing tirade.

"You *can't*," Tom continued, "be a 'little bit' of a vampire, Vi. Impossible," he proclaimed theatrically, with his usual air of someone who hadn't been scolded enough as a child. "You're either dead or you're not."

"Again, *undead*," Vi corrected. "It's like you're not even listening to me—"

"Or it's like you're still trying to sell *my house*," Tom stubbornly countered, "and I am putting my foot down!"

Her condition may have been eternal, but her patience was not. "Thomas," Vi said, to which he grimaced, successfully registering her change in tone. "Put your foot down all you like," she invited. "I can't say it'll make much of a difference."

This, like most things, he did not take well.

"You have to disclose a ghost in the house," Tom reminded her. "Seriously, look it up."

"I don't have to disclose shit," Vi retorted, taking a page from Isis's handbook of casual obscenity. "Not yet, anyway. And besides," she added, her voice nearly drifting an octave in a renewed attempt at forced optimism as she returned to the foyer for her meats, "by the time this behemoth of a house is purchased, I doubt you'll still be in it, Thomas Parker."

"Is that so, Viola Marek?" Tom called after her with an air of retributive mockery. "I'd like to see you force me out!"

"So would I, Tom," Vi murmured, pausing by the front door to scan for buyers she knew with a dismal certainty weren't coming. "Believe me, so would I."

# IV

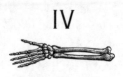

## REAPERS AND SOWERS

A person living in a city tends to learn the different kinds of knocks, and the distinct oddness of hearing them. After all, with seven grocery stores and corner markets existing within a stone's throw, it's hardly a common impulse to turn to one's neighbor for a cup of sugar—*particularly* when one cannot help being aware, thin walls be damned, that one's neighbor was unapologetically playing saccharine alt-pop ballads until three in the morning, and therefore probably isn't awake at 8 A.M.

A person in a city knows the knocks of habit (the UPS delivery man, for example, who opts for three perfunctory beats) and the knocks of expectation (the ones belonging to the Thai delivery man who raps twice, hurriedly). There's a sense of impermanence to these knocks; of *I am here, and soon I will be gone,* and these are the knocks that one learns to anticipate.

*This* knock, however, was clipped and purposeful.

Once, twice; a pregnant pause.

Ominous. The way poetic reflexes might tell you that death would knock, really.

Except that Fox, the recipient of this particular knock, knew his godfather well, and Death had never once been respectful of his boundaries.

Fox frowned, glancing preemptively out his window at the street; nobody there. An unexpected knock was an odd thing on its own, made odder still by the absence of a prerequisite buzz at the intercom. He headed to the door and glanced through the peephole for political canvassers (or worse, the new tenant next door) before chuckling to himself and pulling it open.

It wasn't death, no; but it wasn't nearly *not,* either.

"Cal," Fox sighed, as a hooded reaper turned from where he'd apparently been reading the very interesting literature (a Ninety-five Theses–type sign expressing malcontent about the shared mail area) across the hall. "You can walk through walls, brother. You don't have to knock."

Calix Sanna slid the black hood from his head, his languid dark curls as unmussed as ever as he offered Fox a congenial shrug. "I try to afford you a modicum of dignity, Fox," he replied. "Is that so wrong?"

"Well, efficiency over antiquity, I always say," Fox returned, shifting aside in the doorway and gesturing for him to come in. "What's got you in Chicago?"

"Bit of a lull," Cal supplied, glancing around the apartment's usual off-duty state of misuse with a characteristically charitable reservation of judgment. (In Fox's defense, the boxers on the floor were clean, and so, probably, were the wine glasses.) "Boss is a bit worked up about something. See you haven't changed much since my last visit," he added tangentially, still scouring the room. "I'm glad."

Fox would have guessed as much. Aside from being a soldier of Lucifer, Cal was also a creature of habit.

"Going to war again?" Fox asked him, and walked into his kitchen, sniffing a forgotten cup of coffee and determining it to be cold.

"Don't think so," Cal replied, shrugging in Fox's wake. "Maybe. Hard to tell. You know how he is," he added gravely, wandering over to Fox's bookshelf. "It's always about balance with him. 'Balance is king,' he says. 'Without me, no one would know God was good.' He says it ten times a day, at least."

"Well, he's not wrong," Fox agreed, giving the coffee a testing sip. (It wasn't ideal, but neither was the prospect of making a new batch.) "Want anything?" he called over his shoulder, concealing a grin at the sound of Cal's predictable sigh.

"Fox," he muttered. "You know perfectly well that I haven't had anything to eat or drink in nearly a thousand years."

"Modicum of dignity," Fox reminded him, taking another sip (honestly, it was fine) before moving to join Cal in the living room. "So you're just here for a visit, then?"

Cal nodded. "Not for a job, if you know what I mean," he clarified.

"I always know what you mean," Fox returned, and in response, Cal gave him one of his smiles, drifting from the bookcase to settle awkwardly into the love seat.

Cal Sanna was a relatively serious man—had always been, even while he'd been alive—but he was good company, and however serious he may have been, Fox had never considered him joyless. Cal had, in fact, five different smiles. One for when he was genuinely contented, which Fox had seen on perhaps a dozen different occasions; a second for when he was angry, but was patiently forcing his lips to curl around his teeth; a third for when he wished to convey humor, indulging a moment of amusement; a fourth (far more common) for when he did *not* wish to convey humor, but couldn't quite prevent it (of which this particular smile was one); and, lastly—

"You haven't seen Mayra lately, have you?" Cal asked innocently.

—a fifth, which Fox happened to know was reserved for Mayra Kaleka.

"I haven't," Fox said. "Though I can certainly summon her, if you'd like."

Cal's gaze drifted.

"No, no," he murmured, a bit vacantly. "I don't want to bother her."

Fox, then, smiled one of his own many smiles, each one more alarming than the next; Cal, of course, missed it, involved as he was in the rosy horizon of his thoughts.

"Calix," Fox admonished briskly, with another sip of cold coffee. "Must we play this game every time?"

"It's not a game," Cal insisted, though his fingers closed reflexively around the small wooden box in his hand. Fox glanced up, noting where the box had been removed from the top shelf of his bookcase, and sighed, shaking his head.

"You're already holding her relic," he pointed out. "It wouldn't take much to call her."

"Says you," Cal muttered, but Fox, lacking patience, relinquished the cup of coffee that was better off forgotten and stood, snatching the box from Cal's hand to pull out the gold bracelet that had been tucked carefully inside. "No," Cal said hastily, "no, Fox, *wait*—"

"Mayra," Fox said to the bracelet as Cal leapt to his feet, pointlessly adjusting the buttons on the military uniform beneath his hood. "Will you come and have a visit, please?"

There was a quiet popping sound; a hitch in the fabric of reality, like a lag, wherein sight and sound drifted momentarily apart and then returned, joining up with a loud burst of suction. Illumination in the room grew blinding, settling in waves, and by the time the sunspots of Fox's vision cleared, the light had wrapped itself around the form of a woman swathed in white and gold, her wings lined with a familiar heavenly glimmer.

She was like autumn afternoons, Fox had always thought, and thought it now, again. She had that glow of late September, soft and solemn as it drifted out of reach. She was the last breath of summer—that quiet little gasp just before the end that feels somehow like sadness, like a burdensome loss, just before all the beauty and freedom dies away.

"What," sighed Mayra, "could you possibly want now, Fox D'Mora?"

At the sight of her, he smiled.

— Ω —

Mayra Kaleka was a study in contradictions. She wore her lovely ebony hair twisted up and braided around her head like a crown, with sun-kissed bronze skin that set off unlikely eyes of jade-like green, soft and undeniably celestial. Beauty she possessed in spades; in abundance; in riches. Her voice, though, and the posture of her shoulders, were combatant, strident and harsh, and served to set her apart from other angels Fox had known.

That, of course, in addition to the fact that Mayra Kaleka had very nearly not been an angel at all.

When it came to heavenly reckoning, there were numerous areas in which Mayra had fallen quite short. Her temper, for one. She had rather a violent one, and a great proclivity for anger, much of which was directed at her profession—which was yet another considerable shortage of points. A brilliant and lovely courtesan, Mayra had known perfectly well that her position in the Mughal Empire, particularly as the daughter of an emigrated Hindi family, resided largely in her talents at drawing men into her web. Mayra was shrewd and cunning, brilliant and poised, and ruthless with regard to her competition; and indeed, when the archangel Gabriel told her as much—and his compatriot the archangel Raphael had agreed—she had unabashedly told them both to go fuck themselves, or, if they wished, each other.

The trouble was that Mayra had *also* been a font of noble deeds.

There's something about women, and in particular, women whose survival depends on conscienceless men. Men who have everything are careless with trinkets, and so those trinkets, like Mayra Kaleka, learn to care for themselves, and sometimes, if they are either very blessed or very cursed, they learn to care for others. When the Mughal began to fall to the Maratha and Delhi was no longer safe, Mayra had ushered several women and children to safety, removing them from harm's reach—at the expense of her own corporeal well-being.

In the end she had been summoned as all souls were summoned to what looked, to her, like the bedroom of a noble. (To others it might look like the lobby of a train station or the atrium of a church, or the waiting room of a dental practice.)

"You are selfless," Raphael noted upon her death, to which Mayra scoffed.

"Don't impress your morals upon me," she said. "Where were you while we were dying? While we were suffering, where were you?"

"Watching," he said, and Gabriel nodded. "There must be balance in this world, or how would we recognize evil when we saw it?"

"Who cares whether you recognize it?" she demanded. "If heaven means casting your gaze aside, then I want none of it. You're not my gods," she added stiffly. "You have no claim to me."

Raphael and Gabriel exchanged irritatingly furtive glances.

"True," Raphael admitted. "We offer you something else entirely."

"Had you considered the possibility of afterlife employment?" Gabriel ventured.

Now that she was able, Mayra indulged a sour face.

"Disgusting," she muttered. "Even in death, men wish me to coddle their pricks."

"Nothing like that," Raphael said hastily. "No, I mean—as an angel."

She stared at him.

"Do I look like an angel to you?" she asked him. "Seriously. Do I?"

"A bit," Gabriel admitted. "But that's really not the important part. And granted, there are certainly other things you can do—"

"Weave for the Fates," Raphael enumerated, ticking them off on his fingers. "Serve the Olympians. Fight for Lucifer—"

"But why should I be made to do anything at all?" Mayra demanded. "I'm tired. Life has exhausted me. I want to rest."

The other two sighed.

"Unfortunately," Raphael said, gesturing to a chart that materialized behind him, "you're not quite *there*, I'm afraid."

"What's that?" Mayra asked, frowning at it. It looked like a scroll, marked with figures she didn't understand but assumed to be a method of accounting.

"Your ledger," Gabriel supplied. "As you can see, you qualify to exist in your afterlife without cosmic punishment—which is, of course, not guaranteed, and certainly not unremarkable," he said with an air of generosity. "You do have the option to merely bide your time in lieu of your ledger being more forcibly altered. A variety of venues *do* exist for that purpose," he conceded, "though I confess none of them are much worth visiting. So, as I said, you may suspend yourself in one of the various forms of purgatory, *or*—" Here he paused ceremoniously. "You can make use of your extra time, Mayra Kaleka."

She glowered at him.

"What would I have to do to change my ending?" she asked, brusquely.

"Nothing too strenuous," Raphael assured her. "Keep track of other ledgers. Deliver messages. Provide counsel, of course," he added, "where necessary."

"I never received counsel," Mayra snapped. "Heaven knows I asked."

"Times can change, Mayra Kaleka," Gabriel told her. "We can also grant you miracles. Limited, of course," he said, glancing at Raphael for approval and continuing as he nodded. "Perhaps . . . five miracles a year? But you would have discretion."

She paused, considering it.

"This is power, then," Mayra said slowly. "You're offering me power?"

"We're offering you a means to change your destination," Raphael corrected. "Your ledger will shift slower than it did while you were alive, but it will shift nonetheless, if you work for it."

"So who would I work for, then?" Mayra asked. "You?"

"Him," they corrected in unison, gesturing upward, and Mayra frowned.

"He is not my god," she said, and they shrugged.

"Your gods would have you sent back," Gabriel reminded her. "To earth."

She shuddered.

"So," Raphael prompted. "Do you accept?"

Mayra considered it another moment before deciding this, at least, was a choice. And she had had so precious few of those before.

"Fine," she said.

And that was how Mayra Kaleka became an angel.

— Ω —

"Always a pleasure, Mayra," Fox remarked, and she sniffed her disagreement, catching sight of Cal in the room.

"Oh," she said, her expression shifting. "Cal, I didn't—"

"Hello, Mayra," he said, swallowing. "I hope you haven't been taken from something important."

She opened her mouth, and then closed it.

"Ah, well, not a bother. I'm out of miracles," she admitted to Cal, shifting to sit in what she knew very well was Fox's chair and leaving him to move to the love seat with a grimace. "I'm afraid I'm rather useless for the time being, with the exception of the ledgers."

"What did you do with your last miracle?" Fox asked neutrally, picking up a copy of the *Chicago Tribune* and snapping it open. "Something interesting, I hope."

"Rather not, unfortunately," Mayra grumbled. "I turned up a bit of extra coin for a soup kitchen in Detroit."

"That's meaningful," Cal said, leaning toward her. "What's uninteresting about that?"

"They closed it anyway," Mayra remarked tightly, her lips pressed thin. "Sometimes I wonder if it would not be kinder to simply give this whole country a flood. Or a bubonic plague." She dissolved into something of a daydream. "If I had my way, I'd flip some tables on the moneylenders myself and then go ahead and start from scratch."

"Who are the moneylenders in this analogy?" asked Cal.

"Oh, where to start? Billionaires, lifetime politicians, health insurance companies, megachurches, the NRA—"

"Ah, your celestial humor," Fox remarked, licking his finger to turn the page of his paper. "Ceaseless delights, my dove."

"She does have a point," Cal said, not surprisingly.

"Thank you, Calix, but Fox knows that," she said. "He's simply unbearable for his own amusement. How have you been, by the way?" she asked, as if Cal's welfare were an afterthought or a fleeting remark upon the weather, and Fox listened with amusement as she shifted toward Cal. "I haven't seen you for quite a while, Sanna."

"Well, you know the Boss. Had us on campaign for a bit," Cal said. "A decade or so."

"I'll never understand how you can fall in line so comfortably," Mayra commented, resting her sandaled feet on Fox's side table. "Are you just a fighter at heart, soldier?"

"Yeah," Cal said gruffly. "Yeah. Something like that."

— Ω —

In reality Calix Sanna had belonged to a very small village; an island, in fact. He had not known the world was quite so large—had not imagined it to be so limitless, so vast—and even though he would have told you without hesitation that the sea as he had known it over the course of his insignificant lifetime had no end and no beginning, he still wouldn't have been capable of putting the world's true vastness into words, nor had he ever considered the magnitude of what it might be like to bear witness to its beauty.

Cal's world was only a matter of how far his feet could take him, until the day he became a soldier.

Cal Sanna had been neither selfish nor selfless; neither moral nor indecent. He'd never lain with a prostitute nor slain a man over a petty disagreement, but neither had he fed the poor, nor saved the children. His world was small, and his brother the biggest thing in it, so when Stavros Sanna decided to drunkenly steal back his gambling losses from a muscled tavern owner with too many knives, Cal had thought only to come to his brother's defense.

The blade to his carotid, then, had been something of an abrupt awakening.

"Calix Sanna," the archangel Raphael sighed in displeasure when Cal opened his eyes to a dusty view of pebbled hills, his own feet planted partway up the incline of a mountain. "This is unfortunate."

Cal, who'd never had much aptitude for conversation, stared at him.

"You," he remarked eventually, "are no three-headed dog."

"True," the archangel Gabriel acknowledged. "Cerberus is elsewhere."

"As is Hades," Raphael agreed. "We offer you something else entirely."

"Something aside from the River Styx," Gabriel clarified. "Which, I assure you, is no great use of time."

"You're angels," Cal remarked, having seen paintings of them before. "Am I to be an angel, then?"

"I'm afraid not," Raphael said. "You're on the lower end of things."

"Quite low," Gabriel regretfully contributed. "But you're useful enough, we suspect."

"Ah," said Cal. "So you're putting me to work."

He didn't mind work. He didn't mind much, really; nor, he supposed, did he particularly care for much. Still, he wasn't without some measure of curiosity.

"May I see the world first?" Cal asked the archangels, and then paused. "I thought . . . perhaps in death I might finally see it. Just once," he added, wondering if he'd asked for too much. "If it's not too much trouble."

"What—now?" Raphael asked, taken aback; but at a shrug from Gabriel, the archangel sighed. "If you insist, I suppose."

He waved a hand, and somehow, despite the hill and its apparent ascent to nowhere, a window materialized out of nothing, out of air. Gabriel obligingly drew aside a gauzy curtain—which had not been there a moment ago, not that Cal was keeping track any longer of these or other such oddities—and Cal, astonished, took a step closer to look upon the view.

"Where's my village?" he asked. "Is it behind that blue orb?"

"No, no," Raphael said, with the slightest brush of impatience. "The blue orb *is* the world. Your world, anyway," he clarified carefully. "There are, of course, many others."

Cal suddenly felt he was shrinking.

He felt very scared, and very small.

"If this is the world—" Cal began tentatively, but cut himself off.

Gabriel nodded slowly, in apparent sympathy. "You've seen almost none of it, Cal Sanna," he agreed. "But it doesn't have to stay that way."

Cal pressed his fingers to the glass, still staring.

"Where is Chora?" he asked, turning over his shoulder for direction, and Raphael gestured to another window that had not been there before, drawing Cal toward a second ledge.

"Here," he said, gesturing through the pane, and Cal saw the familiar fishing houses, walls chapped by wind and sea; the village with its mottled stone that would later become bright whites and brilliant blues. "But over there," Raphael added, pointing to the first window as Gabriel spun the world around his finger, indicating the island of Mykonos, "you can see how small it really is."

Cal realized, then, that he had seen nothing, and knew less than nothing, and that this could not possibly be the end.

"What can I do?" he asked, turning slowly to Raphael. "I have to see it."

"See what?" Raphael asked.

"Everything," Cal said, and in a seraphic gesture of kindness that Cal would later learn was highly uncharacteristic, Gabriel settled a hand on his shoulder.

"Come," he beckoned softly. "We'll find you a uniform."

— Ω —

"Well," Mayra said, clearing her throat after Cal had spoken and putting on an elaborate display of normalcy. "In any case, this is an unexpected pleasure, if inconvenient. I've missed you," she added, the words bright and multifaceted, as if something darker might lie beneath.

"Have you?" Cal asked her quietly.

Fox, knowing a private moment when he saw one, flipped his copy of the *Tribune* shut and rose promptly to his feet.

"Well," he began, tucking the paper under his arm and wondering once again what he'd done with his cup of coffee. "I suppose I'll just—"

Then he stopped, something catching his ear. A knock at the door.

A first beat, hesitant, followed by two slightly hasty raps, and then a moment of silence. The usual urban reflex—*who could that be?*—swept over Fox, who remained frozen where he stood, head tilted in bemusement.

"Expecting someone?" asked Mayra.

Fox frowned.

"No," he said.

Living in a city is a study in knocks.

But even Fox could not have known how this one would change things.

# V

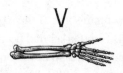

# THE BEAUTIFUL AND DAMNED

Thomas Edward Parker was born a poor man. An agrarian one, at that. His family and friends called him Tom, and he was a working-class sort of man—the kind you could grab a pint with at the end of a long day working the family farm, having both served your names and country well. But when the crops turned bad one year and Tom Parker decided to open a dry goods store with the surplus he'd reserved from years prior, he'd turned into something of a patron for the area; and then he opened another store, and then another, until he wasn't much of a working-class man anymore, but an entrepreneurial one. Still, he maintained that sense of camaraderie with the neighborhood, and before long, Tom Parker was a very rich man.

Thomas Edward Parker Jr., Tom's only son, was a lively young man called Ned (so as not to be confused with his father), and he took the Parker chain of dry goods purveyors into the future by developing Chicago's urban real estate, attracting other, similar businesses and transforming the city into something of a commercial success. He was a bit of a lady's man, and, in most respects, a man's man (a man about town, shall we say, and certainly no everyman, unlike his father), so it was a surprise to everyone when Ned took a lovely, no-nonsense wife quite late in life. It was Ned who'd built the Parker mansion in the Gold Coast, who coaxed the city along until it, too, flourished; and while Tom Parker had been rich, Ned Parker was *filthy* rich. By the time he mysteriously died, passing on his wealth and business acumen to his eldest son, the Parker family was quite firmly established among the Chicago elite.

Thomas Edward Parker III, the eldest son of Ned Parker, was a very serious man called Ed, who took his father's contacts and his father's father's riches and turned them both into a string of developments along

Lake Shore Drive, investing in some of the city's most desirable housing developments. While Tom Parker had been a beacon of the people and Ned Parker the blazing emblem of the nouveau riche, Ed Parker had enough of a bloodline to establish himself a foothold among Chicago's so-called Old Money, catering to luxury and making a name on the strength of his impeccable taste. By the time that *he* stumbled upon an unnatural death, many felt it was a result of envy, or perhaps spite. After all, Ed Parker had not been a particularly kind man, nor a very liked one. It was ultimately ruled a tragic accident and everyone quickly moved on.

Thomas Edward Parker IV, long enough down the line to once again be called Tom, was rather another matter altogether. His was the era of social media, of influence and lifestyle and unavoidable ennui, and as a result, Tom Parker was as much a commodity as he was a creator—far more than, in fact. His was a life of moderate celebrity, his every move recorded throughout the city, a *Forbes*-flavored heartthrob just waiting to be won. By then, the Parker empire was in satisfactory hands. It possessed a board of directors, of which Tom's uncle Benjamin James Parker assumed regency as chairman until Tom's expected graduation from the University of Chicago Booth School of Business. (Or at least, Uncle Benji was *intended* to serve until then, up to the point that Benjamin Parker, too, was killed, as the result of a botched heart operation—or so the public was informed.)

Ultimately, Tom's only job was to keep his nose clean, make sure the Parker machine was running smoothly, and placate his board and their donors by having all the right opinions until the time eventually came for him to rule.

Needless to say, the young Tom Parker was an exceedingly charismatic young man, if a bit of an archetype that was going out of fashion, and it was a great loss to everyone when he was found stabbed to death in the middle of his family's elaborate mansion.

THE PARKER CURSE STRIKES AGAIN, claimed the *Tribune,* plastering it across the front page and then sending waves out on Twitter.

#ParkerCurse was trending within an hour, shocking Chicago's elite.

*A break-in?* they whispered, presumably to clutched strands of pearls. *But our wealth, our prestige! Is nothing sacred?*

*If he had a gun!* they said (he did), or *if he'd had security!* (he had), *then perhaps he might have been saved;*

*Perhaps, perhaps, perhaps;*

But money can buy nearly everything, peace included (however false it may or may not be), and so when the rest of the Gold Coast had paid some segment of their family's fortunes to upgrade their alarm systems and militarize for the advent of cold-blooded thieves, they gradually forgot what had happened in the Parker mansion.

It took about a month before the house was put on the market. It was an architectural marvel, built from the American dream and yet flooded with European finery, and had Tom Parker IV been alive when it was placed on the market (or had he otherwise offered up a house with bloodless walls) it would have sold in an instant, or perhaps even less.

But as it was, the house sat unwanted for weeks that stretched into months.

Largely because it was haunted.

— Ω —

When Tom Parker had first opened his eyes and found himself incorporeal, he'd been more than a little inconvenienced.

"Fuck," he'd announced, looking down at his body. "That's a lot of blood."

Nobody answered.

He understood very quickly that he was dead. He wasn't an idiot (sure, he was privileged, but he'd certainly done a thing or two to deserve his spot at U Chicago—aside from the massive, massive Parker endowment which had done nothing to undermine the element of merit, probably) and it hadn't taken much time to realize that he couldn't touch anything, or do much to get anyone's attention. He had *some* control over his environment (he often toyed with the lights in the various parlors, if only to entertain himself when people came through to fuss with his family's belongings), but in the broad scheme of things, he was little more than a piece of furniture.

It was also no great reassurance that he was trapped in his family home.

Rather, it was the first on the list of things he couldn't explain. Despite some minor memory glitches he seemed to be having, he knew perfectly well that he no longer lived there. The mansion had been largely a museum in more recent years, part of it open for tours since the early passing of his mother, and Tom himself had lived in a Streeterville penthouse, artfully sparse, with a style defined mostly by clean lines and space and the efforts of a highly regarded designer. Tom had never cared much for the Parker mansion, in fact, and wasn't pleased in the slightest to be trapped there for what could conceivably be eternity.

When the house was put up for sale, however, Tom was even *less* pleased, which he tried desperately to let people know, resorting to electricity failures and noises that were regularly blamed, foolishly, on old, substandard wiring. (As if anyone in his family would have settled for anything less than the best, he'd thought, scoffing.)

It was only when Viola Marek came to sell Tom Parker's house that everything changed.

"HEY," he shouted, scowling, with the presumption that he would once again go unheard, but the practical sense that boredom and lethargy would only be needlessly gloomy. "YOUR MOTHER'S A WHORE, AND YOUR FATHER'S A—"

"Well that hardly seems polite," said the girl who had turned out to be Vi, and like a toddler shocked out of a tantrum, Tom promptly stopped flailing, pausing instead to stare at her.

"You—" He paused, glancing around. "You can see me?"

"Yes," she confirmed, with a brisk sort of impatience that he might have expected from a prettier girl; not that she was *unattractive*, per se, but—

"How did you get in here?" she demanded.

He stared at her, and then looked down, wondering if perhaps the bloody mass at his chest was less visible in the dim light of the hallway leading to his mother's second-best sitting room.

"Are you with the contractor?" Vi pressed, her brow furrowing. "Because I thought we said next Tues—"

She paused, frowning at him. Then, unbelievably, she groaned, throwing her hands up as if *he* were the nuisance in question and not, in fact, the obvious victim here.

"Oh *no*," she said, rubbing her temple. "Are you not really there?"

"What?" Tom demanded, managing to find his voice despite the shock of his first conversation in over a month. "Of course I'm here."

"But are you—" Vi sighed. "Are you *alive*?"

"No," Tom said, and narrowed his eyes in suspicion. "Are you?"

"Yes, obviously," she said, attempting to shove her hand through the corridor wall and of course failing immediately, and awkwardly. "Look." Another bang of wrist to mahogany. "See?"

He looked. He saw.

He found he was a bit let down.

"You don't seem very startled," he commented. "I'm disappointed."

"I've seen weirder things," she admitted, though in a measure of what seemed to be politeness she added, "You're my first ghost, though."

"What do you think?" Tom asked, swooping down to stand beside her. "Good, right?"

She considered him. "A little translucent, maybe."

"I mean, I'd prefer to change shirts," he agreed, gesturing to the stabbing in his chest. "But, you know. Whatever." He had the strangest feeling, like he was trying very hard to win her over, a thing he did not normally do. He could see why, now. It seemed exhausting.

"Well, I take it you have unfinished business, then," she said, returning her progress to what seemed to be the kitchen, a room he did not use and certainly hadn't touched since the beginning of the sharing economy (in fairness, it was philanthropic to support local

restaurants and a drain on resources—specifically: his—to cook).
"Are you Tom Parker?" she asked, flipping on the lights.

"Yeah," he confirmed, pleased enough, though admittedly he would
have been far more surprised if she hadn't known. "And you are?"

"Viola Marek," she said. "Call me Vi."

He was wrong about her not being pretty. Or right, he supposed,
since he'd known she was, she just wasn't the type of girl he normally saw or spoke to, which sounded . . . well, insufferable, which
he wasn't. Mostly. Most of the time.

Sometimes.

"What are you doing?" he asked, gesturing to the rustic Italian
loaf she was slicing in thick, crusty slabs. "Who let you in?"

"I did," she said, gesturing to the keys on the table. "I'm selling
the house."

He'd guessed that by then.

"Who gets the money?" Tom asked. He'd never cared much to
discuss such things while he'd been alive, but lately he found that
most of his poignant theories on social norms seemed far less worthwhile when nobody was available to applaud them.

"Dunno who specifically," Vi said, shrugging. "I'm selling on behalf of your trust, I believe. They're the ones who hired my agency.
But," she added emphatically, sweeping the crumbs away before
arranging the bread slabs onto his grandmother's second-worst
platter—no, god, not even, it was *Ikea*, she'd left the sticker on the
bottom!—"I'm just the sales agent, so—"

It occurred to him once again that he might be stuck there, in
that house, for all eternity. It was a feeling very much like coming
apart at the seams or being stabbed mysteriously in the sternum.
And suddenly it mattered very much that the surprisingly interesting
woman slicing up delicious-looking bread was functionally shitting
on everything Tom's family had ever owned, and therefore in some
way shitting upon Tom himself. And while he could not necessarily
follow this train of thought or explain how or when it had occurred
to him, he knew with a very grave certainty that she should be as
forcibly stuck to the situation as he was.

"Wait," Tom insisted, stomping a foot that set off an ear-ringing current of static. "You can't sell the house."

She looked consummately unamused. (This expression, he found, seemed to suit her far more than all the previous ones, as if it were a natural reflex. Somehow even her sardonic eyes were wide and warm and lovely, and he felt a pang of something square in his bloody chest.)

(Hatred.)

"I *can*, actually," she informed him, and suddenly he could picture her doing things like knitting pussy hats and haranguing him about how he never looked up from his phone. "Though it's been on the market for an awfully long time, so—"

"No, you can't," he said. "I refuse to share it."

"Well, then, get out," she invited, gesturing to the door, and he scowled.

"I thought I was going to like you," he said. "But I don't think I do."

"Why?" she asked. "Because I'm selling your house?"

"BECAUSE YOU'RE SELLING MY HOUSE," he confirmed, not altogether quietly. "Is this supposed to be some kind of joke? You obviously can't just sell it while I'm *still inside it*—"

"How'd you die?" she interrupted. She rested her palms on the counter and pulled herself up, swinging her legs once she'd perched godlessly atop it. "I mean. *Knife*, obviously," she acknowledged, reaching for some bread and waving it at the blood on his shirt. "But in terms of details—"

"Get off," he commanded, swiping a hand at where she'd seated herself. She shrugged, ignoring him, which had the enraging effect of forcing him to become defensive of every square inch of a house he had never even liked. (Frankly, he found it gaudy in the extreme, like winking at a guillotine.) "Come on, it's *Carrara marble*—"

"Maybe so, but it's not your Carrara marble," she reminded him, knocking twice on the counter for emphasis. "So, you know. Can't tell me what to do."

"Can too," he said briskly, and he quite figured he could. As a living person, he'd very successfully gotten his way without much trouble, and didn't see why that had anything to do with the physical possession of bones. "Have some respect for my home, would you?"

"I respect it," she informed him. "I'm trying to sell it, aren't I? It quite literally has value to me."

"Maybe it's me I'd like you to respect, then," he said, which he wished he had not said, because she looked overcome with indifference. "It's my house. You're treating it like . . . like . . ." he fumbled for an appropriately damning turn of phrase. "Like it's nothing. Like it's soulless. But it's not." He felt insane, but also like he should keep going, because even if the words were meaningless he'd at least stumbled onto a crescendo. "I'm in it!"

"You and this house are not symbiotic," she pointed out. "If anything, you're the parasite."

He reeled back, stung. "Well, that's quite an attitude," he managed to say without deflating like a small balloon animal.

She smiled at him, or smirked.

It irritated him, or aroused him.

Neither observation seemed helpful.

"So, your death," Vi continued, swinging her legs again. "What happened?"

He grunted his opposition.

"I don't know," he muttered. "I don't remember."

"Well, there's your unfinished business, then," she commented, and he frowned.

"Who says I have unfinished business? You don't know me."

"You're a ghost," she reminded him. "You're not haunting a person, right?" she added, gesturing to the empty house. "Nobody lives here."

"No," he confirmed. "But why haunt my house? Seems restrictive."

"It is," she agreed, without a trace of anything even passably resembling compassion. "But I really don't make the rules."

He was quite certain that he hated her.

But then he remembered that she was the only person he'd spoken to in weeks, and that perhaps she'd be the last person he'd *ever* speak to, and it seemed to strike him with a thunderclap of divine epiphany that perhaps that wasn't a coincidence at all.

"I think you're wrong," he realized, glaring at her. "I think my unfinished business is to prevent you from selling my house!"

She paused, considering it.

"Nah," she disagreed, shaking her head. "Seems unlikely. Maybe something happened here," she postulated. "Besides the murder, obviously. Was anything taken?"

"How should I know?" he demanded. "It's not like I can use the internet."

"You really don't remember anything?" she pressed him, looking for the first time as if she felt something beyond impartiality. "I mean, why were you here?"

"I really don't know." Tom sucked in his cheeks, sighing over his unintentional candor. Not the words, obviously, which were factual, and true. But more of the tonal suggestion that actually it had been haunting him (pun notwithstanding). "Honestly. I remember very little about the entire day."

"Well," she prompted. "What *do* you remember?"

He paused, considering it.

— Ω —

*"Tom." Lainey's voice, purring into the phone. "Please."*

*"Thank you for the offer, Elaine," he said, "but it'll have to be a no." He glanced over at the woman beside him, who had miraculously not woken. "I'm busy."*

*"It's just one small favor," she said. "Just a tiny one."*

*"That's what you said before, but—"*

— Ω —

"Hold on," interrupted Vi. "Who's Lainey?"

"My girlfriend," Tom said, and Vi frowned.

"I thought you said you were with a girl?"

"Well, my *ex*-girlfriend," he clarified, registering belatedly that the picture he was painting for Vi's benefit seemed a little flat. Was it worth defending? Likely not. He could tell based on feelings he was having that Vi was unlikely to be sympathetic to his plight either way. His feelings about Lainey were not, then, a matter of significance, and anyway Tom Parker did not require sympathy. He did not beg. "Still, I was probably going to marry her regardless."

"Oh?" Vi asked with precisely the brand of skepticism Tom anticipated. He would not get the benefit of the doubt from her, that was for certain. "Why's that?"

"Good for the company," he supplied listlessly. "She's a Wood."

"A what?"

"A *Wood*," Tom repeated emphatically, aware he was digging himself a hole, but what did it matter now what she thought of him? She didn't have to like him, and besides, it was kind of fun. "Don't you know anything?"

"I take it that's like Parker?" she asked, and Tom shrugged.

"Older name, but slightly less money," he said. "You've heard of the Cubs, haven't you?"

"Yes," Vi confirmed. "Obviously."

Tom shrugged again.

"Then you've heard of Lainey."

— Ω —

*"The last time you asked me to do a 'small thing,' I nearly got arrested," Tom replied, as the girl beside him stirred; Sarah, or Lauren, or possibly Megan, which was a name he'd encountered a lot in the aughts and hadn't seen much of since. Point being, they were not well-acquainted. "I swear, if I'd been any younger, Uncle Benji would've smacked me."*

*"You're still not too old for a spanking, Tom," Lainey said.*

*He glanced at the woman at his side.*

*"Down, girl," he murmured into the phone, and Lainey laughed.*

*"Come on, Tom. Just this one thing."*

*He scoffed. "No."*

*"Not even if I wear the—"*

*"No."*

*"But I'll bring the—"*

*"No!"*

*"I'll suck you off so hard you'll cry,"* she whispered, and to his dismay, he shuddered.

*"Don't need you,"* he told her, eyeing his fingernails. *"I'm over it, Elaine."*

He could practically taste her displeasure through the phone.

*"Stop calling me that."*

*"Stop calling me at all, then—"*

*"Never."*

*"—Elaine—"*

— Ω —

"I don't understand," Vi cut in, as Tom groaned over the constancy of her interruption. "What exactly is your relationship with Lainey? Or is it Elaine?"

"She preferred Lainey," he sniffed. "I, on the other hand, preferred to unnerve her."

"What makes you think you did?" Vi asked, and Tom frowned.

"Of course I did," he snapped, and then shook himself, unwilling to reframe what had heretofore been an extremely straightforward matter between himself and a woman who was not Vi. "And anyway, that's not important."

"Yes, actually, it is," Vi pointed out, rather obnoxiously. "You don't seem to have had any power in the relationship, did you?"

"What?" Tom asked, aghast. "Of course I did."

"You were in bed with *another woman*," Vi reminded him, "talking to your ex on the phone."

"Yes, telling her to leave me alone," Tom countered. "How is that not having power?"

"She called," Vi said. "You answered."

"Yes, but—"

"You *answered*," she repeated, and he glared at her. She smiled.

"What was the 'small thing' she'd wanted from you before? The thing you'd get smacked for," she clarified, and he rolled his eyes.

"I came to pick her up from somewhere once," he said. "It was three in the morning."

He thought it sufficient to stop there, but Vi obviously disagreed.

"Well?" she prompted, expectant. "Where were you picking her up from?"

He cleared his throat.

"Her house," he said, and Vi frowned.

"Why'd you almost get arrested, then?"

"Well," Tom sighed. "Because she'd just robbed it."

— Ω —

*"Tom," Lainey said. "Last thing, and I'll leave you alone forever."*

*"I don't believe you."*

*"It's not a big deal—"*

*"You always say that."*

*"You're too careful, Tom," she lamented. "One of these days you'll rub off on me."*

*"Frankly, I wish I would."*

*"Tom."*

*"Elaine."*

*"This is no fun," she whined. "Come over."*

*"Why?"*

*"Because saying things like 'rub off on me' with no physical component is boring."*

*"I thought you said we were done, Lainey."*

*"We're never done, Tom."*

*"Yes, we ar—"*

*"I'll let you do that thing you like," she interrupted. "You know. That thing you always want."*

*He paused, swallowing.*

*"I told you—"*

*"I know you, Tom. I heard your voice change. You want me to, don't you? Want me handcuffed to your bed," she said with a laugh. "That's the only way you can keep me, isn't it?"*

*He sighed. "Elaine."*

*"Tom."*

*"This isn't funny."*

*"It's not, no," she agreed. "It'd be funnier if I could watch."*

*"Watch what?"*

*"Watch you struggle," she murmured. "You have a tell, you know."*

*"What's that?"*

*"Your dick." She laughed.*

*He glanced down at his lap, overcome with a sudden desire to die very slowly in her arms.*

*"Come over," she whispered.*

*He swallowed.*

*"Ten minutes."*

— Ω —

"Oh my *god*," Vi said with a laugh, more of a bray than a cackle. "She *owns* you!"

"She doesn't," Tom insisted, to which Vi shook her head.

"You poor sap," she said, chuckling.

— Ω —

*His last concrete memory was of Lainey's blue dress.*

*On her, firstly, and then as it looked on the floor.*

*He remembered the sex. Sex with Lainey was always memorable, not because she was flexible (though she was), or because she was adventurous (though, again, she was), but because there was something intuitive about her; about the way they were together. It was poetic, really, in a filthy sort of way, in a way that robbed them of their hard-fought independence, lessening them to halves. There was a mutual longing when they were together, and it had never, ever been filled by anything except her sigh in his ear, or his gasp in her mouth.*

*It wasn't an evening gown. It wasn't silk.*

*It was a sundress, he remembered. He remembered the feel of cotton beneath his fingers.*

*It was summer.*

*It was hot.*

*He was sweating but her air conditioning was off; she hated the sound. Hated most sounds, most things; hated him, too, most of the time, except when her nails were digging into his hips and then she loved him, told him so, told him just how much.*

*"You're bad for me," she whispered, hair slicked to the back of her neck and clinging to her shoulders. "Aren't you?"*

*"I'm good for you," he told her. "I make you so good, Lainey, so fucking good—"*

*"Stop," she interrupted, her fingers on his lips. "I'm serious."*

*He stopped.*

*"You're bad for me," she said again, staring at him.*

*He met her eye; held his breath.*

*Counted the seconds, the heartbeats.*

*One Mississippi, two Mississippi, three Mississippi, four—*

*"I need this, Tom," she said, slipping her thumb across his jaw. "I need you to do this for me, baby, please."*

*He wanted to ask why, but he knew she'd never tell him.*

*"I'm still inside you," he offered in demurral. Which was the same, really, as saying yes, yes, yes.*

*She smiled.*

*"Rock my world, Tom," she invited, falling back, stretching out, shamelessly luxuriant beneath him. "And when you're finished with that, we'll talk."*

— Ω —

"So you slept with her," Vi said, unceremoniously. "Then what?"

"That's it," Tom replied, shrugging. "All I know is I woke up here. *There,* actually," he corrected, pointing to where there had once been a rug on the floor—a Persian, and a favorite of his mother's, which had clearly been besmirched by his apparently grisly murder. "Well," he amended. "*I* didn't wake up, but—"

"I get it," Vi assured him. "Spiritually, you awoke. A*rose,*" she amended fancifully.

"Arose," he agreed, and then grimaced. "Fucked, isn't it?"

Vi gave him something of a half smile.

"So where's Lainey now?" she asked. "Obvious question, I guess—"

"I don't know," Tom said honestly. "At some point I heard the detectives mention that she'd arrived on the scene when she heard I was dead, but after that they couldn't find her, so . . ."

He trailed off.

"Any chance she asked you to steal from *your* house?" Vi asked thoughtfully. She seemed to be mulling it over, toying with it, analyzing the story from every angle, and he couldn't tell if he appreciated it or not. It was effort, obviously, but he didn't quite relish the implication, especially since he was 80 percent sure he hated her very much.

"I mean," Vi clarified, "if she's the type of person to rob her *own* house, then maybe she needed the money."

"Lainey never needed money." It was laughable that she'd even suggest it, but then again, Vi was obviously no Lainey. Vi would have never been in any of Tom's circles, in fact, which was a thought meant to be bolstering in some way but achieving only the effect of making him feel worse about himself. (Tom didn't care for the existential clarity of death, which presumably explained all these unnecessary feelings.) "She never did anything because she *needed* to."

"Except you," Vi pointed out.

Tom frowned.

Considered it.

Rejected it.

"Nah," he said eventually. "Doubt she ever really needed me. She didn't come to the funeral," he added. "A lot of people came to the house to 'pay their respects' or whatever, but—" He paused, an unintentional voicelessness that felt profoundly implicating, and forced a shrug. "She didn't."

"Huh," Vi said, tapping her fingers on the counter. They were ordinary nails, maybe a little long. Later he would notice how routinely she scrubbed them and that somehow, despite this, her hands often had a slightly earthy scent. "Any chance *she* killed you?"

"Seems like that would be the obvious answer, wouldn't it?" Tom asked. "And honestly, it wouldn't surprise me if she wanted me dead, whatever her reasons might have been. If she even had them," he added. "She didn't always find them useful."

"What, reasons?" Vi asked.

"Yeah," he said ambiguously, having meant something even more vague, or something even vaster in scope. The thing about Lainey that had both tormented and fascinated him was that she didn't seem to find anything useful; didn't seem to categorize things by their use at all. It wasn't an uncommon attitude for someone of their background, but—and obviously there was no way to explain this to Vi—there had always been something heavier there for Lainey, something deeper than the tedium of excess wealth. It wasn't just apathy, it was weariness, down to the bone. Something darker and more culpable than boredom, more desperate than the next convenient high.

"But anyway—" Tom cleared his throat. "Whether she had reasons or not, I don't think she did it. I mean, she could have at any time," he pointed out. "I guarantee she kept a gun in her nightstand. A knife, even. Could've just gutted me. I mean, she *did*," he offered drolly, forcing a laugh when it came out too sad. "But I meant, you know. Literally."

Vi gave him a sympathetic look.

He ticked the plausible hatred up to 90 percent.

"So not Lainey, then," she said.

He cleared his throat.

"Not Lainey," he confirmed.

Vi opened her mouth to speak, and then closed it. She tried again, tilting her head, but then she looked up, both of them catching the faint echo of a sound from down the hall.

"Potential buyers," she said, glancing back at him. "They want to turn the house into a rehab facility for rich people."

"Mm," he said. "Well." He paused. "I'm going to probably break something." Fair warning.

"Fine." She seemed indifferent. He squinted at her, looking for evidence to the contrary, but she looked genuine enough. "I would prefer if you didn't, of course, but—"

"Vi," he said, facing her. It was a trick his father had always used; face the person, lock eyes, and very deliberately use their name. Sort of an imitation of intimacy, Ed had always said, and Tom had always made a point to listen.

"Listen," Tom said now, conspiratorially. "The thing is, I like you." He paused. "Actually, that might be a lie."

She nodded. "Understood. Go on."

"I like you, *probably*," he amended, "so this is nothing personal, but—"

How to put it into words? The mess of things, the blink of consciousness he knew now to be fleeting, the gutting revelation that eventually, life was little more than the countertops you used to hate?

"I get it," she interrupted him, waving a hand. "Haunt away."

"Really?" he asked.

She nodded. "Really."

She slid from the counter, turning to leave the room, and for whatever reason, he suffered a blister of disappointment at the idea that she was going, and that it meant he would inevitably be left alone.

"Talk later?" he asked in a fit of self-sabotage.

She rolled her eyes, picking up the platter of bread and dusting off her blazer.

"Why not?" she muttered, more to herself than to him, before heading for the door.

# VI

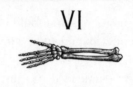

## MODERN MYTHS

"So you've got a ghost," Isis had said.

"I've got a ghost," Vi confirmed. "A very chatty one."

*Very* chatty. She'd thought at first that if Tom simply warmed to her he might ease up on the haunting, but that had not been the case. The last potential buyers had all suffered some variety of electromagnetic shock from every surface in the house. *Just a hot day,* she'd assured them, but they seemed about as willing to buy her excuses as they were to buy the house.

Fair enough. She wouldn't have, either. Many things about the house were not to her taste, including but not limited to the occupant moping incurably inside it.

"And, I take it," Isis continued, "people aren't really into the idea of buying a haunted house?"

"Most people just think the house's pipes are old, or that there's something off with the materials, but the cost of tearing a historical building apart and redoing it all, and with all the city permits required—" Vi shrugged. "Scarier to them than a ghost, really."

"Rich people," tutted Isis, lips pursed in disapproval. "Why are they always so fucking cheap?"

"Human people," contributed Sylvester, the computer-hacking fae called Sly for short, who was sitting two chairs to their left in the circle. "The worst."

"Dead people," Louisa the siren interrupted from Vi's right, shaking her head. "Or was that not the topic at hand?"

"Right, dead people," Vi confirmed. "*One* dead person, actually."

"A dead *Parker,*" Isis told them pointedly, and Sly frowned.

"Which one?"

"Which *one*?" Vi asked, bewildered. "Is this a thing?"

"The curse," supplied Isis, nodding.

"The *curse*," Louisa sighed wistfully. "I miss curses."

"*You* miss curses?" Sly demanded. "I should think *I'm* the one who—"

"Stop," Isis warned, snapping her fingers. "Focus."

"The curse," Vi pressed, turning to Isis. "You mentioned this before, about the Parkers being cursed. Is that a—" She paused. "Like, a *human* thing? Like a rumor, or—?"

"Humans talk about it," Isis replied ambiguously, and the other two nodded. "Sort of like a modern mythology type of thing." Her gaze drifted, somewhat longingly. "Reminds me of the old days, really."

"Yes, exactly," Louisa agreed. There was a slight singsong of enthusiasm to her tone that flared wildly around the room, prompting a visible thrill up the spine of every creature present except for Lupo, who as usual was drowning out the pre-meeting din with an incredibly cheap pair of knockoff AirPods. (They almost never successfully connected to Bluetooth but retained formidable siren protection, being glorified earplugs.) "You know, like the stories."

"Stories?" Vi asked, once she'd recovered from Louisa's effect. (Sexuality was a spectrum, she reasoned, which made all of this very normal and fine.)

"Stories," Sly said firmly, dragging his chair around to face her. "Once upon a time, there was a man who cheated Death, and so, on the third day, after a donkey shed its skin and a snake made a wish on a bridge, Death took him for his own." He shrugged. "You know. That sort of thing."

"People used to believe those things," Louisa told her, pulling her chair over to Sly's. "They don't now. People sort of embrace coincidence now," she added, picking listlessly at her nail polish. "They welcome chaos."

"Not everyone," Isis countered. "Clearly. Or they wouldn't still call it a curse, would they?"

"Okay, so, hold on a minute," Vi said again, holding up a hand. "I take it more than one Parker has died, then?"

"*All* the Parkers have died from something that's been either fully unexplained or highly improbable," Isis said. "And this one was stabbed, right?"

"Right," Vi confirmed, thinking of the gory mess on Tom's chest that had followed him into his afterlife. "But nothing was stolen from the house, and no alarms went off, and—"

"—there was nothing on the security footage," Sly finished, sounding bored. "Not that that means much. If you can hack into the alarm system—"

"But nobody *did*," Isis reminded him. "Remember? It was a whole thing. We checked."

"*You* checked?" Vi asked, frowning. "Why?"

"Sort of obligated to. Creatures are always suspected first," Louisa explained. "Lupo thought one of us had something to do with it."

"Not really," Isis assured her hastily, as Vi glanced around the room, helplessly searching it for evidence of criminal activity. "Not seriously. But hey, you gotta ask, right?"

"I guess," she permitted warily. "So, a billionaire—"

"Millionaire," corrected Sly. "Actually, you'd be surprised how much money the Parkers give away every year—"

"—*millionaire*, then," Vi amended quickly, hoping to avoid a lesson on the Parker endowment and any pursuing discourse on whether it was or wasn't immoral to build a fortune off the backs of unlivable minimum wage. "A millionaire was murdered, *mysteriously*, and with no suspects, and nobody knows how or why?"

"Not a soul," Isis confirmed. "Creature or otherwise."

"Not true," Louisa said. "I bet Death knows."

Vi laughed.

She stopped laughing, though, when the others didn't.

"What?" she asked, disbelieving. "*Death*?"

"You know, he has a godson," Sly suggested, as though he were talking about a distant relative and not, as it were, a manifestation of natural phenomena. "Lives in Wicker Park."

Louisa: "Bucktown."

Sly: "Ack."

Louisa, soothingly: "Common mistake."

Vi: "Hold on." (Conversation had gotten very fast at that point, like a ping-pong match.) "Death has a godson?"

"He's a medium." (That was Isis.) "He's not technically a creature, but we know about him."

Vi: "How?"

"Disruptions, you know," Sly said, waving ambiguously around their heads. "Haziness between realms, if you want to call them that. Rumor has it he's been alive for hundreds of years."

Louisa: "Though who hasn't, really."

Sly: "Well, precisely."

"But he's human?" Vi interrupted, confused. "So—"

Isis: "He's human, yes. Entirely mortal. But I think when you're raised by Death, there's a good chance you can sort of do whatever you want. He's definitely mortal, he's just also—" she shrugged "—*privileged*, I guess you could say."

"Nepotism," muttered Sly, disapproving, and Vi frowned.

"You said he's a medium?"

"A fraud, more likely," Louisa cheerfully supplied. "But he might be a good place to start, if you're wanting to get rid of your ghost."

"I am," Vi confirmed. "Very much wanting to."

She was getting quite tired of fielding calls about it. It cut into her evening time, and she had never developed a fondness for speaking while in feline form. There was an unpleasantness to it; hurt her throat.

(Small things, she figured, but still. If she'd lost her chance at happily ever after, then a reasonably untroubled afterlife seemed aspirational, if not fair.)

"You sure?" Isis asked, grinning. "You seem a little fond of Mr. Parker. It's that aura of concern you have," she explained, nudging her. "Makes it seem like you kind of like him."

Vi scowled.

*Like* was a definite stretch.

"I feel bad for him," Vi corrected, and she did—that much she could readily admit. "I'd hate to be in his position. To be trapped like that. *But*," she emphasized with a shake of her head, recalling her own position, which wasn't exactly a picnic. "The bottom line is that I need to sell the fucking house, and there's really no getting around that."

"Fair enough," Isis said. "I can come with you to see the medium, if you want. I've always been curious."

Louisa, with a nod: "Same. But he knows a creature when he sees one."

Sly: "He's not exactly friendly, or so I've heard."

That, Vi thought, sounded less than promising, but she wasn't about to press the issue.

"What's his name?" she asked instead.

Isis smiled.

"Fox D'Mora," she supplied. "The motherfucking godson of Death."

# VII

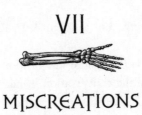

# MISCREATIONS

"Expecting anyone?"

"No," Fox said warily, and approached the door, glancing through the peephole. He frowned, taking in the sight of two women. One was fairly innocuous, with a subdued, nonthreatening look to her. The other, unnervingly, was eyeing *him* through the peephole, as though she were looking directly back at him from the other side. Fox shuddered, forcing the feeling aside, and cracked the door just far enough to speak.

"Yes?" he asked, not altogether patiently.

The women exchanged glances. One, the unnerving one, who was athletically built and coppery-toned in an idealized Amazonian kind of way, nudged the other forward.

"Hi," the other one said. She was sort of olive-skinned; mixed race, maybe white and something island-y if he had to guess, though he was comfortably certain he'd have just as easily overlooked her altogether. "Are you Fox D'Mora?"

"I am," he confirmed, though he wasn't happy about admitting it. "And you are?"

"I'm Viola Marek," she supplied, and took a breath, as many of his visitors often did before admitting their intentions. *I need to speak to someone*, the supplicants might prepare to say, wringing their hands, or *I need to access the other side*. Most of them had labored with it; after all, the need to visit with the dead was often a compulsion. An obsession, for some. A need, and many struggled with themselves before confessing upon arrival.

Not this woman.

"I have a ghost problem," she said flatly.

Fox blinked.

It wasn't *new*, exactly, but the delivery was surprisingly unbur-
dened.

"Interesting," he said, without elaboration. He had not yet determined the value of the conversation. It had been a quiet week so
far, but then again, silence was golden and this seemed annoying.
There was something off about the entire visit, from the eerie knock
with its portentous timing to the strange sense that the other one
had been looking at him through the door. Even now his skin was
pebbled slightly, as if from static. Perhaps if he said nothing of consequence they would both spontaneously disappear.

Viola glanced at the woman beside her, who shrugged.

"The thing is," Viola pressed on, interpreting Fox's silence as an
invitation to continue despite that being only sort of true, "I'm a real
estate agent. I need to sell this house, right?" she added, with a spirited air of conspiracy. "But I can't—"

"Because of the ghost?" Fox guessed, and Viola nodded.

"—because of the ghost," she confirmed.

He paused, considering it. It definitely sounded annoying, and
also, he couldn't be sure in this lighting, but he had the strange sense
that his reflection in Viola's otherwise normal brown eyes was somehow upside down.

"How's Death?" the other one interrupted, teeth cutting giddily
against her lip as she smiled.

Fox blinked again. (Perhaps he'd misheard, or misattributed a
proper noun where none had been intended?)

Then he frowned. (By the look on her face, he'd understood her
perfectly well.)

"Sorry," he said, though he wasn't. "What?"

"Is it true you call him Papa?" the unnamed woman asked, and
at that, Fox's suspicions were confirmed. He gave an impatient
growl as recognition dawned with an irritating clang of clarity, like
a summoning via gong.

"You're creatures," he deduced without pleasure, realizing now why
he'd found them so unsettling. "I don't do creatures. Best of luck," he
offered, moving to shut the door. "Really, good luck selling the h—"

The was a loud bang against the door as Viola's hand shot out, preventing it from closing.

"Sorry," she said, though she didn't look any more remorseful than he had been, and Fox wondered how long their mutual insincerity could persist. "I'm kind of not going to let you go that easily, I'm afraid."

"Bold claim," Fox commented.

"Oh, come on," Mayra coaxed behind him, and he jumped, startled by the reminder of her presence in his apartment. "Let them in, would you?"

"Oh, hi," the other woman said, peering at Mayra in Fox's apartment through the crack in the doorway. "Angel?"

"Ironically, yes," Mayra said, "as clearly, you're a demon." She nudged Fox aside to look more closely at Viola, humming to herself in thought. "You're something else, though," she noted, tilting her head with curiosity.

"Yes," Viola agreed, glancing warily over her shoulder. "Though I'm not sure it's appropriate for the entire hallway to hear."

"Something dead," Mayra ruled, apparently still trying to sort out Viola's particular brand of miscreation, and then brightened. "Huh," she remarked to herself, and pulled the door open farther, dragging Fox back by the collar of his shirt to allow the two women entrance. "Come in."

"Yes, welcome to *my home*," Fox muttered irritably, glaring at Mayra. "Never mind that rules are rules, and no matter how interesting you happen to find them, I *still* don't work for creatures—"

"What's going on?" Cal asked, rising to his feet as they processed into the living room, Fox sulking behind Mayra as she led the two creatures inside. "Who's this?"

"Isis," the demon offered, extending a hand. "You're a reaper, then? Hey," she said, gesturing between them and smirking. "Same team."

"Sure," Cal said warily, as Viola frowned.

"What's a reaper?"

"A soldier of Lucifer," Isis supplied, with the air of someone who was usually in possession of the answer—which was, relatedly, one of Fox's least favorite qualities for other people to have. "And *this* one," she went on, gesturing to Mayra, "is an accountant of God—"

"I prefer auditor as a term," Mayra corrected. "More accurate."

"True, true, must have lost that one in translation—"

"Okay, first of all, *stop bonding*," Fox announced, and both Isis and Mayra gave him skeptical looks of disapproval, but gestured for him to speak. "Look," he said, turning to Viola, "I understand that you need help—"

"I do," she said. "He—the ghost," she clarified, while the demon, Isis, nodded encouragingly (some might even say enablingly) beside her. "Anyway," Viola continued, "he doesn't know how he died, or why he's still there—"

"Which, as I said, is totally understandable as a problem," Fox assured her, unmoved by the knowledge of the ghost's pronouns or any other details of his situation. "But still, I don't work with creatures. No creatures, no gods, no demigods. Always ends up being something complicated," he added in explanation, since Mayra was glaring at him in a way that routinely made him feel like one of the small children in *Mary Poppins*. "Curses, you know, that sort of thing. Comes with the territory. Not my forte, and always more sacrifice involved than I'd like."

Which, as far as explanations went, was true. (Though, *always* was a bit of a stretch; in reality, one time had been enough for Fox to swear off the undead and/or immortal altogether.)

"Well, can't you at least talk to him?" Viola asked, in a tone Fox uncharitably associated with a request to speak to his manager. "The ghost, I mean. Or, you know. To Death?"

Fox scoffed loudly. "Believe me, Death would be even more opposed to this than I am," he informed her. "It would be *quite* a favor, and I'm not even sure you have anything to make it worth my while."

"He says, lyingly," Mayra contributed, and Fox rounded on her with a glare.

"What's that supposed to mean?"

"You're a collector, Fox," she reminded him, gesturing around the room to the furniture, the various trinkets lining the walls and shelves, the things a normal person would call décor that Mayra apparently considered the refuse of a compulsive magpie. "It's why you kept my relic, and why you have Cal's tags—and don't get me started on that watch—"

Fox shifted uneasily, tucking the watch beneath his cuff as he caught the demon's eyes wandering greedily to his wrist.

"So?" he muttered.

"*So,*" Mayra said, "I'm sure that a demon and a—vampire?" she guessed, and Viola nodded, prompting Mayra's golden cheeks to flush celestially with satisfaction. "Surely they have *something* of value to you, don't you think?"

"Not to mention that the ghost in question is a Parker," Viola added as if she'd only just remembered, with an imploring step toward him as if proximity might help. "The house is *full* of heirlooms, so—"

"A Parker?" Fox echoed, surprised. "Not Tom Parker? No, wait," he amended, frowning. "He's dead."

"Well, yes," Viola said impatiently. "You know, which tends to happen, what with the whole *ghost* thing—"

"No, I meant the first Tom Parker," Fox corrected her. "I heard about him once or twice. A long time ago," he clarified, shaking his head at the thought. "Clearly, seeing as we were contemporaries when I first came here. But this must be the . . ." He trailed off, thinking. "Fourth?"

"Yes, fourth," Viola confirmed with a nod. "Thomas Edward Parker the fourth."

It did not seem ideal. But then again Mayra was watching, and Cal was looking steadily at him in a way that suggested they both knew Mayra was watching, and anyway it was only one question. One call.

"Well, *fine*, then," Fox sighed, sucking his teeth a little with displeasure when Mayra preened again, content. "I guess I can call my godfather now—*if* you promise to keep it brief," he growled, "and to leave, quietly and calmly, regardless of his ans—"

"Oh, no," Viola cut in quickly. "Actually, we need you to come to the house, because he can't seem to leave it."

Fox felt his mouth tighten, both at the interruption and the new information, which was very upsetting. This was now infringing on two rules. And it could so easily have been an email.

"I don't make house calls," he began to say when Mayra cut him off, groaning aloud.

"Do you need me to pull out your ledger, Fox D'Mora?" she demanded, snapping her fingers to produce a golden scroll from midair. "Sorry to inform you that once again, you're in the negative," she said. (Isis the demon leaned over, struggling to view the scroll's contents as Mayra pulled it out of her sight.) "*Deeply* in the negative, actually, just as you've been since the middle of the nineteenth centur—"

"Doesn't matter," Fox reminded her, uninterested in the details of his tiresome moral existence. "Or do I really need to remind you that I'm not dying anytime soon?"

"See? Nepotism," Isis whispered to Viola, which Fox resolutely ignored.

"Come *on*," Mayra urged, adjusting her wings to accommodate a coaxing shrug. "I'm out of miracles, Fox. I need something to do."

"Oh, so then you're coming, too?" Fox demanded, feeling as if all of this had gotten very quickly out of hand. Just the other day he'd been a perfectly respectable businessman with his head between a client's legs and now he was being bossed around by an angel for no benefit whatsoever (except some unquantifiable advantage to his soul, which he had never cared about before and certainly wasn't concerning himself with now). "You're suddenly interested in ghost stories, are you, Mayra Kaleka?"

"I'll come," Cal offered, with his usual quiet solemnity. "What?" he asked when Fox deliberately stared at him, arching an admonishing brow. "I've never been inside the Parker mansion. Seems like it could be interesting."

"Oh, sure," Fox muttered, narrowing his eyes as Mayra innocently considered the ceiling. "*Of course* that's why—"

"I," Cal said with one of his insufferable smiles, "have no stake in this matter, Fox D'Mora, and certainly no agenda to speak of, so naturally I cannot imagine the source of your tone."

"Okay, well, great," Viola judged aloud uncertainly, somehow gauging the back-and-forth between Fox's extremely unhelpful associates to be affirmation of her cause. "Tomorrow there's an open house in the afternoon, but if you can come right after that—"

"Now you want to *schedule* me?" demanded Fox, who had already parted with so much of his dignity today and could not for the life of him remember where he'd put his cup of coffee. "What's wrong with right now?"

"What's wrong with right now," Viola retorted without expression, "is that if I don't get on the L quite soon, I'm going to turn into a terrifying hell-beast."

"She means a cat," said Isis.

"I meant what I said," said Vi, and Fox, clearly outnumbered and suddenly ravenous, gave a loud, long-suffering sigh.

"Fine," he said. "Tomorrow, then—"

"Excellent," contributed a delighted Mayra, plucking a loose feather from her wing and gifting it with theatrical ceremony to Viola. "When you're ready for me to arrive, make a wish on that feather, would you?"

"A wish?" Viola said, looking as if she couldn't decide whether to laugh. "How . . . fanciful."

"Fanciful bullshit, more like," Isis said, and Mayra nodded.

"Inconvenient," she agreed. "Overly whimsical, certainly, but not wholly without its merits."

"And you?" Viola asked, turning to Cal. "How do I find you?"

"Oh, I'm just staying with Fox," he said.

"The hell you are," Fox retorted.

"Mayra," Cal said, turning to her. "What was that about Fox's ledger?"

Mayra gravely cleared her throat. "Deeply in the negative, beginning with the time he first stole a bit of—"

"OKAY," Fox said, rolling his eyes. "Fine. *Fine.* So, in summary,

I have an appointment with some creatures at a dead man's house and a reaper sleeping on my couch—"

"I don't sleep," Cal reminded him, and Fox threw his hands up.

"You seem stressed," Isis commented. "Is this by chance triggering some complicated feelings for you? If so, I'm sure we have time to fit in a workout. Have you tried a body scan meditation?"

"Don't talk anymore," Fox told her. "You're hurting my head."

"Great," Viola declared again, turning to the door. "See you tomorrow, then."

"Not great," Fox corrected. "Decidedly not great, but yes, tomorrow."

The demon paused at his side, glancing oddly at him.

"How old are you?" she asked, and he groaned.

"Didn't I tell you to stop talking?"

"I'm just curious—"

"How old are *you*?" he snapped, and she smiled.

"Ageless," she replied, with an air of eternality.

He pursed his lips.

"Fine. I'm twenty-seven," Fox said. "Happy now?"

She smirked. "Been twenty-seven for long?"

Once again, the hair along Fox's arms stood on end, like static. This time he had an additional, primal sense of having been unopened, like a knife had applied itself thinly to some adhesive layer of his mind.

"Very mortal of you to wonder," he commented in lieu of the truth, and she laughed, dazzlingly.

"Well, I strive to make myself relatable," she returned.

His stomach twisted. A thousand thoughts contorted in his mind, birthing a thousand more. He swallowed them all. He dragged them from his soul and cast them aside.

"You remind me of someone I used to know," he said eventually, traveling a long way down steep paths of his memory. "And for the record, I hate them."

She looked oddly triumphant.

"Fair enough," she agreed, and smiled.

It was an unsettling smile, and Fox, lost for words, headed to the door, holding it open and ushering them through it.

"Goodbye," he said, without watching them go.

— Ω —

"You think she knows?" Mayra asked later, curling her hand around Fox's shoulder.

Of course she doesn't know, he thinks.

She cannot know.

(Can she?)

(This is why he doesn't work with creatures.)

"Yes," he said, frowning.

Mayra smiled warmly. One of her smaller miracles, for which there was no price.

"Sleep well, Fox," she said, and kissed his cheek.

"Goodnight," he whispered.

— Ω —

"Juice pack?" Isis offered, holding one out to Vi as they took the Blue Line to the Red Line, taking the slightly complicated but largely timely route back to their respective homes. Vi accepted, glancing uneasily around the train.

"Something feels off," Vi commented, puncturing the box and pausing, bringing it carefully to her lips. "Something just feels . . . *wrong*." She tried to shake away the intangible off-ness of it all, instead letting the blood spread gradually across her tongue like a full-bodied Syrah, which was effective for a bit, if fleeting. "It's nothing to do with Fox," she added after she swallowed, because while their visit hadn't been a *delight*, there was nothing about the encounter to give her this kind of unease. Vi knew difficult clients, persnickety vendors, recalcitrant sellers. They were all functionally the same, and Fox was, after all, only human. "I can't explain it."

Isis looked around in apparent agreement.

"There are more creatures here than normal," she noted, in apparent confirmation of Vi's theory. "There's a general undeadness to the air."

Closest to them on the train was a man in a suit, a woman in athleisure. Neither looked suspicious or even out of the ordinary. Further down was the usual passenger blaring unsolicited music from their phone, a woman with a baby stroller, a teenager in a school uniform. None of them looked especially paranormal, but then again, neither did Isis or Vi.

"How can you tell?" Vi said, pinching the plastic straw thoughtfully between her teeth.

"I can tell a lot of things," Isis said, shrugging. "Sort of comes with the territory." She nudged her chin in the direction of the stroller. "Whatever's in there is extremely ancient," she said in an undertone, "so try not to look it in the eyes."

"You know, I never really asked what being a demon entailed," Vi noted, glancing again at Isis. (She often seemed so normal that Vi forgot to wonder what else was involved.) "You've always said that like it means something, but I guess I just never asked."

"Well, there's some poeticism to it, I suppose—the whole 'casting off your demons' thing, you know," Isis replied, waving a hand. "Abilities vary, obviously, but down to the quick of it, we exist to remind mortals of their inner selves. I daresay being around the godson of Death will do wonders for my complexion," she added, turning to preen in her reflection from the train's scratched up windows. "We really thrive on blood sacrifice, but psychological trauma will do in a pinch. Especially the kind he's been through."

"Seems—" Vi paused. "Slightly immoral, doesn't it? Taking advantage of him like that?"

Isis nodded, but shrugged. "Can't do much about that. Demons feed on misery. It's why I always live in a city—plenty of that to come by, especially with weather conditions like this. I tried L.A. once," she added, with a bit of winsome nostalgia. "There's sort of a vacuousness there, though. Too many transplants, too many artists. Melancholia and misery aren't really the same, you know?"

"I don't think I realized this about you," Vi remarked, and Isis shrugged again.

"You're a creature," she said, with a fraternal sort of nod. "I leave creatures alone. Got their own thing going on, and anyway, I'm a demon, not a monster. But Fox, on the other hand—"

"Why was he so upset?" Vi asked. "It seemed like you were reading his mind, but that's—"

"I was," Isis confirmed bluntly. "Well, less *reading* it—that's a bit, you know, elementary. It's more like catching imprints of it. Tracing the bits of it that matter and feeling out the pressure points."

Interesting. "And what are Fox's pressure points?"

"Abandonment," Isis said without hesitation. "Disillusionment. Resentment. Guilt."

"Guilt? Really?"

"Yes, guilt," Isis confirmed, nodding. "Tends to happen when one lives for several hundred years. Can't really help picking up a crime or two along the way."

Vi gave a perfunctory nod, her attention already drifting by then to thoughts of open houses and noisy ghosts, and took another sip of her juice box, looking around. This time, she noticed that several heads had swiveled her way the moment she raised it to her lips, various passengers registering the presence of blood. There was an eerie sort of creeping up her spine now, as if too many eyes rested on the back of her neck.

She forced a swallow and shifted closer to Isis.

"So, do you think Fox is going to be able to fix this?" Vi asked, aiming for neutrality, and Isis smiled.

"Well, I certainly hope so," she said. "I mean, if we're going to go through all this trouble," she added, glaring at the man in the suit, who now seemed to be helplessly reaching out for her juice pack. "Here," she said, tossing it to him. "Drink your own and move along, would you?"

He seemed surprised but nodded gruffly, stumbling down the train.

"Ghoul," Isis offered in explanation, as Vi raised a brow. "I think.

Something dead, for sure. Probably something that likes corpses, too, by the looks of it."

"Gross," Vi determined, shuddering.

"Says the vampire," Isis reminded her with a firm nudge. "The *aswang*, even. Don't you have a whole thing with unborn babies?"

Vi forced herself not to let her eyes drift toward the woman with the stroller. Easier now that Isis had as good as told her it wasn't human after all.

"Yes," Vi permitted, "but I'm managing it."

"You can't manage everything," Isis remarked with a put-on sense of foreboding, like the narrator opening a tale of such woe. "And anyway, I'm not totally sure you've thought this through. You know that if Fox is successful, Tom will be *gone*, right?"

"It had occurred to me, yes," Vi replied dryly. "Only in the sense that it's my primary goal."

"Gone," Isis said again, *"forever."*

"Yes," Vi agreed. "Correct."

"Are you sure that's what you want?" Isis prompted. "No little nigglings of opposition?"

Vi battled the strangest feeling that she was being thoroughly invaded.

"I thought you said you leave creatures alone?" she asked tartly, and Isis smiled.

"Sorry," she sang in reply, without a trace of apology. "Force of habit."

# INTERLUDE I:

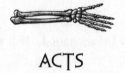

## ACTS

Fox is human, and so he dreams. That night, he has the same dream; the same dream he always has, every night. He watches it like a play.

— Ω —

[The scene opens upon two lovers in bed. The candles are low, and the bed, meant for a single occupant, is far too small for the both of them. Still, they huddle together, bathed in each other's warmth, and they whisper; not because they fear they will be overheard, but because they fear retribution. They fear their words will come back to haunt them, and so they restrict them, hold them close.]

[The scene begins with a young man; too young. Young men are fools.]

[Act I, Scene I. Begin play.]

**The fool:** Will you still love me, do you think? If we are ever to be old and gray.

**The thief:** You'll never be old, Fox. And I certainly will never be gray.

**The fool:** You will. Someday.

**The thief:** How mortal of you.

**The fool:** You're mostly mortal too, you know, despite your efforts to hide it.

**The thief:** Well, I strive to make myself relatable.

**The fool:** You know, sometimes I wonder . . .

**The thief:** Wonder what?

**The fool:** If I hate you.

**The thief:** You don't hate me. Didn't you just say you loved me?

**The fool:** No. I asked if you would still love *me*.

**The thief:** Ah.

**The fool:** Well?

**The thief:** The question doesn't apply, Fox. Go to sleep.

**The fool:** Why?

**The thief:** Because.

**The fool:** That's not an answer.

**The thief:** You're a child.

**The fool:** I'm not a child.

**The thief:**—he says, childishly.

**The fool:** It's a simple question. Will you love me still?

**The thief:** You'll never grow old, Fox, and neither will I. I won't let us, remember?

**The fool:** But you see my concept, don't you? Say we don't get old. Say we live forever. Will you love me, then? Well into forever?

**The thief:** Fox.

**The fool:** It's a simple question.

**The thief:** Yes, but it's not a simple answer.

**The fool:** So it's a no, then. Do you even love me now?

      [Silence.]

**The thief:** What if I tell you that I will love you, Fox D'Mora, every day that I walk this earth—would that make you happy? Is that what you want?

      [More silence.]

**The fool:** Are you lying?

**The thief:** Impossible to tell. Do you think I'm lying?

**The fool:** I think you enjoy lying to me.

**The thief:** Then why do you love me?

**The fool:** Because I'm a fool. Why do you love me?

**The thief:** Because you're a fool.

**The fool:** And because you're a thief.

**The thief:** And what, pray tell, am I supposed to have stolen?

**The fool:** This watch, for one. My affections, for another.

**The thief:** Ah, yes. Rather an incidental theft.

**The fool:** Do you regret it?

**The thief:** For your sake? Perhaps.

**The fool:** How philanthropic of you.

**The thief:** Go to bed, Fox.

**The fool:** You go to bed.

**The thief:** Clever, aren't you?

**The fool:** Kiss me.

**The thief:** Clever and demanding, it seems.

**The fool:** Please?

[A kiss occurs; it is neither given nor taken. The kiss is shared.]

**The thief:** Happy now?

**The fool:** You taste funny.

**The thief:** Well, that's what I get for indulging you, I suppose. Mockery.

**The fool:** No, I mean—you taste *different*.

**The thief:** Different how?

**The fool:** Different, like . . . like how the air smells different after rain.

**The thief:** Like change, you mean?

**The fool:** Yes, I suppose. Like change.

[They marinate in silence.]

[It drags, and falters, and pulses.]

**The thief:** I'm afraid I will cost you quite greatly, Fox, and I'm desperately sorry for it.

[The fool battles his folly. Temporarily, he wins.]

**The fool:** I think perhaps I'll go to bed now.

[The thief swallows heavily.]

**The thief:** All right.

**The fool:** Will you stay until I fall asleep?

[A pause.]

**The thief:** Always.

**The fool:** Are you lying now?

[Yes, and they both know it.]

**The thief:** No way to tell, is there?

[There is no Scene II. The fool wakes alone. End Play.]

# VIII

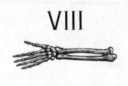

## OPEN SEASON

"I remembered something else today," Tom announced, and Vi inclined her head, acknowledging him discreetly as she watched prospective buyers wander around the Parker home, speculating widely about rehabilitation facilities, institutional libraries, and/or personal saunas.

"I remembered that it was someone's birthday that day. You know," Tom added, gesturing to his chest. "*That* day."

"I didn't realize you'd want to chat right now," Vi commented warily, not looking at him. "Thought you'd be busy poltergeist-ing." She waved a hand, gesturing ambiguously around the sitting room, which was one of Tom's favorite settings for mischief. "What with all these potential new owners here, I mean. Your opportunities for mayhem are spectacularly boundless."

"None of these people are serious buyers," he admonished her with a scoff, to which Vi arched a brow, permitting a wary show of interest (this, unlike most of Tom's opinions, was worth knowing, given her position as the seller in this particular case). "My dad always had an eye for this sort of thing. Look at that guy," Tom explained, pointing at someone in the corner. "He's studying that painting *far* too closely for that not to be what he's really here for. Probably expecting it to show up at an estate sale or something. And that woman," he noted, gesturing, "her suit's been re-tailored more than once; the buttons are imperfectly matched. She doesn't have the money for this."

"Maybe she works for someone else," Vi suggested. "There are people who want to turn it into a government building, you know."

"Nah," Tom sniffed. "She'd be taking notes, taking pictures; some-one else buying the house would want details on the investment, presumably. If you ask me, she looks like a blogger," he guessed. "She's checked all the rugs, and I swear she's looking for blood stains."

"God, what a bunch of vultures," Vi murmured, shaking her head in disapproval. "But maybe she just likes the suit?"

"She doesn't," Tom corrected. "Watch," he added, and Vi obliged, considering the woman from afar as she shifted, tugging at her pencil skirt. "I think she finds the material uncomfortable. More likely it's her only suit. She's gained some weight, I think," he noted. "Hence the re-tailoring."

"You're good at this," Vi grudgingly allowed.

"Nothing better to do," Tom replied. "Plus, I checked her purse, and the receipt from the tailor's in there."

Vi rolled her eyes. "You're the worst," she said, which he did not contest.

"So anyway," he continued instead, as if she'd simply remarked upon the weather. "It was someone's birthday."

"Not yours," Vi said. "I looked it up."

Tom made a delighted, terribly irritating cooing sound. "*Vi*-ola," he sang, holding his hand over his bloodied heart. "You know my birthday?"

"More like I know it wasn't your birthday because it also wasn't Christmas," she reminded him smartly. "Because as you might recall, to the rest of the world, December twenty-fifth registers as something slightly more significant than simply Thomas Edward Parker's birthday."

"Thomas Edward Parker *the fourth*," he reminded her with a wag of a finger. "Important distinction."

"Quite," she said, stifling a yawn. "So, whose birthday, then?" she pressed, glancing over at him. "Lainey's?"

"Nah," he said. "It wasn't, and anyway one of us would have mentioned it in the phone call. Besides, usually on her birthday I take her to this diner she likes in the South Loop. She likes the red velvet there because they add a side of whipped cream to the cream cheese frost—" He broke off, catching the look on her face. "What?"

"You take your ex-girlfriend to dinner on her birthday?" Vi asked, amused. "What was all that about 'we're done here,' then? Just you playing games?"

Tom gave her a look of singular irritation.

"We'd fought," he explained. "We had our ups and downs, and that was definitely a down—but still, I'd have taken her out for her birthday. Tradition, you know. When you're the fourth person with the same fucking name," he muttered, more to himself than to Vi, "you tend to attach to things that feel meaningfully repetitive."

Vi shrugged. This, like much of Tom's life and personal history, was a very *can't relate* state of affairs. "What'd you fight about?"

"Not sure," Tom admitted, grimacing. "I keep trying to remember, but it feels like something's blocking me somehow." He leaned forward, rubbing his temples. "Makes my head hurt, actually."

"Odd," Vi remarked, which, unlike most things she said to Tom, she meant in an authentic way. "Seems like you shouldn't feel things like that." She herself didn't feel much in the way of aches and pains. Just hunger.

"I sort of thought I'd feel less in general," Tom agreed, and brightened. "Remind me to ask Death about it when we see him."

"Did you not see him before?" Vi asked. "I mean. Presumably he came for you, right?" *She* hadn't seen him, but she supposed her death hadn't really counted. Her condition was more of a loophole of a life than a real, proper end.

"Maybe I did, maybe I didn't." Tom shrugged. "The memory lapses, you know. Who knows. Maybe he performed a full, grim reaper-y rendition of 'I Ran' and I just lost the whole thing—"

"That," Vi interrupted, "is a classic, whatever anyone says."

"I know," Tom said stiffly, "which is why I imagine it's in Death's repertoire."

"Excuse me," someone ventured, interrupting their conversation and sidling up to Vi. His golden-blond hair, which contrasted strangely with his pale blue eyes—a bit like mixed metals, Vi thought, abruptly reminded of flashes of gold and silver—was slicked back neatly from his face. She caught the slim, jagged line of a scar across his upper lip and watched it level itself as the man smiled, the white line of it stretching idly above his canines. "You're the real estate agent, yes?" he asked. "Ms. Marek?"

"Yes, that's me," Vi confirmed, offering him a hand. "May I help you?"

"I'm just curious," he began, accepting her proffered grip with a firm but unremarkable amount of pressure, "I know there are sometimes tours hosted in this house." He gestured vaguely around the room as she nodded in confirmation. "When are those?"

"Weekends, late morning," Vi supplied in answer. "Which will, of course, willingly cease once the house is purchased. For now, though, the Parker Foundation has a controlling stake in both the house and the offices. They say that Wynona Parker—the wife of Ned Parker, who built the house—started the tours herself nearly a hundred years ago," Vi added, leaning into a bit of anecdotal charm. "She was particularly fond of the solarium."

"Yes, yes, interesting," the man said disingenuously, glancing around the room. "What's the security like here?"

"Poor," Tom said. "Clearly."

"Hush," Vi said through her teeth, as the man continued to inspect the ceilings. "It's excellent, sir—though most things in the house are insured," she added, sensing something off about his behavior. "And protected by dogs," she threw out wildly, in a fit of inspiration.

"No it isn't," Tom scoffed. "Dad was allergic, so—"

The man shifted, glancing at precisely the spot where Tom was standing.

"Good try," the man said blandly to Vi, "but there's no reason to frighten me off. You don't think I'm a serious buyer?" he prompted, offering her a full spin so as to appreciate the finery of his sartorial choices. "I assure you, if I decide I want the house, it's as good as mine."

"Oh, no, sir," Vi assured him, "I just—"

"Viola," the man interrupted, and then glanced warily at her. "May I call you Viola?"

"Sure," she allowed with a sense of foreboding, and he nodded, pleased.

"I see I've given you the entirely wrong impression, but you should know that you do some lovely work with staging, and that I've slipped myself one of your cards for future use. Not a bad picture, by the way," he commented, holding it up between two fingers. "You pull off a collarless blouse with aplomb."

"Maybe not with aplomb," Tom disagreed. "Something slightly lower. I mean, you look fine, but—"

"Thank you," Vi told the man, speaking pointedly over Tom despite the fact that no one could hear him. (*She* could, which felt like reason enough.) "It's a good blouse."

"Isn't it funny how objects endear themselves to us?" the man asked, reaching into his pocket and producing, oddly, a small yellow apple, almost like one of the apple-pear hybrids Vi knew they sold in an obscure corner of the supermarket. He buffed part of it, shrugging, and then took a bite, chewing quietly and politely waiting to speak until after he'd swallowed. "Like, this blouse," he continued, holding up the card again. "It's good because it makes your neck look, you know—" He gestured, using the hand with the apple. "Makes it look *regal*. You know. Like a pillar."

"I suppose," Vi permitted, and then, for reasons she could not explain, she allowed the conversation to continue, adding, "possibly a bit more to it, though. Material and all that." She shrugged. "Fits right every time, et cetera."

"Yes, sure, but to that point, nobody's questioning *your* material," the man said, in something of a baseless tangent. "Anyone ask you what you're made of lately? I'd guess not," he answered himself, taking another bite into the apple. "Because *you* are good or bad separate from who you serve, right?"

"Well," Vi said, glancing askance at Tom, who looked equally bewildered. "What's your philosophy on houses, then?"

The man paused, thinking it over.

"Well, what makes a house good or bad? Its foundation, I suppose," he postulated, nodding to himself. "It's got anatomy too, though. Guts and stuff. *This* house," he said, abruptly tapping his foot against the floor. "It's got guts, for sure. Good bones. Good face. How's its soul?"

He stopped, waiting, and she blinked.

"I—" Vi faltered. "What?"

"How's the house's soul?" the man asked again, less patiently. "Has it got one, firstly?"

"It's an inanimate object," Vi reminded him slowly, and he shrugged.

"Houses've got souls," he said. "You know when you walk into a house and you can smell the home cooking, hear the children laughing, playing? That's the soul of it. *A* soul, anyway, but not this one's soul. *This* house, well—" He shrugged again. "If I had to guess, I'd say it's got a soul like a church, you know? Seen too much. Seen everything. Austere. Real sense of hierarchy to it." He shifted, taking another bite, and gestured toward the ceilings, sweeping his arm around to reference the room. "Churches, man. *They've* got tears on the floor, though," he said, somewhat thoughtfully. "You can feel them. Taste them. This place isn't quite that."

He paused again, chewing slowly.

"This place's got blood on the walls," he said, somewhat eerily.

Vi, uncomfortable, felt it best the conversation come to an end before someone else overheard them. "Are you—" she began, and stopped. "Is this . . . are you a blogger or something? Because if so—"

"Nah," he said, getting down to the core of his apple and tossing it in the garbage at her side. "Why?"

"That's—I just—"

"Oh, is there actually blood on the walls?" he asked, laughing. "Just a guess, *jenta mi*."

Vi didn't recognize the term, but she frowned anyway, ambiguously displeased.

"Not that it changes anything for me," he assured her. "I've got blood in my veins, haven't I? Haven't *you*?" he prompted. "Why should it scare me if it also lives in the plumbing?"

Someone a few feet away looked up, frowning at their conversation.

"Could you possibly not say things like that?" Vi asked, as politely as she could manage.

The man grinned, the thin scar on his lip stretching up again. "Sure thing, my."

"'My'?" Vi echoed, and he shook his head.

"My," he said again, and because she couldn't hear the distinction, he reached up to draw it into the air. *Møy*, he wrote, and that time, she nodded. "Means *pretty girl*," he explained, "so take it as a compliment."

"Mansplaining," Tom muttered, rolling his eyes. "Even I know that's passé."

"Isn't the whole thing with compliments that they sort of . . . give off a complimentary impression?" Vi asked the man dryly, and he laughed.

"Not to worry, *møy*," he told her, "my intentions are pure. Or, at least, purer than you suspect, I imagine."

"I'm mostly curious about your purchasing intentions," she reminded him.

"Ah, right," he agreed. "Well, those too, I think, are not what you expect."

"So you're interested, then?"

"Oh, certainly I'm interested," he agreed. "But I can see I have monopolized your time, so I think at this point, I've seen what I need to. Best of luck, Viola Marek," he offered, and tipped his head as if he were wearing a hat. "And you, I think, could possibly use some laundering, but best wishes to you as well," he added to Tom, and then walked away, leaving the other two to stare at each other in confusion.

Vi frowned. "Did he just—?"

"Wait," Tom said, glancing at Vi. "Hold on."

He disappeared, and as instructed, Vi waited, watching the crowd.

The man was clearly strange, she thought firstly, though she didn't know what to make of him, and so she didn't think it worth the time to consider.

Her second thought, shortly after, was that the juice box in her purse was particularly tempting at this moment; though, again, she wasn't quite sure what to make of that either.

She felt *off*, slightly, which was difficult to explain, even to someone who understood it, like Isis. For whatever reason, Vi felt extremely conscious of her teeth. Wanted to sink them into something. She glanced over at the woman in the hastily tailored suit, trying not to eye her stomach. Anything that attracted her attention these days was something to be avoided, and she was growing increasingly confident this was one of those.

Yes, drat, there it was, all the signs. The waft of ginger tea for nausea from the thermos in the woman's hand, the swollen ankles, bandages showing precisely where her shoes had started to cut in, the weight gain that forced her to wear the uncomfortable suit. She hadn't touched the wine or any of the soft cheeses, the cured deli meats.

Taken along with Vi's heightened senses, there was only one reasonable conclusion.

"How far along?" Vi asked the woman. It was a question Vi had worried about asking as a human, but not so much as . . . whatever she was now. By now, she knew a pregnant woman when she saw one—knew the pulse of a living thing, even when it was inside of another—which was, in truth, far more disconcerting than practical.

Though the practicality of it was, obviously, not altogether forgone.

The woman looked surprised. "Fourteen weeks," she answered. "Just at the start of my second trimester. Do you have children yourself?" she asked, though she looked dubious. "My coworkers just assume I'm getting fat."

"People," Vi sighed with a shake of her head. "They're all just the worst, aren't they?"

The woman stepped closer, and Vi's heart, were it functional, might have raced.

"Listen, I have to be honest," the woman said, appearing to think they'd bonded somewhat over shared possession of a uterus. "I'm not actually here to buy this house. I'm writing a book on the Parker family, and—"

*Don't come closer,* Vi thought instantly, and forced herself to focus.

"It's okay," she managed to respond, feeling a bit dazed. "Naturally people are curious. But you—" She paused, feeling a twitch in her fingers, salivation gathering on her tongue. A strange sensation shot up her spine, like she wanted the woman to run, to dart away so she could chase her. "You should probably go," Vi finished hoarsely, and the woman's brow furrowed.

"Sorry," she said, looking delicately betrayed. "I just thought—"

The tension in Vi's spine roared through her limbs and her hand shot out, closing around the woman's arm. The woman blinked, staring down at Vi's fingers, and Vi—remembering at the very last moment that she may have been a vampire but she was, importantly, a broker first—gave herself another internal shake.

*Don't you have a thing about unborn babies?* Isis had said.

(Yes. Just a small thing, otherwise known as a taste for flesh.)

"Sorry," Vi managed, forcing herself to turn the motion into a reassuring pat. "I understand, of course it's your job, but in the future, try to make an appointment with the Foundation. This is about the sale," she clarified, "so I'd rather not be distracted."

The woman nodded, stepping away. Vi let out a breath of relief.

"Thanks," Vi exhaled.

"No problem," the woman replied, and glanced over at the food spread before gesturing to the tapenade Vi had set out beside the bread. "I'm feeling a bit guilty now about partaking," she added, "but I swear, all the baby seems to want is oliv—"

"I have to go," Vi cut in, turning sharply. She looked around, trying to spot Tom, and then checked her watch, wondering where he'd gone.

Ten minutes.

What was he possibly doing?

— Ω —

"Hey," Tom called, chasing the blond man from the house's west entrance (near the garage, which had once been a stable). He grimaced as the stranger nearly left the premises, already mere steps away from the limit of what Viola referred to charmingly (defined here as *in a manner befitting an unpleasant, if passably pretty, nuisance*) as Tom's perimeter of haunting. "HEY," Tom shouted again, sending a wave of electromagnetic tension through the air for emphasis (Vi likened this effect to the sensation of having a horrible, unprompted recollection of middle school) before finally, the man paused.

For a moment, he stood perfectly still, staring into nothing.

"I've missed something," the man remarked, "haven't I?"

Then he pivoted sharply and faced Tom, narrowing his eyes.

"Ah yes," he said, nodding with certainty. "You're dead. My mistake."

Tom gaped at him.

"That," Tom eventually remarked, "is not the usual reaction."

"Well, I suppose I'm not all that usual either, but thanks," the man replied. "The lines between realms are inherently faint, I'm afraid. Sometimes it doesn't occur to me to wonder if one has been crossed."

Tom gauged him for truth; arrived at certainty.

"Christ" was all he came up with for a response. "What are you?"

"Unimportant," the man said. "What are you?"

There was another pause; this time for estimation.

"A ghost, I think," Tom answered. "Vi thinks I'm a poltergeist."

"Vi?"

"Viola," Tom clarified. "The vampire in there. Sorry," he realized, amending the statement. "I meant the Realtor."

"Oh shit, no kidding," the man said. "Missed that too, I guess."

"You don't seem too concerned," Tom commented. "Come across us supernatural types often?"

"Well, like I said, there's only a distinction if you make one," the man told him, with a strange sort of dignified ease that struck Tom as though his grandfather might have said it. "A short redhead served me my coffee this morning, but that doesn't mean he's a leprechaun. Doesn't mean he's *not*, either," the man conceded, "but the coffee was good, so the distinction is moot."

"I guess that's one way to look at it," Tom said slowly, and then frowned. "But I don't think you're here to buy my house."

"Oh, it's your house?" the man asked. "Interesting."

"Yeah. I'm Tom," explained Tom. "Tom Parker."

"Brandt," the man returned. "Solberg."

"Is that an alias?"

"It's been updated to suit the times," Brandt confirmed. "Americans have a hell of a time with Old Norse."

"How old is your Old Norse, exactly?" Tom asked.

"Old enough," Brandt said. "Otherwise I'd have just said Norse." That was fair, Tom thought.

"So," he pressed. "About the house—"

"I'm not going to buy it," Brandt said, confirming Tom's suspicions. "Actually, I'm going to rob it."

Tom blinked. "What?"

"Look, it's not like you can do much with the stuff in here," Brandt reminded him. "And you seem like a nice enough guy. Not sure I can base that on much," he amended, gesturing vaguely to Tom's knife wound, "since most nice guys I know have never been stabbed in the chest, but, you know." He shrugged. "I'm not really the lying type."

"You seem like you probably are," Tom pointed out, and again, Brandt shrugged.

"No real way to tell, is there?" he asked.

Tom, by that point, felt vaguely dizzied.

"I'm just not sure I want you to rob my house," he determined after a moment.

"Well, that's fair," Brandt agreed. "Most people don't."

There was a pause.

"I'm still going to," Brandt assured him, somewhat apologetically. "There's something I need."

"Oh," said Tom.

"Besides," Brandt added, "it's technically mine."

Ha. "Doubt that."

"People often do," Brandt charitably allowed.

Tom paused again, thinking it over.

On the one hand, even if he accepted the premise that the stuff in the house was of no further value to Tom (arguable, depending on the items in question), a robbery—especially a burglary—would draw quite a lot of attention to the house, making it a crime scene once again. It would *also* once again expose the house as a high-profile place with deeply ineffective security, which would contribute to its continuing lack of sale.

On the other hand, Vi would be furious.

Or perhaps that was still the first hand.

"I could help you," Tom offered.

"That," Brandt remarked, "would be transcendent."

— Ω —

"There you are," Vi said, catching sight of Tom as he hovered back into the living room. "It's been nearly twenty minutes!"

"Missed me, did you?" Tom prompted obnoxiously, to which (need she specify each occurrence out loud?) she rolled her eyes.

"What'd he say?"

"Not much. He's something weird, though, that's for sure." Tom did not seem shaken by this admission, which was promising. "Said something about not seeing lines between realms."

"Realms?" Vi echoed with a frown. "That just sounds fake."

"Didn't you say that an angel, a reaper, and the *godson of Death* were coming this afternoon?" Tom countered. "I hardly think you're one to discuss what is or isn't real, Viola."

"Viola," she noted, tutting. "Are you trying to 'Elaine' me now?"

"No," Tom said. "If I were, I'd call you Elaine."

There was simply no adequate method by which to describe the agony of trying to have a conversation with Tom.

"Whatever," Vi said, an exercise of restraint in a longer, more futile battle for sanity. "In any case—"

"In any case," Tom agreed, "he's gone now. And I don't think he's a buyer."

Vi didn't think so either, but what else was new there, really. Confessing it aloud would only make Tom's day. "I'm thinking I'll try talking to commercial developers next," she commented instead, glancing around. "This place might make a lovely boutique hotel, you know?"

"God, you have no imagination," Tom said, rolling his eyes. "This is just now occurring to you? Uncle Benji tried to get the board's approval for that about twenty years ago. They never agreed to it."

"Well, maybe they will now," Vi said, aiming for optimism. "Unless it's expressly stated somewhere that they can't, obviously—"

"It is," Tom informed her. "It's a stipulation in the house's ownership. People have to *live here*—don't know why, but Wynona made sure Ned Parker put it in his will. My grandmother," he clarified unnecessarily. "She said it was important."

"Of course she did," Vi sighed, shaking her head. To her it sounded like one of those absurd celebrity riders, like having only blue M&M's. The type of entitled frippery that only occurred to the overly wealthy. "Your family's a bunch of oddballs," she added. "No wonder they're cursed."

"Hey, don't joke about curses," Tom warned in a somewhat droll manner, gesturing pointedly to himself. "I did, and look at me."

"I don't think you died from a curse," Vi said. "I think you died from a violent stabbing."

"Well, you can think whatever you like, Viola Marek," Tom said. "Doesn't mean you'll be right."

It shouldn't have sounded ominous, of course, because it was Tom Parker, who was incapable of any meaningful threat beyond the one he posed to her patience, but he looked a smidge too pleased with himself for someone who was about to be supernaturally evicted, and therein lay the rub.

"Fair enough" was her only reply, to cover the slight chill of her unsettling.

# IX

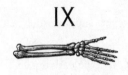

## CAUSE AND EFFECT

"We have a problem," the archangel Raphael announced, his weightless footfall disturbing little of the nebula below him save for the airy breeze it conjured in his wake, apple-scented and crisp. "Death appears to have shirked his duty."

"Shirked," echoed his colleague, the archangel Gabriel, who lifted his head from where he'd been busily sorting employment records at his desk. "Sounds serious."

"It is," Raphael confirmed. "He's nowhere to be found."

"Who, Death?" Gabriel prompted with a frown, stretching upright with a yawn. "Impossible. Something must be wrong."

"Hence the problem," Raphael agreed. "I should think that would be obvious."

(And it was, of course, but still.)

(Some things simply needed to be said.)

"Well, pause for a moment," Gabriel said, and Raphael folded his arms over his chest, waiting. "Which job are we talking about, specifically?"

"The main one," Raphael supplied. "The transportation bit," he added for further clarification, "not the security part."

"Well, presumably the thing is safe, then," Gabriel said, exhaling. "That's a relief."

"Not nearly as reassuring as I'd like," Raphael countered gruffly. "You'll notice there's no receiving line."

(Gabriel *had* noticed, but rather hadn't wished to remark. He'd quite hoped that if he ignored it, it might simply go away, or better yet trickle down to someone well beneath him on the payroll.)

(Proverbially speaking, of course. They weren't paid, this wasn't

Reaganomics, and to even suggest such a thing would be prodigiously undignified.)

"So there have been no Ends, then," he guessed, as Raphael grimaced.

"Not quite," he said. "The Ends are still going ahead as scheduled."

Gabriel waited, perplexed.

"But—"

"But without Death to transport them, they're not arriving at the gates," Raphael continued, having indulged his irritating love of dramatic pauses. "There is . . . much unrest."

"Wait," Gabriel said. "So then where are they? The dead, I mean."

Raphael hesitated. "They're—" He paused, coughing. "Not quite dead."

Again, Gabriel frowned. "How 'not quite' are we talking?"

"Let's just say this," Raphael offered. "We should probably pay a visit to Death's abode."

Gabriel shuddered.

"Not my favorite abode," he lamented.

"Hence the problem," Raphael confirmed.

$$-\Omega-$$

Where does Death reside?

In the dead, of course, and in the souls of the living; in their fears of the future and in the losses of their pasts. Death lives in the too-quiet silences, in the deepest parts of night. Death makes a home in the moments of stiffness, the seconds before a fall; in the heavy-hearted candor of the surgeon's hands, the archer's bow, the executioner's axe, the injectioner's needle. Death lurks, he stalks, he *waits*—or so we would believe, anyway, in our selfish vanities and prides, because Death lives so vibrantly in our consciousness that it is exceedingly difficult to imagine he might actually have a home of his own.

But despite our misconceptions, he does have a place, as do most people and things and beings, and Death's abode is not a grim Tudor manor house, nor a hard stone castle, nor a spindly Victorian. Death resides, rather, in the Tree of Life, which sits above a cave of his own making. He sleeps (metaphorically, of course) in a treehouse of sorts, built from enchanted wood lent to him by the Tree, but he *lives* down below, where the jeweled interior of a solitary cavern reflects the light of his many treasures.

Death's cave is illuminated by itself, and to see the inside is to see the manifestation of wishes, of fanciful wonder, for Death is a collector by trade, and his private collection is quite grand.

"Well," Raphael said, careful not to drag his seraphic wings on the mossy, damp ground of Death's cave. "I'd say he's not here."

"I'd say you're right," Gabriel agreed. "Much as I abhor it."

They paused, considering their predicament.

"He's never been gone before," Raphael commented to nobody in particular. "I really don't like it."

"Well, I doubt he meant to upset you personally," Gabriel offered kindly, to which Raphael sighed.

"Do you think anyone else has noticed? You know the others will want to be alerted as soon as possible. Him," he said, pointing upward, "and *him*," he determined, tapping his foot against the floor.

"Unless we can find him first," Gabriel suggested. "Him, I mean," he clarified, gesturing around Death's cave.

At that, Raphael brightened.

"Perhaps we find him first," he agreed, and paused. "We'll have to fetch someone," he realized. "But who?"

Gabriel tilted his head, weighing their options. "It *is* a matter of urgency," he ventured tentatively. "So while it would certainly be unorthodox, per—"

"Don't say it," Raphael muttered, flinching.

"—haps we should simply summon both sides?"

Raphael sighed.

"I was afraid you'd say that," he lamented.

"Hence the problem," Gabriel contributed sagely.

"Hence the problem," Raphael agreed.

# INTERLUDE II:

## WISHES

There is nothing more telling about a person's character than the silent wishes they keep to themselves, buried in the little nooks and crannies of their hearts. Mayra Kaleka has been borne aloft on many a person's wish and can say with requisite authority that some hearts are darker than others, and can possess an intriguing opalescence; but however dark or light or multifaceted a heart may be, all things pertaining to a person's true self can be read and measured by someone (like Mayra, for example) who knows precisely where to look.

Were Mayra to impart one piece of wisdom for your benefit, it would be that wishes are darker things than we imagine because they are so close to wants, and from there only inches from desires, and thus can so easily devolve headlong into vices—which are the precise business that Mayra is employed to tally and, when possible, prevent. She is a soldier of her own kind, fighting her many tiny wars, and in her experience, even the darkest of human natures can be read by the intent of something as fanciful as a wish.

To believe a wish is always pure and good is to embrace a misconception.

To glimpse what a person's heart beats for, though, is to understand who they are.

At the moment when Mayra is not-awake-not-asleep, she hears a distant whisper that gently rustles the gauzy plumage of her wings. She cannot refuse when a heart calls for her, and so her eyes flutter open as she listens.

*I wish to feel something,* she hears, and it has the somber pain belonging to exhaustion, which is a feeling Mayra remembers well. She still feels an echo of it from time to time, resonating in her feather-light bones, and though death and life and afterlife have very little in common, Mayra is as she always was, and memory has not escaped her.

She sends a little ripple through the air; the supplicant will feel it as a delicate breeze that alights around her shoulders.

*Good or bad?* Mayra asks.

The shudder of the question climbs the notches of the supplicant's spine.

*I wish to feel something much, much larger than I am,* the supplicant's heart replies.

*I wish to stand on the edge of ruination and defeat, to leap into a chasm full of danger.*

*I wish to feel my blood turn cold with fear and my cheeks burn bright with shame; I wish to feel joy that fills my lungs, and sadness that swells within me like a current. I wish to feel so much and so deeply that it washes over me in waves. I wish to drag myself toward something; I wish to lose pieces of myself along the way. I wish for hunger that drives me, for passion that fulfills me, for sensations of taking and having and losing and wanting, and I wish for all of it to come with a price, and a steep one*

*—and then I wish for the courage to pay.*

*Isn't it all good because it's something?* the supplicant asks.

*Isn't it all bad because beneath it—any of it,* the wish sighs—*I may collapse?*

Mayra listens and she wonders.

She is out of miracles, she knows, and this one would be no small feat.

But some things only need a little push.

— Ω —

"What'd you wish for?" asks Isis, swinging her legs from atop the kitchen counter as Tom glares at her from across the room.

"World peace," Vi quips, tucking the feather back into her pocket.

"Should've aimed for something more likely," Isis says. "Like calorie-free cheese."

It's a valid point. Though, in fairness, Vi has some familiarity with impossibilities.

"Next time," is all she says, pairing the statement with an evasive shrug.

# X

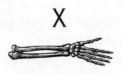

# CALL AND RESPONSE

To say that the Parker mansion is gaudy is rather an unrepentant understatement, though Fox has seen houses like it before. One of the hazards of having lived through history is having witnessed the many cycles between opulence and devastation, and ultimately having learned to distrust them. Thus, Fox no longer possesses much patience for turrets or balconies or vines; he knows they all turn to rot eventually.

The house is beautiful to most eyes, though, Fox is sure—or if not truly beautiful, then at least in possession of a certain kind of grandeur; the untouchable, inimitable kind. It stands alone on a smaller-than-average city block near Lake Shore Drive, and it seems more in communion with the lake than it does with the streets and homes around it. It has been cared for, of course, in all the superficial ways, but still a sense of longing remains, like that of an older generation. Around the house, for instance, time has visibly moved forward. Architecture has changed, neighborhoods have grown and aged and flourished. Around the Parker house, the city has been reborn in different forms, bigger and smaller and new and different, but still always in conversation with the busy city streets.

The Parker mansion, however, sits alone and speaks to no one. It faces its back to the city and its inhabitants and sulks wistfully toward Michigan, as if it would rather sink below the surface of the lake than continue to stand.

At first glance, the house seems stiff and haughty. Even birds seem unwilling to rest on the shoulders of the house, opting instead to circle overhead.

After a few moments of contemplation, though, it seems lonely, in the way that people who have outlived their purpose seem lonely, and then it seems to be a little sad.

After about a minute of staring, Fox thinks that perhaps he understands.

— Ω —

"Oh good," Viola said, granting them entry through the front double doors and stepping deftly to the side for them to pass. "You're here, then."

"Yes," Fox sighed, Cal at his side peering curiously around the Parker house's marble-laden foyer. "I said I would be, didn't I?"

She didn't say aloud how little his word clearly meant to her, but he could see it plain enough. "Well, either way, it's appreciated," Viola said, turning over her shoulder and leading them through the foyer and down a corridor that seemed devoted to a sequence of pointless rooms. "Have you been here before?" she asked, briskly making small talk as Cal dragged along in their wake.

Fox shook his head. "No, never seen it," he admitted. "I only really knew anything about the original Parker; the first one, with the dry goods store. He was the only one remotely in my circles at the time. But this house was built by—"

He paused, shuddering from a sudden, violent chill, and Viola paused to glare at what appeared to be the air beside Fox's right shoulder before turning her attention back to Fox.

"Ned Parker," she supplied for him. "Tom's grandfather."

"Ah," Fox said, glancing at his right side with a grimace. "That must be the ghost, then."

Viola didn't appear to be listening, having already turned her attention back to empty air.

"Yes, I *know* it's Thomas Edward Parker the fourth," she was sighing irritably, talking to the space between Fox and an aged gallery wall featuring dead Dutch herrings and delicately spiraling lemon peels. "I just thought, you know, *Tom*, seeing as that's the name you actually *use*—"

"Tom, hm?" Fox echoed, still eyeing what he assumed must have been the ghost. Just beyond him was a room with mahogany paneling and walls of what could only be described as a moneyed shade of green. "Like his ancestor, then," Fox mused, hazily recalling his experience with the first Tom Parker, whom he'd bumped into at a pub over a century ago.

"Did you know him well?" Viola asked, and then immediately let out a loud groan.

"No, as I mentioned, I didn't, but—" Fox began, disgruntled, but again, she held up a hand, addressing the ghost instead of him.

"I don't know what you expect," she informed the air. "You are hardly the first person in the world named Tom." She paused, or listened, her expression melding to a stiffness obviously intended to blur the extent of her impatience. (It did not work.) "I'm not going to ask him that, Tom. Because I don't have all the time in the world, that's why, and I'm also not in the business of antagonizing people whose help I need." Another pause. "Yes, Thomas, I know very well that it's your preferred business, but once again, I continue to not share enthusiasm for your hobbies—"

"So," Fox noted, equally speaking to empty air. "This is fun."

At that, Viola paused, her gaze sliding to his with a slow, contemplative, and poorly concealed air of distaste.

"You know," she commented, "I thought the whole point of being a medium was that you would be able to speak to him yourself."

"Oh," Fox said grumpily, "so are you talking to me now?"

Viola folded her arms over her chest, exchanging what looked to be a snotty glance with the ghost next to him.

"He's not a fraud, Tom," she said flatly, before glancing at Fox. "He'd better not be, anyway."

"I have a process," Fox reminded her. "And anyway, you've dragged me out here, haven't you? Would I have bothered to come if I weren't actually capable of doing what I claim?"

Viola's grimace tightened.

"Yes, I know it's a good argument," she muttered to the ghost, and Fox sighed.

"Is there even a ghost?" he demanded. "Or might your problems be better suited to a medical practitioner?"

"You're right, Tom," she replied. "He *is* deeply unpleasant."

"Did you see the engravings beside the stairs, Fox?" Cal observed, having finally caught up to them in the corridor. He nudged Fox with childlike insistence, pointing indiscriminately over his shoulder. "Ornate. Immaculate. And really quite—"

"Showy," Fox supplied, indifferent.

"You've no appreciation for the arts, Fox D'Mora," Cal said gravely, as Viola led them into the kitchen. Mayra and Isis were waiting there, the demon chewing idly on a carrot stick before smiling at Fox with all of her teeth.

Mayra, of course, was distracted by Cal immediately upon his arrival. "It's a beautiful house, objectively speaking," she remarked in agreement, nodding in greeting to Cal first before proceeding sequentially to Fox. "Not to my taste, really, but to be honest, very little is."

"And it's really not to many buyers' tastes," Viola confirmed with a grimace as she reached for something in the refrigerator, proceeding to lay out a hummus spread as if this were some kind of congenial get-together. "Though, admittedly, the inseverable poltergeist that haunts it without respite might have something to do with that, but I suppose I haven't conducted a thorough survey—yes, *I know,* Tom, that you don't appreciate the reference, but I don't know what you want me to tell you—"

"He's telling the demon to get off the 'very expensive' marble," Cal commented, leaning toward Fox and providing a fully unsolicited translation. "She's ignoring him."

"I can see that, Calix," Fox muttered, rolling his eyes. "Thank you."

"You're welcome," said Cal. "And now he's—"

He broke off as the foundation of the house gave a brief, violent tremor.

"He's displeased?" Fox dryly guessed.

"Yes," Cal said, unironically. "He's shouting 'HELLO'—"

"No need," Fox assured him. "Thank you, but I'm good."

"Yes, hello," Isis flippantly agreed in the ghost's direction, and Vi sighed.

"Well, now that you've all met Tom," she continued, turning to Fox, "I presume we can get started?"

"What exactly does this whole thing entail?" Isis asked before Fox could answer, finally removing herself from the kitchen counter (presumably so that she could stand nearer to him, and thereby more effectively obstruct his life). "Is there some sort of blood-and-bone ritual involved?"

"Oh no," Viola said, looking queasy. "Please no."

"Well, a magician never reveals his secrets," Fox informed her, suffering again the demon's unnerving proximity. (Unclear how much of that was paranormal versus the discomfort of her personality.) "But no, there's little to no blood involved."

Isis, however, did not look disappointed.

"Interesting that you would liken yourself to a magician, you know," she remarked. "So you admit this is all smoke and mirrors, then?"

Fox opened his mouth, about to argue that she was quite obviously oversimplifying matters, but at the last moment managed to recall that this was meant to be a very simple and time efficient errand, and if he did not want this to be a faff, then it simply need not be one.

"Do you want my help," he prompted bluntly, "or do you want to antagonize me?"

"Me? Antagonize you, obviously," Isis said, gesturing to Viola. "*Vi* wants help."

"I do," Vi agreed. "To sell the house."

"Among other things," Isis chirped.

"No," Vi corrected, glaring at her. "One thing."

"The ghost says 'how unspeakably rude,'" supplied Cal, leaning into Fox's ear again. "I don't think it's about you," he added unhelpfully.

"It's fine. She's lying," Isis assured the vacancy of the ghost's presumed location, at which point Fox finally threw out a hand, silencing them both.

"Listen," he said. "I'll call Death, we'll get a few answers, and then we'll part ways for the rest of time. Understood?"

"Sure," Vi permitted.

Cal leaned in again. "The ghost says 'still rude,' so—"

"Brilliant," declared Fox, with another measuring glance around the room before deciding no, best not to speculate about the quality of his audience. "Now," he sighed. "Let's get started."

— Ω —

Upstairs, Brandt Solberg paused his search through the carved wooden chests of the antiquated Parker nursery, catching the sounds of conversation below.

"This," he murmured to nobody in particular, "is less than ideal."

And it was.

Less than, that was.

The ideal in question? Silence, presumably, though a thief must always know not to trust silence too implicitly. While some might hear silence and assume innocence for a lack of something more troubling, a thief knows better. Silence only means something too quiet to hear, an unnatural state of affairs too noticeably tampered. Anything so calculatedly furtive as to make no sound and cast no shadow more often means misbehavior underfoot. In this case, a *bit* of noise would be fine—the natural creaking of the old house, the hum of the air conditioning and plumbing, empty aching of the swollen floorboards— but the sounds of voices down below were fully unanticipated, and therefore wholly undesirable.

Brandt's displeasure (more accurately, the break in his agile disposition upon realizing there were several people elsewhere in the house) was due to several factors; not the least of which being his ongoing burglary.

Well, not a burglary, per se. He hadn't *broken in*, exactly. The ghost, Tom Parker, had told him where to go, which door to enter through, and how to avoid detection, so Brandt supposed it was less a matter of breaking and entering than it was simply entering.

If anything, he'd been invited, so the burgling was more or less theoretical.

Really, the intent to commit a crime was somewhat opaque as well, if one were so inclined to get into the particulars. Sure, theft was *involved*, but on a more cerebral plane of analysis, was anything really theft when the item in question was something that belonged so deservedly to oneself?

Essentially, Brandt had been invited into the Parker mansion and had then proceeded to go about his extremely normal business; if anything, the unanticipated crowd was only a minor inconvenience.

Less than ideal, yes, but not catastrophic.

It was certainly not devastating in the slightest.

Or, at least—it *wouldn't* have been, had Brandt Solberg not recognized a voice he'd once been quite positive he would never hear again.

— Ω —

"This dining room seats *fifty people*," Cal declared, looking around this latest rendition of obscenity with its pink Numidian marble floors and candy-apple upholstery, all set off with actual gilts of gold. "My entire village could have eaten in here, Fox, and it wouldn't even have been *crowded*—"

"Calix, I don't know if you've noticed, but I'm busy," Fox told him, arbitrarily instructing Viola, Isis, and Mayra to stand at various points around the room (mostly to ensure they came no nearer to his own position). "You," he said, snapping his fingers into empty air for Tom, "come over here."

"He says 'yes, wonderful, please summon me like an animal,'" Cal supplied from where he lingered near the door, dragging his gaze from the room's crown molding to once again serve as extraneous intermediary. "He also adds, 'I love it, I live for it,' and—"

"You don't live at all," Vi snapped at the ghost. "Will you just follow instructions?"

Cal, still whispering loudly: "He says no. And he also says to voice his dissent for the record."

Fox, clearly struck by lunacy for even bothering to ask: "Whose record?"

Cal: "Posterity, he says."

"Okay, great," Fox exhaled, shaking his head and wondering when, if ever, he would learn. "Cal, if you would?" he prompted, gesturing purposefully to a spot beside Mayra because he was a moderately decent friend if not an excellent human being, and the reaper nodded, abandoning his place beside Fox's ear to set off as instructed. "Okay. Are we ready?"

Isis, who was unfortunately still present: "There's not some kind of meditation involved, is there? Not to be redundant, but if there's no human sacrifice, then I don't know if I want to stay."

Fox: "I'd love for you to leave, but I'd love even more to get this over with."

Across from him, Cal tentatively raised a finger. "The ghost says that if he's not going to be considered a priority in his own exorcism—"

Fox: "This is not an exorcism. I feel that it should be very clear that he is not possessed."

Vi, thoughtfully: "True, he'd be the possess*or*, wouldn't he? Seems like the *house* is possessed, really, which would make *Tom* some type of—I don't know, vengeful spirit, perhaps?"

Cal: "He says 'that, as ever, is exceedingly unflattering'—"

Vi, with the pinched look of thinking something ruder than she spoke aloud, which Fox was beginning to consider her primary facial expression: "To clarify, I can *hear him*—"

Cal, with the sort of impossible affability that ought not to be so easily forgiven but was, somehow: "Right! Sorry, I'd gotten a bit caught up in the excitement of it all—"

Vi: "Well, it's no problem, really—"

"Oh, for fuck's sake," Fox cut in, and then grimaced with dismay, snapping the rubber band on his wrist. (He half expected to spontaneously summon his godfather just for the amateur mistake.) "Let's just get on with it."

Fox closed his eyes, both for show and to briefly massage out his sinus cavity before reaching down to surreptitiously twist the ring on his left hand, feeling the demon's eyes on him from well across the room. "Listen, Papa," he began, letting out a heavy sigh, "I know this is unorthodox, but the thing is—"

"Who are you talking to?" Isis interrupted.

Fox paused, opening his eyes.

"Oh," he said, glancing back down at his ring. "Huh."

He gave it another twist, waiting.

"Papa?" he asked, looking around the room.

Isis grinned. "That's super cute."

"We're German," Fox informed her. "It's not cute. Nothing is cute in German."

"Isn't it, though? Papa," Isis repeated with a winsome smile. "Adorable."

"Not now," he muttered at her, frowning around the room as if he might have missed something the first time. (It wasn't as if Death was Santa Claus but still, it was all he could do not to check the chimney.)

Vi: "Is everything all right? Yes I *know*, Tom, shut up—"

Mayra: "Fox?"

Fox, in a mix of shame and concern for which a German word would likely do quite nicely: "It *should* just work, but—"

He heard a sound behind him and sighed with relief.

"Thank *god*," he exhaled, turning to face the doorway in which Death must have belatedly appeared. "Papa, it's really not funny when you—"

He froze, the air swelling in his lungs, and blinked.

"Hello, Fox," said Brandt Solberg.

Fox closed his eyes.

The room spun.

The walls collapsed.

It all came back in a rush.

— Ω —

"You've kidnapped my godfather? You can't kidnap my godfather!"

"In fairness, I didn't realize he was your godfather. I was simply informed that he existed on this plane sometimes—though, admittedly, that's in fairness to me. In fairness to you, I suppose I should mention that I don't happen to care whether he is or isn't of any particular relation to you. Also, he isn't kidnapped. And anyway, if that's all—"

"Who are you?"

"Is that relevant? We'll likely never see each other again—"

"The hell we won't! Where is he?"

"I'll bring him right back, I promise. Well, if he is where I think he is, anyway, he'll be back soon enough regardless—"

"But—"

"—I simply needed to see if he cared to help me with something, but as he's not here and you most certainly can't help—"

"Help with what?"

"None of your business, is it?"

"Of course it's my business, he's my godfather!"

"I fail to see how that's pertinent to your line of questioning, but since you obviously won't be leaving me alone—"

"I certainly will not, seeing as I'm still waiting for an answer to my question!"

"—the long and short of it is that we've made deals before, your godfather and I, so I'm back to try and make another one. But obviously I've just missed him, so now I'll be off—"

"Wait, what do you mean you've made deals with him before?"

"Before, meaning prior to this moment, or, alternatively, none of your concern—"

"Don't do that. Don't be—"

"What? Clever?"

"Flippant!"

"I'm never flippant. I am, however, quite busy, so—"

"Tell me who you are, or I swear, I'll—"

"My goodness, no need to escalate in pitch. If you really must know, I'm Brandt, derived from Brandr, of little repute and littler consequence. Lovely to make your acquaintance, and you are?"

"I . . . Listen, you can't just—you can't—"

"Oh, what a relief. I was worried you'd be exceptionally articulate."

"You're a thief!"

"Well, yes, and you're clearly a fool. And on that note, goodbye forever—"

"Don't you dare walk out on me! Where's my godfather?"

"Haven't I already made that clear? I feel as if we're going in circles. If he's not here, then he'll be at the tables, so if you'll just excuse me—"

"What tables? Never mind, I'll just come with you—"

"Ah—no. No thanks. Not interested. Goodbye, best wishes, enjoy whatever remains of your vacuous adolescence, and—"

"I said I'm coming with you!"

"And I said you aren't, didn't I? Which is frankly the only position that makes sense, isn't it, seeing as you haven't the faintest idea who or what I am—"

"I don't care who you are, or what. If it comes down to your will and mine, I promise you, mine will win."

"You really are a fool, then, aren't you?"

"I just don't like being kept in the dark."

"Exactly a fool's position on the matter."

— Ω —

The Parker house's elaborate dining room contained the ghost called Tom, the vampire real estate agent called Vi, and a number of additional strangers. There was an angel, her lovely eyes narrowed with either concern or suspicion; a reaper, his faintly curious expression tainted only slightly by surprise; and a demon, her eyes flaming with a certain worrying delight.

And then, of course, there was Fox, who hadn't yet spoken, and looked highly unlikely to speak anytime soon.

"Ooh," the demon trumpeted with relish, pivoting wide-eyed toward Brandt. "Who's this?"

Tom the ghost, however, was thoroughly unamused. "You were supposed to come later," he told Brandt with a frankly unthreatening glower of petulance. "Don't you listen? Or is your conception of instruction limited to realms, too?"

Across the room, the reaper took a step toward Fox. "He says," the reaper began, and then paused. "I actually have no idea what he's saying. Lack of context," he offered apologetically, as Fox finally managed the presence of mind to blink. "I'll wait."

"Wait a minute." Vi, too, was staring at Brandt, albeit with less of Fox's apparent paralysis. "Aren't you that buyer from the open house?"

"Hm? Not technically," Brandt said, and then paused. "Well, not at all, really. Sorry," he added insincerely, before she abruptly rounded on Tom.

"What do you mean he was supposed to come later?" Vi demanded. "Did you hatch some sort of deviant plot about the house, Thomas?"

"Obviously," Tom replied with a flourish of annoyance that sank upon the rest of them like claggy, incorporeal sponge. "But clearly that's just not in the cards for me, is it?"

Had the vampire been capable of smoking from the ears, Brandt figured she would have been. "What exactly did you think was going t—"

"Fox?" The angel had placed a hand gently on Fox's shoulder. "Fox, are you with us?"

— Ω —

"What is this?"

"I told you what it is. It's a game."

"Looks . . . seedy."

"Well, looks can be deceiving."

"Can they?"

"Theoretically? Of course. Not this time, though. In this particular instance, I'd say seedy is spot on."

"Are you always this infuriating?"

"Hopefully. I certainly aim to be, but everyone has off days."

"I think I might hate you."

"Ah, but you might not, and more's the pity for that, frankly."

"What's that supposed to mean?"

*"Nothing. Nothing much, anyway. Just that you'd have been wiser leaving me to my business and waiting for your godfather to return—which, again, he will. The tables close at dawn, and then he'll be right back in your little cottage. Or hut. Dwelling?"*

*"Sorry, but I find it difficult to believe that Death is some sort of gambling aficionado. Doesn't that strike you as immensely . . . odd?"*

*"I find it substantially more odd that he has a godson, truth be told. I've played several games with him, and at no point did he mention you—though I suppose I wouldn't either, if I had a vulnerability I couldn't protect. Never a good thing to reveal a pressure point, and particularly not with this crowd. He'll kill me for bringing you here—ha ha, death by Death. Anyway, you said your name was Fox?"*

*"I—yes, but go back to the part about—"*

*"Fox what?"*

*"Just Fox, it's not like I need a surname. And when you say a pressure point—"*

*"I don't need a surname either, but I have one, and so should you."*

*"What's yours?"*

*"Solberg. Sort of."*

*"'Sort of'?"*

*"What do you think about D'Mora? For a surname, I mean. You know—of Death. Seems fitting."*

*"That's—stop it, you're distracting me. Where's my godfather now?"*

*"Usually at the head of the table. He generally takes on the winners."*

*"Winners of what?"*

*"The game, Fox, keep up—"*

*"What game? And why the winners? Does he always win?"*

*"Well, hard to say. The game is unusual. Sometimes there isn't a winner. Sometimes both players win—which is I suppose the same outcome, depending on how you look at it."*

*"How does that make any sense?"*

*"Because the object of the game is to win the game, not to beat your opponent. So yes, Death always wins, but sometimes there's another winner, and in that case it can be equal parts win and loss. I've beaten him once myself."*

"*You have?*"

"*Yes.*"

"*And what did you get for beating him?*"

"*A secret.*"

"*Well, fine—*"

"*No, I mean that's what I got: a secret. I asked him for a particular secret, and he gave it to me as a prize for beating him. There was a trade involved, but—that's a longer story, really.*"

"*What did you beat him in? Is this . . . cards?*"

"*No, not exactly. The game is more a battle of wits. Well, and wills, I suppose. More like a gauging of wills.*"

"*What does that mean?*"

"*Hard to explain.*"

"*Can't be that hard. What was the secret you won?*"

"*Can't tell you, can I? Or the purse for winning will be worth nothing, since it would no longer be a secret.*"

"*He'll tell me if I ask.*"

"*Perhaps he will. Perhaps I'll even tell you. Or perhaps you'll never know. All equal possibilities, I think. Do you ever think about the world that way? In the many slivered pieces of what could be? Astronomically unending possibilities, but with infinitesimally small likelihoods of each—*"

"*You're unbearable. You said it was a battle of wits?*"

"*No, I've said repeatedly that it's a game. And thanks ever so for listening, by the way—*"

"*If it's just a game, then teach me the rules.*"

"*No. You're a child. And who says there are rules?*"

"*Everything has rules. And also, I'm not a child.*"

"*You are, and this is not a game for you.*"

"*You don't even know me!*"

"*Don't I? You're clearly loyal. You're obviously good-hearted, good-natured. A good and worthy fool, all in all.*"

"*Oh, and I suppose in your world that's a bad thing?*"

"*In my world? Absolutely. Well—more accurately, it's dangerous. You're quite dangerous, whether you realize it or not.*"

"*For what? For whom?*"

*"Isn't it obvious? For me. For Death. For everyone here."*

*"What does that mean?"*

*"If you don't already know, then you're a bigger, sadder fool than I thought."*

— Ω —

Fox felt the resurgence of time and place suddenly hit him like a wall of bricks.

"Where is he?" he demanded.

There was a moment where Brandt seemed to struggle with his response, and Fox took advantage of this uncharacteristic absence of (circular, convoluted) wit to scrutinize the man who now stood before him.

Brandt Solberg looked the same, really, and it was maddening. He looked *the same,* as though hundreds of years and crippling heart-break had not stood so inescapably between them, and it stung like a blistering slap to Fox's sensibilities that nothing—not the betrayal, not the lies, not even the absence of Fox himself—had been enough to carve even a single line of age or sorrow around Brandt Solberg's mouth.

Not that Fox had expected him to look different. He'd known, after all, that Brandt was never going to get older. Fox had lamented countless times, in fact, that he could not even presume Brandt Solberg to be dead, because such a thing was so laughably impossible as to be struck, useless, from consideration of what might have possibly gone wrong. Eternal youth had been a process Brandt had begun long before their lives had crossed, and clearly the brief window of his dalliance with Fox had not made enough of an impact to change it.

But still. It would have been gratifying to see his hair appear less golden, at least.

"I didn't take him, if that's what you're implying," Brandt said.

"You've said that before," Fox muttered.

Brandt sighed.

"Centuries, Fox," he murmured, "and all you have for me are accusations?"

"Don't patronize me. Where *is* he?" Fox demanded, with a bullish step forward to where Brandt had lingered near the door. "You can't possibly tell me that you being here like this is some kind of meaningless coincidence."

"And yet it is," Brandt replied with his usual languid insincerity. "You know how possibility can be. Astronomically large," he added, "and yet infinitesimally small."

Fox swallowed hard.

"Don't," was all he managed.

"Fox," Mayra attempted again, stepping toward him. "Are you—" She paused, tilting her head, as if she were listening to something that hummed overhead. "Oh balls," she murmured, and promptly disappeared.

"Okay then," Brandt remarked. "Didn't realize I'd insulted her, too."

"You didn't," Cal said, mournfully eyeing the place Mayra had been. "She's clearly been—"

He broke off, looking a tinge green, and glanced down at his ankles.

"Rats," he muttered.

And then, with a small pop, Cal vanished into the floor.

"Well," Brandt exhaled. "That's—"

"They've been summoned," Fox said gruffly, crossing his arms over his chest. "It's no concern of yours, and more importantly, *you* need to answer the question, Brandt. What the hell are you doing here?"

Brandt paused, opening his mouth.

Then he snapped it shut, which—by the feel of the suddenly crackling air in the room between them—seemed to have disgruntled their translucent host.

"Be quiet," Vi hissed at him, as another unsettling shockwave manifested underfoot. "None of us need reminding of your 'gruesome murder,' we all know perfectly well why we're here—" A pause. "Did *I* do this? Are you serious? First of all, *you're* the one who apparently conspired to have your own house robbed, and secondly, I was trying to *help* you—"

"Please," Isis told them, eyes darting between Brandt and Fox. "I'm trying to enjoy this deafening silence, if you don't mind—"

"You know what, maybe I should just hand this off to some other broker and be on my way," Vi growled, but Fox, having previously wanted to strangle every creature in the room, was now incapable of following their conversation.

All of his senses were dulled in the presence of Brandt Solberg, and rather than indulge the mindless chatter of the woefully undead, he instead turned his attention to the man from his past, staring him down from his side of history.

"Hey," he snarled, taking another threatening step toward Brandt. "I asked you a question. It's—"

*It's a simple question,* Fox nearly said, and stopped, momentarily faltering.

*Yes, but it's not a simple answer,* he heard the ghost of Brandt reply— easily, as if it had not come from the confines of Fox's memory. As if it had not been from centuries and lives away while the real one stared down at him, offering nothing more than an uneasy swallow. A careless, expressionless blink.

"So this is that voice in your head," Isis commented, jarring Fox out of his reverie with a delighted clasp of her hands as she looked from Fox to Brandt.

Fox turned to glare at her, finally determining the source of his intuited violation. "What's that supposed to mean? Don't tell me you've been *reading* it—"

"I'm a demon," she reminded him curtly. "What did you think that meant?"

"I see your choice of company hasn't improved much," Brandt murmured with what might have been a chuckle, and Fox rounded on him.

For a second, Fox almost yelled; he'd always been quick-tempered. He—and surely Mayra and Cal if they'd still been there—would have expected himself to rant with fury, to accidentally (or intentionally, and at the top of his lungs) spill out the many, many items on his list of grievances and demand an explanation, an apology, a supplication. Part of him wanted to hold out his empty hands and wait for Brandt to fill them with everything he had so achingly been without, but he didn't.

Instead his limbs dangled at his side, useless.

*Lillegutt,* Brandt would say if Fox yelled (*child,* as if that had ever been fair), and Fox was certain he would break beneath the sound of it—of mockery and affection and history combining to shatter him all at once.

"You don't deserve to talk to me like that," Fox croaked instead.

Brandt shut his eyes; opened them.

"I know," he said eventually.

— Ω —

*"He's not so innocent, you know. Your godfather."*

*"What does that mean?"*

*"That he cheats, of course."*

*"But you said there are no rules."*

*"I didn't say that."*

*"Then what are the rules?"*

*"There aren't really rules."*

*"You just said—"*

*"Well, fine, there's one rule. Don't lose."*

*". . . and to think I thought you might be vague about it."*

*"But you see why you can't afford to lose, though, don't you? Because Death cheats. He takes from you either way, but if you win, he gives you something, too. Sort of a shadowed reward."*

*"He takes?"*

*"Yes."*

*"He took from you?"*

*"Yes, when I won the secret."*

*"Is what he took from you a secret, too?"*

*"No. Not at all, actually."*

*"So what was it, then?"*

*"I can't tell you that."*

*"What? Why even bring it up if you didn't plan t—"*

"No, I mean it—I physically can't tell you, Fox. That's part of what he took."

"I—but I don't understand. Why would you agree to that?"

"Why would anyone agree to anything? Because I wanted something else more, of course. You have to be willing to sacrifice everything to gain one thing that matters most. Of course, the problem with the game is that the more you have to lose, the harder it is to win. I had nothing to lose then, and I still don't, so—"

"Hardly seems like much of a victory, then."

"Well, that's precisely it, isn't it? You have to win. The ideal situation is the other player losing, but Death never loses, so—"

"But this just doesn't seem like him."

"What, because he's Death, he's incapable of vice? This is the problem with the immortals, you know. This is why the game is so very dangerous—because they have played the game for so long and understand so easily that which can seem so inconceivable, so ineffable. But they are still subject to addictions and boredoms, just like any other beings. The stakes for them are so low that they're impossible to beat; it's simply a matter of outlasting their opponents, which their very natures render inevitable."

"Still. Papa curses sometimes; he has a temper. But an addiction?"

"Do you not have addictions, Fox?"

"Not that I know of."

"Well, then never play the game. You might find it to be one."

"Doubtful."

"You seem certain. Foolishly certain, in fact."

"I am. Certain, I mean. Not a fool."

"That's up for debate. You're quite young, aren't you?"

"Aren't you?"

"No. Yes, but no. I've been young for quite a long time."

"You said I would be dangerous for you."

"You will be. Or would be, if I were dumb enough to let you. Luckily we'll never see each other again, so I doubt it's worth contemplating."

"Luckily?"

"Yes, luckily. Apple?"

"No thanks, I'm—wait, what kind of apple is that?"

"The immortal kind."

"What?"

"Ever heard of Iðunn?"

"Who?"

"Iðunn. Goddess of youth—wife of Bragi, god of poetry. She guards the golden apples that are eaten by the Norse gods that allow them to live until Ragnarok, the battle of the end of the world."

"I didn't realize you were a . . . god?"

"I'm not. Well, half-not. My father is a god. A rather neglectful one, too, but I can't say I blame him for the inattention, much as I rather don't care for it. I understand it, I think. Frankly, I'm not sure I'd be thrilled to discover my son was a thieving rapscallion either."

"So I was right. You are a thief."

"I already told you I was. But as I said, I didn't steal your godfather, so—"

"Wait a minute. Did you just offer me a bite of an immortal apple?"

"I did."

"Why?"

"Seemed rude not to."

"That's an insane thing to say."

"Well, we all have our flaws."

"Aside from being a thief, or in addition to?"

"Well, fine. So I'm a thief and I suppose technically also a liar. But I'm certainly not impolite."

"A liar?"

"Yes. Technically."

"That's—"

"Opaque? I know. See what I mean? Lucky you hate me."

"Did I say I hated you?"

"Well, if you don't hate me by now, Fox, then you're simply not paying attention."

— Ω —

"I can't do this right now," Fox muttered with a pivot in the opposite direction, only to be reminded that his only plausible exit route was currently obstructed. Unless he intended to walk past Brandt, he had nowhere else to go.

Not that it mattered. A variety of protests swiftly broke out at his back while a crisp, intangible chill manifested in the air in front of him, freezing Fox in his tracks.

"He's not wrong, you know," Vi said, presumably referring to whatever the ghost had just expressed. "Did you somehow manage to *lose* Death? You said you weren't a fraud, Fox D'Mora," she warned as if she planned to write him up to the Better Business Bureau, "but excuse me if I'm not entirely convinced—"

"You're both *so troubled*," chuckled Isis tangentially, volleying her glee between Fox and Brandt. "Oh, Fox, we're just getting started—"

Vi: "Seems quite irresponsible, frankly—oh yes, funny *you* would say that, Mr. 'Let-A-Thief-In-Unchaperoned'—right, yes, *my sincere apologies*, that would be Mr. 'Let-A-Thief-In-Unchaperoned' *the fourth*—"

Isis: "—not sure if I should start with the abandonment and *then* work my way to the heartache? Or perhaps heartache, betrayal, and *then* abandonment—"

"Fox," he heard in the midst of the chaos, and paused at the sound of it, ringing like a bell through the matter of his conscience. "Fox, please don't leave."

For a moment, Fox was struck by the quietude of the request. The tenderness of it.

But then the brittle truth of it registered and he clenched a fist, spinning in place.

"Don't you *dare* say that to me!" he shouted at Brandt.

The others abruptly fell silent, startled from their bickering into sudden, suspended pause.

"Perfect," Isis whispered, but Fox had already forced her to the periphery of his attention as he waited for Brandt's response.

Which was, in a word, underwhelming.

"I know you don't want to hear this," Brandt said blandly, "but you have to, Fox. The fact that this happened—that we—" He broke off, shaking his head. "The fact that I'm here, Fox. It means something's wrong. It means something's gone very wrong."

"Don't." Fox's jaw felt tight, his throat sore. "Don't try t—"

"Something's happened to Death, Fox," Brandt said. "I shouldn't be here. I *couldn't* be here otherwise, and you should know that. Do you really think I didn't look for you?" That was quiet, almost inaudible, as if the two of them were alone. "Did you really not look for me?"

Fox reeled backward at that; for all that he'd imagined this or something like it, he had never really believed that Brandt would ever give him an answer. "I—"

"What's going on?" Vi asked, curiously leaning toward them, and the ghost swept directly through Fox, sending him convulsing in a shiver as it must have manifested on his other side.

Fox, though, looked helplessly at Brandt.

"Death's gone," Brandt informed the room, holding Fox's gaze as he said it. "He has to be, or else I couldn't have found you."

# XI

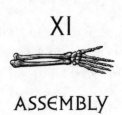

# ASSEMBLY

Everyone present, immortal and creature alike, generally agreed that they had never seen the man at the head of the room before. This, unsurprisingly, contributed to several different layers of confusion. The first of which was the source of their own presence in the unknown chamber—a disruption wholly inconvenient by any stretch of the imagination, and when had they all been faced with each other collectively before? (The answer being never, except of course for one time, but we'll get to that here shortly.)

The second layer was that the mortal addressing them from the opulent golden pulpit did not register with any familiarity, despite the literal eternality of memory through which to sift. Third was that although he (the mortal) was unrecognizable by face, something about him struck them all with an eerie shiver of déjà vu, as if from a past life, or a half-remembered dream, or a prophetic glimpse into the future.

His voice, his mannerisms—and particularly the way his magic (for that was the easiest thing to name it) effervesced from his lips like vapor, or the smoldering tip of a cigar—were an unwelcome familiarity.

And if that were not enough, the ostentatious crown rather gave it away.

"It is my understanding," the king began, "that you have all been part of something from which I have been reprehensibly excluded. I must tell you, this does not thrill me. In fact, I find myself singularly displeased."

Artemis, who by contrast found the whole ordeal immediately tiresome, drew her bow.

"Careful," the king warned, waving a hand that served at once to dissipate her weapon. "I come in peace. Or, you know, something like it. Something mutually beneficial, at very least." He shrugged. "Entirely dependent on your priorities, and whether or not you care to live."

The immortals, who by definition always lived, found this both laughable (who could possibly disrupt that which simply *was*, ineffably?) and vaguely troubling (Artemis, for example, stared at her hands as if her bow had gone invisible, or chosen of its own volition to hide).

It was Artemis's twin, Apollo, who spoke first. "Is that supposed to be a threat?"

"Oh, very nearly," the king replied. "But more accurately, it's a proposition. This," he clarified, "is primarily about Death."

There was a pause.

"He's no friend of ours," commented one of the Muses slowly; then, bolstered by the collective nods of agreement, she added with a more concentrated proclamation, "He has taken something from each of us."

"He cheats," contributed a small deity in the form of a rabbit. "He's cheated us all out of something."

"Which is precisely my point," the king agreed, nodding his approval. "He has been without consequence for too long, don't you think? It's about time his actions be met with remonstration."

"Where is he?" asked the venerable Count Dracula. (Accounts of his death had been greatly exaggerated.) "Shouldn't he answer for his grievances himself?"

"Oh, I have him," the king replied, shrugging. "And he *will* answer for his grievances. In supremely fitting fashion, he will suffer as we have suffered."

"We, you mean," one of the grandmother spirits maintained. "*You* have suffered for nothing."

"Haven't I?" the king argued, and almost at once the podium at which he stood began to perilously smoke. "I have suffered exclusion. The particular cruelty of . . . how shall I put it?" he pondered to himself, before determining aloud, "Missing out."

"Your pain is not our pain," grumbled a blue deity, who despite the signs of danger chose to recklessly continue. "What right do you have to our injustices?"

The mortal eyes of the king shifted blandly to the deity, who then melted to a puddle on the floor.

"This," announced the king with a sudden return to bonhomie, "is hardly the time for pointless philosophizing. Death will pay, and I will make him pay, and you will all help."

"Why would we?" protested a dauntless fate. "We owe you nothing."

"True. Should the promise of satisfaction at seeing Death brought low be insufficient motivation, then consider this: you are all beholden to someone," the king pointed out with a ghastly smile. "You each serve the will of something above you, woven as you are within the tapestry of your various worlds. You all stand to lose, therefore, by your disobedience. By the debts of your crimes," he added, referencing a thin leather-bound volume, "which have, I believe, gone unpaid."

The king held up the book between a trident of three fingers, pausing to lick the pad of his thumb before gingerly turning the page.

"It appears Death and his keepers have been rather careless," the king announced, holding the pages up for the audience to see. "I have in my hands each of your names—" (dangerous enough, and so the crowd collectively intuited) "—and each of your winnings and losses. I have, therefore, your cooperation. Assuming you wish to avoid the consequences of your own misconduct, that is."

Immediately, the figures in the crowd grew uneasy; they realized now what had transpired to lead to each of their summons, and what, in particular, they all had in common.

"There are rules, aren't there? Even for you," the king prompted with a cutting smile. "You've all broken the codified expectations of your positions. Boredom," the king remarked, "is rather a faultless trap, and Vice Himself such an indulgent master. Aren't I?"

Silence.

"Very well," the king continued loftily, judging the lack of argument to be suitable compliance. "I am not unreasonable. You may be trapped, but you're hardly powerless. Do as you're told," he advised them, "and all of this is merely temporary. I assure you, once I've assumed mastery of Death, all of this will have been in the name of a far brighter future."

"Is that what you told the mortal," Fortune postured slowly, "before you stole his skin?"

The king's smile faltered only slightly. (The podium, however, turned black with rot.)

"Nothing was stolen, and the deals I make with mortals are none of your concern," the king said blithely. "Any other questions?"

"How did you get that?" asked the Unseelie queen, pointing tartly to the book. "It should have been kept safe—"

"And why now?" asked a serpent god, tongue flicking between his teeth. "Why is this the time to challenge Death?"

"Because I can," the king replied simply, "and as for the book—" He shrugged. "The past is passed, and that's a story for another time. Suffice it to say," he continued, "I expect you all to comply with my wishes, and in return, I will continue to guard your secrets. I'm really not so terrible," he remarked, flashing his mortal teeth, "am I?"

"What do you want with us?" Artemis asked, having since realized her bow was not returning. "There are more of us than you, and by your own admission we are by no means powerless; say we wish to fight you rather than submit?"

For a moment, the king's expression darkened.

"I don't want *you*," he said, the air around him warping with noxious effluvium as he spoke. "Once again, your egos befall you. You are not the ends; merely the means by which I take my rightful place, and you forget the vulnerable state you presently occupy. I ask for little and offer much, and for my silence, you each owe me one simple thing: one turn each at the tables, wherein each of you will lose."

"Lose?" a jinni blurted. "But—"

"I am not Death," the king cut in. "I will not cheat you. Once the tables are opened, you will have no choice but to play; such is the consequence of contracts," he clarified knowingly, holding up the book. "Many of you have lost before, and now you will simply lose again. All I ask is that you do so expeditiously, as I'm in something of a hurry. Death's sovereignty has already been suspended," he added. "With your help, it can be removed."

"This was only supposed to be a game," said a satyr, with wary recognition of entrapment.

"It was a game," permitted the king. "Now it's a war."

To that, there was no answer.

"Excellent," proclaimed the king. "Now. Where can I find the two in charge? A game is yet to be played."

# XII

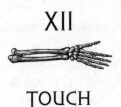

# TOUCH

You have your expectations of heaven and hell. The fact that you call them such things—that there is a polarity in your mind at all, and that they are indeed poles; opposites; a study in contrasts, and with such poetically alliterative names—is already a misunderstanding, but there is only so much that mortal minds can see. True, there is a duality of sorts; balance is king in all things, after all. But there is also a hinge you cannot see, and this is the place where the members of both sides are summoned.

You have your expectations of heaven and hell. Don't you?

Now subvert them.

What is the holiest place you have been? A place of righteousness, a place of austerity, of gravity? Surely not among the clouds. No, the holiest place you have been is solid, from the floors to the walls to the authority, to the assurance of consequence; and perhaps it is expansive, but it isn't *free*, is it? You are restrained by the limitations of your own smallness. You are caged by the littleness of what you are.

What is holy? That which makes you fall to your knees.

What is the most sinful place you have been? A place of decadence, of opulence, of wrongs? Surely not cast out in flames. No, the most sinful place you have been is comfortable, isn't it? In a sleepless way; in a too-full, swollen sort of languor, pressing down on your intestines even as your cheeks burn with pleasure, as your head rushes, your vision swims?

You are restrained here, too, though you may not realize it when the taste of hedonism on your tongue is so undeniably sweet. You are fooled, more likely. You are deceived by the pleasure of a freedom so clever it knows to seek you out for payment later, and thus, what is sin? It is the most fleeting of pleasures, and the true torment is in the waiting for whatever will inevitably come.

For ease of mortal conception, there is a place precisely at the midpoint of heaven and hell, and it is both holy and bolstered with sin, and all who sit within it wait for something they understand, somehow, that they cannot possibly know. The walls are gilded, dressed in untouchable finery, and though the ceilings are impossibly high—too high for fixtures or for windows—light shines in from somewhere, casting you in shadow all the same. Your voice, were you able to speak, would echo from the marble floors; would bounce from the columns and return to your lips in a whisper. The air is still and stiff, filled with uncertainty and the frizzle of transition, like the calm before the storm, because this is merely an axis. This is the hinge, and no one can remain here for long.

Perhaps you would walk inside and call it a courtroom, and perhaps you are right.

There is no telling what is real and what is not.

But here is where they meet.

$$-\,\Omega\,-$$

"Well," Gabriel announced, clapping his hands stiffly to call the room to order. "Now that you're all here."

"Naturally, you must have curiosities," Raphael offered, gesturing around the room. "As you can see, we've felt it necessary to call in both sides."

"Privately," Gabriel added. "For now, we must ask this to remain between us."

"And by ask," Raphael contributed, "we do mean unequivocally require."

"On pain of further servitude," Gabriel unnecessarily clarified, "and additionally, outright pain."

"Not good," one of the angels beside Mayra muttered. "You realize this is highly unorthodox, don't you?"

"Oh, is it?" Raphael mocked with a glare. "I'd simply no idea. *None.*"

"By which he means that we *know*," Gabriel barked. "And also, nobody asked you, Clement."

"Tempers," Clement tutted, displeased. "Surely I don't need to remind you, of all people, of the requisite point value—"

"Will you get to the point?" one of the reapers asked, a brass commendation of merit winking from her chest.

Behind her in the room, Mayra caught a glimpse of Cal; she furtively adjusted her place in the assembly, taking a few steps back to reach the perimeter of the crowd. Cal, meanwhile, caught the motion of Mayra's wandering and unobtrusively managed to attempt the same, weaving toward her from his position along the periphery of clustered souls.

"We would explain," Raphael was informing the reaper (who was, in fact, of highly distinguished rank), "if you would all shut your gaping pieholes."

"Name-calling," observed Clement, his voice piercing the tepid chatter rising from the center of the crowd. "What is that, a loss of three? Perhaps five under the circumstances?"

"Clement, one more word and that's a miracle gone," Gabriel snapped, to which the angel sighed, shaking his head and scribbling something down on his golden parchment with tacit disapproval. "As my esteemed colleague was saying," Gabriel continued, promptly vanishing the parchment from Clement's hands, "we have a problem. Death is missing," he finally announced.

(Clement immediately opened his mouth to speak but produced only the soothing sound of a harp. Thus beaten, he crossed his arms and resigned himself, grudgingly, to a charming, light-fingered rendition of Saint-Saëns.)

"It is of the utmost importance," Gabriel continued, "that we determine Death's whereabouts immediately, if not sooner."

"Does that mean Ends are not being met?" someone asked from where Mayra had previously been standing. (Mayra, meanwhile, continued stepping quietly through the crowd toward the reapers, hoping not to attract attention. Elsewhere, she caught sight of Cal edging in her direction, evidently intending to meet her halfway.)

"Ends are being met," Raphael confirmed. "Destinations, however, are not."

"Messy," remarked an angel named Beatrice. "Very messy."

"WE KNOW," yelped Gabriel and Raphael in unison.

"And you really have no idea where he is?" the first reaper asked. "Problematic, don't you think? We're trackers, certainly, but not psychics—"

"And we're archangels, not detective-twins," Gabriel snapped, his wings ruffling on a sharply conjured breeze.

"We recognize the difficulties," Raphael offered, taking over the role of good cop as Gabriel attempted to cool off with a few meditative breaths, "but circumstances notwithstanding, I'm sure we all understand that Death must be found, and with unutterable haste."

"Do we, though?" contributed a reaper beside Cal, who froze, having been just about to cross over to the angel side of the assembly. "This really seems like your problem, doesn't it?"

Raphael paused before answering, having noticed (despite Cal's best efforts) the steady progress Cal had been making through the crowd, which in turn led him to search, narrow-eyed, for Mayra.

(She grimaced, noting that his hawkish gaze subsequently found her with ease.)

"That's quite an attitude," Gabriel snapped to the reaper, not having noticed Raphael's distraction. "Clearly you're in no hurry to amend your destination, are you, Rupert?"

With that, the reaper promptly closed his mouth, warily eyeing Clement as the latter soared wildly into the climactic trilling of a stirring rendition of Opus 95.

"Just find him," Raphael snapped to the crowd, nudging Gabriel.

What followed was the typical chaos of dismissal, angels embracing angels while reapers stoically came together in a rigid forward-march. Mayra, however, let out an unwilling sigh as both archangels swiveled in unison to glare at her, just catching Cal's arrival at her side.

She reached down, letting her fingers hover above Cal's.

"They see us," she murmured to him.

"Let them," Cal whispered back.

For a moment, then, Mayra closed her eyes, toying with the air between their hands. She curled her fingers inward toward her palm, crafting a delicate, patient current between them that rustled the down of her wings, the raven edge of his cloak; a careful, conscious not-a-touch.

"Kaleka," Gabriel said, his voice familiarly curt. "Sanna."

Mayra's eyes snapped open. They were alone now, the room abruptly shrinking to contain only the four of them.

"What now?" Mayra sighed, abruptly folding her arms over her chest. "I thought you'd had enough of scolding us for one millennium."

"First of all, impossible," Gabriel replied. "Admonishment is quite literally the foundation of our respective constitutions. That, of course, and divinity." He scoffed. "Obviously."

"Secondly, much as we find . . . this," Raphael continued with a wary glance between Mayra and Cal, "*repulsive,* this particular case isn't about the two of you or your clandestine avocations. Though, as a reminder, if you've done anything untoward since our last little talking-to—"

"What, you'll charge us with more time?" Mayra demanded, rolling her eyes. "Astounding. As if a *longer eternity* could possibly mean anything anymore."

"Mayra," Cal warned softly.

With a grimace, she grudgingly backed down. "Fine. So then what is it you want from us, if not to meddle in our personal affairs?" she asked the archangels. "You've lost track of Death, clearly."

"We're not his nannies," Gabriel said.

"Could've fooled me," muttered Mayra, who was feeling obstinate now.

"Kaleka, your opposition to us is hardly wise. We only keep Death's secret because he keeps *our* secret, as you know," Raphael reminded her, and Gabriel spared her a smug, intolerable nod. "Surely we don't need to remind you of the importance of finding him, given what he tasked you with from the start."

She did not need reminding. In fact, the archangel's reminding of her not-needing reminding was as unnecessary as it was annoying, making it increasingly difficult to stifle her disdain.

"You know," Mayra began, lips pursed, "if anyone knew how corrupt you two really were—"

"Corruption is such an unpleasant way to put it," Gabriel cut in. "And as I recall, Mayra Kaleka, you're not so innocent yourself."

An unhelpful observation.

An irritating one, really.

"I genuinely don't know what you want me to do," she told him, with little (well, slightly less) derision to her tone. "Fox already tried calling his godfather and did not succeed in reaching him. As Fox's guardian angel, I can really only know as much as he does—by your own rule, I might add," she pointed out, this time indulging her contempt (which felt appropriate).

"Am I to assume this is the first time Death's failed to materialize at his godson's behest?" Raphael asked with a questioning glance at Cal, who hesitated for a moment, but ultimately nodded in confirmation.

"That we know of," Cal agreed. (Mayra, who knew better than to indulge a sidelong look of suspicion, instead focused on the mental picture of Raphael suddenly bursting into flames.) "Given the circumstances, this summons was rather unsurprising. Well," Cal amended, "the summons themselves, I should say, though I admit the nature of it was very unexpected. I didn't realize we could both be summoned."

"Unusual circumstances," Gabriel said somberly. "They call for unusual means."

"You seem nervous," Mayra noted. "I take it this is about the tables, then?"

Raphael and Gabriel exchanged a glance.

"Not entirely. The lack of fundamental transportation *is* distressing," Raphael said, obviously hedging. "Traveling the worlds is tricky business—"

"The security bit alone being of quite impressive scale. Which you, of course, lack the capacity to grasp," Gabriel added loftily, to which Mayra rolled her eyes.

"I know you consider yourselves exceedingly clever and duplicitous, but you're terrible liars," she reminded Gabriel, with an additional glare at Raphael. "Obviously you're concerned about Death's extracurriculars, aren't you? As I certainly would be," she added darkly, "if I were you."

"Which you're not," Raphael reminded her gruffly.

"No," she agreed, "I'm not. And therefore, why should his ability to guard your ledger concern me?"

Beside her, she felt Cal's disposition change. Mayra, a woman who'd been cursed by touch all her life (both its oppressive monotony and its fleeting absence), had learned Cal Sanna's motions from afar well enough to feel that he was wary now, and coiled; tensed. She could taste it in the air, as plainly as if he'd taken her by the shoulders and shaken the truth from her lips.

"A ledger?" he asked, and though the untrained ear would hear nothing but curiosity, Mayra Kaleka could sense the stirring of consternation in his voice.

"*The* ledger," she corrected. "For the game."

"Ah," Cal said. "The game."

"Yes," Raphael said, grimacing. "The game."

# INTERLUDE III:

## GAMES

There is a game that the immortals play.

It is played around tables that open at dusk, and close at dawn.

The stakes are impossibly high, and yet laughably low.

There is only one secret: *The more you have to lose, the harder it is to win.*

There is only one rule: *Don't lose.*

At first, the immortals only played each other; god against god, and all against Death, who could cost them nothing, and could ask for nothing in return.

But what is the fun in winning when there is so little to lose?

What is the point of playing when there is so little available to take?

Eventually, the tables were open to others on occasion.

(Though a sad fool you are indeed, to play the immortals' game.)

— Ω —

The son of a god plays for immortality; for what should be his birthright, he thinks, though the world disagrees, and his father does, too.

The son plays the game and wins it, and in his celebratory haze, he beckons Death for one thing: for the secret to a goddess's heart, that he may possess the eternal youth he so desperately desires.

Death agrees. In exchange, he takes the son's truth for his own reward.

"I have no truths," the son says, and signs it away easily, greedily, thinking himself the victor; thinking that Death himself is fooled.

Death is not fooled, however, and he smiles.

"You will have one someday," he replies, once the son of the god has gone.

— Ω —

The son returns once more, as Death had known that he would, to play for the truth that he has lost.

The outcome of this game cannot be told.

It is a truth too heavily guarded.

— Ω —

An angel plays for love; for the freedom to covet another's heart without secrecy or remorse, but there is such a thing as asking too much, even for the heaven-bound.

She does not win; she *cannot* win—she wants it too badly, and to want anything at such great risk to yourself is a cardinal sin in the game—but Death takes pity on her, and so he cushions her loss.

"These are things that I can't give you," he tells her, "but I can offer you this instead."

He hands her the gold bracelet she once wore, gifted to her by a suitor she'd almost come to care for during her lifetime; or perhaps she would have, if the inequity of belonging to him had not been such a constant, and thus true love an impossibility.

"There is a man for whom your predicament will mean something," Death says in a rare display of sympathy. "It will echo in his soul as if he is living your pain himself, and this is the most I can do for either of you."

She looks up at him, bemused.

"But I lost the game," she says.

"Yes," Death agrees, "and for your loss, you will have to do something for me in return. You will have to look after him. I will hold you responsible for his heart, and at times, this will disappoint you. He's a right little shit," he adds, which startles the angel into laughter.

"I will watch over him," she solemnly agrees, and Death smiles.

"And for your troubles, you will have windows of love," he says. "They will be brief and wonderful and rapturous; they will fill your heart until it bursts. You will feel a kinship like you've never known, and pain like you've never imagined, and each parting will tear the breath from your lungs and fill you with a longing that will never be quieted. Agony inseverable from ecstasy," he says, "neither of which can ever be taken from you."

She takes the bracelet, her relic, and nods.

"Thank you," she whispers.

— Ω —

A mortal plays for success where others have failed; it is a selfish wish, and Death does not challenge him too greatly, as he knows this man's desires will cripple his humanity, and therefore it will be a loss whether the table determines so or not. (Death would ask how the mortal came by the tables, but he suspects he knows, and because Death himself is breaking a promise already by returning to the tables, he does not invite confirmation of his suspicions.)

Death does not tell the mortal the cost; that his success will come with insatiability.

That this win will be not the filling of a vacancy, but the igniting of a fire.

That this mortal will die with hunger on his tongue, a hunger that cannot be assuaged, even as he possesses all that he could ever desire.

The mortal thinks he has cheated Death.

Death thinks he has cheated the mortal.

Both are wrong.

Neither knows it yet.

— Ω —

A water spirit—an aquatic sprite, a so-called mermaid, born from the sea foam itself—wishes for legs; *not just legs,* she laughs as she details the circumstances of her prize. *Nothing quite so primitive as that,* she amends, but rather, she wishes for humanity; specifically, for carnal pleasures: the toe-curling ache of sex, the heart-pounding thrill of the chase, the adrenaline of theft and the swollenness of guilt; and addiction that can only be soothed by the process renewing itself, cycling endlessly on repeat.

Death, who has heard this one before, finds himself fairly uninvested in the outcome, but because this particular deity cares so little for anything at all there is no denying that she will win, so he doesn't bother to cheat.

"You'll have all the pleasure you want," he tells her, "but you will care so deeply that it ails you, and you will suffer the pain of your wrongs like knives."

She laughs like the rush of the sea, and smiles like the crescent of a wave.

"At least I will suffer for something," she replies.

He sees trouble on her horizon.

But she welcomes it, so he relents.

— Ω —

A mortal who is no longer a mortal returns with a crippling debt to pay, but Death is no longer willing to entertain his supplication.

"You should not have played this game," Death warns.

"Past is passed," the indebted mortal replies.

— Ω —

There is a game that the immortals play.

It has no rules (save one, and a simple one at that) but it does have a keeper, and a ledger, and every success and failure is marked and bound in celestial ink, and so the keeper of the ledger maintains a power that even the players themselves do not understand.

For he who controls the ledger controls the game, and whoever controls the game controls all of the players; even the players, like Death, who never lose.

The game has no rules, save one: *Don't lose.*

The game has no tricks, save one: *You may play to beat the player, but even so, you must always play to beat the game.*

The tables have been closed for many years, but they are open on occasion, and an occasion is about to arise.

(Though a sad fool you are indeed, to play the immortals' game.)

# XIII

## PRIZED POSSESSIONS

"You played again, then, didn't you?" Fox said flatly. "That stupid game."

An accusation, clearly, but a bland one, unfaceted, as if he'd only arrived at the answer because no reasonable alternatives were left. Brandt supposed that over the course of the centuries between them, Fox must have considered every possibility, striking them out on a list until only one option remained.

"As I've mentioned many times to you, Fox, the nature of the game is that it's impossibly addictive," Brandt reminded him, dancing knowingly around the core of the issue. "You can hardly be surprised, then, if I went back—"

"What game?" Tom and Vi interrupted in unison, pausing to exchange a dissatisfied grimace.

"There's a game that the immortals play," Brandt said. "The stakes are impossibly high, and yet laughably l—"

"It's gambling," Fox cut in, as impatient and ruffled as ever. "Plain and simple, and after you left the first time—" He broke off. "After you," he amended tightly, "Papa promised me he would no longer play."

"Oh, and *you've* kept all your promises?" chuckled the demon, whom Brandt had to admit possessed quite a skill at getting under Fox's skin.

("Why are you still here?" Fox demanded from her.

"This is good stuff" was all she had to say.)

"I'm sure Death meant to keep his promise at the time," Brandt assured Fox, "but again, that's the nature of addiction. It always comes to call, and the game is especially alluring."

"I've heard of that game," the demon offered, as Vi glanced questioningly at her, frowning with bemusement. "I've also heard Death cheats."

"He does," Brandt said, just as Fox scoffed, "He doesn't."

"He *does*," Brandt repeated, shaking his head at Fox. "Shamelessly, too, though not how you'd think."

"Controlling the results isn't *cheating*, Brandt, it's a simple matter of consequences. You can't blame the house every time the players lose. And are you really suggesting that he's playing right now?" Fox prompted crossly, scowling.

"No," Brandt said, shaking his head. "It must be worse than that if I'm here."

"What do you mean here?" Tom asked gruffly. "Here as in my house?"

Brandt paused, trying to consider an explanation that would satisfy all interested parties.

"Not exactly," he conceded after a moment. "Well, your house, sure, but the house as it exists at precisely *this moment*, more specifically. The house ten minutes ago, or perhaps a year from now—not so much." He let his gaze travel warily to Fox's. "I presume you know what that means?"

Fox's mouth tightened.

"So you gambled me, then," he judged flatly. "I wondered if you had."

Brandt hesitated, biting his tongue on the words *I'm sorry* and ultimately opting for silence.

No truth would satisfy Fox D'Mora, even if Brandt still had one to give.

"So is that how little I meant to you?" Fox pressed him, but gratifyingly, the vampire cleared her throat, stepping between them.

"Much as I'm enjoying the obvious surplus of history in the room," Vi said, "I do still have a ghost I need exterminated." Predictably, Tom opened his mouth, but Vi continued, "Where exactly could Death have gone, and how are we supposed to reach him?"

"Unknowable, I'm afraid," Brandt informed her. "Death is more enigma than man, and ironically, he's not as constant as you might think. And now that we're all on the same page," he added, "considering my lack of contribution to the situation, I suppose I should be the one to take my leave—"

"Oh, no you don't," Fox snarled, lunging out to grip his arm.

At the contact, Brandt felt his breath catch, lodging itself firmly in his throat; he forced himself not to look down at where Fox's slender fingers, always so deft and clever, pressed tightly around the fabric of his sleeve.

If Fox noticed anything between them, he was angry enough to ignore it. "You're not going anywhere, Brandt. You can't tell me your appearance here now is just some kind of *fluke,* or I don't know, some sort of—"

"Coincidence?" Brandt supplied irritably, yanking his arm free. "That's absolutely what I'm saying. Just because the convergence of these events happens to be *this house* doesn't mean that I'm somehow involved in your predicament."

All at once there was a cacophony of opposition.

"Well—"

"But then—"

"What exactly were you here to steal?" Vi and Tom finally trumpeted in unison, and then froze, each once again sparing the other a narrowed, indignant glance.

"Nothing important," Brandt informed them. "And alternatively, none of your business."

"It *is* my business, actually," Tom corrected stiffly, "considering that this is my house—"

"And even if it weren't our business—seeing as this is *no longer your house,*" Vi reminded Tom before turning back to Brandt, "it seems relevant, don't you think?"

"Oh, more than," the demon remarked, delighted. "I'm Isis, by the way."

"Brandt. And what are you all doing here, anyway?" Brandt ventured, abruptly changing the subject.

Vi: "I'm trying to sell the house."

Tom: "I'm trying to *leave* the house."

Isis: "I couldn't give a fuck about the house. I'm just here to feed on whatever energy comes out of it."

"Fine." Brandt paused, turning to Fox. "And you?" he asked expectantly.

Fox resisted for a moment, as he often did. He was always so juvenile that way, so childish, with a flimsy line between subtle mirth and outright tantrum that had to be born from an adolescence spoilt by strangeness, by the interspecial and inconstant. Brandt may have possessed eternal youth much earlier than Fox had, but Fox always wore it so perfectly, so *authentically*, with that ennui, the melancholy something-nothing-everything curled warily around his mouth and furrowed stubbornly in his brow. If anything, that little rivet of youth jarred the handsomeness of his face; soured him a bit, like a bruise on the otherwise unblemished surface of a peach. Fox would be undeniable to anyone, without a doubt, if he would ever learn to set his sullenness aside.

Though on a personal note, Brandt had always found him quite perfect as he was.

"I'm working," Fox muttered.

"Of course you are," Brandt indulged him. "Doing what, again?"

"My job."

"Ah, and I was so worried you'd be specific."

Fox's expression angled itself downward, sloping to displeasure. "It's none of your business."

"No, it isn't," Brandt agreed, turning facetiously to leave, "so I suppose I *should* go, after all—"

"Fine," Fox said through gritted teeth, pausing him in place. "If you must know, I'm a medium."

Brandt turned slowly.

Frowned.

Stared at him.

Then barked, "You're a *what*?"

"A medium." Fox's mouth tightened. "You might be familiar with the term?" he prompted. "I communicate with the dead."

Brandt paused for a moment in continued disbelief, and then

watched Fox's glower turn sallow as he promptly doubled over, succumbing to the ridiculous notion that Fox D'Mora, ruler of the moral high ground, would be able to say something so absurd without any remorse whatsoever.

"*Now* who's a thief!" Brandt crowed, with another harsh bray of laughter. "You can't even *identify* the other side, Fox, much less *communicate* with it—you can't even see the *ghost,* for fuck's sake—"

"Helpful," Fox grumbled, looking skyward. "Incredibly helpful."

"So, is this what you've been doing, then?" Brandt asked, stepping toward him. "Fox," he murmured, catching the tail end of a breath Fox had been holding. "You tried so hard to make me better," Brandt lamented, "and instead you just made yourself worse, didn't you?"

Fox was a different man now. His anger was old, his sadness even older.

"Don't you think you owe me enough to try to help?" Fox asked bitterly. "Or would you rather continue making a mockery of me?"

"Neither," Brandt said, and paused. "Both."

"He called you a liar," Isis whispered to Fox, leaning toward him and placing a hand merrily on his shoulder. "That has to sting, doesn't it?"

Fox wrenched himself free, stepping furiously toward Brandt.

"Take me to my godfather," he demanded. "You did it once, didn't you? You can do it again."

"Yes, I did do that once, and it didn't go very well the first time," Brandt reminded him. "Not to mention that I don't technically know where he is."

"Where else would he be?" Fox snapped. "You said it yourself. You said so, just now, that the game is addictive—"

"Of course it is," Brandt said without thinking, "but I still wouldn't know. Something's gone wrong, and anyway, I haven't played in—"

He stopped, faltering just shy of a confession, and then forced it out anyway, determining it more fact than truth.

"I haven't played the immortals' game," he said as tonelessly as he could manage, "in one hundred and seventy-five years. And if

Death's back at the tables again, there's no guarantee I can actually get there. In fact, I'm almost positive I can't. Unless—"

He broke off, grimacing, and again—in another sequence of tepid, gamified choreography, one step forward for two steps back— Fox moved toward him.

"What were you here to steal?" Fox's expression, Brandt could tell, was held carefully, pointedly blank, which on Fox had the effect of looking seasick. "It had to do with the tables, didn't it?"

"Yes," Vi chimed in from behind him, nodding firmly. "Whatever those are," she added with a shrug, and the ghost nodded along.

"Your purpose here does seem increasingly relevant," said Tom, making a face. "And frankly, I don't appreciate how long it's taken to bring that to your attention—"

"There's nothing else to tell," Brandt attempted firmly, but he could see there was no escaping it. The others were advancing on him, expectant, and for better or worse, he knew there was no way they'd let him go now.

"It has to be about the tables, about the game. I know it couldn't be about the house or anything in it," Fox was saying, having undertaken another step in Brandt's direction. (Yes, Brandt was certain now, Fox could feel it. He knew the cost of every step, of every breath.)

"Nonsense, Fox, haven't you any idea how much that table is worth?" asked Brandt with a nod to the center of the dining room. "Those chairs? That painting? Any one of the fucking knives— including," he added with a pointed gesture to the ghost Fox couldn't even see, "the one stabbed through your client's chest?"

"I think technically Vi's the client," said Isis, while Fox shook his head, still doing a decent job of ignoring her.

"Brandt, please. You've never needed money. You've never wanted anything from people like this—"

"Unlike you, apparently," Brandt commented in an undertone, but Fox didn't waver.

"If there's something *extraordinarily* valuable in this house then maybe that could be it, but I doubt it," he continued. "It's a house full of mortals, Brandt, and I've only ever known you to venture out for two things. One of them was the game," he said knowingly. "The other was me."

He paused, waiting. Their little dance was suspended, Fox mere inches from reach. Even prolonged eye contact would be an answer. Even a glance would be enough.

So Brandt looked away.

"Well," Fox said, mouth visibly strained, "since it couldn't have been me, it was obviously the game. Wasn't it?"

There was no way around it now.

Conveniently, it wasn't a truth; it was always true, but now it was also fact.

"There is . . . a ledger of sorts," Brandt said. "Inside of a book."

"What?" Vi and Tom asked, confused, but Fox's face immediately went pale.

"You didn't," he said. (Beside him, Isis clapped her hands with glee.)

Brandt heaved a sigh.

"I did," he finally confessed.

# INTERLUDE IV:

## SNIPPETS

"You told me I would be done soon," a woman who is not a woman whispers in the dark.

"You will be done when I am done," returns a creature who was once a man.

"I can't keep doing this," she says.

"You should have thought of that before you agreed to play the game," he reminds her, not for the first time, "and especially before you agreed to make a deal with me."

"Do you really feel nothing?" Her voice is low, private, hushed. "No remorse whatsoever?"

"Me? Of course not," he replies with a chuckle. "My host, on the other hand—"

"It must be killing him," she murmurs.

"His debt to me is what's killing him, as you well know. If he had ever truly wanted a life worth living, he would have been more specific about what he asked."

"And you blame the mortal for that? You do realize this is Death's fault, don't you?"

"Ironic, isn't it? Or it would be—but then again, it's not precisely Death's fault. It's Death's *doing*, obviously, but if we're being more specific, it's actually *life's* fault—though that leaves us with so little to blame. In any case, he's withering, and I'll need more."

"And what exactly is 'more'?"

"What I am owed. No more, no less. I'm not unreasonable."

"What has he promised you?"

"The mortal? Never mind what he's promised me. Your debt is unrelated to his."

"Is it, though?"

"Well, I suppose not in the grand scheme of things. But I don't think it worth your time to worry prematurely."

"But if you can't get what you want from your host—"

"I won't take it from you, if that's what you're asking."

"Not *just* me, you mean."

"Ah, true. I do have my eyes set on a larger prize."

"Then why am I still necessary?"

"Because the ledger is of no use to me on its own. Surely you realize? The game must still be played, and the process is draining, even for me. Well—for *us*, I should say. Might I presume you know where I'm going with this?"

"You're . . . you're saying I'll have to play the game again? You can't be serious—"

"Of course I'm serious. Dead serious, in fact, which is another delightful irony. Mortals do produce the best phrasing—"

"But how can you even know your host is right? You know how unreliable the game can be, and he could easily be trying to appease you."

"True enough; desperate mortals do have a tendency to make grim pleas. But it's a win-win, in my view. Those archangels are far too comfortable with their corruption, and as for Death, he's come far enough without any retribution. Didn't you say so yourself?"

"No, I didn't, and I won't. I don't want any further part in this. I won't do it."

"Actually," he says, "I rather think you will, Elaine."

She shudders.

"Don't call me that," she says, swallowing hard.

He conjures a smile, or something like one.

"Get that under control," he advises, gesturing to the torment that's currently written on her face. "Or it'll be a hard loss, and there's only one rule, isn't there?"

"Don't lose," she whispers in confirmation.

He nods his approval.

"Don't lose," he confirms, rising to his feet and tipping his hat in her direction. "Now if you'll excuse me," he says genially, "I have somewhere else I need to be."

— Ω —

Two archangels, the appointed stewards of righteousness, continue a lengthy discussion that has been ongoing since nearly the birth of Time.

"I don't care if it's love between them or not," one says, "that shouldn't change anything."

"You care about nothing," the second chides the first.

"I'm not built to care," the first says. "Only to last."

This they agree on. In general, though, they agree.

"Boredom," the second tangentially laments. "An affliction of the everliving."

"The forevermores," the first agrees. "Truly, this isn't our fault."

"Not in the least," the second says. "If anything it's a matter of faulty construction."

"No consequences," contributes the first. "No integral system of punishment and reward."

"Not for us," agrees the second. "And not for Death, either."

"Flawed," the first one says. "And him being such a king of vice."

"Careful, or Volos will hear you," the second warns. "Being the *actual* king of vice."

They both look apprehensively over their shoulders, wings skittishly ruffled.

"He flatters himself," sniffs the first, after a moment.

"He does," agrees the second, because again, in general they agree. "A very good thing we managed to exclude him from the game."

"Should we have excluded Fortune, too?" the first comments thoughtfully.

"Why? Fortune never beats Death," says the second. "She sometimes even loses to Destiny."

"Hence her hands being so precariously tied," sighs the first. "A lovely fool, Fortune."

"And we *her* fools if we don't sort this out," reminds the second. "If anyone takes hold of the ledger, we are all at risk. Death most of all, I would think."

"Mortals, you mean," the first says. "Not us. Only mortals suffer in the aftermath of Death's conceivable loss. He has no power over us."

"But we are more connected than that, aren't we?" the second philosophizes (or less charitably, corrects). "Isn't that the very danger of the ledger, how terribly connected we all are? How inescapably? If one of the players falls victim to the game's control," he says solemnly, "don't we all have something to lose?"

"The entire game *is* sacrifice," the first thoughtfully contributes. "It's not a game at all without some universal risk of loss, I suppose."

"So we'll have to keep it safe," the second determines, and pauses. "There are no other copies, are there, aside from Death's?"

"Who would be fool enough to make one?" the first scoffs. "Someone stupid."

"Someone desperate," the second corrects.

"Same thing," acknowledges the first. "Though who has lost so badly in the game that they'd risk this much just to recover it?"

They lock eyes, afraid to answer.

"You don't think," the first one begins, and the second grimaces.

"It couldn't possibly be," he says, though even he looks as though he might be wrong.

Soon, though, they discover that they both are.

Within seconds, a man who is not a man (though he looks very like one) arrives in their courtroom, snapping his fingers.

The celestial argument is frozen.

"Time to go," says the not-man, cheerily. "A game is yet to be played."

# XIV

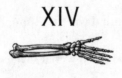

## SOMETHING WICKED

"How did you possibly get ahold of the *ledger*?" Fox demanded, just as the angel and reaper reappeared.

"Oh, good, you're still here," the angel said, marching up to Brandt with her finger brandished at his face. "I'm Mayra, that's Cal," she said, gesturing wildly to herself and the reaper respectively, "and we have a thing or two to say to you, Brandt Solberg—"

"Who are you?" he cut in, frowning.

(Isis, in a loud whisper to Vi: "Ahhh, she's his guardian angel—*that's* why he has her relic."

Vi, now hopelessly bemused: "Her . . . relic?"

Isis, nodding: "It's rare, but some angels have an item from their mortal lives that binds them to earth. Fox has hers.")

"It's only *a* ledger," Brandt told Fox, ignoring the others. "An unofficial one, which I *happened* to scribble down in a book, so really, it's more of an imitation."

The reaper, Cal, looked green.

"Not *Death's* ledger though, surely?" he asked uneasily, sounding as if he very much needed the answer to be no but was confident it wouldn't be. (Beside him, Mayra's wings seemed momentarily affected by static, or possibly dread.)

(Isis, greedily, with a glance at Vi: "Ooh. Now this is getting good.")

"Not Death's ledger," Brandt confirmed. "*My* ledger. Well, the ledger I've been working on," he amended, "though I've kept it here for the past several decades."

"Here?" Tom echoed. "How is that possible?"

Brandt opened his mouth to answer before deciding against it.

"You know, you're all getting excessively worked up over this," he noted. "So I suppose, rather than spin you all into an unnecessary frenzy, I should just remind you that I simply need to find it and be on my way—"

"That's it," Fox announced with a shake of his head. "Cal, if you would?"

"Are you sure?" Cal asked, hesitating.

"He's clearly a flight risk," Fox hissed in confirmation, and Cal sighed, grudgingly snapping his fingers to make a pair of cast-iron handcuffs appear around Brandt's wrists.

"Fox," Brandt growled, trying and failing to wrest his hands apart, "is this really necessary?"

"Yes," Fox replied curtly, "it is, and I'll tell you why. If my godfather is missing, then he's at the tables. If you have a ledger and *it* is also missing, then someone else is at the tables, too. And seeing as you're the only one who can get me there—"

"Can't your angel do it?" Brandt countered, to which Mayra replied with a pursed look of annoyance.

"First of all, I'm not *his,* I'm mine. Secondly, I'm out of miracles," she informed him. "Traveling between conceptions of reality isn't in my employment contract, so without miracles, I can only function within the constructs of the reality I'm currently in."

"How is it *you* can do it?" Isis interrupted, staring incredulously at Brandt. "Even I can't, at least not easily. Not without, you know." She shrugged. "A fair amount of murder, several uninterrupted hours of yoga, and for real expediency, an orgasm."

"I have a key," Brandt said, "not that it's any of your business."

"Well, it's our business now," Fox informed him reflexively, and then grimaced. "I mean," he amended, "it's *mine,* anyway—"

"And mine," Mayra said. "Fox isn't going anywhere without me."

"And mine," Cal agreed. "I'll keep an eye on—" He broke off, his gaze narrowing as it settled on a fidgeting Brandt, "*this* one."

"And mine," Isis said. "And also Vi's. Just because."

"Wait a minute," Vi interrupted. "I don't see why—"

She paused, startled, as a low chime flooded the house, clanging through the foyer and flooding the high ceilings of the dining room.

"Doorbell," barked Tom, zooming out of sight. "I'll take care of it."

"He will, too," Vi lamented as he went. "This is just another in a long list of reasons why the house still isn't sold. But anyway, as we were saying—"

"As *I* was saying, I'm not going," Brandt informed the group, choosing that moment to exit the room (the shackles were really far more aesthetic than useful) while the others, panicked, scuttled frantically after him. "Death banned me from the tables a long time ago, Fox," Brandt narrated over his shoulder, selecting a predominantly green sitting room that suited his complexion, "so I couldn't even if I wanted to. Which, to be clear," he added, falling back against the sofa amid the cushions' soft cough of dust, "I do not."

"Oi." Tom abruptly reappeared just as the others filed into the parlor after Brandt, Fox taking up the helm with an impressively manic look of frustration. "Someone's at the door for the medium."

Cal, slightly winded in Fox's wake: "He says 'it's for the medium.'"

Brandt, under his breath: "He's not a medium."

"It's not for me!" Fox agreed. "And for *fuck's sake*—"

"Band," Brandt said, and Fox rolled his eyes, dutifully reaching for the rubber band on his wrist before pausing abruptly, freezing in place.

"I—" Fox began, and stopped, staring at Brandt. "How did you know about that?"

"I said I was banned from the tables," Brandt informed him, crossing one leg over the other. "I never said I hadn't seen Death."

Again, Fox was staring at him, waiting for something unspoken. "But how would you—"

"They had wings," Tom supplied. "Big ones. Bigger than hers," he clarified, pointing to Mayra, whose eyes widened. "They were also—and while this is true for almost everyone in the room, try not to let that undermine what I'm about to say—extremely annoying," he added, as Mayra and Cal exchanged a glance.

"Were they, by chance," Mayra began tepidly, "finishing each other's sentences?"

"Yes," Tom said, making a face. "Definitely."

"Well, rats," Cal sighed.

"What is it?" Fox demanded. "Honestly, Calix, the one time I actually need you to translate for me—"

"Let me put it to you this way," Cal said. "If it's who I think it is, then everything is much worse than we thought."

# XV

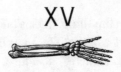

## WORSE THAN THEY THOUGHT

### One Hour Ago

"Oh balls," Raphael muttered, regaining proper use of his voice once the knots had been tightened around his hands and feet. "You again."

"Yes," the man curtly replied. "Ta-dah!"

"I see you've found yourself a new mask, Volos," Gabriel commented sourly. "Was the last one not to your liking?"

"Well, this one's a bit tight," the demon king called Volos agreed, sighing in lamentation. "I'd prefer a better fit, but then again, this mortal's turned out to be rather useful. And you know I never maintain any particular skin for very long—dulls my edge," he explained, plucking lint from his cuff. "As the experts say, better to diversify the portfolio."

"Why are you even here?" Raphael asked, exasperated. "You know we don't allow you to play the game."

"Correction," Volos countered. "You don't allow *Volos* to play the game."

"Minor detail," Gabriel grumbled. "Easily loopholed."

"Yes—*so* easily loopholed, in fact, that here I am," Volos reminded them, with something of a showman's pirouette for emphasis. "Along with a couple of other unfortunate souls. You do know Elaine, don't you?" he added, snapping his fingers to make Lainey appear beside him. "She had the misfortune of making a couple of extremely flawed deals with me after she played the game with Death—"

"As did the mortal, I presume," Raphael muttered knowingly, "but that doesn't mean we'll allow you to play simply because you wear someone else's skin. You are Volos, no matter whose corporeal state you occupy."

"Well, see, this is the fun thing," Volos informed them, appearing quite pleased they had asked. "The mortal played the game—as did my little friend Elaine, here," he added, tapping her nose. "So, once I initiate the ledger, they will both have to play again, by virtue of the ledger itself."

"We don't have the ledger," Gabriel reminded him gruffly. "So you've miscalculated, haven't you?"

"Actually, I have one of my own," Volos said with a flourish, holding up what looked to be a slim leather volume with some of the pages torn out. "All I need *you* to do, gentlemen, is enforce the rules. Which, as I recall, is *your job*," he pointed out, "and therefore hardly too much to ask."

"You know perfectly well that there's only one rule," Raphael reminded him.

"*Everyone* knows that," Gabriel agreed. "Our enforcement of it is highly unnecessary."

(A mistake. Volos now appeared agitated, and the ground beneath them began to smart the soles of their heavenly feet.)

"That may be the case for the game, but the tables themselves answer to you," Volos clarified, forcing a smile, "as you both know. The game cannot start until you permit it. Now, I have Death," he explained, cooler heads apparently prevailing. "I have the ledger, I have my players, and I have my prize. Now all I need are the tables awoken."

"What do you mean your prize?" Raphael demanded, balking at this very unfortunate turn of events. "What exactly is your goal, Volos?"

"You already have possession of a mortal. And a water deity, by the looks of it," Gabriel commented, eyeing the almost certainly not-a-woman. "Don't you think you've gotten a bit greedy, Volos? You know what they say, after all—"

"—balance is king," he and Raphael concluded in unison.

(This, too, was unwise. Gabriel sputtered a cough, the air before them churning with smoke, while Raphael suffered the beginnings of what he had no reason to know was a migraine.)

"Correction," Volos informed them, "*Volos* is king, and I'm tired of being relegated to less. Besides, the mortal owes me more than simply the use of his body. *Far* more. Frankly," he added with a scoff, "a mortal capable of this sort of debt should have never been allowed to play at all, don't you think?"

Gabriel and Raphael exchanged a look.

"That wasn't our fault," Gabriel said tightly, as Raphael nodded his agreement. "Mortals aren't permitted at the tables."

"Well, neither was I," Volos said cheerily, "and now look! It seems there are even fewer rules than you thought, seeing as your exclusions about who can sit at the tables don't seem to hold."

"Shows how much you know," Gabriel muttered through a hacking fit of coughs. "Nobody *sits* at the tables—"

"Oh yes, antagonize me," Volos mused aloud. "What an excellent decision for which there will surely be no consequences whatsoever—"

"I don't see what you want us to do about this, Volos," Raphael said, the banging behind his temples beginning to crowd his more sensible thoughts. "We'd be stupid to let you play."

"You *are* stupid," Volos confirmed. "You're *immensely* stupid, and no pun intended, but your hands are clearly tied. I'll turn you in," he added, gesturing upward. "I'll turn all of you in, and then what will you do, when you have God and Lucifer to contend with along with every other creature and immortal who's ever played the game? A precarious position," he warned, though Gabriel and Raphael already knew as much, and exchanged apprehensive glances.

"You have to give us a chance to win, Volos," Raphael attempted. "There has to be a way we can win, or else there's no fun in playing at all, is there?"

"That's true," Gabriel chimed in, catching a momentary glint of opportunity in Volos's pause. "The game does require an opponent to be worthwhile."

"The opponent is Death," Volos said, clearly sensing the intimations of a trap, but Raphael hastily shook his head.

"No, the *prize* is Death," he corrected. "In order to achieve your intended result, Death is merely the last of the players. You need a true opponent; a *challenger*. Let us choose one," he offered. "Let us choose our opponent in the game, and then we'll open the table."

"It won't be any fun," Gabriel warned, "unless there's a chance you could lose."

Volos hesitated.

"Winning is fun," he protested suspiciously.

"Yes," Raphael permitted, "but it's not the *most* fun."

"After all, you have to beat both your opponent *and* the game," Gabriel reminded him. "There's no satisfaction without sacrifice. Is there, Volos?" he asked expectantly. "Otherwise, why would the king of vice himself stoop so low as to toy with a mere mortal?"

Volos narrowed his eyes.

"I won't share my ledger," he said. "Your opponent will have to find his own way to reach me at the end."

"Fine," Raphael said, shrugging. "Doable."

"And if I win, I win outright," Volos said. "No deals. If I win, I play for mastery of Death."

"Yes," Gabriel agreed. "And if we win—"

"If your *opponent* wins," Volos corrected.

"Fine," Raphael said again. "If our opponent wins, they take mastery."

"No ties," Volos warned. "The game must be won, *properly*, and the opponent must be defeated."

"Fine," Gabriel said. "Then do we have a deal?"

Volos considered it, toying with his options one last time.

"Who is to be your chosen opponent?" he asked, still guarded. "None of the deities will play for you," he added. "I've already se-cured their loyalty. None of them would dare to challenge me—not with the leverage I possess."

Raphael and Gabriel exchanged another searching look.

"Not an immortal, then," Raphael postured slowly.

"Right," Gabriel agreed, and frowned. "So . . . a mortal?"

"A mortal?" Volos scoffed.

"Yes," Raphael said, blinking rapidly. "Yes, a mortal."

"A mortal," Gabriel exhaled, "called—"

"—Fox D'Mora," they said in unison.

"Never heard of him," Volos said, frowning. "Who in the cosmos is that?"

"A mortal," Raphael said.

"Just a normal mortal," Gabriel added.

"Low born," Raphael inserted hastily.

"Generally talentless," added Gabriel.

Volos scoffed.

"A mortal?" His lips curled up indolently, stretching to accommodate a slow, wicked smile. "Well then, gentlemen, you have yourself a deal."

## Thirty Minutes Ago

"So," Volos began, adjusting his crown before addressing the vast sea of immortals from his slightly blackened podium, "now that I have you all here again—"

"We never left," one of the minor domestic gods grumbled, sitting up from where he'd been lying morose across the floorboards. "Or have you forgotten that you imprisoned us here?"

"I haven't forgotten," Volos informed him, "nor have you been imprisoned."

"Strange," Aphrodite said, "but *don't move* and *don't argue* seem a bit like imprisonment, Volos."

For a moment, the king of vice was silent, letting his gaze slide coolly around the room.

"Do you all feel this way?" Volos prompted, pausing to glance at each of the immortals under his purview. "You think I've trapped you?"

"You have, haven't you?" asked one of the ancestral spirits. "We are no friends of Death, true, but neither are we friends of you."

"You threatened us all with exposure," a shapeshifter said, trans-forming from hawk to golden-scaled dragon and back again in her fury. "You've essentially *blackmailed* us—"

"And all but put us in cages," Artemis added thunderously, still smarting from the loss of her bow.

Thus began an annoying, thankless discord of mutters and nods of agreement around the room, none of which the king of vice had time for.

"Well," Volos hummed to himself. "If that's how you feel—"

He waved a hand, prompting a series of twining gold bars to rise up from the floor, towering up from underfoot, while above them, thick strands lowered like vines from the ceiling and snaked out from the walls, hooking around crooks of elbows and hollows of necks to anchor each immortal in place. Shouts of protestation echoed throughout the fold between worlds, sound casting out into the voids, while Volos himself waited, falling back into a throne that grew up from the ground and sprung up in spires, embracing him just as fully as his soon-to-be uncontested reign.

"There," he said, eyeing his fingernails once every immortal had been bound immovably in place. "Now there's no need for *all buts*. Comfortable?"

Expectantly, the others glared at him.

"You cannot hold us," a fire-god said. "You should not even be able to now, but—"

"But you're all bound to the game," Volos answered for him, pointedly holding up the book that contained the ledger. "So long as the game is in play—with all of you bound to your own errors," he added pointedly, gesturing to the restraints that seemed to hold tighter the more they struggled, "you are all more subject than ever to the particularities of my gifts. Not to worry, though. I expect it will all be over soon."

"How?" one of the moon's purveyors pressed, as a plague beside them frowned. "Even if you win against Death—"

"When," Volos corrected. "*When* I win against Death."

"—what will you do?" the plague-deity demanded. "Put all of humanity in chains, too?"

"Maybe I will, maybe I won't," Volos replied, shrugging. "After all, they entertain me much more than all of you. Look at this one," he added, gesturing again to his current host; the mortal whose bones and flesh he presently wore. "He simply let me in, didn't he? I knocked and he answered, with none of this whining to slow us down."

"You can't keep us forever," a sylph insisted. "Once the game is over—"

"Once the game is over, I will possess mastery of Death, and will not need any of you," Volos reminded them. "I tried to do this civilly," he added, sighing in feigned lamentation. "I told you we were all on the same team, did I not? But seeing as none of you turned out to be my friends, I will simply have to keep you here until the game is through."

"Are we prisoners of the game, or of you?" asked one of the fae queens.

"Both," Volos said, "and also, neither. Prisoners of your own boredom, aren't you? And by the way, the two who run the tables can't save you," he added, lest they consider seeking the archangels out. "They're as afraid of their own masters as you are, and as ineffectual as ever. When all of this is over, you may take your anger out on them," he offered graciously, turning away. "In the meantime, I have a game to attend to—"

"Did the archangels at least choose an opponent?" one of the ancient spirits asked, her voice ringing out through space and time.

At that, Volos paused, turning over his shoulder.

"Yes," he ventured, toying carefully with his response. "Which reminds me—has anyone ever heard of a mortal called Fox D'Mora?"

A few heads shook; mostly, though, silence reigned.

"Is he some type of hero?" Volos pressed. "An Achilles, perhaps? A Jason or a Hercules?"

More scattered murmurs.

"Arthur, even," Volos attempted. "Karna? Sigurd?"

A few groans of defeat.

"I see," Volos determined cheerfully. "So he really is a nobody, then?"

This time, nobody dared to speak, choked to silence by their own impending losses.

"Well," Volos said, straightening his lapel and trotting toward the tables, "then I suspect we'll all be done here quite soon indeed."

## Ten Minutes Ago

The two archangels departed the Red Line stop at Chicago Avenue, ducking their heads and hurrying east toward the lake. The sun had nearly slipped below the horizon at their backs, bathing the city in a hint of autumnal pink.

"I don't see why we had to do it this way," Gabriel muttered, shaking out his wings and shivering as a gust of wind smacked abruptly into their faces. "Couldn't we have simply summoned him to our realm? It's not as though we have much time before we're required to oversee the tables—"

"Oh, sure, so we should just zap him to a netherworld and then say, 'hi, hello, we need you to play an elaborate game to gain mastery over your godfather, who by the way has been kidnapped'?" Raphael said sarcastically, nudging Gabriel past a large group of tourists. (His head, needless to say, still ached.) "Yes, I'm sure he would have taken that quite well."

"How he takes it is hardly the issue," Gabriel hissed in reply. "I recognize that he's our only choice, but still, if he doesn't win against Vol—"

"Don't say his name," Raphael warned, glancing uneasily over his shoulder. "I'm beginning to wonder if that doesn't summon him directly."

Gabriel sighed, not wanting to be agreeable. (Though for the record, he fully agreed.)

"I simply don't see how he's occupying a mortal's body," Gabriel muttered instead, turning his agitation back to the so-called king of vice. "Just being *around* mortals is disturbing enough, personally. Have you looked at them lately?"

At that, Raphael paused, looking more closely at his earthly surroundings for the first time.

To his right, something that was almost certainly not a mortal was sorting through the rubbish bin, moaning quietly; across the street, a zombie-looking creature clutched at a crinkled Dunkin' Donuts mug, stumbling drunkenly through traffic. On the wind, too, Raphael noted a translucent form that gave a wretched, impatient howl as it flew, joining up with a thick cloud of fog that lingered ominously atop Lake Michigan's glassy surface.

"*Have* you looked at them?" Raphael echoed, frowning. "Because I hate to say it, but I don't believe these are normal mortals."

Gabriel's eyes widened, noticing the ghoul nearby in a suit, clutching a child's juice box while sorting blithely through the trash.

"Oh balls," he said, snapping his fingers to change the stoplight and darting in front of several screeching cars. "It appears we're going to have to hurry."

# XVI

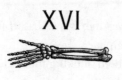

## PUT IT ON MY TAB

By then, Fox knew better than to answer an unexpected knock (or in this case, the sound of the Parkers' melancholy doorbell), but as was becoming a thematic consistency, his refusal to budge was insufficient to keep the outsides out.

"You know, it's very impolite to keep us waiting," one of the archangels began, gratuitously parting one of the house's walls to step into the Parker dining room.

"Is it?" Fox muttered dryly. (Mayra, who had already given him detailed instructions—"don't antagonize them, don't ask about the meaning of life, and for heaven's sake, don't be a dick"—flashed him an impatient glare.)

"Be sure to add this to his mortal ledger, Kaleka," the other added, glaring at Mayra as he followed behind the first. His gaze then flicked briefly to Cal. "Imprisoning people, are you, Sanna?" he asked, gesturing to where Brandt sat handcuffed on the sofa. "Tsk, tsk."

"Not that we care much for the godling either," the first acknowledged.

"Raphael," Brandt muttered in greeting to the first. "Gabriel," he added to the second.

"Godling," they replied tartly in unison.

"Nice to see you've managed to stay out of trouble," said the one called Gabriel, before adding facetiously, "Oh, wait—"

"What are you two doing here?" Mayra prompted, her brow furrowed. "I thought you were supposed to be looking for Death."

"Yes, well, we found him," Raphael said.

"Yes," Gabriel agreed. "We did."

"More like he found us," Raphael amended.

"Yes, and if we're really aiming for accuracy, then what we mean is that his captor found us," Gabriel corrected, glancing again at Raphael. "But who has the time for exactitude, really?"

"Where is he?" Fox demanded, stepping toward them.

"Ah, how to put this delicately," Raphael murmured to himself. "Well, you see, Fox D'Mora, your godfather is—"

"Bound to an immortal game by a reprehensible demon king," Gabriel generously provided. "And as a result, we're going to need you to do a few things for us."

"*Another* demon?" Fox scoffed, and looked around, realizing suddenly that Isis had disappeared. "Wait. Speaking of demons—"

"So you agree, then?" Raphael ventured hopefully. "It's really rather important that you do so expeditiously."

"By which he means now," Gabriel contributed, "so take whatever you need. A coat, perhaps, and—" He frowned, turning to Raphael. "What else do mortals require for travel? A discus? Some small shampoos?"

Raphael: "There was something about a grail at one point, wasn't there?"

Fox: "I'm sorry, what?"

Brandt: "The holy grail is for dinner parties, not for travel."

Raphael, frowning: "I thought that sounded wrong."

Fox, with palpable frustration: "No, I mean—*what*? Where is it you want me to go? Where is my godfather?"

Gabriel: "Metaphysically? Trapped."

Fox, irritably: "I meant geographically."

Raphael: "Oh. Well, then he's at the tables."

Fox, with both annoyance and relief: "So then he *is* just playing the game."

Gabriel, with a glance at Raphael: "Not exactly."

Raphael, with a perfunctory nod: "Not of his own volition."

"By which we mean," Gabriel clarified delicately, "no."

"I'd like to know more about this game," commented Vi, whom Fox had entirely forgotten about until the air beside her rippled slightly. "Yes, I'm glad you agree, Tom, but that's hardly the point at the moment—"

"I'm sorry," Gabriel trumpeted, glancing at Raphael, "but did she just say *Tom*?"

"Tom Parker?" Raphael asked, producing a golden scroll from nowhere and giving it a brief, hasty scan. "Yes, yes, I see, Thom—"

"—as Edward Parker *the fourth*," Vi finished, rolling her eyes. "We *know*, Thomas—"

"Right, okay then, two more things," Raphael determined, turning back to Fox. "One, as we were saying, we need you to play the game against Volos, the demon king."

"Right," Fox said. "Yeah, I'm not doing that."

"Secondly, we need you t—I'm sorry, what?" Gabriel broke off, turning to Raphael. "Did he just say no?"

"Can he do that?" Raphael asked in apparent disbelief. "Is that—can he—?"

"He isn't dead," Brandt reminded them. "He's alive, he's a mortal, and he's out of your jurisdiction, so you can't make him do anything. Believe me," he added meaningfully, "I've tried."

"Still." Gabriel was visibly aghast. "He's—why—"

Cal, once again displaying a singular talent as well-intentioned intermediary: "Maybe if you just explained *why* you want him to do this—"

Fox, unhelpfully: "No."

Gabriel, dazed: "Did he just do it again? Did I hear that correctly?"

Brandt, to Gabriel: "You must have dreamt it."

Raphael, to Brandt: "Shut up, godling."

Brandt, to Raphael: "Temper, temper."

Gabriel, to Brandt: "SHUT UP."

"Fox," Mayra sighed, drifting ethereally toward him. "You might want to listen to them." She glanced uneasily over her shoulder, nudging him aside to speak with him in pseudo-private. "They're terrible, but they wouldn't have come if it weren't very much necessary."

"No," Fox replied, with no attempt to lower his voice. "I'm not playing any games, certainly not this one, and I'm not going anywhere with them—"

"Oh, you can't come with us," Gabriel chimed in from afar. "We have a demon on our tail, and you're a mortal. We can't exactly hold your hand and help you discover the wheel—"

"They already have that," Brandt cut in. "It's been reinvented several times, actually."

"Really?" asked Raphael, scoffing. "That sounds wildly impractical. Isn't one wheel enough?"

"I don't know what to tell you," Brandt replied, stone-faced. "They just love wheels."

"Hold on." Fox spared Brandt a silencing glare before turning his attention back to the archangels. "I can't travel between worlds. If you weren't planning to transport me yourselves, then how was I supposed to get from place to place?"

"Kaleka?" Raphael asked Mayra expectantly, and she grimaced.

"We already played this game," she assured them. "None of us can do it, except for . . ."

She trailed off, everyone in the room slowly turning to look at Brandt.

"What?" he asked.

Cal, with a frown: "You have a key."

Brandt: "Hm? No I don't."

Vi, with apparent agreement from the ghost beside her: "He's right, you just said you did."

Brandt: "Did not."

"There's only one key," Raphael informed them, raising a hand to presumably summon it from elsewhere. "I keep it right—" He paused, paling, as he opened his palm to nothing but empty air. "Oh." He turned to Gabriel. "How long have we been missing a key?"

"It's just a spare," Gabriel said.

"Well, it's also gone," Raphael muttered, glaring at Brandt as Gabriel rounded on him.

Gabriel, to Brandt: "Did you take our key, godling?"

Brandt, to the ceiling: "No."

Fox, to the archangels: "It's *your* key? Because he definitely has one."

They both turned back to Brandt, expectant.

Brandt, to the archangels: "What does he know? He's a mortal."

Fox, to Brandt: a wordless glare.

"Fine," Raphael said, throwing his hands in the air. "You can keep the key, godling, if you use it to transport the godson of Death."

"Come to think of it," Brandt mused, "I might have a key."

"Your ledger," Mayra sighed at him, shaking her head. "It's a *mess*."

"Speaking of ledgers," Raphael said, "that's the second thing we need."

"Yes," Gabriel agreed. "We need you to get Death's ledger."

"Why?" Fox demanded. "And also, no."

"Yes," Raphael corrected, "and because in order to beat the demon king in the game, you need to determine who to play to reach him."

Brandt, to Fox: "Like a tournament."

Fox, irritably, to Brandt: "How would you know?"

Brandt shrugged. "Fairly straightforward," he said, though he didn't meet Fox's eye as he said it.

"Okay, so," Raphael concluded, "we just need you to find the ledger, win the game, and—" He paused, thinking. "That's it, I think."

"Oh, is that *it*?" Fox echoed sarcastically. "And here I thought it was going to be *complicated* or *difficult*, but no, I see, I merely have to travel through worlds with a *known liar*—"

"None taken," said Brandt, lifting his shackled hands to brush away a piece of lint.

"—and then beat a demon king by winning an immortal game with no rules that everyone famously loses," Fox concluded with a scowl. "Very simple, what could possibly go wrong?"

"The game has a rule, first of all, and it's very simple so don't forget it. Secondly, there's one other thing," Gabriel said, snapping his fingers in a fit of seraphic epiphany. "Tom Parker."

"Ah yes, Tom Parker," Raphael instantly agreed. "He needs to come."

Beside them, a glass lamp rattled unsteadily, edging toward the floor.

Vi, in an impressively unironic deadpan: "He says he doesn't want to."

Cal, to Fox: "That, plus a few more things inappropriate for present company."

Gabriel, in obvious frustration: "It's really rather important. Haven't we made this clear? You don't seem to have grasped that all of mankind is at stake."

Brandt, lifting a shackled hand: "In fairness, you hadn't technically mentioned that."

Raphael, with a frown: "Oh. Didn't we say something?"

Gabriel, nodding: "Yes, I distinctly recall saying that with Death kidnapped, all recent Ends have been improperly transported, leaving restless creatures to roam the planet untended and bereft of hope for ever reaching their appropriate destinations—"

Raphael: "Right, and then *I* said that if the demon king defeats Death, all mortals will fall within his purview, leading to a world wracked with vice—"

Gabriel: "And I continued that only one person can save us, of course, and that, for reasons unknown, is Fox D'Mora, the best-kept secret in all of the worlds—"

Raphael: "Which isn't saying much, except that we are not so good with secrets."

"You said absolutely none of that," Fox informed them in disbelief. "Could I really have refused if you'd said all those things?"

"Oh," Raphael said, glancing sideways at Gabriel. "Did we not say them?"

"Mortal brains work slower," Gabriel said. "It's possible he missed it."

"Seems irresponsible not to listen attentively," Raphael commented, flashing Fox a brief glare. "Aren't you paying attention? Your *world* is at *stake*—"

"I grasp the concept *now*," Fox muttered, turning to Cal. "And I take it this is what you meant when you said things were worse than you thought?"

"Yes," Cal said simply.

"Fox," Mayra attempted, "the reverberations of this decision will be felt in every world, not just this one. The consequences of the game falling into Vol—"

"SHHHH," Raphael and Gabriel snapped in unison.

"—the demon king's hands," she amended, as they nodded in relief, "and of *Death himself* falling into his hands—beyond the outcome of this game, those consequences would be severe for everyone." She glanced down, eyeing her feet. "More people than you think."

"But," Fox began, and withered, watching Mayra interlace her fingers tightly.

He sighed, feeling immensely trapped.

"You wanted to find your godfather," Brandt reminded him unhelpfully. "You found him, and this time he's not coming back unless you do something."

"Why do you care?" Fox asked, hurling the question at him.

Brandt didn't answer. Instead he eyed his restrained hands carefully before looking up, his gaze falling steadily on the ring on Fox's finger.

"I care," he said quietly, and Fox, recalling another moment from their past, shuddered and said nothing, resigning himself to silence.

"So, will you do it?" Raphael asked, interrupting Fox's silent, pained meandering.

Everyone's gazes swiveled to Fox, who let out a troubled sigh.

"Maybe," he muttered eventually.

"That's a yes, right?" Gabriel prompted, turning to Raphael. "It sounds like a yes."

"It's a yes," Brandt assured them, glancing at Fox. "He'll do it."

"It's a maybe," Fox corrected.

"Which, in Fox-speak, is a yes," Brandt told the archangels, unfazed.

"You know, we actually speak fox," Raphael commented. "They're a much less evasive species than you'd think."

"Very true," Brandt said. "But shouldn't you go?"

"We have this handled," Mayra assured them, glancing at Fox. "Don't we?"

Fox shrugged.

"Maybe," he said again.

Raphael, with a glance at Gabriel: "We do have a few problems on our hands."

Gabriel, agreeably: "There's been a bit of a management crisis."

Vi, with a frown: "What does that mean?"

Raphael: "There may or may not be some imprisoned immortals to deal with."

Gabriel, with a corrective air: "Allegedly."

Raphael: "Yes, precisely—"

At which point Fox let out a groan.

"Fine," he snapped. "Brandt will take me. I'll get the ledger and meet you at the tables."

"And bring the ghost," Raphael reminded him.

"Don't forget the ghost," Gabriel said.

"The ghost is very important," Raphael agreed.

"The ghost is *stuck*, though," Vi pointed out, raising a hand. "Sorry, but—any ideas how to actually get him out of this house?"

Raphael and Gabriel exchanged a glance.

"Nope," said Raphael.

"Best of luck, though," offered Gabriel.

"You two are the worst," Fox informed them.

"We know," they said in unison, and all at once, they were gone, leaving the others to wonder if they had ever, in fact, been there at all.

— Ω —

For a moment after the archangels disappeared, the room was engulfed by a potent, bewildered silence.

It didn't last.

"Wait a minute," said Fox, whom Brandt was amused to see had shaken himself to cognizance like a dog. "What just happened?"

"I agree," said Isis, who was suddenly standing at Fox's side.

"Oh," Vi chirped, "you're back," just as Tom groaned, "Ah fuck, you're back."

It was all going very poorly, and very madly, and very promisingly indeed.

"Well, if I'm going to do this, I want the handcuffs off," Brandt informed the room, taking advantage of their collective confusion. "I mean, *if* you plan to follow the instructions you were given, that is. Which, to be clear, is my inarguable condition for involvement."

"You're bound by previous thefts," Fox reminded him. "You don't get a condition."

"Well, I want one," Brandt replied, "and I can be quite difficult, you know."

"Oh, can you?" scoffed Fox. "I can't imagine how that escaped my notice."

"Wait," Tom said, disappearing from his place beside Vi to rematerialize next to Brandt. "Why me?"

"He says 'why me,'" said Cal to Fox, who glared at him.

"Don't know," Brandt said smoothly. "Only have guesses, but I'm going to assume it has something to do with the ledger. Possibly your blood, or your name—"

Isis, happily: "Oh, his blood! That would be fun, wouldn't it?"

Tom: "Excuse me?"

Vi, cutting in with a frown: "I'm confused about ledgers. How many are there? I thought that Mayra said they were for some sort of mortal deficit—"

Tom, interrupting Vi (interestingly, a thing he appeared to do less often than she made it seem) to stare at Brandt: "What exactly are your guesses? What would my blood or my name have to do with anything?"

"A few things," Brandt replied. "By which I mean possibly everything, but I don't see why that should be important for you to know."

"How exactly are we supposed to bring him?" Fox demanded. "He's a *ghost*—"

"So, about the ledger," Vi attempted loudly, only to be interrupted again by Brandt.

"If a live mortal can come, I don't see why a dead one can't," he admonished Fox. "You've been there yourself, haven't you? What's the difference?"

Tom: "Well, for one thing, I can't leave the house. Ask Vi."

Vi: "Yes, and on the topic of me, and questions—"

"I'm sure that's simple enough, isn't it?" Brandt prompted. "Probably just a flaw in the house's foundation."

"Actually, it has very solid bones," Vi said, "but—"

"Not *that* foundation," Brandt corrected her. "Its *moral* foundation."

Fox, with a long-suffering sigh: "It's a house, Brandt. Can you manage not to philosophize wildly for just a single productive moment?"

Brandt, with an equal air of suffering: "No, Fox, I can't, because my 'philosophizing' is the crux of the thing, whether you like it or not. The house has a foundational structure of moral intent that, when corrupted, upsets the natural balance of things. Creeps up on its inhabitants. Et cetera."

"The will!" Isis exclaimed at once, turning to Vi. "Didn't you say there's a provision in the house's legal documents that says it has to be used as a residence?"

"Yes," Vi said, "but I don't see why that would—"

"There it is," Brandt agreed, pointing both cuffed hands toward Isis. "*That's* the flaw in the foundation. The demon's got it."

Isis, smartly: "Well, I'm a demon. I'm always right, especially when it's annoying."

Fox, still being Fox: "What are we supposed to do about that, then? I just want you to take me to my godfather, Brandt—"

"—and I, meanwhile, already told you my conditions," Brandt cut in firmly, raising his hands again. "The handcuffs go, Fox, or I won't help you—"

"And Vi has to come as well," Tom interrupted, "or *I* won't go."

Cal opened his mouth. "He says—"

"Calix," Fox growled, "when I want to know, *I will ask*. In the meantime—"

"Listen, I'm still waiting for—wait, what?" Vi asked, turning to stare at Tom. "Why me?"

"Because I know you won't let anything happen to me," Tom replied. "Self-preservation."

"Nothing's going to happen to you," Brandt informed him, to which Tom scoffed.

"I'm sorry, but nobody ever says 'possibly your blood' in a story where everyone comes home with all their limbs," he said. "*Forgive me* if I want some sort of insurance—"

"You're already dead," Brandt reminded him. "What on earth do you think is going to happen next?"

"That's the point—*I don't know*," Tom shouted, ruffling Mayra's feathers from afar.

"Okay, listen," Mayra said, stepping forward to play the necessary role of referee. "I'm legally obligated to tell all of you that each of your motivations are highly suspect. Yours is generally fine," she assured Fox, "but the kidnapping is going to cost you in terms of your ledger. If you decide to help Raphael and Gabriel and to let Brandt help you of his own free will rather than forcing him to do so, that would be the morally responsible, and therefore celestially preferred, method of action. As for you," she said, turning to Brandt, "you're so far gone as to be rendered relatively defunct in terms of ledger, so I'm not going to bother—"

"None taken," he interrupted grandly, inclining his head.

"—and as for the matter of the ghost—"

"TOM," contributed said ghost, prompting the lights to flicker.

"He says Tom," Cal clarified.

"—obliging *his* wishes would be the morally right alternative as well, meaning that, ethically, Viola will have to come." She glanced between Fox and Brandt. "Have I made myself clear?"

"I still don't think I'm necessary," Vi ventured tentatively, "but if I have to go, then Isis is going."

"Oh *no*," said Fox and Tom in unison.

"Thank you, I accept," Isis graciously replied.

"But the house," Cal ventured, quietly raising a hand. "If the ghost—" He paused, hesitating, as the fireplace threatened to flame. "I mean, if *Tom* can't leave the house, then—"

"I have a thought about that," Isis said, and as their attention swiveled to her, she smiled, sighing contentedly. "Look at me," she remarked, nudging Vi. "Useful already."

— Ω —

Fox waited until the two creatures (three, including the ghost he still couldn't see but now had a very good sense for) had left the room to place a mysterious phone call before turning to Brandt, crossing his arms over his chest.

"Tell me everything," he said flatly.

"Well, where to start?" Brandt pondered aloud, evidence that everything to follow would almost certainly be false. "I'm fine, by the way, thanks for asking. I've recently mastered the perfect braise, so all's well on my end, you might say—"

"I meant with the ledger," Fox cut in, feeling very aware of his fists. "And you know that."

"Ah, yes, well, I've always advised you to be more specific, Fox," Brandt said. "Efficiency is king—"

"*Balance* is king," Mayra corrected him. "And also, answer the question."

"You know, I'm not sure I like you," Brandt informed her, leaning back to scrutinize her fully. "But don't think I haven't caught the aura of wrongdoing. You're a little more ambiguous than the average angel, aren't you?"

"Focus," Fox snapped, to which Cal nodded his agreement, narrowing his eyes. "Why were you making a ledger to begin with?"

"You know I keep a book," Brandt said, and paused. "Well, many books, actually."

"Yes," Fox grumbled, ignoring Cal's sidelong glance at him for recognition, "but still, I don't see why you'd record the details of a game that you were apparently banned from playing."

"Because, Fox, *I'm banned from playing it,*" Brandt emphatically replied. "I needed to keep tabs on it to get back in."

"Why would it even matter?" Cal asked. "It's only a game."

Beside him, Mayra looked down, meticulously eyeing her feet.

"It's not 'only a game' once you've played it," Brandt informed the reaper. "Especially since Death cheats."

"He doesn't *cheat*," Fox muttered, "which you should really understand by now, considering how many times I've said it—"

"Still, why did you make a ledger?" Mayra asked, daintily sidestepping Fox's comment. "How would that get you back into the game?"

"Well, there was a rumor," Brandt explained, "which the archangels have clearly confirmed. The game has its own ledger, a record of every win and loss kept safe by Death, which they use to keep track of everyone who's ever played. A token of leverage, most likely," he added, as Mayra eyed her fingernails this time, and Cal turned questioningly toward her. "The other Norse gods used to postulate that if you could challenge your way through the previous players, you could theoretically compel Death to sit at the tables again by virtue of enacting a new game."

"That's what you meant? A tournament?" Cal asked, and Brandt nodded.

"Just a rumor, though," he warned. "Until a few minutes ago, that is."

"One that you clearly believed to begin with," Fox pointed out, "or else you wouldn't have summoned the effort. Creating a replica of that ledger couldn't possibly have been easy."

"It wasn't," Brandt agreed. "As you may have noticed, I've been trying to replicate it in full for the last two centuries." He glanced up at Fox, considering him from afar. "For something worth playing for, I might add."

This time, Fox felt keenly aware of his mouth.

"You shouldn't have gambled something you couldn't afford to lose," he said, clearing his throat. "Or did that thought not occur to you?"

"Sometimes, Fox, the purse is more important than the cost," Brandt answered with agonizing ease. "Sometimes, the reward is more important than anything."

"Said like a loser," Fox replied.

"It's not all that easy to win," Mayra murmured, and they turned, looking at her with surprise. "Not that I would know, of course," she said quickly. "It's just . . . you know. Celestial wisdom and all that. In any case, I could have told you that at least one part of the rumor was true," she added, turning briskly to Brandt. "Raphael and Gabriel have always kept track of who plays at the tables, and most of the angels know it."

"What about the second half?" Cal asked. "Clearly it's true that Death could be compelled to play again, but how?"

"I don't know," Mayra said, and Brandt let out a scoff.

"The same way any bit of leverage works," he said irritably, as if explaining to children that Santa Claus didn't exist. (Though he did, and Fox had met him.) "However, if it's really my ledger the demon king has," Brandt continued, "then it's incomplete. I never sorted everyone out; I was always missing at least one player."

"You do realize how dangerous it was to have recorded that, don't you?" Mayra asked him, with Mayra's particular method of pointing out when someone (usually Fox) had recently been dumb. "Whether Death could be forced to sit at the end or not, every immortal who's ever played the game can be manipulated by the mere presence of a record. Knowing who's lost to whom is dangerous information in the wrong hands."

"In the right ones, too," Cal said. "I wouldn't want Raphael and Gabriel knowing things like that. Would you?"

"Of course I know how dangerous it is," Brandt informed them tartly. "This isn't the only bit of dangerous information I've recorded, which is why I took precautions. It was well hidden," he added. "And inaccessible—"

"Except it *was* accessed, wasn't it?" Fox muttered gruffly. "And now Tom's dead in the place you apparently kept it. The very last of the Parker line was murdered, and you don't think that's a coincidence?"

"I didn't say I didn't," Brandt replied. "I was just hoping you hadn't noticed as well."

— Ω —

"Well, they're a mess," Isis said with a sigh of contentment, hanging up the phone and gesturing into the sitting room where the others still remained. "This is going to be an utter fiasco. The only problem," she murmured to herself in idle contemplation, "is that I don't know who the fuck to root for."

"Huh," said Vi, who disagreed. "I got the feeling we were supposed to be pro-Fox. Right?"

"Well, he is technically the injured party," Isis allowed. "I think there's more to it, but the other one—"

"Brandt?"

"Yes, him," Isis confirmed. "Yes. He's not totally mortal. Obviously, since he can see Tom, but—" She broke off. "Well anyway, I can't quite sort him out. But I will," she murmured happily to herself. "I will, and then I'll get back to you on what it is."

Vi nodded, still thinking.

"So what is this 'immortal game' like?" she asked, aiming for indifference, and Isis shrugged.

"Interesting, I hope. I mean, if we're going to go through all this trouble," she clarified. "But for the record, I've never played. Demons are sort of unofficially banned from the tables."

"Would you even want to?" Vi couldn't imagine why anyone would. "I mean, by the sounds of it, it would be a terrible mistake to attempt, don't you think?"

"Depends how you view it," Isis replied with another ambivalent shrug. "Also depends what you would be willing to sacrifice for the things you desire most."

"What," Vi scoffed, "like riches? Treasure?"

"Yes and no," Isis said. "I mean, if you're a pirate, then yes and yes. But it's an *immortal* game, Viola, and immortals can do a hell of a lot more than creatures. They can give and take life. They can give and take beauty, fortune, fame. The things on earth like victory and success that take a lifetime to achieve—and which still always come with a price," she added, "—those can be gifted in the bat of an eye by an immortal. And there's no way to get an immortal's gift without sacrificing something for it."

Vi thought instantly of her own wish, shoving it brusquely from her mind.

"Still," she said uneasily. "Seems risky."

"True. But everything is a risk," Isis hedged, "and that sort of thing is far more intoxicating to someone with no stakes—someone, for example, who can't die. But it would be absolutely terrible to play the game as a mortal," she added with a shudder. "Mortals are so short-sighted, and creatures are only marginally better. We still have eternity to contend with, so the consequences are different, but the draw of it for us is fundamentally the same."

"I don't really see it as much of a draw," Vi said, but Isis looked skeptical.

"Maybe not yet," she said, "but you do have a creature's urges, no matter how hard you suppress them, and with Death missing, they're going to be considerably stronger. Especially the more you're around mortals," she warned. "Be sure you don't actually play the game yourself. You probably shouldn't even touch the tables."

Vi looked away, grimacing in the direction Tom had gone, apparently to think.

"Maybe we shouldn't do this, then," she murmured.

"Ha," Isis agreed, looking smug. "No, we certainly should not. But it'll be fun, won't it?"

Vi sighed.

"Doubtful," she determined.

# XVII

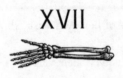

## REINFORCEMENTS

The doorbell's moody minor key dinged again exactly twenty minutes after Vi and Isis had placed the phone call.

"Oh, good," Isis said, opening the door. "I see you brought the loon brigade."

"Well, I figured I should have reinforcements," Lupo replied in earnest. "Juice box?"

"Yes, please," Isis said happily, stepping aside for Louisa and Sly to enter behind him. "May I ask why you thought to bring these *particular* reinforcements?"

"Well, mostly they were there," Lupo said as Louisa immediately began to explore the foyer. "But Sly's, you know, Fair Folk. They're a slippery bunch under the best of circumstances, and considering you need a bit of slipping—"

"If you need a loophole," Sly supplied, "I'm your man. I don't just hack computers," he added. "I can hack anything—legal contracts included."

"Ooh," Louisa exclaimed, stepping far enough inside to catch sight of the sitting room where Brandt remained on the sofa, hands still cuffed. "Are we taking prisoners, too? Fun!"

The others followed her to the sitting room where Fox was pacing what seemed to be a rigid six-foot radius from Brandt, both arms crossed firmly over his chest.

"How is this supposed to help, exactly?" Fox demanded, as Lupo removed his hat, stepping forward to greet him.

"You must be Fox D'Mora," he said, scratching at his beard in awe before offering his hand. "I'm Lupo. Werewolf."

"I—yes," Fox agreed faintly. "So it would seem."

"He won't bite, you big mortal baby," Isis sniffed. "And anyway, to continue the introductions: Louisa's a siren," she explained, gesturing. "Sly's fae; Fox is a mortal with an abandonment complex; Brandt's a random thief we don't really know anything about yet, short of his romantic falling-out with Fox; Mayra's a guardian angel who's almost certainly hiding something; Cal's a reaper who's very clearly obsessed with Mayra; Tom's a poltergeist who won't be quiet—"

"Excuse me?" they all protested in unison, and Isis shrugged.

"Just catching everyone up," she explained, and frowned. "What? You all look upset."

"Let's just get this over with," Vi sighed, shaking her head before turning her attention back to Sly. "Do you want to look over the contracts?"

"Sure," he said. "Though any particular summary would probably do."

"Good," Vi said, "because it's nearly dark, and then I'm going to start having very strong urges to chase balls of string."

"The house has to be lived in," Tom supplied for him, swooping down from overhead. "My grandmother's stipulation. It can't be occupied by a business—or a rehab center," he sniffed with displeasure, "despite Viola's insistence on selling it—"

"It's not *my* insistence," Vi reminded him, for what was easily the hundredth time. "I keep telling you, I'm just the real estate agent. I'm employed by the house, basically, so—"

"So who owns it now?" Sly interrupted.

"The Parker family trust," said Vi. "Which is currently being operated by the board of trustees, as there are no direct living heirs to the Parker family."

"Well, there's your answer," Louisa contributed. "That's not a person, is it?"

"Well, no," Vi agreed, "but—"

"That's why Tom's here," Lupo agreed. "Is it okay if I call you Tom, by the way?"

"FINALLY," blasted Tom.

"He says 'finally,'" Cal informed Fox, who glared at him.

"So what does that mean, then?" Vi asked, amazed to have found the whole thing resolved so simply. "I just have to find a person to buy the house and live in it, and then Tom can go?"

"Sounds that way," Brandt contributed, leaning forward. "Not that anybody asked the man in handcuffs, but that's my uninvited thought on the matter."

"We can buy it," Lupo offered, waving awkwardly to Brandt before turning back to Vi. "I mean, we can live in it for a bit until you get back. Provided you can make the price reasonable," he added, glancing back at Sly. "Do you have cash?"

"I had ten dollars. Seven now," Sly said, holding up a Diet Coke. "I bought a pop on the way here."

Louisa, gaping: "For *three dollars*? That's thievery!"

Sly, taking a languid sip: "Capitalism. The worst of all mortal inventions."

Brandt, to no one, and to no one's notice: "Not sure Greed would agree."

Vi, with a shake of her head: "I can't just sell the Parker mansion for *ten dollars*. I'd have to get the approval of the board, first of all, and seeing as they aren't clinically insane—"

Sly, interrupting: "Firstly, as I mentioned, it's actually seven dollars, and secondly, you don't need to amend the mortal contract, considering that the consequences are outside the mortal realm of control. We can make an addendum to the supernatural clause—"

Vi, bemused: "What supernatural clause? I've read the deed from cover to cover and I promise, there's no supernatural clause anywhere in it."

"You have to read the fine print," Louisa cut in primly, taking the paperwork from Vi's hand and scanning it quickly before letting out a sigh. "Hang on," she requested, and stepped back, placing the buyer's agreement on the floor, humming a quick sailor's shanty, and then picking it up again, frowning up at the glazed eyes in the room. "Oi," she called to them, snapping her fingers. "Focus. We're here to work."

"Thanks," Brandt said, roughly shaking out the frame of his shoulders, and Louisa shrugged, indifferent.

"Right here," she said, pointing to the clause she'd summoned. "*'Supernatural events notwithstanding, the house shall necessarily be occupied by a member of the Parker bloodline, or by someone granted express approval by the last remaining heir.'* Simple enough, I'd say. Tom just needs to approve and then boom, it's ours."

"I'm not giving away my house," Tom said, horrified. "Certainly not for *seven dollars,* which is an outright travesty—"

"It's only temporary," Ludo assured him kindly. "You can have it back when you come back from . . . what was it again?"

"Traveling to an immortal realm to rescue Death," Isis supplied.

"What is that, a day or two, tops?" Sly asked. "There's only a marginal chance we'll have ruined it by then."

Vi turned to Isis, murmuring quietly to her. "But what if Tom doesn't come back?" she asked in a whisper. "If he isn't bound to the house, then—?"

"Hush," Isis warned with a silencing glance before stepping forward as if Vi had said nothing at all. "Do we have a deal, then?" she prompted, searching pointedly around the room. "Lupo will buy *and live in* the house for as long as it takes us to master Death—"

"Master him?" Fox echoed. "Excuse me?"

"What? You misheard," Isis assured him. "I said rescue him."

"You most certainly did n—"

"Is this about the immortals' game?" Louisa asked. "God, I've always wanted to play that. Sly," she suddenly exclaimed, turning to him in a fit of ardor, "do you remember that mermaid who played it and won? She used to come to the meetings *all the time,* always going off about how bored she was, blah blah—she played the game and then tried making a deal with that demon king and skipped off somewhere—"

"Demon king?" Vi echoed, noticing Isis's face going slightly green, but the other two continued their manic chattering.

Sly: "Oh, right—wasn't she some sort of changeling?"

Louisa: "Yes, like an adult changeling—is there a word for that?"

Sly: "Not an English one."

Isis, who was clearly (albeit mysteriously) perturbed: "Can we stop babbling? First of all, none of this is relevant. Secondly, if we're going to torment people, let's not have it be me—"

Sly, ignoring her: "She had one of those nicknames. Remember? Hated the full name—"

Louisa: "Ooh, yes, hated her name, said it was too depressingly mortal—what was it? Ellen? Eleanor?"

Sly: "Elbow."

Louisa: "Eldridge?"

Sly: "Elphaba!"

"Elaine," Lupo interrupted, rolling his eyes. "You two can never remember shit."

"Elaine! *Lainey,* actually," Louisa said. "That's it—"

"Lainey?" Tom asked, abruptly choking. "Lainey Wood?"

"That's the one," Sly said. "Why, do you know her?"

Vi and Tom instantly found each other in the room, locking eyes in slow, tensed recognition.

"Well," Brandt said with a chuckle. "I'm going to go ahead and make a judgment on behalf of the group, I'm afraid. You're going to have to sign these contracts, *moy,*" he told Vi, "because it's a small world after all."

# XVIII

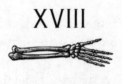

## DEMONS

"You really think this is going to work?" Tom asked, peering over Vi's shoulder as she flipped through the contract Sly had altered. "Paperwork, really?"

"I'm beginning to understand that the supernatural has its own flavor of tedium," Vi replied. "I'm starting to wonder if there's anything in this world that doesn't ultimately amount to minutiae. Or any other world, for that matter," she amended, shrugging, "considering we're all about to be brought down by irresponsible accountancy."

"And to think," Tom remarked. "For this I went to business school."

"You know, I'm surprised you didn't think of this first," Vi commented, glancing over at him. They were alone in the upstairs office, situated on either side of a hulking executive desk with the Parker monogram engraved in the wood. "Shouldn't you be an expert in contracts?"

"That's for the lawyers," Tom sniffed. "Though, thank you for finally acknowledging my intellect."

Vi read the same sentence three times as Tom fidgeted beside her.

"You haven't said anything about Lainey," she finally voiced aloud, not taking her eyes from the contract in her hand.

"What about her?" Tom scoffed, a little too quickly for truth. "So what if she was a—"

He stopped.

"Mermaid," Vi supplied. "I think. Which, if true, feels strangely fairy tale–esque."

"Maybe it would," Tom grumbled, "if our relationship had ever been remotely like a fairy tale."

"Well," Vi said primly, "there was a bit of love in there, don't you think?"

"Who knows now," Tom said, his expression darkening. "If she's a mermaid then she's basically a siren, isn't she? So how could I ever know what was real?"

"Louisa's a siren," Vi corrected. "From the sound of it, Lainey is different. Some sort of water spirit, I guess."

"Ah, yes," Tom muttered. "Much better."

Vi pretended once again to scan the contract.

"So," she said, not looking up, "are you okay, then?"

"Of course," said Tom. "Why wouldn't I be?"

Vi pointedly flipped a page.

"Oh," Tom said. "You mean because a couple of angels need me for a mysterious world-ending tournament that might require bloodshed, and Lainey's a—" He paused again to swallow. "She's . . . oh, I don't know, a—"

"Creature," Vi supplied helpfully.

Tom forced a smile. "Right. So then I should be what, exactly? Upset?"

"I don't think it would be unreasonable if you were." Vi considered other potentially helpful things to say before settling unimpressively on "It's a lot to take in."

"Says you," Tom said gruffly. "*You* are the one living in denial, after all."

"I'm not living in denial," Vi retorted. "I'm just—"

"*Managing your condition,* I know," Tom said. "Which is stupid."

"Well," Vi said carefully, having re-read the first sentence of the supernatural amendment so many times that words had lost all meaning, "if I'm so stupid, then maybe I should just stay here." She glanced up then, too sadistic (or possibly masochistic?) to miss whatever his reaction would be. "To be honest, I don't understand why you want me to come in the first place."

He shifted, folding his arms over the stab wound in his chest.

"Well, Viola, whether or not you understand my motives is entirely on you" was evidently the best he could come up with. "In any case, I don't see what you have going on that's better."

"I have a job, Tom," she reminded him. "I have a *life*, you know—"

"You quite literally don't," Tom countered, transitioning rapidly from moody, tepid avoidance to his more comfortable state of antagonism. "At best, you have an '*un*-death,' Vi, which to my understanding is hardly the same thing."

"You're not answering the question," she pointed out. "I'm asking you why you want me to come, Tom. Weren't you just trying to undermine me with the thief?" she added, gesturing to where Fox and Brandt remained in the other room. "He wouldn't even be here if not for you telling him how to get into the house!"

"Yes, well, that's about the *house*, not you," Tom muttered, as if semantics could really make a difference. "As I keep telling you, I don't want you to *sell it*—"

"And yet selling it is what's going to get you out of it, isn't it?"

"Well, that's a very new development," Tom countered stiffly. "Really, Vi, you're going to have to keep up."

"You're still not answering the question." Vi abandoned the pretense of reading and set the contract on the table. "Why do you want me to come?"

"Obviously because you're my only entertainment," Tom replied, which, while clearly not the answer they'd been dancing around, did not seem entirely a lie. "I can't *move*, Viola. I can't leave. I can't do anything except push your buttons, and you're my only—"

"Friend?" Vi asked, watching Tom promptly stumble over hesitation.

But then he looked stricken, and she suddenly felt cruel.

"Tell me I'm your friend, Tom," she teased, adopting a lighter tone, "and maybe I'll come."

"Maybe?" he echoed.

"Maybe," she confirmed. "Depends on what you have to say."

Tom frowned.

"But why do I have to bend?" he demanded. "You're the one trying to help me. *You*," he emphasized firmly, "should be the one admitting that you like *me*."

Masochist, Vi realized abruptly. She was definitely a masochist. "Once again, Tom, I'm not trying to help you. I'm trying to get *rid* of you—"

"See?" he announced, triumphant. "You're being just as difficult, aren't you?"

"I need to sell this house," Vi began, but Tom smugly held up a hand.

"Your job is to sell this house," he corrected, "but you *want* to help me."

Then he paused, watching her face just as she had watched his.

"Tell me I'm right," he added quietly, "and I'll tell you why I want you to come."

She hesitated.

"Fine," she exhaled grumpily. "Fine. So maybe I do want to help you. It's hard not to," she added defensively. "You're always just floating around here moping, you don't have any memory of how you got here, you have no answers and no hope and no—"

"Friends," he supplied grimly.

"Yeah," she confirmed, wondering why she suddenly felt so bereft. "No friends."

She gave herself permission to see the muscle jump beside his jaw. To notice the tension wrought exquisitely below his cheekbones.

"The truth is," Tom admitted, "I'm afraid that if you're not there, no one will see me. You were the only person who could before, and I'm afraid that if you don't come, then—"

He stopped.

"I don't think there's any significance to why I can see you," Vi said. "The others can see you, too. Minus Fox, though he's apparently nothing out of the ordinary. I mean, that's what Isis says," she mumbled, "but that seems sort of like . . . I don't know, a terribly obvious understatement, so—"

"I would just feel better," Tom interrupted, "if you were there."

This time, Vi gave herself permission to notice his eyes; the way they met hers.

"Is this you asking nicely?" she remarked.

He shrugged.

"Probably," he admitted.

"Then I guess I'll have to go," she murmured, and turned away, doing them both the favor of not letting him see her smile.

— Ω —

"So," Mayra commented in the kitchen, glancing over at Isis, who was the only one of them with any appetite for hummus. "You've heard of this demon king, haven't you?"

"Is it that obvious?" Isis asked, and Mayra shrugged.

"A bit," she admitted, passing Isis a smirk. "You're afraid of him, aren't you?"

Isis hesitated.

"We shouldn't talk about him," she said. "Calling him by name is, in essence, to summon him."

"But he *is* a demon, then," Mayra noted. "Like you?"

"Not much like me," Isis said with a shudder. "More powerful. Less constrained by any sort of code. Older, too—ancient, in fact. Much less flexible. Bad at yoga." She smiled wryly at Mayra, who obliged her with a laugh. "But he calls himself the king of vice, and mostly feeds on mortals."

"Feeds on them?"

"Uses them. Wears them," Isis grunted. "Then sheds them like a snakeskin and moves on."

"And this is disturbing even to you?" Mayra asked evenly.

"Almost as disturbing to me as the game is disturbing to you," Isis knowingly replied.

Mayra fought the impulse to retort, biting her tongue.

"Don't worry," Isis assured her. "I won't tell them you played if you don't want me to."

"It was—" Mayra inhaled, holding it in, then exhaled. "It was a long time ago, and—"

"The past is passed," Isis assured her. "And besides—"

She broke off, a slight smile twitching at her lips.

"Besides?" Mayra prompted, waiting.

"Well," Isis said, half-laughing. "Everyone has demons, don't they?"

— Ω —

"Fox," Brandt sighed for the dozenth time, "take the shackles off."

"Sorry," Fox replied, not bothering to conceal the ring of falsehood to his apology. "Can't. You have a tendency to leave, remember? And clearly, we need you."

"Fox," Brandt said again, shaking his head. "A pair of reaper's handcuffs isn't exactly binding."

"It's more binding than anything else I have on hand," Fox irritably replied. "And you can't convince me to take them off just by saying there's more danger in doing nothing. I'm not a total fool, Brandt."

"I know you aren't—"

"Do you?" Fox cut in, narrowing his eyes. "*Do* you know that, Brandt? Because the past version of you always thought otherwise, didn't you? Or is this the benefit of you leaving," he muttered, bitterness pooling like bile on his tongue. "That now, finally, I have the presumption of adequate intellect?"

"Fox, listen to me—"

"So I'm not a child anymore, Brandt?" he taunted. "Am I not your *lillegutt* now?"

"Fox," Brandt warned again, harsher this time, and Fox made the unforgivable mistake of meeting his eye.

He fought a rush of memory, a crash of it, an axe against his heart; the things he'd tried so helplessly to bury rushing out of it in waves, in droves, in swarms. How many times had he heard Brandt Solberg say his name? How many ways? He'd heard it low and reverent, a whisper in his ear. He'd heard it sharp and strident, an assault on all his senses, a weapon and a blow. He'd heard it mournful and blissful; he'd heard it heated in anger, cool in warning, warm again in the late hours of night. He'd heard the sound of his name from

Brandt Solberg's lips so many times, in so many ways, that it almost seemed cruel to suffer it now.

They both struggled for a moment with familiarity; they'd already lived through so much history that witnessing theirs again was paralyzing to them both.

The grandfather clock in the corner ticked several times, punctuating the sound of their uneven breaths before Brandt spoke again, inhaling wearily and letting the words out in a sigh.

"If you had held me in handcuffs two centuries ago, Fox," Brandt told him, "you still would not have kept me."

Fox reeled back, taking the impact of the statement like a slap.

"I just meant," Brandt supplied hurriedly, "that you can't undo the past—"

"No, I can't," Fox confirmed, his voice clipped. "I know that. Don't you think I know that?" he asked. "Do you even know what the past would look like if I could?"

Instead of answering, Brandt let a moment of silence pass, neither of them speaking.

"Did you look for me?" he asked neutrally.

Fox stared at him.

The question—that Brandt would even dare to *ask,* much less that he could manage to do it so carelessly—was so abjectly horrifying as to render it unthinkable. Callous.

"No," Fox lied, as nastily as he could manage. "You'd already made it plenty clear how little I meant to you, Brandt. I didn't look for you because I knew I wouldn't find you, not if you didn't want to be found. And if I couldn't keep you then—" He faltered painfully, though he disguised it, curling his hand around his mouth and imagining he could swipe the bitterness from his tongue. "If I couldn't keep you then, I certainly can't keep you now. But it's different this time," he warned, breaking off. "This time, I'm not—"

Another break. "This is about my godfather. Not about—" A crisp, unpreventable shattering. "Not about us. That past is passed."

"Fox—"

"*Brandt,*" he spat in return, tired of hearing his name weaponized against him so easily, as if it could be said without thought or remorse. "I don't care what Mayra says, I'm not having Cal remove the handcuffs until I've gotten the ledger and freed my godfather. What you do from there is up to you." Fox did not say: *I know that given the choice, you'll only walk away again, unscathed, as you always do, and I cannot bear to watch you do it.* "For as long as there is something I need from you, I will not be the fool I was once. I will not be the fool who lets you go."

He heard what he'd said and flinched. "I meant that I won't be the idiot who lets you escape. Not when there's this much on the line."

"I know what you meant," Brandt replied quietly.

Fox glared at him. "Don't flatter yourself."

"I would never," Brandt drawled, but Fox was in no mood for his games. He rose to his feet, turning to leave the room.

"Wait," Brandt called after him, and though Fox wanted very much not to stop, it seemed his feet were conditioned. Muscle memory of sorts, which he assumed was one of the terrible flaws of mortality. "You know about the ledger. How?"

Fox indulged a moment of recalcitrance, choosing whatever small pains he could inflict. "What ledger?" he asked from the doorway.

He turned to find Brandt giving him a look of unfiltered irritation. "You knew the game had a ledger even before the archangels got here. You recognized what I'd done before I even mentioned I had done it. How did you know that? And don't lie," Brandt added in warning. "I know you love the moral high ground, Fox, but you can't expect to keep it if you choose obstinacy every chance you get."

"Don't tell me what to do," Fox snapped. "I'm over two centuries old."

"Well," Brandt muttered, "act like it, then."

Fox suppressed a scowl before determining that anything, including answering the question directly, would be preferable to remaining in this room. "Fine. Papa told me. I made him tell me everything, after . . ."

Another terrible, undermining falter. "After everything."

"After me, you mean," Brandt said, with a gentleness that made Fox want to strangle him.

"After you *left*," Fox spat, "yes. I made him tell me everything."

"But he didn't," Brandt commented, gesturing to where the shackles bound his wrists. "Clearly."

"No," Fox muttered in agreement, "but I'll take that up with him later. He told me about the ledger. *And* he promised me he wouldn't play again," he added. "And as far as I know, he hasn't."

"Well." Brandt leaned forward, contemplating something in Fox's eyes for a long moment before abruptly breaking the spell with a murmured "'As far as you know' does not take us very far at all, does it, Fox?'"

Annoyed, Fox opened his mouth to answer, but Brandt exhaled and shook his head.

"As I said, my copy of the ledger is incomplete. There is at least one game that was played with Death that I know nothing about. I have some suspicions, though," he added carefully, "and I have very long wondered what information about that you might possess."

"Me?" Fox echoed, both surprised and, somehow, offended. "What would I know? I'm not involved in any of this. You're the one who's been stealing things, hiding things—"

"Did you ever lend your ring to anyone?" Brandt cut in seriously, resting his elbows on his knees. "Anyone, Fox. It's critical that you remember."

"I—are you serious?" Fox demanded, gaping at him. "First of all, how is this possibly the question that you're asking me? After everything?"

To Brandt's apparently guiltless silence, Fox gave in to another rush of bitterness.

"You see this?" Fox growled, lunging forward with his right hand outstretched. "This is the ring *you* gave me, Brandt. And this?" he prompted, holding up his left arm to gesture to the watch. "*You* again, Brandt. My own name, in fact," he said painfully. "Fox *D'Mora*. You gave that to me too, didn't you? I could never sever you from me,

Brandt, and you think it's fair to ask me questions as if all of that time was nothing?"

He stared, but Brandt said nothing.

"Why did you leave?" Fox finally asked, his voice hoarse. "Why?"

"Fox—"

"Tell me," Fox demanded. "Tell me why you left, Brandt, it's hardly too much to ask—"

"I can't," Brandt said, flinching. "I can't tell you, Fox."

"Why not?"

"Fox—"

*"Brandt—"*

"As you say, the past is passed," Brandt said sharply. "And it may seem unfair, Fox, but there could be more at stake here than you realize. More than the wrongs I have committed against you, as much as I know what I've done. Do you really think I can't see what you've been through? How you've changed?" he asked, almost roughly. "Don't you think that if I could answer you, I—"

He broke off, his lips closing around nothing; as if his throat itself had been suspended.

Fox, unable to bear his silence, turned away.

"Fox," Brandt attempted again, his voice a hollow rasp, but Fox shook his head, thoroughly defeated.

"You're right," he said flatly. "The past is passed."

# INTERLUDE V:

## PAST IS PASSED, PART I

Brandt Solberg
1833

"There's your godfather," Brandt informed the mortal, pointing to the shadowed figure at the head of the center table. "Right where I told you he would be. But again, it's nearly dawn," he warned, gesturing to the window that had no end and no beginning, manifesting from nothing and ending in a cloud of refracted dust. "He's almost finished now, so——"

But the young man called Fox wasn't listening, instead razing a path toward his godfather until the specter at the end of the table flickered with alarm, transitioning from something hazy and insubstantial into solid, admonishable form, the eyes of the man-resembling figure's head blowing wide at the sight of his young ward.

Brandt paused, amused, and made a mental note to scribble it all down in his book later before following in Fox's wake.

"Papa," the mortal was calling tartly, folding his arms over his chest. "I see you've left something out about where you've been, haven't you?"

Death paused, obviously gauging how much he could conceivably cover up with a lie.

"Well," he began, and then caught sight of Brandt, his hazel eyes (an interesting choice, a mirror of the young mortal's own) promptly narrowing. *"Well,"* Death amended, sharpening his voice to sour disapproval. "Of course you're here, godling. Can't keep a secret worth a damn, can you?"

"Not worth having one, is it?" Brandt replied knowingly, with a shrug. "And anyway, this is hardly my fault."

"No more deals," Death warned, brandishing a finger at him. "Your spot at the table's been rescinded, and I expect you to hand over that book of yours, too—"

"What book?" Brandt chirped. "Why, *Papa,* surely I know of no such thing."

"You have no idea how dangerous that book could be, godling," Death growled. "I expect you to hand it over immediately. And in the meantime—"

"Can't the logistics wait?" Fox growled, glaring at his godfather. (Brandt had already taken ample notice that Fox wasn't actually a child, but still, his youth shone irredeemably as he scowled.) "I didn't realize you were a *gambler,* Papa."

"Stop calling me that," Death warned, grabbing Fox's arm and pulling him aside.

Brandt, too curious not to follow, hung in the shadows for only a moment before darting after them.

"Didn't the godling explain this to you?" Death hissed to his god-son, dropping his voice. "I can't have people knowing about you, Fox. It's far too dangerous."

"Oh, so now you're *dangerous*?" Fox pressed, jerking his arm free. "Were you ever going to tell me about this?"

"No," Death said, and rolled his eyes. "In case you've forgotten, I'm a timeless, incorporeal being, Fox, and you are a mortal. You don't need to know everything."

Fox paused, his brow furrowing, and opened and closed his mouth.

Brandt, finding himself inexplicably moved by the sight of the young man's dismay, stepped forward. "Perhaps *mortal* is as much an oversimplification as *gambler,* then," Brandt suggested, careful to keep his voice light and breezy. "Surely you're aware your own godson's life could never be that of any normal mortal."

Death grimaced, sparing him a flash of ire.

"Take Fox home," he said to Brandt, spinning on his heel, "and be certain you don't come back here, godling, or there's no telling what the others will do."

Fox blinked in disbelief, reeling from his dismissal. "But Papa, I—"

"That's awfully rude," Brandt retorted to Death. "I hardly think I deserve *banishment*—and more importantly, why am I relegated to babysitting? *You* take him home."

"He shouldn't be here and you know it," Death reminded Brandt, his gaze flicking sharply to his godson and then hastily away, as if he could not stand to look. "You knew better than to bring him here, godling, and now you ought to know well enough to leave."

Brandt felt his eyes narrow in irritation. "Perhaps *you* should have known better than to keep secrets. He's a very nosy mortal, as you surely must know," he accused, "and perhaps, all things considered, he has a right to be."

"Will you stop talking about me like I'm a child?" Fox demanded, hands characteristically on hips. "I'm *right here*."

"Yes, you are," Brandt snapped, "and it's problematic for both of us, seeing as I'm clearly being blamed for it." He turned back to Death with a glare. "For the record, I tried to shake him," he added, which was true, "but you've raised a relentless little boil of a man."

"I," Death muttered under his breath, "will deal with my godson later. Just get him out of the game. You know he doesn't belong here."

"And what will be my payment, then?" Brandt prompted. "Since, after all, I now know something we both know could be your undoing."

Death's eyes narrowed, displeased. "I'm not letting you play again, not even for this. Every time you come here, Brandt Solberg, something priceless goes missing—and don't think for a moment that I haven't pieced that together."

"Oh, don't be such a stiff," Brandt sighed. "What's the point of an illegal gambling ring if no one gets robbed?"

"Just give Time back his watch," Death growled. "He hasn't stopped yapping about it since the solstice."

Fox turned, eyeing Brandt; a careful glance this time, excessive and scrutinizing as if considering something he hadn't before, and Brandt found it supremely unnerving.

Distracting, even, and therefore entirely unhelpful.

"I can't give it back," Brandt replied neutrally, shifting his focus from Fox back to Death. "It's broken."

Death's eyes widened. "You *broke* it?"

"He can make another," Brandt assured him. "But this one is definitely broken, yes."

Death sighed wearily, his mouth twitching at the corners.

(This iteration of him was extremely unsettling, Brandt thought.)

(*Far* too human.)

"Fine," Fox said dully, turning to Brandt. "Take me back, then. I don't want to be here anyway."

"You're a child," Brandt sighed, shaking his head, "and as for you—"

He paused, looking around for Death, but found him nowhere in sight.

"He's gone," Fox informed him bluntly, as Brandt blinked.

The two of them now stood alone.

"Apparently," Fox muttered, "he has somewhere better to be."

Brandt watched the young man's gaze drift to his godfather at the head of the long wooden table, something twitchy and bitter and sad forming around the corners of his mouth. Something familiar, and therefore both troubled and troubling.

And then, with an inward grimace, Brandt sighed.

"Come on, then, *lillegutt*," he muttered, taking hold of Fox's shoulder and drawing him away from the tables. "Before you have a tantrum."

"Let go of me," Fox snapped in return, ripping free of Brandt's hold and storming forward the way they'd come. "I don't need you to escort me out."

"Yes, actually, you do," Brandt sighed after him lazily, not bothering to give chase. "You can't find your way out of here alone."

"Yes I c—"

"No," Brandt repeated firmly, "you *can't*. You're a mortal, and this form of transportation will not occur to the blood in your veins, Fox—"

The young man spun so swiftly that Brandt momentarily faltered, taken aback by the look on his face.

"I *know* that I'm a mortal," Fox snapped. "Do you think Pap—" He stopped, swallowing. "Do you think Death ever lets me forget?"

Brandt waited a moment, feeling his shoulders stitch together in the tension of the moment.

"There is no shame in mortality," he said slowly, and Fox let out a bark of laughter.

"You don't believe that."

"I do, actually—"

"Your life says otherwise, *godling.*"

"Don't read me by my life," Brandt warned. "Important to have all the facts."

"I don't want them," Fox muttered.

Brandt, feeling again an itch of irritation that nagged somewhere in his chest, fought a pointless retort.

"Let's get you home, then," he suggested flatly, "and be rid of each other for the entirety of your mortal existence, shall we?"

Fox glared at him.

"Yes," he said, pawing at the frustration that had creased in his brow. "Let's."

— Ω —

"Well," Brandt offered cheerily, waltzing into the bucolic scene that was the village dairyman's barn. "I see you've been keeping out of trouble, then."

Fox looked up, tearing his face away from the pretty maid's lips with a loud, suctioning sound of displacement.

He blinked once, registering Brandt's presence.

"Oh," said Fox.

"Oh, indeed," Brandt agreed, glancing down at the girl. "And who is this?"

"Not any of your business, I should think," Fox told him briskly, tightening his arms around her waist and brandishing her like a shield. "And what do you care?"

"I don't," Brandt assured him. "I just felt it rude not to ask."

"Um," the girl said, glancing uneasily between them. "Should I go?"

"No," Fox told her, in the same moment that Brandt said, "Yes, thank you."

"Excuse you?" Fox demanded, glaring at Brandt with that same youthful scowl. "You don't get to tell—" He hesitated, pausing over the vacancy of her name. "I mean," he amended, "seeing as this, um—"

"Wonderful," the girl sighed in displeasure, rising to her feet. "Enjoy your life, Fox D'Mora," she yelped over her shoulder, storming out of sight as Brandt turned to Fox with patent amusement, pulling his book from the pocket sewn into the lining of his coat.

"D'Mora?" Brandt prompted knowingly, opening to the next available page and withdrawing some charcoal to write with. "I told you it was a good name."

Fox glared at him, or so Brandt assumed, being busy writing.

"What do you want?" Fox demanded, with the impatience that Brandt had come to expect.

"Just visiting," Brandt supplied, as he scribbled and Fox grimaced.

"I thought you said you wouldn't visit," he muttered. "Didn't you specifically tell me we'd never see each other again?"

"I did," Brandt confirmed, finishing the sentence in his slim leather volume before tucking it back into his pocket. "But then I was in town," he clarified, settling smoothly into the lie, "and there is so little else to do here, so—"

"Is my godfather at the tables again?" Fox asked, his eyes darkening with displeasure. They were woodsy, maple, autumn in nature. Unlike Brandt, who was himself a winter, or so he'd been told. "I've suggested he desist," Fox added gloomily, "but he seems unconcerned with my opinion on the matter."

"An understandable tendency," Brandt acknowledged. "Seeing that he will outlast you quite significantly, that is." He paused, taking a bite of his apple, and then held it out to Fox. "Apple?"

"I hardly possess the same need for immortality that you do,"

Fox reminded him, rising to his feet and dusting off his trousers. "Is there something you wanted to do while you were here?"

"Antagonize you," Brandt said, taking another bite.

Fox rolled his eyes, waltzing out of the barn in the direction of the town's central market.

Obligingly, Brandt followed.

"How do you get those, anyway?" Fox asked, and Brandt paused, considering how best to answer.

"You know how there's a goddess?" he prompted, glancing askance.

Fox nodded. "Yes. You told me."

"Right, well—" Brandt shrugged. "I have something that she wants."

"What is it?" Fox asked, and Brandt quirked a brow.

"Can't tell."

"Of course you can't," Fox grumbled to himself.

"Yes. See?" Brandt prompted. "You understand."

Fox groaned. "Why are you even here?"

"Why not?"

A passing villager nodded to Fox, who riffled a hand through his hair before mirroring him in greeting. A convenient excuse to leave, though Fox did not. "You're exhausting."

"Yes, and you and Death are still on the outs, I see," Brandt returned, disregarding the comment. "You seem angstier than usual, *lillegutt.*"

"Angstier? What's angst?"

"Something Kierkegaard made up," Brandt said. "Nice guy," he added. "Minus all the, you know. Anxiety and dread."

"I don't know what that means," Fox replied stiffly, "but in any case, I'm positive it's not true. About me, I mean," he amended. "Papa and I are fine."

"You aren't," Brandt corrected. "You haven't seen him in some time, have you?"

The motion of Fox's knuckles whitening confirmed it.

"That's none of your business," muttered Fox.

Brandt smiled.

"Shall I go, then?" he asked. "You seem displeased to see me."

"I am," Fox assured him. "Deeply."

"Very well, then," Brandt permitted, and paused as they reached a fork in the road. "Same time next month?"

Fox stared at him.

And stared.

And stared.

"Yes," he said eventually, managing a nod. "Yes, all right. Fine."

— Ω —

"What do you give the goddess?" Fox asked, skipping a stone across the river. Forestry suited him. Perhaps it was the autumnal eyes. Perhaps just the contrast between his restlessness and nature's.

"You never tire of asking me that, do you?" Brandt prompted, tucking his book back in his pocket after finishing a quick sketch of the landscape. "And yet, imagine it: I tire of your questioning."

"It's a fairly natural curiosity," Fox said. "Don't you think?"

"Perhaps," Brandt replied. "Though, considering how often I tell you it's unwise to ask, you'd think eventually you'd come to learn your lesson."

"Maybe eventually," Fox remarked with a sidelong grin, or perhaps a smirk. "But not yet."

"What'd you tell that girl?" Brandt asked, changing the subject. "The one you were with this time."

"Nothing," Fox said bluntly. "What would I tell her? I have no trade, really. Nothing of value, and she'll want a provider, a husband. I hardly need a reason not to see her again."

"She seemed keen to see you," Brandt attempted, aiming for reassurance.

"Yes, well, they all are for a time," Fox said. "But it's all just a cycle of impermanence."

"Ah, yes, my favorite cycle." Brandt chuckled, and Fox glanced questioningly at him. "Not to worry," Brandt assured him. "Times change, you know. It hasn't always been like this, and if anything in the universe is constant, it's that any given *this* will not remain so for long."

"It will for me," Fox reminded him. "This is my only *this*, remember?"

"Doesn't have to be," Brandt said, shining an apple on the rolled-up cuff of his shirt before offering it to Fox. "Bite?"

Fox glanced at it, then shook his head slowly.

"Why do you do that?" he asked.

"Do what?"

"You know." He waved a hand. "Offer me your immortality like it's nothing."

"It *is* nothing," Brandt assured him. "For one thing, you'd need a lot more than just a bite. And for another thing, eternity itself is nothing," he said with a shrug. "Meaningless, really, unless you do something with it."

Fox frowned. "So why cling to a meaningless eternity, then?"

"I'm not clinging," Brandt told him, "and it's not meaningless."

"Seems like it is," Fox countered. "You never actually *do* anything, do you?"

"Aimless and meaningless are different things, Fox."

"Fine. So what's your meaning, then?"

Brandt shrugged again. "Vengeance?" he suggested. "Well, more like—" He paused, frowning. "What's a word that means *stick it to you*, you know? Something that means existing for the purpose of someone else's discomfort, if only to remind them of the injustices they've committed."

"Something a bit softer than vengeance," Fox said thoughtfully. "Reprisal?"

Brandt considered it. "Mm, no. More like—"

"Recompense. Compensation? No," Fox realized, blinking. "Restitution."

Brandt tilted his head.

"Paying them back," Fox clarified, and Brandt nodded slowly.

"Yes," he permitted. "Quite."

Then he looked at Fox.

Fox looked at him.

Elsewhere, a twig snapped; a breeze displaced a branch; a bird took flight.

"Well," Fox exhaled, turning back to the river. "I suppose I see that. Though it seems rather—"

"Stupid?"

"I was going to say unsatisfying."

Brandt paused.

"Yes," he agreed. "I suppose it is, in some trivial way."

"Trivial?"

"Well—yes, I think. In the grand scheme, I find it largely rewarding. In a very mortal, deeply selfish way, actually."

"But the smaller scheme is—"

"Frustrating?"

"I was going to say unfulfilled. Or, malcontented, or perhaps—"

"Lonely," Brandt murmured, before he could prevent it slipping out.

Fox turned to face him.

"Is this why you come back to visit me?" he asked.

Brandt said nothing.

"I only ask," Fox offered neutrally, "because you could come back more frequently. If you wanted. I wouldn't mind."

"Twice a month?" Brandt suggested.

Fox turned, facing the river and shading his eyes from the sun.

"That could work," he permitted.

— Ω —

"What do you have for me today, *gudssønn*?" Iðunn asked from beneath the golden blossoms of her apple tree, crooning at the sight of Brandt and holding her hand out for his book. "Something good, I hope."

"Would you like to hear another story about the godson of Death?" Brandt asked, nudging her fingers toward the bookmark, and she brightened as she turned to the most recently written page.

"Yes, my favorite," she agreed, smiling indulgently. "Tell me."

"He's a little older now," Brandt said, gesturing to his notes on the page. "Definitely old enough to take a wife, have some sons of his own—"

"Oh, but he doesn't," Iðunn pouted. "Does he?"

"No, he doesn't," Brandt assured her. "Frankly, I doubt he will. I think he finds himself continuously searching for something he can't quite find."

"He lives an extraordinary story," she commented, humming with thought as she pored over the pages. "An ordinary woman would only bring him a temporary sort of pleasure, don't you think?"

"I agree," said Brandt neutrally. "And I think he knows it himself."

"Poor thing," the goddess sighed. "Then where do you suppose he finds joy?"

"Well, joy and pleasure are hardly the same thing," Brandt reminded her. "One is more lasting than the other, or I would not have to consistently return here, would I?"

"Pleasure, then," she amended, and Brandt laughed.

"He has plenty of that."

"Companionship?"

"That, too," Brandt said. "At least I think so."

A blossom floated gently to the ground, resting on the sodden earth between them.

"Do you see him twice a month still?" Iðunn asked, and Brandt nodded. "Why?"

"Why? I like him. He amuses me. And anyway, it was you who asked me to go back the first time, wasn't it?"

"No," she corrected him softly, shaking her head. "I meant—why *only* twice a month, *gudssønn*?"

Brandt hesitated before forcing something like a smile.

"Do you remember the last time you left here?" he asked, gesturing to the garden around them, and she wilted slightly, her fingers resting on the bark of the apple tree behind her as she let the book drop slowly from her hand in reverie.

"Only a little," she admitted, staring wistfully at the falling blossoms. "And it was wonderful, and now it haunts me like a nightmare."

"That's how I feel." Brandt nodded once, stiffly. "Like if I take too much, then the time away will only haunt me."

Helplessly, Iðunn's nails dug into the bark of the tree.

"Hm," she said. "So you are trapped too, then, yes?" Brandt nodded. "But only by fear," she told him softly, "and not by the gods, so perhaps we are not entirely the same."

"No, we aren't," he agreed, and she leaned back with a sigh.

"Does he know about me?" she asked him. "This godson of Death. Does he know I am your goddess?"

"In a sense. He knows about the apples. He asks about you," Brandt added. "Often. *Quite* often. But I can't tell him, of course."

"Mm, no," she agreed, "you can't. I understand now," she added. "What you are trapped by, I mean."

"Do you?"

"Oh, yes," she said. "And it's worse than the gods, I'm afraid."

Brandt arched a brow. "Not sure you're right about that."

"Well, perhaps not *worse*," she permitted. "I suppose I've seen very little outside this garden, haven't I? I must know very little about anything."

"I wouldn't go that far. You are a goddess, after all."

"A bit of a useless one," she lamented.

"Use*ful*," he corrected, "which is the problem. You have so much to give, and nothing you're permitted to take—"

"Nothing but one," she cut in, taking his hand, and pulled him toward her. "There is one thing I can take, isn't there?" she sighed, the feel of her breath curling like a filigree around the curve of Brandt's neck as he leaned against her, resting his hands on her hips. "A pity I must take so shamelessly from the godson of Death."

Brandt paused, unsteady and uncertain.

"What could you take from him?" he asked, forcing gaiety, and Iðunn smiled.

"Don't you see it, *gudssønn*?" she whispered. "Don't you see it yet?"

He swallowed, and she laughed.

"Perhaps I am not so useless a goddess, then," she remarked, and pulled him down to the grassy base of her tree, tugging at his trousers. "One of these days I will let you go," she told him, a blossom landing in her hair while she shifted to hover above him, "but today is not that day."

He nodded, leaning upward to brush a kiss against her cheek.

"How shall I love you today, then, Iðunn?" he asked, tucking a golden curl behind her ear.

"With deceit, and a liar's finesse," she said. "Like you always do."

"With pleasure, then," he assured her, watching her close her eyes.

— Ω —

"I don't understand what you're writing."

This time it was summer and hot. Too hot. Fox was floating in the water, idling on his back.

"It's a book," Brandt informed him from where he sat on the riverbank, and then paused. "Well, really more like a journal, I suppose."

Fox's eyes were closed, his hair slicked back from his face. "Do you always keep it with you like that?"

"Not always. This is my current book, but I have others. I hide them, usually," Brandt clarified, gesturing vaguely. "When they fill up, I put them somewhere for safekeeping."

"When they fill up?" Fox asked, frowning, and Brandt nodded. "But what do you write in them?"

"Nothing," Brandt said, shutting it, and shrugged. "Or everything, I guess."

Fox's eyes were open now, and keenly on Brandt's. "That doesn't answer the question."

"I know," Brandt agreed, and Fox rolled his eyes. "By the way," Brandt continued, "I brought you this." He reached into his pocket and dug out the ring, holding it out as Fox swam toward him. "It's been too long."

He eyed the ground while Fox approached, water dripping from his hair, his underthings. His increasingly golden limbs.

"What do you mean it's been too long?" Fox asked, reaching tentatively for the ring in Brandt's palm and picking it up, eyeing it in the sun. "You were just here last week."

"No, I meant—" Brandt growled to himself in frustration. "I meant it's been too long since you last spoke to your godfather. Summon him," he suggested. "That's what the ring is for."

Fox glanced down at it, studying it as he toweled himself off with his shirt. "Where did you get it? And by that, I obviously mean—"

"I didn't steal it. I made it."

Fox barked a laugh. "Liar."

Brandt picked at the fraying edge of his cuff.

"What does it matter?" he managed, with something like nonchalance. "It works."

"Still. I don't enjoy being privy to your crimes," Fox reminded him. "It's been nearly five years of this, Brandt, and you never get any less suspect."

"Well, I aim for distinction."

"And you succeed," Fox murmured, but let out a sigh, still eyeing the ring. "What would I even say to him?"

"Nothing, perhaps. But *if* there's something, then . . ."

Brandt trailed off, shrugging.

Fox, meanwhile, seemed to be contemplating something of his own.

"This is thoughtful," Fox remarked, glancing up at him. "I didn't know you had it in you."

"What, thought?" Brandt asked dryly.

"Yes. Well, no. Consideration."

Brandt closed his eyes, leaning back to tilt his chin up toward the sun. "I consider everything at length, as you well know."

"Fine," Fox rumbled impatiently, giving him what must have been another sulky glare. "If you *must* be difficult—"

"Yes," Brandt agreed, "I must, but surely you're used to it by now."

Fox opened his mouth, paused, and then closed it. He sat down beside Brandt, who did not move.

"This makes three times this month," Fox commented tangentially.

Brandt shrugged. "I have some free time."

"Iðunn not keeping you?" Fox teased.

"She doesn't keep me."

"Yes, she does," Fox corrected, without pause for breath. "Do you love her, or are you simply indebted to her?"

Brandt opened his eyes to stare at him. Fox was very close.

Too close.

"Is there something you'd like to say, Fox?" Brandt asked.

"Yes. Many things."

"Like?"

Fox was beginning to freckle around the eyes.

"Answer the question first," he said.

"I—" Brandt looked away. "I can't."

"Can't," Fox mused, "or won't?"

"Does it matter?" Brandt demanded, rising sharply to his feet. "I have to go."

Fox's expression was indolent, unchanged. "Well, that's easy. Don't."

"Stop it," Brandt snapped, and Fox rose to his feet. "Just—stop it. *Stop*."

He closed his eyes. He opened them.

Fox, however, hadn't moved.

"You said once I was dangerous for you," Fox remarked. "Is it because I make it harder to give whatever it is you offer the goddess in exchange for your youth?" He paused, but Brandt didn't respond. "Is it sex?" Fox guessed, looking thoughtful. "I could forgive sex, I think. A small thing, really. An easy thing, and not to be totally unbearable, but I would certainly know."

"I didn't ask for your forgiveness," Brandt muttered.

"No, but I would give it," Fox told him, standing far too close to him now. "If you asked."

Brandt swallowed. "I didn't."

"So it's sex, then," Fox pressed, in his irritatingly juvenile way. "In exchange for immortality—or is it technically youth?" He paused again, waiting, but still, Brandt said nothing. "A little unoriginal. Funny how you repeatedly insist that things will change, but some things are just a tale as old as time, aren't they?"

And then, horribly, Fox laughed, and Brandt felt the sound of it resonating in his lungs, as if he'd cast the breath of it himself.

"As usual, you oversimplify everything," Brandt retorted stiffly. "And what does it matter to you how I am kept, or by whom?"

Fox furrowed his brow at that, eyeing him, and took another step.

"If you can't see by now that you belong to me," Fox told him quietly, "then you're a bigger fool than I am, Brandt Solberg."

Shuddering, Brandt closed his eyes.

"Deny it if you like, but you're mine, godling," Fox whispered, his fingers hovering over Brandt's lips and catching the sound of his hesitant breath.

Brandt opened his mouth.

Nothing came out.

And by the time he opened his eyes, Fox was already gone.

— Ω —

"What does the godson of Death do now, *gudssønn*?"

"He tells me I belong to him," Brandt said, shivering beneath the weight of it, and Iðunn sighed, resting her cheek against Brandt's chest as she slipped the slim leather-bound volume from his pocket.

"This book is almost full," she noted tangentially, eyeing the spine of it, and Brandt shrugged.

"I suppose I've seen a lot of things recently." He paused. "Had a lot of thoughts."

The goddess hummed her agreement. "All about the godson of Death?"

Brandt hesitated.

"Mostly," he admitted. "I suppose you find that boring," he added guiltily, "but—"

"But he is your world," Iðunn commented softly, and Brandt felt a twinge of what he hoped was disagreement, but worried was something more like recognition, or truth.

"No," he said, and couldn't say more.

Iðunn's lips curled up in a smile.

"Would it be so bad, *gudssønn*," she murmured to him, "to be free?"

"You know what that would cost me," he reminded her, and she nodded, her chin digging into his sternum.

"You know my secret," she replied simply, "and I, in turn, know yours. You shared with me the secrets of your world, and in so doing, you gave a lonely goddess powerful dominion over your heart. I can feel its allegiances changing. But perhaps we are something like friends, now," she mused, sitting up to look at him, "and so perhaps I can give you something now, too."

"You do," he reminded her, gesturing to the apples overhead. "My youth, remember?"

"Yes, and I do expect something for it. But if I could choose, I would wish you to enrich your life, and your heart," she suggested. "It is far more valuable to me that way."

"How?"

She gave a divine shrug; a little hovering of nonchalance.

"You know as well as I do what has been stolen from you," she reminded him. "Take it from the keeper of a garden—no love can bloom without it. You are not whole, *gudssønn*," she told him softly, nurturingly, her fingers sliding along the lines of his chest. "Your time with the godson of Death will be brief, I'm afraid."

Brandt flinched.

"He told me he would forgive sex," he said dully, and Iðunn laughed.

"Yes, of course. An easy thing to forgive," she said, "and likewise, easily done without. I release you from it."

"But—"

"You will come back," she predicted firmly, before taking his hand and placing the book carefully in his palm. "You will return to me in time."

He sat up, dazed and grateful. Captivated and fearful.

"Why does that sound more like a curse than a blessing?"

"Because, *gudssønn*," the goddess sighed, cupping her hand around his cheek as she brushed a finger down the book's spine. "Like all things an immortal bestows, it is a little bit of both."

# XIX

## ROOTS

Fox was seeking quiet in one of the other rooms—a purple one this time, clearly and ridiculously modeled after the hall of mirrors at Versailles—when he unintentionally came upon Vi.

He didn't notice at first, of course, and he jumped when she turned her head from where she'd been staring idly out of the lake-facing window, tail flicking back and forth across the silk of a lavender upholstered chaise.

"Right," she confirmed, nodding. "Forgot?"

"I," he began, then abandoned his efforts. "You're a cat," he voiced aloud, catching the sheen from the chandelier as light slid languidly over the ebony pitch of her fur.

"Perceptive," Vi agreed, idly eyeing her paw. "As I said, it tends to happen when the sun goes down."

"Mind if I sit with you?" Fox asked, glancing over his shoulder. "I'm avoiding the demon."

"And Brandt too, I imagine," Vi said.

"That's the one I meant," Fox replied, and Vi gave a strange, feline chuckle.

"Right," she said again, staring back out over the lake.

Fox sighed quietly, taking a seat beside her. "The ghost isn't here, is he?" he asked, glancing around, and Vi shook her head.

"You've never actually talked to a ghost, have you?" she commented, and Fox shook his head. "So you're, like, totally a fraud."

"Yes," he said. "Almost entirely, actually."

"Huh," Vi said. "I take it I don't have to pay you, then."

"Well, let's not be so hasty," said Fox, with a genial shrug. "I'm getting him out of the house, so don't the ends justify the means?"

Even as a cat her expression was similarly inscrutable. "You can't even see the ghost I'm paying you to remove."

"True," Fox conceded. "I don't see him or much of anything, and yet I'm apparently responsible for saving mankind anyway, aren't I?"

It came out a little more bitterly than he intended, and graciously, Vi relieved him of any necessarily traumatic response. Instead she turned her head, tail flicking again as she eyed a piece of lint that fell slowly through the air.

"So," she said. "You're a thief."

"No," Fox corrected, shaking his head. "Brandt's a thief. It's in his nature, down to the quick of it, down to his bones—he takes things." This, too, was worse than he intended. Not because of bitterness. Because it sounded admirable, almost fond. "He's clever enough to know how to make use of something better than its owner can, and then, somehow, he makes it his." Fox cleared the melancholy from his throat. "It comes naturally to him, but not to me."

"So if he's the thief, what does that make you?" Vi asked.

"I don't know." Fox shrugged. "Just lazy, mostly."

Her amber cat-eyes slid to his.

"I don't believe that," she said.

Fox sighed.

"I'm not really anything," he told her.

He planned to stop there, but for whatever reason—perhaps because talking to a cat was its own form of meditation—he kept going.

"I always thought that I would be, you know?" he prompted, shifting awkwardly beside her; facing the lake, as she did, though it was a difficult thing to accomplish, sitting backward on the edge of a stiff Victorian chaise. "Something, I mean. Godson of Death," Fox pronounced grandly, spreading his hand wide, as if to envision it on a marquee. "Beloved by a god, once," he added under his breath, slowly letting his hand fall in defeat.

Vi let a few seconds pass, allowing the statement its proper despondency and weight.

"So what happened?" she asked eventually, and Fox opened his mouth.

Then he closed it.

Opened it again.

Sighed.

"The thing is," he attempted, frowning slightly, "you can see angels, you know. Anyone can, I mean, if they look closely enough. So yes, I can't see the ghost," he conceded, and she nodded, "but I saw my first angel when I was a boy. My godfather pointed her out to me." He shifted again, fidgeting through the anecdote. "I remember thinking she was so beautiful, and so bored. And nobody else noticed her. She was just walking around, watching but not actually meeting anyone's eye, and I thought—*maybe*," he parsed out slowly, "maybe, if I just kept looking that closely, then one day I'd be able to see everything. Maybe if I just kept *trying*, if I just kept *looking*—"

He broke off, staring at his empty hands.

"I'm not really anything special," he finished, shaking his head. "I don't have any real talents. No real skills. I have this one thing," he explained, raising his hand for her to see the ring on his smallest finger, "which is that I can speak to Death."

"That's not all," Vi attempted, but Fox shook his head.

"I thought there was more," he said. "I did, I really did, until I realized that I was just a normal mortal, doomed for an ordinary life. And it's not like I wanted more, really—not like I wanted immortality or anything, not like Brandt—but after a while I just didn't want to die," he admitted. "I didn't want to age. But I didn't want to work, either, and I didn't want to travel, and I didn't want to change, and I didn't want to *move*, really, and I didn't want to—"

He stopped again.

"I didn't want to feel," he said. "But nobody could ever do anything about that. No amount of sex or thrills or number of lifetimes could stop it, any of it, and—" Another shaky pause. "I wish I could just stop feeling," Fox admitted, watching a pair of joggers run by the basin of the lake shore path like tiny, careless specks of nothing, the waves of Lake Michigan swelling beside them. "You know what I mean?"

Vi made a slight retching sound, like a rasping cough.

"Sorry," she said, and then added, "sort of."

"Sort of?" he echoed.

She tilted her head.

"Sort of," she confirmed.

He figured that was the best he was going to get.

"What does it feel like?" Fox asked, watching her resume her vacant staring out toward the lake.

"Being a cat?" she asked. "Or being a creature?"

Fox shrugged.

"Either," he said. "Both."

She cocked her head, considering it.

"You know, I don't feel anything anymore," she admitted. "And I swear, I used to feel everything."

She turned to look at him, her eyes settling unnervingly on his face.

"Pain," she remarked. "I sort of remember it."

Fox swallowed.

"It's not great," he said. "Neither is anger, or confusion, or betrayal—"

"No," Vi agreed. "I understand."

Something about the way she said it, though, made Fox feel the need to apologize.

"Sorry," he said, giving into his impulses, and she glanced up at him.

"Thanks," she said, and he nodded, satisfied.

He stood up to leave, but Vi shifted her paw out to stop him.

"You should take the handcuffs off him," she said, stretching out until she looked unnaturally long, as cats did. "I don't think he's going to run."

Fox suppressed a scoff. (Barely.) "You don't know him."

"No," Vi agreed. "But I know a person who's running, I think, and it's not him."

"Big words," Fox muttered.

"It also seems to bother you," she pointed out. "Seeing him in chains."

For a moment he said nothing.

Then he reminded her, "You don't know me."

"No," she agreed. "So why'd you tell me everything you just did?"

"Don't know," he admitted. "I guess because you're the most normal person here," he remarked to the cat-shaped vampire, who spared him a decidedly human laugh.

"I am pretty normal," she agreed. "Almost aggressively normal, I'd say."

"Oi," Isis interrupted, sticking her head into the sitting room. "The contract worked."

"So the ghost can leave the house?" Fox asked, rising sharply to his feet. "Did you try it?"

"Totally," Isis confirmed. "We took him to Starbucks," she added, holding up her cup.

Fox glanced at Vi, who shrugged. "Do demons drink coffee?" Fox asked.

"We do when it tastes like diabetes," Isis replied, just as Cal appeared behind her.

"Tom says we should go," he said, and turned to Vi. "He also says you make a nice cat, and I agree."

"I can hear him," Vi said, and then marginally softened. "But thank you, anyway."

"Come on," Isis beckoned, crooking a finger. "Here kitty, kitty—"

"Stop it," Vi said. "That's undignified."

"Viola, my little meow meow," crooned Isis.

"Tom's right, you know. You *are* the worst—"

"Cal," Fox interrupted, calling after him to pause him before he left the room. "Wait," he said, spotting the cup in the reaper's hand. "Does that say caramel macchiato?"

"With extra foam," Cal confirmed. "I know I don't *need* food or beverages," he added, "but some things are just luxuries, Fox."

"Whatever," Fox sighed, shaking his head. "Anyway, before you go, take the handcuffs off Brandt, would you, Calix?"

"Why?" Cal asked, taking a dainty sip. "I thought you said—"

"I know what I said," Fox grumbled. "And if I end up being wrong—"

"I know, I know," Cal cheerfully confirmed. "Keep my *I-told-you-so*s to myself."

— Ω —

"Don't destroy the house," Tom said firmly. "Okay? I know it's basically palatial Georgian vomit with the occasional Venetian piece thrown in for drama, but you're not allowed to burn it to the ground. Got it?"

"I don't know why you think that's our goal," Louisa replied, propping her feet up on the Italian marble side table.

"That's—" Tom growled. "Don't *do* that—"

"Listen, about the mermaid," Sly cut in, setting his Frappuccino onto the table beside Luisa's feet. "She probably didn't kill you, okay? If that's what you were thinking."

"I wasn't," Tom barked, "but NOW I AM—"

"Tom," cat-Vi sighed, leaping up onto the couch beside Louisa. "Would you please not yell? They're doing us a favor, you know."

"Time to go," Fox called into the room, poking his head in. "Ready?"

Tom, lacking any reasonable alternative, grimaced.

"Don't break that vase," he said in parting, swooping over to it and startling Lupo into dropping his croissant. "This one," he clarified, gesturing to it. "Okay?"

"Why?" Sly asked. "Is it valuable?"

"Extremely," Tom told him. "But more importantly, I'd like to be the one to break it."

"Come on, Tom," Vi groaned, shaking her head. "Let's go."

"Yes," Isis contributed. "I don't want to miss a moment of Fox reliving two centuries' worth of trauma. Take care of everything here, will you? And use a coaster," she added to Sly, smacking his foot. "We're creatures, not animals."

"YEAH," said Tom, before realizing who he was agreeing with. "Oh."

"There's a ghoul outside," said Louisa, gesturing toward the view of the lake path. "Is that normal? It seems new."

"Super new," Sly agreed.

"LET'S GO," Fox shouted from the hall, and Tom sighed, eyeing the house one more time before catching Vi's eye from the doorway.

"Come on, noisy ghost," she called to him. "I promise to find you somewhere new to haunt."

"It won't be any fun unless you're actively trying to get rid of me," he grunted back.

She was a cat, so she couldn't smile, but he could have sworn he'd made her laugh.

"Well," she said, "then at the very least, you can still haunt me."

"Thanks," said Tom, who hated her 8 percent less, or maybe 5 percent more. "I suppose I'll cling to that."

$$- \Omega -$$

It wasn't the first time Fox had passed through one world into the next with Brandt, but this particular journey was definitely the strangest, owing to the creatures trudging along behind him in a mad procession from demigod to cat. They'd filed out of the house and directly into a pocket of spacetime, which of course looked and felt like empty air.

"Ouch," Mayra said from somewhere near the rear. "Someone's stepping on my wing."

"Sorry," Vi's voice offered sheepishly. "I didn't realize I wouldn't be a cat anymore once we got . . . here."

"That," Brandt explained to the confederation of idiots who paused collectively in the threshold of the door between worlds, "is because there is no day and night here, nor any particular environmental limitations. You can occupy whichever form you choose. That goes for all of you that possess different forms," he added, his gaze falling meaningfully on Isis. "No?" he prompted, and she pursed her lips. "All right then. Off we go."

"What about the ghost?" Fox asked, looking around for him. "I don't see him."

"He's right here," Cal said, gesturing to the vacancy between himself and Vi. "He's very testy at the moment. I think it's the caffeine."

"He didn't have any caffeine," Vi said.

"Yes," Cal agreed, "and I think that's the problem."

"Tom's form is the same," Brandt informed them. "It's his material that can't change. Sorry," he added to the ghost. "You're still incorporeal. And it's fine," he grunted before Cal could open his mouth, "Fox doesn't need to know his reply."

Fox arched a brow, and Brandt shrugged.

"What?" he said. "You don't."

"Fine," Fox permitted, gesturing forward to the verdant glimpse beyond the doorway Brandt had opened. "What's this?"

"Death's abode," Brandt supplied, stepping further inside to join Fox where he stood at the bottom of a massive, knotted tree, or what must have been a tree, although it was too large to take in all at once.

"The Tree of Life," Brandt clarified, gesturing to it, "with his treehouse up there," where there was, aptly, the glimpse of a gleaming wood treehouse, "and his cavern down here."

The cavern in question was the mouth of a dark cave below a twisted tangle of roots, each one approximately the size of the Lincoln tunnel.

Brandt paused beside Fox as the others shuffled in, Cal politely shutting the door behind them. "I thought," Brandt ventured carefully, his voice just low enough for Fox alone to hear, "that you would know where to find the ledger?"

"I don't," Fox said. "Not really." He didn't have to remind Brandt that he'd never been there before. It was the cottage where Fox had been raised that Brandt had found him in the first time, a secret place where Death only temporarily lived but which Brandt had managed to uncover because, apparently, Brandt had always known more about Death than anyone—certainly more than Fox—ever had. (Which was, ultimately, little more than salt in the wound, or so Fox was repeatedly telling himself.)

"Well," Brandt said, gesturing ahead. "Then I'd start with the cave."

"The cavern of mysteries?" Isis trumpeted from behind them. "Coincidentally, that's what I call my—"

"*Don't*," Vi groaned, and Cal chuckled.

"That's a good one," Mayra said. "I like that."

"I'm going in alone," Fox announced, making a face. "You can all wait out here."

"Are you sure?" Cal asked, stepping forward to eye the mouth of the cave, from which a twinkle of light suggested a multitude of shiny objects. "Don't you need help looking? It looks like there's a lot of stuff in there," he added, and Fox, who hadn't wanted to admit it, had to concede that in that specific account, Cal was correct.

Even from the mouth of the cave, it was obvious the innards were lousy with objects. This could take days, weeks. Months. Eons. Time they simply did not have, if the two archangels were right about the stakes of their ill-conceived mission.

"I—" Fox began, and stopped, gritting his teeth before turning to Brandt. "You've been here before," he prompted gruffly, "haven't you?"

Brandt nodded, but said nothing else.

"Fine," Fox said flatly, not bothering to wait for him to follow. "Then you're coming, too."

— Ω —

For the first few minutes, picking over the countless trinkets and baubles in the near darkness of the cave, neither of them spoke.

Eventually, though, Brandt found that uncomfortable silence had been preferable.

"This is a fiasco," came Fox's interminable grumbling as he picked through the items, growling incoherently into space. "This isn't locked, anyone can get in, so where would he keep something that would literally *destroy the world*—"

(Every few minutes, more of the same.)

"Ridiculous," Fox snapped at nothing, the comment directed at no one. "All that time making him watch his mouth when clearly what I needed to do was solve his fucking hoarding. *Shut up*," he added to Brandt, even before the latter could think the word *band*.

It wasn't until an uneasy muteness befell them that Brandt paused his search, turning to check on Fox. The other man, who'd been stooped and irritable the entire time, was now standing with his spine erect, staring vacantly into nothing.

"What is it?" Brandt asked neutrally, wondering if Fox would tell him.

He wasn't surprised when he did; Fox had never been a very good liar, and he'd been even worse at concealing his feelings.

"He doesn't have anything of mine," Fox said.

"Of course he does," Brandt countered, and Fox turned, frowning at him.

"He doesn't," he said again. "No mementos, nothing. All this stuff, it's just—" He held up a candelabra, giving it a firm shake until it promptly lit itself. "It's just *stuff*. And I know he always said I was just a mortal, but I thought—"

He stopped, looking stricken.

"Death is a being with a secret, Fox," Brandt reminded him. "People with secrets don't keep things in plain sight. They can't afford to." He wandered over to where Fox stood, scrutinizing the ground first, and then the shapes of the stalagmites that jutted out from beneath it. "What we need to do," he murmured, testing various spots on the cavern floor, "is find his treasure."

"He's not a pirate," Fox sighed, exasperated. "And I thought you'd been here before?"

"Once," Brandt said. "And as you might have guessed, I wasn't welcome to stay long. He also certainly didn't show me where he kept things," he added, knocking lightly on one of the nearby walls, "so it's not like I have all the answers, Fox."

"Why were you here?" Fox pressed. "When?"

Brandt paused, disguising his hesitation as an attempt to listen closely for echoes.

"There was a time," he said simply, "when I wanted something very badly from Death, and he refused to see me. I traded something of mine for the location of his abode, and—"

"What was it?" Fox asked. "That you traded."

"A month," Brandt said.

"A month? Of time?"

"Of my life," Brandt corrected, testing the solidity of an alleged boulder. (Confirmed, it was, in fact, a rock.) "I traded with Persephone. You know, daughter of Demeter, queen of the Underworld?"

"You went to the Underworld for a month?" Fox asked, bemused, and Brandt scoffed.

"What, and be forced to fuck Hades for a month in her place? No. I stayed with her mother," he corrected, prowling through one of the aisles of the cave. "I'm not going to lie, it was a very strange experience. Crops that year? Not great, truth be told. Probably won't be making that deal again anytime s—"

He broke off, catching the stillness of Fox's gaze lingering on something.

"What?" he prompted, shifting over to him, and Fox pointed.

"It's a box of rubber bands," Fox said, briefly eyeing the one on his own wrist.

Brandt reached over, picking it up.

"This," he determined, shaking it slightly, "has something more than rubber bands in it."

"Open it."

"*You* open it."

"Don't be stupid."

"Don't be a child."

"Don't call me that!"

"Don't *be* that—"

"Give it to me," Fox snapped, yanking the box from Brandt's hands and prying it open, the slight tremor in his hands hastily concealed. Or would have been, to someone who knew him less well.

"Well?" Brandt prompted, and Fox paused, blinking, as he looked over the items contained in the box.

"Oh," said Fox, and Brandt shifted over, eyeing the box's contents over his shoulder.

"Oh," he agreed, and Fox set the box down, withdrawing the items one by one.

"Baby shoes," Brandt noted, picking one up after Fox set it aside. "Very cute. Little foxes on the toes."

"Stop," grumbled Fox. "That's—stop it."

"Oh, look," Brandt crowed, reaching for a schoolbook with small, tentative lettering. "Is this where you learned to write?"

"Oh, for the love of fuck—"

"And you thought he didn't have anything of yours," Brandt chided him, picking up a small, shapeless doll. "Look at *this*, how *precious*—"

"Give me that—"

Fox reached for it, stumbling over a chest full of Mayan jewelry, and Brandt caught his elbow, steadying him.

"Careful," he cautioned, and swallowed uneasily as Fox looked up, blinking.

Fox had always had such expressive eyes, and now they expressed something vulnerable and terrible and loudly, violently dismayed, and Brandt could not breathe for having looked at them.

"Careful," he said again, and Fox drew away, searching through the box again.

"Here," Fox muttered absently, withdrawing an angel's scroll from the box. "This has to be it. All the names are here—"

"A scroll," Brandt lamented, rolling his eyes as he came closer again to glance over Fox's shoulder. "How utterly predictable of them."

Fox turned slightly, appearing to register the nearness between them as Brandt reached around for the ledger, brushing his arm.

Instantly, Brandt froze, the air in his lungs briefly collapsing.

"What did you want from him?" Fox asked without looking up. "From Death. When you came here looking for him."

Brandt sighed. "I can't tell you."

"Can't?" Fox countered, pivoting to face him. "Or won't?"

"Do you really want to do this now, Fox?"

"Do what?" Fox demanded. "You haven't given me an *answer*, Brandt, and I just want to know what you were—what you—whether this was *before*," he stammered miserably, "or if you—if he—"

"You want to know whether you should be angry with me," Brandt supplied for him, "or angry with your godfather, or both."

To that, Fox said nothing, visibly deflating.

"The truth is, Fox, that it doesn't really matter, does it? You can be angry with Death and still want to save him," Brandt said. "You can acknowledge that he kept things from you, and that he cheated, but that perhaps he still matters." He paused, and still, Fox said nothing. "You can be angry with me," he added quietly, "and still be happy to see me. Can't you?"

Immediately, Brandt could see it had been the wrong thing to say.

"You think I'm—*happy*?" Fox choked out in disbelief, the word seeming toxic from his throat. "You think that's what I feel? 'Happy,' like nothing *happened*, like I've just been—like I've just been *waiting*—"

"Fox," Brandt attempted, reaching for him. "Fox, I didn't mean it like that—"

"No, no, you're right," Fox returned bluntly, turning away. "The past is passed, and there's no reason to discuss it. I knew as much when I said it the first time. Never mind what, exactly, passed in the meantime; the life I led after you. Why would you care, after all? Where I went, or who I—"

He stopped, freezing in place, and stared down at the ledger in his hand.

"What is it?" Brandt asked, one hand reflexively outstretched. Thankfully he curled his fingers just before reaching Fox's shoulder, letting the hand fall limply in the space between them before Fox took notice of what he'd done. "What do you see?"

It took a moment; clearly, something was churning through Fox's head.

"After you disappeared, I left Frankfurt," Fox explained slowly, still looking lost in thought. "Years later, but still—after you were gone, I couldn't stay. I came here. I came to New York first, but I was restless, I kept moving. I came to Chicago during the Civil War, stayed there, and there was one night. One night when someone—"

He shook himself.

"Who do you think it is?" Fox asked, rotating slowly to face Brandt. "The missing game in the ledger, I mean. Why did you think it had anything to do with me?"

For a moment, Brandt stared at him. It was the most Fox had thus far revealed to him about their time apart, and yet it was also the least. It was a moment that felt ripe with significance, but it wasn't the time. This wasn't the place.

"I think it was a mortal," Brandt eventually admitted.

Wordlessly, Fox's eyes blew wide.

"Fox?" Brandt prompted, waiting, and Fox shoved the ledger into his hand.

"What exactly does the ghost look like?" he asked, apropos of nothing, and Brandt, taken aback by the question, frowned.

"I don't know," he said. "Brown hair? One nose, two eyes—"

Fox growled in frustration. "Just look," he said, pointing at the ledger, and Brandt glanced down at the name beneath his finger.

"Tom Parker," Brandt read aloud, looking up in time to catch Fox's bloodless expression.

"This is why the angels want the ghost," Fox determined, one hand pressed to his mouth. "And I think," he added painfully, "that this might all be my fault."

# INTERLUDE VI:

## PAST IS PASSED, PART II

### Fox D'Mora
### 1835

"Where do you go?" Fox asked, turning to Brandt. It was the usual spot in the woods; the usual stolen moment, a tree in the forest with no one but Fox and Brandt to hear it fall. "When you're not here with me, where are you?"

Brandt gave his usual ambiguous shrug.

"Elsewhere," he said. "Into an ongoing state of wandering."

"I meant a place," Fox said.

"Yes. I know what you meant."

"Then why don't you just——"

"Because," Brandt cut in irritably, "not everything is a *place*, Fox. Not everything can be identified on a map, or understood by a——"

"Mortal," Fox supplied gruffly, kicking aimlessly at the dirt.

"Yes," Brandt said, looking ruffled with discomfort. "Which I realize is a sore subject, *lillegutt*, but some things are simply facts. Consider them lessons."

Fox stubbornly lifted his head. "I could do better than having a teacher like you."

"Yes," Brandt said. "On that we agree."

He seemed different. Fox considered the change, glancing sideways at him.

"Let me try again," Fox suggested, trying very hard not to be too sulky. "Why do you return? If you're in a constant state of wandering," he clarified, knowing as he did that Brandt would take the circular route if allowed, "then surely this is the one place you go that has . . . I don't know, intention. As in, coming here *intentionally* is the antithesis of wandering, and thus——"

"I'm here because you're here," Brandt said plainly. "After a year, Fox, I should think we can admit some things to ourselves. As I've said, some things are simply facts."

Fox couldn't see why Brandt could say as much so easily now when he'd chosen to be difficult a mere five minutes prior.

"So you admit, then, that you come here to see me," Fox deduced slowly.

"Yes," Brandt replied, equally slowly. "All evidence points to it."

"Meaning that you come here," Fox attempted in a meaningful alternative, "*for* me."

"Yes," Brandt confirmed, with a sense of resignation. "Another reasonable conclusion."

"You say that as if you have no choice," Fox commented.

"And I don't. Not really."

"But I've never forced you to," Fox countered.

"No." Brandt looked amused. "I was rather under the impression that you'd prefer it if I did not, actually."

"That was true once," Fox admitted. "But you persisted, and now I think you've lured me into some outrageous sense of expectation."

"Ah, poetic. Persisted like a troubadour, you mean?"

"More like a virus."

"Fair. I do find I have a feverish effect on others."

"Don't lie," Fox scoffed. "There are no others."

He'd meant it to be a playful jab, but Brandt's easy smile wavered.

"No," Brandt agreed. "There are no others," he said, a declarative statement so rare and precious Fox wished he could capture it in his hands; hold a feast in its honor; commit the occasion to stone beneath his feet; "and there never will be."

Fox paused, surprised.

"Is that true?" he asked.

Brandt sighed.

"Some things are just facts," he finished morosely, and leaned against their usual tree, closing his eyes.

— Ω —

"Put it on," Brandt said, holding the watch out. "There's a reason I broke it, Fox. Though," he added uneasily, "don't tell your godfather I said that. Tell him I dropped it. Timepieces are, after all, notoriously fragile." He paused. "Perhaps, when the subject arises, you should suggest that it's time for new industry standards."

"*You* use it," Fox suggested instead, warily eyeing the watch. It looked normal. An unremarkable silver face with a nondescript leather band, only it was anything but. "If you use it, you won't need the apples."

Brandt shook his head. "There's a difference between stopping time to preserve my youth and claiming the immortality that should be mine," he explained, though Fox didn't grasp the significance of drawing the distinction. "Besides, it's too late now. I already have my method of eternality, and now it's your turn."

"Why?" Fox asked. "I'll still only be a mortal. I'll still belong to this world, so won't it become, I don't know—somewhat worrisome to others when I mysteriously fail to age?"

"Not if you go far enough," Brandt replied smartly. "Get good enough at disappearing, *lillegutt*, and nothing ever becomes a problem."

"You realize," Fox sighed, "that disappearing means leaving people behind, doesn't it?"

Brandt shrugged. "You can't simply look at time as a function of comings and goings. Time is always in motion, even if you personally opt to desist. Whether you come or go or leave or stay, time continues. People are left. People are found. To think that resigning yourself to permanence is itself a state of permanence is already made in error."

As usual, Brandt's logic was dizzying, and Fox tried desperately not to stumble.

"You act like because you're not a mortal, you're not even human," Fox said. "Is it really that easy to just . . . continue?"

"Of course it isn't easy," Brandt said. "What could be easy about outlasting your own existence, your own time? History is a cycle, you know. It's a function of gains and losses, of ups and downs. A single lifetime contains enough highs and lows to imitate completion, to simulate satisfaction, like any narrative given an end. But if you persist, as time does, then you will only encounter infinite highs, infinite lows.

"How can one ever be satisfied, then? Impossible," Brandt ruled with finality, taking a bite of his golden apple, and Fox, beaten to submission by the usual laborious pretension, finally rolled his eyes.

"So why should I wear it then?" he prompted. "Give me one good reason."

Brandt's gaze slid carefully to his.

"For me," he said.

"That's it?" Fox stared expectantly at Brandt, searching his face as if there might be more to it if he managed to look closely enough. "You want me to wear a stolen watch and cling to eternal youth so that, what? You won't have to be alone?"

"Yes," said Brandt. "Naturally, Fox, I don't relish a future where you've gotten old."

Fox frowned. "You say that like you'll be around for it." His life, he meant. His narrative, as Brandt put it.

His story.

Predictably, Brandt shrugged. "Can't rule it out," he said.

— Ω —

Brandt gasped, his lip caught between Fox's teeth.

"Funny," Fox mused. "Immortality doesn't rid you of *all* mortal sensations, then, I take it?"

"Not quite," Brandt permitted gutturally, throwing Fox down on the bed. "Not all sensations, anyway."

"What else can you still feel?" Fox asked. (It came out less studiously than he intended. Embarrassingly, it sounded more like *I missed you* or *tell me to stay*.)

Brandt brought his lips to Fox's neck, nudging his chin up. "I feel everything," he said into Fox's skin. "I feel it all, but I will never feel anything as you will feel it. Things are so much sweeter when they have an ending; things are so much more painful when they can be ripped away."

Fox paused, gripping the hair at the back of Brandt's head to still him.

"Are you telling me this will end?" he whispered.

Brandt opened his mouth, then closed it, something forcibly caught on the tip of his tongue.

"You never listen," he said gruffly, fingers digging into Fox's hips. "You only hear what you want to hear, *lillegutt,* no matter what I say."

"Don't call me that," Fox growled, forcing Brandt onto his back. "I'm not a child."

Brandt hit the mattress with a dull thud, tracing the lines of Fox's face with the path of his gaze.

"No, you aren't, are you," he agreed quietly. "But what will I call you, then?"

It took a moment; Fox fought it as resolutely as he could.

"Call me yours," he begged, burying his forehead in the crook of Brandt's shoulder so as not to see him refuse.

Around him, Brandt's arms stiffened for a moment, and then relaxed.

They slid tightly around Fox's ribs, holding him steady.

"Some things are just facts," he said, and Fox wished desperately to believe him.

— Ω —

"Papa," Fox croaked, his head bent. "Papa, he's gone."

Death hesitated, his mouth slipping into a crescent moon of tentative sympathy.

"The godling," he began uncomfortably, "is not a very good man, Fox."

The idea that he could say so, Fox thought, and somehow manage to not devolve into laughter at the intensity of the understatement was putrefyingly sad, grotesquely unfunny, insurmountably crushing; sickening, to the basest corners of his stomach.

Brandt Solberg had never been a good man, but what did that matter?

Fox hadn't fallen in love with his goodness.

(At least—not in any obvious way.)

"I might have told you that sooner," Death added, "if you had tried to speak to me at any point over the last five years."

It was so close to the sound of Brandt calling him a fool or a child that Fox wanted to crumble under the weight of it; to seep into the grains of the wooden floor and melt into the ground below.

"You didn't look for me, either," Fox pointed out, which served at least to shame them both.

"I'm—" Death began, and broke off. "I am simply unaccustomed to the expectations of humanity. Which is not to say I didn't worry about you," he added, "but seeing as you were in the throes of rebellion, or something along those lines—"

He trailed off.

"I am relieved, at least," Death determined quietly, "that you have chosen to come to me in the godling's absence. You will be better off without him, Fox," he added. "You may choose a different path without him, and I promise you, you will be better for it."

Privately, Fox doubted it.

In truth, he'd never before wanted so badly to break things; to shatter them. To place something beneath his heel and deliver it to shards; to send the tiny, indistinguishable grains of his anguish out to sea on a gust of wind. He wanted to part with his fragile illusions of rightness; to abandon his many worthless moral qualms. To take the youthful pieces of himself and carry on without them, leaving them—and the remnants of a life he'd once shared with Brandt—behind, scattered for someone else to find and choke on.

"Papa," Fox sighed eventually, confessing at last. "You were right, you know. Brandt is the one who broke Time's watch."

"I know," Death said, as Fox had been certain he already had. "He has a habit of breaking things."

"Stealing them," Fox added glumly.

"Gambling them," Death muttered, and Fox looked up.

"What?"

"Nothing," Death said firmly. "But it goes without saying that the godling was never especially admirable, Fox. He was," he began, and sighed, apparently not having produced any new descriptors, "not a very good man."

"He wasn't a man at all," Fox reminded him. "He was a god."

"A demigod," Death corrected.

Fox swallowed.

"Right," he agreed. "Right."

— Ω —

"What's this?" Death asked gruffly, staring at the rubber band as if it might come to life and bite him.

"Aversion therapy," Fox replied. "We're going to cure you of your bad habits."

"And what about *your* bad habits?" Death demanded.

"Which ones?"

"The thefts, the shenanigans, the constant sleeping around—"

"Symptoms of mortality, Papa," Fox said with a shrug.

Death glared at him. "You should at least be punished for your expletives, too, Fox."

"Fine. Then I'll wear one, too. Does that make you happy, Papa?"

"Fuck no," said Death.

"No, that's—" Fox shook his head, concealing a certain mad fondness. "You see what I mean? Now you have to snap the band."

Death looked reticent. "*Fuck* is a good word, Fox. I like it. It fits nicely in my mouth. I like the way it feels like a weapon."

"Yes, Papa, but most people don't care for it."

"Who people? What people? Fuck them."

"Papa." He fought a laugh. "Just snap the band."

"Why?"

"Look, I'll do it too, see? I'll say 'fuck,' and—*fuck*, ouch—"

"Not so easy, is it, Fox?" asked Death smugly.

Fox rubbed the skin of his wrist, rolling his eyes. "It's not supposed to be easy."

"Does this mean you're feeling better, then?"

It was such an abrupt shift that the laughter died in Fox's throat.

"What do you mean?" he asked neutrally, and Death sighed.

"It's been over a year, Fox," Death said. "Perhaps you should consider moving on. Finding a hobby. Or, I don't know, a fucking vocation."

"Band, Papa. And I don't want a vocation."

"You're becoming just like him," Death warned. "You're as much a thief now as he was."

"Am I? Doubtful." Brandt was better. It came more naturally to him.

"Fox."

"Yes, Papa?"

"Fox, listen to me."

"I'm listening."

"Why are you doing this?" Death pressed. "You seem so—"

(Aimless.)

(Broken.)

(Sad.)

"I'm looking for something," Fox said.

"For what?"

(A book.)

"Nothing," Fox lied.

"Fox," Death sighed.

(A warning.)

"I'm fine," Fox said again.

"Like hell you are," Death scoffed.

"Band, Papa."

"Why? It's a fucking *place*, Fox—"

"*Band,* Papa."

"Fi-OUCH."

"Thank you."

(A sigh.)

"Someone should really keep an eye on you," muttered Death.

— Ω —

"I'm sorry," Fox said, frowning. "Who are you?"

"Mayra," the sharp-voiced angel said, adjusting her wings beneath his highly dubious scrutiny. "Mayra Kaleka. And just for reference, *this*," she pointed out, gesturing to where Fox was climbing out the window of the Frankfurt pub, "is really not going to reflect favorably upon you in your ledger."

"Well, my apologies," he said, "but considering I won't be dying anytime soon, I'm not too concerned with my ledger, thanks. I've diminished my purpose to restitution."

"Yes, well, be that as it may," Mayra sighed, alighting beside him in the window, "since I can't actually stop you, I suppose I'm here to help."

"Help . . . what?" Fox echoed, bemused. "And why, may I ask, is there an angel following me around to begin with?"

"Right, yes, about that. This thing you've just stolen," she informed him, gesturing to the bracelet he clutched in his hand. "It's mine. So, now that you possess it, you can call on me whenever you like."

"Oh, so you're my babysitter, then?" Fox asked, making a face. "In that case, you can most definitely have the bracelet back."

"Actually, I can't," Mayra said. "I used my last miracle for the year making sure you would find it, so." She shrugged, ignoring his puzzled expression of disbelief. "You're going to have to hold on to it, I'm afraid."

"For what possible purpose?" Fox asked, and Mayra shrugged again.

"Well, anything I can provide, I suppose. Advice?" she suggested. "Miracles, when I can spare them. Conversation. Book recommendations. Consultation on your ledger, I imagine, though I should really warn you, Fox D'Mora, that things are *decidedly* not going well in that department—"

"Wait a minute," Fox cut in. "Are you saying you're my guardian angel?"

"Yes, essentially," Mayra agreed. "Do you need help getting out of here or something?"

"Well, I wouldn't say no," Fox agreed, glancing down below. "I believe I angered the owner of this pub the last time I was here, so if there's some way to, you know, magically vanish me elsewhere, that'd be much appreciated."

"Oh, no, I can't do that," Mayra told him gravely. "I'm out of miracles, and really, my abilities are quite limited. Bureaucracy, you know. Exceptional amounts of red tape. Vanishing people requires all sorts of immortal permits. It's a real nightmare."

"Okay," Fox allowed uncertainly. "Well, then can you warn me if someone's coming?"

"Morally? No," she said, shaking her head. "That would be, as my employer puts it, a sin. Which is, coincidentally, against the celestial rules. I am very firmly not allowed to foster instances of crime."

"Right," Fox grumbled. "Well, you realize that's sort of inconvenient."

"I do," Mayra confirmed. "But still, I want you to know that I'm here for you."

"Can you tell me where to find the book I'm looking for, then?" Fox attempted. "Someone I knew made it. It's a book of the Oth—"

"The Otherworlds, yes, I know," Mayra confirmed. "As I said, I've been keeping an eye on your activities, but I'm afraid I don't know where to find the book you're looking for. Wherever it's hidden, it's hidden quite well."

"So what exactly *can* you do for me, then?" Fox demanded. "It's starting to look like nothing."

"That's incredibly rude," she informed him, though it seemed more purely fact than evidence of offense. "I'm mostly here for your mental state," she added in clarification. "Your psyche."

"My psyche?" Fox echoed, repulsed. "I'm mildly in the midst of a one-man heist for a book that seems to not exist. So I think, in the scheme of things, that my psyche might have to wait."

"Well, it's not my fault that this is when you chose to steal my bracelet," Mayra informed him. "I can easily come back later, you know. That is the whole idea of the relic."

"Relic?"

"Yes, the relic," she said, pointing again to the bracelet in his hand. "My relic. All you have to do is call for me while you're hold-ing it, and I'll be here."

"But again," Fox said, "you can't actually help me, right?"

"Not if it involves the commission of a crime," she said, "or if it requires a miracle and I happen to be out of them."

"So, to be honest, I probably won't call on you, then," Fox in-formed her. "Nothing personal, but it's not like I really need to chat."

"Fair enough," Mayra said. "Nice to have met you, Fox D'Mora, even if it was only briefly."

He gave her a vacant smile, thoroughly bemused.

"And you, Mayra Kaleka," he replied, reaching from the pub's upstairs window to the tree branch outside.

— Ω —

"You know, I know I'm biased, but this Brandt character sounds like a real dick," Mayra commented. "You're sure you can't find him? I'd like to give him an extremely firm talking to, personally. Or perhaps some boils at the edge of his nose? I'm sure I could pass it off as a miracle. Presumably some good would come from it, even if it was simply my satisfaction."

"Not sure I could locate him even if I tried," Fox told her, and then grimaced. "Okay, fine, I've tried," he muttered, "but I don't think he's in the mortal world. He rarely was before, so I doubt he's here now."

"Hm," Mayra said. "Well, you know who could help you in the Otherworlds, don't you?"

"Not you, apparently," Fox commented, and Mayra shrugged.

"Sorry," she said. "Five miracles go by fast, you know. Can-didly, I'm afraid I'm a bit soft," she lamented. "I'm rather ashamed of it myself. Plus I regularly underestimate the length of a mortal year."

"Are immortal years different?"

"No," she admitted. "But it still seems worth marking the distinc-tion. In any case," she went on, directing his attention back to the point, "what you need is a reaper. Death could help you find one, if you wanted. I could ask around, but most angels never encounter a reaper, considering we work for different departments."

"A reaper? One of the soldiers of Lucifer, you mean?" Fox clarified, and she nodded. "That seems a bit questionable, doesn't it? Someone who works for the literal devil?"

"Well, they have excellent tracking skills, or so I hear," Mayra said. "And anyway, they're not demons. They just have a different job from angels. Different employer, too," she conceded, "but really, we're like two sides of a coin. Altogether, similar ends."

"Balance is king?" Fox prompted knowingly, and Mayra smiled her approval.

"Balance is king," she confirmed.

— Ω —

"So they've run you out of Frankfurt, huh?" Cal asked.

"Yeah," Fox said, shrugging. "I mean, I could just wait until they all die and then carry on as I was, but Mayra thinks I should get out somewhat more permanently. You know, for my mental health. Which sounds like something she made up, but you know how she can be."

"Not a bad idea," Cal agreed. "And the truth, Fox—in my professional opinion," he clarified, tiptoeing delicately into the point, "is that I don't think you'll ever be able to find Brandt, or his book, for that matter. From what you've told me about him, I think he'd have to find *you*, but if he were actually planning on doing that . . ."

He trailed off, and Fox sighed. The implication was clear enough, even with Cal's characteristically sparing delivery.

*If he wanted to find you,* Cal hadn't wanted to say, *he would have already done it.*

Which Fox already knew was true. After all, it wasn't as if he was a toy that had been somehow carelessly misplaced.

(Or was he?)

(He wasn't.)

(—he hoped.)

"I know," Fox conceded morosely. "And I think I've stayed in

Frankfurt as long as I possibly could. If he wants to find me, he will," he sighed. "He always found me before, even when I didn't want to be found. Especially then, actually."

Cal took a moment, thinking, and then appeared to discard the effort, offering Fox an empty-handed shrug in lieu of sympathy.

"You know, a cliché would be nice here," Cal commented, and tilted his head. "Maybe we should ask Mayra."

At that, Fox glanced askance, fighting a smirk.

"Should I summon her?" he asked neutrally.

Cal shrugged. "If you want," he said, feigning disinterest. "Entirely your decision."

"Perhaps I will," Fox said, and paused. "Unrelated," he ventured, "can an angel and a reaper fall in love, or are there rules against it?"

Cal spared him a wary glance.

"Love is a rather mortal concept," he said, which both of them were quite aware was not an answer. "Don't you think? It can be born; it cannot exist alone; it can die. Love itself, then, is mortal, and thus not within either of our realms."

"A very pretty argument, Calix, but do you actually believe that?" Fox asked. "That love can die?"

"Can't it?" Cal asked. "I wouldn't know myself, but it seems to."

Fox let out a breath, contemplating what might have been his last look at the town before turning his attention back to Cal, and to the road ahead.

"I really thought he would have hidden the book somewhere in Frankfurt," Fox confessed. "I thought perhaps he would have left it here for me to find, or—" He broke off with a heavy swallow. "And besides, there are no places that meant anything to him except for here. Unless I never meant anything to him," he realized, the words turning sour on his tongue. "But that's—that can't be—"

Cal settled a hand on his shoulder, sparing him a warning look.

"Don't go down that road, Fox," he murmured. "There might not be any coming back."

Fox nodded, collecting himself, and turned his back on the setting sun.

"So," he said. "Boat to New York?"

"I don't really care for boats," Cal said.

"You don't have to come," Fox reminded him.

"Oh," Cal said, relieved. "Well. Boat it is, then."

— Ω —

"Papa," Fox said with a hiccup, his arm slung around the shoulders of a pretty schoolteacher he'd been acquainted with for a lovely, intoxicating hour. "Do you mind? Mrs. Greenaway here would like to know how her husband is doing, so if you could be so kind as to inform us if you've seen him—"

"Fox, I'm really quite busy," Death returned grumpily. "There's a bit of a fucking civil war on, in case you missed it, and I'm not exactly swimming in free time."

"Who are you talking to?" the teacher asked with a giggle. "Are you communing with ghosts?"

"Why yes, yes I am," Fox determined loudly. "So, Papa?" he prompted again, glancing over at him. "What do you think? Is John Greenaway resting well in whichever world he happens to be in?"

"He's not dead, Fox," Death informed him, and Fox choked, abruptly sputtering a loud series of coughs.

"What is it?" asked the teacher, whose name he supposed was Mary or Anne or Grace, or something equally Puritanical. "What does the ghost of my husband say?"

"Uh," Fox replied.

"Super alive, Fox," Death reminded him, pinching the bridge of his nose. "Very much alive."

"He—" Fox paused, weighing the value of the woman on his lap and determining an appropriate course of action. "He says," he continued firmly, "that he wishes he could be here to keep the bed warm for you tonight—"

"Don't do it," Death warned.

"—but in his tragic absence, he hopes you'll find a way," Fox concluded, as Death let out a loud, obtrusive groan.

"Fox," Death admonished. "Fox, are you listening? Fox—FOX,

I'm talking to you, you can't just—Fox, this is, I can't, I refuse to stand by and be privy to your—Fox. FOX!"

— Ω —

"That's an interesting ring," a man pointed out, taking a seat across from Fox in the old wooden tavern (the second, after the first one had burned down). A staple for those who worked the shops on Lake Street, it was crowded now, predominantly with men. "Does it mean something?"

Fox glanced down, eyeing the familiar blank face of the signet ring on his pinky.

"Nope," he said, shrugging as he tossed back a gulp of ale. "Nothing at all."

The man eyed him for another long moment.

"You know, I've seen you here the last few weeks," the man commented. "You seem like the sort of man that's running from something."

"Do I?" Fox asked, already a little drunk. The barmaid across the room ducked her head, coyly skirting his gaze. A project for the evening, and so Fox turned obligingly to the man beside him. "Just arrived from the East Coast, so I suppose I am. And what about you, then?"

The man offered his hand. "I'm Tom," he offered. "Tom Parker."

"You certainly are," Fox agreed. "Just come back from service, have you?"

"Yes," Tom said, nodding. "And you?"

"German," Fox told him, gesturing to himself. "Just happen to be caught amongst the fray."

Tom nodded again, raising his tankard to his lips.

"Well," he said. "How do you find our fair country?"

"I find it not to be Germany," Fox told him, "which is approximately my intended result. I also find it to be a bit indulgent, I suppose," he added, glancing up at the barmaid again. "Though, who knows. I'll leave that up to Fortune."

"May I ask what it is you do now?" Tom ventured genially. "Pardon my familiarity, but you seem to have done well for yourself, and I'm sort of in the business of sorting out the rest of my life," he clarified. "Bit hard to do, really, considering."

He paused, then, glancing at Fox's watch. "Seems like you might need a watchsmith," he joked, and Fox glanced down, barely suppressing a grimace.

"Very true," he agreed dully, raising his glass to his lips. "Unfortunately it's something of an heirloom. I'm afraid the sentimental value is considerably higher than its functionality." He paused, holding his tankard against his mouth. "But then again, I suppose you can't really put a price on freezing time."

He'd meant it as a joke, but the other man didn't laugh.

"What's your name?" Tom asked. "Sorry, I don't think I caught it."

"It's Fox," he replied. "Fox D'Mora."

"Fox," Tom repeated, his gaze slipping back to Fox's ring. "You know, I think I've heard of you, actually. They say you can speak to the dead, don't they?" he asked, taking a careful sip of his ale.

"Do they?" Fox asked. "Must be another Fox."

"Must be," Tom agreed, and gestured to Fox's near-empty glass. "Need a refill?"

Fox considered it, squinting at the suspiciously eager man.

*Was* he suspicious?

Perhaps that was just some glitch from his preexisting haze.

"Sure," Fox agreed, draining the tankard and setting it down with a shrug. "Why not?"

# XX

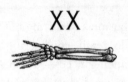

# IMMORTAL PERIL

By the time the others had gathered around outside the cavern to hear what Fox had discovered in the ledger, Brandt had become very sure that everything that could go wrong was gradually doing just that.

"I'm sorry," Vi said when Fox finished talking. "What?"

"Say it all again, but slower," suggested Isis. "Then say it backward and three times fast."

"It's really very simple," Brandt informed Vi, sparing Fox a disapproving head shake because it felt extremely fitting. "Fox here is very careless with his things, and as a result, a mortal has now put us all in the extremely inconvenient position of having to travel through the Otherworlds to win an unwinnable game."

"Although again, we don't know for sure what happened, seeing as I don't remember. Nor can we be sure that it's him," Fox interjected grumpily. "It could very well be some other mortal Tom Parker."

"Yes, he's right. It's a very common name," Tom contributed, in what everyone in the group seemed to agree was a surprising alliance. "Far too common, I'm beginning to think."

"Yes, true," Brandt agreed. "But then how many other Parkers are cursed?"

Tom, insistently: "I'm not cursed."

Isis, eagerly sensing a crisis: "Yes, actually, you very much are."

Tom, with the air of a losing argument: "Says you!"

Fox, in an aside to Cal: "What's he saying? Actually no, never mind. I feel very sure that this is probably a coincidence."

Brandt, in an aside to Fox: "Almost certainly not a coincidence, actually."

Fox, in a retort more aimed at Brandt than spoken to him: "Really? Suddenly it's *not* a coincidence? What happened to the Brandt

Solberg 'astronomically unending possibilities with infinitesimally small likelihoods of each' school of nonsensical thought?"

"It's in perfectly fine working order," Brandt informed him, trying not to read into the precise detail of Fox's recollection. "It simply doesn't apply when one thing very obviously leads to another."

"I maintain that this can't possibly be my great-grandfather," Tom protested. "For one thing, wouldn't he be—I don't know, old?"

"Yes," said Isis, an ageless being.

Tom, sighingly: "Right."

Cal, to Fox: "The ghost just called us all old."

Fox, with a roll of his eyes: "Honestly? Pretend I never asked."

Vi, still confused: "Tom Parker played as a mortal? But I thought it was an immortals' game."

Brandt, with a nod: "It is. It is certainly not designed for a mortal."

Cal, kindly: "Not as an exclusionary principle, I'm sure—"

Isis, brusquely: "*Yes* as an exclusionary principle. Literally, for purposes of exclusion. Mortals were never supposed to play, and neither were demons."

"Well, obviously, nobody wants a demon," Tom muttered. "But what I don't understand is why there's any sort of specific mortal distinction."

At that, Brandt caught the motion of Fox shifting uncomfortably, his fingers tightening around the ledger's scroll. *Just a mortal.*

"Well, there's the whole death thing mortals always have," Isis supplied. "Sort of the main feature, really."

"Yes, but Tom's right," Vi pressed curiously. "Why wouldn't a mortal be able to play the game?"

"Well, they could, clearly," Brandt told her, gesturing to the ledger in Fox's hands. "It's not as if they're physically incapable. But in general, mortals have different rules."

Isis, in an apparent fit of helpfulness: "Different feelings. Different matter, really."

Tom, with a frown: "Are they really so different? Mortality and immortality?"

Mayra, contemplatively: "Sort of. I remember being mortal—I remember the feel of it; the doubt, the pain—"

Cal: "I mostly remember confusion. I'm much less confused now."

Mayra, with a shrug: "Yes, that's true, but—"

"We need to go," Fox announced, apparently no longer willing to carry on the conversation. "We have the ledger, obviously, and we have the now-mobile ghost, so—"

"Yes, that's true, we should go," Mayra agreed, fidgeting slightly. "Soon. I don't have a very good feeling about this."

"Soon as in now, I presume," Isis suggested. "Right?"

"Yes, yes, to the tables, then," Brandt absently agreed, digging around in his jacket pocket and frowning. "Ah, rats, where'd I put that key—"

"Hang on," Fox cut in loudly.

Brandt, startled, took a hasty step back as Fox strode furiously toward him.

"Fox, what the—"

He broke off, grimacing, as Fox unceremoniously proceeded to pat him down, hands smacking with perfunctory ease against Brandt's chest before sloping down to the angles of his hips. Then Fox sank to a crouch, taking care to check Brandt's trouser pockets, and proceeded to groan aloud as he reached under Brandt's trouser leg, revealing the small bottle that Brandt had tucked into his sock.

"Really?" Fox demanded, rising to his feet with the bottle firmly in hand. "Dessert wine from Bacchus?"

His face was so close to Brandt's he could count the freckles, align them like stars.

"In my defense," Brandt replied stiffly, "I'd have taken more if I could have."

"That is *not* a defense!" Fox barked.

"Eh," Isis said, shrugging. "I don't know about that. It checks out."

"How could it possibly—" Fox cut himself off, shaking his head. "No. I just—no. Let's just go—"

"What did you steal from my house?" Tom demanded.

"Nothing," Brandt said, the torn pages of his book nestled securely in the lining of his coat, which Fox had never learned to check. "Everything in your house is terrible."

"That's true," sighed Tom.

"Are we clear?" Fox said. "I said we're leaving!"

"Well, if you said it," Isis sniffed, "then I suppose it *must* be true—"

"Come on," Brandt said, shaking his head and ushering them forward. "Before Fox ruptures his spleen."

— Ω —

"Fox," Cal said, nudging him as they prepared to walk through Brandt's latest invisible Otherworld door. "Can I see the ledger?"

"Why?" Mayra asked, abruptly alarmed. "What interest do you have in it?"

Cal frowned. "I'm just curious," he said. "I've never actually seen a ledger, and I just thought—"

"It's not very interesting," Fox assured him. "Not like a mortal's ledger. This is more like a bookie's."

"I guess," Cal said, still looking vaguely disappointed.

"I'll show you when we get there," Fox promised. "For now, though, you should probably keep the peace," he pointed out, gesturing to where Isis was gleefully baiting what must have been the ghost.

Cal looked over at the crackle of spectral static with a sigh. "Isn't that Mayra's job?"

"No," Mayra replied. "I'm more of a morality police than a peacekeeper."

To that, Cal flashed her his fifth smile; the one Fox knew he reserved for her.

*"Fine,"* Cal said in feigned exasperation, hurrying to catch up to where Isis was now antagonizing Brandt, goading him until he promptly dropped the key, pausing to pinch the bridge of his nose.

"Mayra Kaleka, you troublesome angel," Fox murmured, turning to face her in Cal's absence. "You *do* realize he's going to know eventually."

"I take it you already saw, then," she said, chewing her lip, and he nodded.

"It's not like he won't forgive you," Fox assured her. "He's—" He paused. "You know. Not likely to hold it against you."

"Still," she lamented, jade eyes falling to her clasped hands. "I'm not proud of it."

"So?" He gave her a nudge, hoping to lift her spirits. "I'm not proud of most things I've done."

"I don't know about that," she said with the lift of one brow. "You're pretty boastful of your conquests."

"Don't *objectify* them, Mayra."

"Hush, Fox—"

"Fox," Brandt cut in, calling to him from the door between worlds and gesturing to the threshold the others had already passed through. "Are you coming?"

"Ready?" Mayra asked him, resting her hand fraternally on his shoulder.

Fox sighed.

"Nope," he said.

Mayra smiled, brushing his cheek with her thumb before walking through (reserving a moment for petty vengeance, which in this case was a narrowed glance at Brandt). Fox, meanwhile, prepared himself to step through the frame behind her, pausing only when he noticed that Brandt seemed lost in thought, his eyes alighting with a jolt on Fox's face.

"Will it be as I remember it?" Fox asked quietly, for only Brandt to hear.

"Depends how you remember it," Brandt said.

"A dark room. Maybe a dozen tables?" Fox mused. "I remember the smoke more than anything. The general seediness," he added, making a face, and Brandt shrugged.

"The tables have been closed for years," Brandt reminded him. "Death hasn't been compelled to play in over a century, and this is no normal game. This is a tournament," he clarified. "This will be once in a lifetime, Fox."

"Once in a mortal lifetime, or yours?" Fox asked dryly.

Brandt shrugged again.

"I suppose we'll see," he said, gesturing for Fox to enter.

— Ω —

Stepping through the door was as Fox had hazily recalled. There was a foyer, or perhaps a lobby—there didn't seem to be an appropriate word for whatever it meant to wait for this particular event—that led to a much larger atrium, which wasn't visible from the head of the queue, but which Fox remembered as having vaulted ceilings resembling the celestial sky. (At the time Fox had first seen it, the room containing the tables had looked how he imagined Olympus might look. In more recent times, however, he could more aptly compare it to the Venetian Hotel in Las Vegas.)

In something of a show of solidarity, the others of their motley coalition had stepped aside to allow Fox to go first, giving him the sense that he was walking into some sort of lurid nightclub.

"Names?" asked the guardian spirit at the door to the tables, his (her? *their*) expression solemn.

"Fox D'Mora," Fox supplied.

"New player," the tutelary spirit replied. "Next?"

Cal stepped forward as Fox hung back. "Calix Sanna."

"Observer?"

"Yes," replied Cal.

"Fine." Cal stood beside Fox for less than a second before venturing on ahead toward the tables, unable to deny his curiosity. "Next?"

"Viola Marek," offered a nervous Vi. "Also an observer."

"As you wish. Next?"

"Isis Bernat."

The spirit looked up, alarmed.

"Does he know you're—"

"Observer," Isis said sharply.

The spirit blinked.

"Fine," they said uncomfortably. "Next?"

"Brandt Solberg."

"Existing player. You are required to sit at the tables."

"If you say so," Brandt replied.

"That way," the spirit instructed, gesturing in a different direction than Fox had been directed, though he wasn't given the opportunity to wonder why.

"Hey, Fox," Cal called to him from just inside the atrium. "Come look at this."

"What is it now, Calix?" Fox sighed, abandoning his post just as Tom was about to finish up the queue. "More moldings? The light fixtures, perhaps? Or do you—"

He broke off, astounded, as he joined Cal where he stood, hovering at the threshold of the atrium.

"Fuck," said Fox.

"Band," said Cal.

*"Fuck,"* Fox repeated.

"What are you—oh," Isis exhaled, joining them to stare up at the view.

"'Oh' is right," Cal murmured.

Where there should have been a set of walls there was instead a structure of cages that climbed from floor to ceiling, each one a strangely ornate framework of twisting gold bars. It was as if a series of large, glittering birds had chosen to take up residence against the wall, only instead of feathered occupants, there were a series of figures—some human-looking, some not—that stared down at the perimeter of separate, orderly cubicle-style rooms, each one hosting a table within impossibly thin walls of glass (or ice, Fox thought, bemused) that were watched studiously from above.

At a strange, hollowed-out basin where an apse might have stood in a church, a lone table sat in the shadows. Inside the stadium-style depression of what had once been a suitably normal atrium, the hooded form of Death sat perfectly still, his hands bound with glowing ropes to the wood of the table before him.

"Is this what you remembered?" Vi asked, her voice startling Fox to a shudder.

"No," he confessed, his stomach abruptly manifesting a terrible storm of knots. "No. This isn't what I remember at all."

— Ω —

"Where've you been?" Lainey hissed, grabbing for Brandt's arm once he rounded the corner from the entryway.

"I don't have to answer that," he told her smoothly, detaching himself from her grip. "It's not part of the deal."

"Still." She looked nervous. "You shouldn't have brought so many of them," she muttered. "And you shouldn't have taken so long."

"It's not my fault these were the conditions I had to work with," Brandt said. "And anyway, I'm here, aren't I?"

She muttered something like agreement.

"Do they know?" she asked.

"Know what?"

"Anything."

"No," Brandt replied. "Of course not."

She chewed her lip. "Are you—"

"Sure?" he guessed. "No. But when can one ever really be sure of anything, *jenta mi*?"

"You are infuriating, godling," she forced through her teeth with a glare.

"That I am," he agreed. "But you have to admit," he couldn't help adding, glancing over his shoulder at where Fox stood looking out at the final table, "I'm also wildly effective."

# XXI

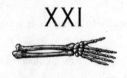

## THE TABLES

When Vi first wandered into one of the partitioned rooms and saw it, she was fairly convinced it was just a normal table.

It wasn't ornate or kitschy. It wasn't especially large, and it had no particular novelties. She'd expected something like a poker table (or—for some reason—a pool table, with that green felt lining along the inside, but that might have simply been because she lacked familiarity with games) but there was nothing much to be said about it when she was actually standing next to it.

It was made of—

She paused, knocking on it.

It was made of wood.

Definitely wood.

Okay. So it was a normal, unremarkable *wooden* table.

There was no special evidence of wear, she noticed, which was probably not unusual considering it was one of many that were owned and operated by two archangels, but it was the sort of table she might have expected to see in a small dining room; maybe somewhere in a starter apartment, or a loft of some sort. Something owned by two artists in Brooklyn, or possibly Bucktown. Just a regular dining table that the young couple—Roxanne-called-Roxy and Martin-called-Barns, Vi decided, opting to give the figments of her imagination appropriately artsy names—found at their first ever merchant fair; or maybe just something they found at a rummage sale and that Roxy decided she just *had* to have, even though she knows that within months, the table, just like every other piece of furniture they own, will have several concentric ring-stains on the surface (from ice-cold beers on too-hot days with no air conditioning, forgotten and left to drip down into the wood while Barns is making love to her on the kitchen floor).

Vi cleared her throat, glancing askance before returning her attention to the empty room.

So, yeah. A normal wooden table.

Fancifully, though, Vi tilted her head to check for marks of imaginary condensation, eyeing the tabletop surface and then crouching down to look at the table legs, following the path of the strange, oddly nostalgic daydream of a life she'd never get to have.

She lurched forward slightly as she bent, losing her balance, and steadied herself against the wood, something searing through her mind; a bright, opalescent sunburst behind her eyes. She faltered, blinking it away, and then straightened, feeling something course through her fingers and buzz through her shoulders, expelling from her system like a shudder as she hastily drew her palm back from the wood. She eyed her fingers, her palm, then reached out again, tentative.

Another sunburst. She gasped, surfacing from the vision, and blinked.

Okay. So maybe it was slightly more than a normal wooden table.

Vi glanced around a second time before resting both palms flat atop its surface, closing her eyes. It was smoother this time, less abrupt, and far less like a lurching free fall—but still, there was a sensation she couldn't put a finger on. Like being in the eye of a hurricane, with everything spun around her while she remained rooted in place. Her feet kissed the ground impossibly lightly despite a rush, a jagged tear through time and place that seemed to have unglued itself from her, coming loose.

*So this is the game,* she thought, and though she knew that somewhere, her eyes were closed and her hands were resting carefully on a normal-abnormal table, a second set of eyes seemed to open, and a second set of hands felt a breeze flutter beneath her palms. She took a breath, smelling the crispness of it—feeling the sun's rays licking solemnly across her skin as a branch rustled gently overhead—and felt another set of lungs come into being, expanding with a force so sharp she felt the aftershocks like needles in the expanse of her chest.

To her right, she heard—no, she recalled, she *sensed*, somehow, because somewhere, in a place more real than this one, her eyes remained closed in an empty room with her hands on a normal-abnormal table—the presence of a waterfall; she was somewhere in a forest, surrounded by foliage so lush she could gauge it only by its color, by its richness, by its spectacular flashes of texture and its corresponding assaults on her delicate, unpracticed senses.

It had been so long since things had been so thoroughly un-spoiled; years, in fact, since she'd last felt anything but a lingering chill up her spine.

She'd never been so conscious of being *dead*, in fact, than she was now, though it seemed that she was as alive as everything around her. To prove it, she headed for the water, making her way through branch and brush, faster and faster, running now, running, jump-ing, leaping, skidding to a halt only when the trees abruptly cleared, giving way to openness. To danger.

She would have flown clear over the cliff's edge, sinking to the depths below, had she kept going without slowing. She swung her arms at the perilous edge, flailing for balance, and felt her heart—her *heart,* pounding out the sound of her name as the blood in her veins matched the rush of the current below—stammer in fear, in panic.

In desperation.

She took a breath, tasting salt.

And then she jumped.

It was no different from an ordinary fall; the vertigo, the sensa-tion of her innards rising to her throat was the same as any drop on a roller coaster, the turbulence of an airplane, all things that had once felt so real that now only seemed like memories compared to *this*—to the gravity of it all. She wondered if she would hit the water, if she would drown, if she would die—and if maybe that had been always the truth about the game. If perhaps there were no cards and there was no luck and in fact there was nothing at all, nothing but this, the feeling of knowing that there was winning and losing and *living*—and coming to understand only moments before she crashed into the mirrored surface of the tide below that living and being alive were not even remotely the same.

She held her breath, preparing for the impact, and—

"What are you doing?" she heard from behind her, and realized she was standing back in the forest where she'd begun. She blinked, startled, and focused on Tom's voice, quieter and more thoughtful than she'd heard it before.

At the table, Vi opened her eyes.

Tom stood across from her, his palms floating above the table on the other side.

"What are you doing?" he repeated.

She paused, considering it.

"I don't know," she confessed.

He nodded.

"Can I come?" he asked.

She blinked.

"*Can* you?" she returned quizzically, in lieu of parsing the meaning of his question. "I mean, you're a ghost."

"Sure. But it's a magic table," he reminded her, and she paused again.

"To be honest, I don't really understand the rules," she admitted, and he smirked.

"Haven't you been listening?" he prompted. "There's only one rule."

"Don't lose?" she recited, and he nodded with a certain juvenile severity, like a child asked to confirm his one truth.

"Don't lose," he confirmed, "and I don't think it counts for a loss if I just come along, does it? Or maybe it does," he amended, frowning.

She considered it again.

"No, I think it would be okay," she decided, steadying herself. "Just, um. Close your eyes."

He nodded.

"Count of three?"

She nodded.

"One. Two. Thr—"

This time there was no forest.

"Well," Tom muttered, appearing beside her. "This is unpleasant."

It was so absurd she almost laughed.

"The Parker house," she sighed, glancing around the familiar foyer. "Of course. Sorry," she added, lacking any better vocabulary to address his disappointment, but she realized as she turned to face him that perhaps they'd been too hasty to presume that nothing had changed.

"Nice shirt," she commented, and he glanced down.

"Chambray," he noted. Quite outrageously, in Vi's opinion, seeing as there were far more pressing observations to be had.

"More relevantly, *unbloodied*," she pointed out. "Which is good, because I think I'd be more susceptible to blood here."

"Would you eat my heart in the marketplace, dear Viola?" he asked, grinning at her, and she rolled her eyes.

"You just love the gore of my predicament, don't you?"

"It just makes you so uncomfortable," he replied, "and seeing as your discomfort is about the only thing I can control, I guess I—"

He trailed off, staring absently into the corner, and Vi frowned.

"You what?" she prompted, but he didn't answer.

Instead, his hand shot out without warning, knocking the crystal vase to the ground.

Vi leapt back, alarmed, as it shattered but Tom only laughed; a full belly laugh with his head thrown back. As he did it, Vi noticed for the first time how much she had missed about him from never knowing him as he had lived. He'd been like a painting before, present and enchanted but fixed, constrained; and now he was awake, he was dynamic and imperfect and free, and he had come vibrantly to life.

His hair had been swept back from his eyes, the corners of them crinkled with humor, and there was something else, too—a *brightness* to him, somehow, that hadn't existed before. He didn't float back to her, either; he *ran*, tearing through the room to collide with her before throwing his arms around her waist and tossing her exuberantly into the air.

"*VI*-O-LAAAA," he sang, letting her down so unsteadily she grabbed behind her for the arm of a hideously upholstered velvet chair. "You have no idea how long I've wanted to break that stupid vase, and—"

He broke off, grinning at her, and held out one hand.

"Want to dance?" he asked, with a strange, alluring recklessness, and she felt her brow furrow; her pulse stutter; her heart bang.

"I don't really d—"

But he wasn't listening, pulling her into his arms and breaking into some sort of spirited, unrefined process of twirling that tore her breath from her chest, leaving her panting as he dropped her back into a supremely unsteady dip and then rose her up again, triumphant.

"Let's go outside," he announced, pulling her hand, and the space around them—the very air itself—shifted to bring them to the water's edge, their toes hovering dangerously above Lake Michigan's troubled, choppy surface.

He turned to face her, the Chicago wind whipping color into his cheeks, and smiled.

"Think we can do it?" he asked her, and she held her breath.

He'd never been this close to her.

Not really.

Not like this.

"Do what?" she rasped, and he leaned in as if he might confess a secret, or snatch the certainty from her lungs, or touch his lips to hers.

"Jump," he whispered, the tips of his hair falling into his eyes.

Her stomach convulsed in fear.

"What?"

But he had already grabbed her hand, pulling her into the lake and dragging her under the current.

She would have gasped if not for the threat of drowning. Instead she floundered, panicked, as the water swept in through her nostrils and filled her lungs, leaving her to kick frantically for the surface, to reach for the sun, the moon, and the stars. She struggled, she was struggling, and it felt real, more real than anything she'd experienced since she'd truly been alive, and for that she wondered at the irony. Because surely she was *dying*, wasn't she? Surely only death could feel like this, like pain and panic and desperation alike, and surely only her death would give her this sense of anticipation, that righteous sense of *now*—surely only death would feel as purely, wildly life-resembling as this—

But then Tom caught her fingers, dragging her up to the surface.

"Tom," she spluttered, coughing up lake water as her fingers shook with cold, and he turned to face her, flicking wet hair from his eyes.

"Vi," he said, and she shivered.

"Could have given me a little more warning," she grumbled, treading water beside him, and he laughed.

"And ruin the fun?" He reached for something, her hair or her mouth. She shoved him away. "You look like a drowned rat."

"Lovely," she muttered.

"It is," he promised, and it was her hair he'd been reaching for. He smoothed it back from her face. "Rats have a certain appeal. Naturally, so do you."

"Wow," Vi said, shaking her head. "Win me over, why don't you."

She looked down, trying to ascertain how deep the water was beneath them. Several feet, at least.

"I'm trying," Tom said, and she glanced up.

He was staring at her.

"I'm trying," he said again, and she swallowed.

"Is this the game?" she asked.

"Is what the game?"

"This," she said. "How do I know you're even really here?"

He pursed his lips. "How rude, Vi. How *dare* you, in fact—"

"Well," she said, sighing, "that helps."

"You believed in me when I was a ghost," he reminded her, "so I don't see why your faith in me should somehow lessen when you have me in your hands."

"Do I?" she asked. "Have you?"

"In the palm of your hand," he said, and it sounded suspiciously like a promise, but she shook her head, pulling away.

"This is the game," she said. "Isn't it?"

"Do you feel something?" he asked. "It doesn't feel like a game to me."

"But it is," she insisted. "And I think I understand it now."

And she did.

(Don't lose.)

(Gamble everything, but don't lose.)

"Careful," Mayra warned.

Vi shuddered to consciousness with a gasp, opening her eyes to find herself face to face with the angel, who leaned casually against the table's edge.

"Be careful," Mayra said again, her dark brow arched. "I wanted you to have a turn at one of the tables, but still—be careful you don't misplace yourself inside it."

Vi looked around for Tom; he had disappeared.

If, that is, he'd ever been there to begin with.

"Was it real?" Vi asked quietly, and Mayra shrugged.

"Isn't it all real?" she asked.

But Vi, who no longer felt capable of placing a finger on the fabric of reality, couldn't find an answer.

"Don't forget I heard your wish, Viola Marek." Mayra's voice was reassuring but firm, soft but steady. "I heard the secrets of your heart, and I can tell you with absolute certainty that you are not meant to play this immortal game."

"I," Vi began, and swallowed. "I wasn't . . . I just—"

"You may be managing things on the outside, Viola, but on the inside, you still cling to your mortal losses," Mayra said. "This game will ruin you, Viola Marek, because you still want much more from it than you could ever win. But some things," she added quietly, "are not meant to be gambled or won except through chance, or perhaps by fate. Or by lovely, foolhardy stubbornness."

"Is this your way of granting my wish, then?" Vi asked, and Mayra nodded.

"Not everything is a miracle," she said.

Vi's attention strayed across the table again to where Tom had stood, imagining his eyes on hers.

"But then again," Mayra said blithely, "perhaps some things are."

Vi swallowed hard, not entirely understanding, but nodded anyway.

"Have you seen Isis?" she asked, abruptly remembering. "She disappeared the moment we got here."

"I wouldn't look for her just now," Mayra said, with the air of knowing a touch too much. "I believe she has her own . . ." She trailed off, half smiling. "Demons."

"And you?" Vi asked. "Why exactly did you come along?"

"Well, two reasons. One is that I worry relentlessly about Fox," Mayra said. "He is very easily frustrated, and this game will not be easy for him. You can only hope that you raise them right," she sighed, flashing Vi a small smile.

"And the other reason?"

To that, Mayra hesitated.

"The truth is, Viola," Mayra said carefully, "that I know the game quite well."

"Ah," Vi said. "You're in the ledger, aren't you?"

Mayra nodded, her eyes drifting to the wood of the table before them. "I suspect I will be summoned at any moment. I was one of the last to play before Death refused to come to the tables. I'm quite certain I will be required to play again."

"How do you know that?" Vi asked. "That you were last, I mean."

Mayra shrugged.

"Some things a person just knows," she replied simply. "And when I faced Death, I could see that his time at the tables was coming to a close."

Vi nodded, watching Mayra's gaze drift along with her thoughts.

She wanted to ask why, but could see the question wouldn't be met with an answer.

"I don't know when I will be summoned to play again," Mayra continued, turning her attention back to Vi. "But Fox often has need of guidance, even if he will never ask. May I rely on you, in my absence?"

To Vi's uncertain blink, Mayra smiled. "You're sensible, Viola. He will need to be clear-eyed in order to win, and much as I adore Cal, he can be easily persuaded by his affection for Fox." She paused, looking saddened. "And he does not always see pain coming."

"But you see it coming?" Vi asked. "Why?"

Mayra spared her a wary glance.

"I see nothing," she demurred, shrugging. "What could I possibly know? I may be celestial now, but once I was only a woman, and a hard one at that. I did not know love during my lifetime. The only thing I ever truly knew was how to sense a storm. How to protect others from it, perhaps—at certain times when I was lucky—but never how not to be destroyed by it." She glanced away. "Perhaps you and I might agree to try our luck at blind faith, though, and see how that serves us."

"Not well, in my experience," Vi grumbled.

"Really?" Mayra asked, arching a brow. "He should be dead, you know," she mused, gesturing to where Tom had been, "as should you. You might have never crossed paths during your lifetimes, and it all might have simply ended there."

"Or we might have met in service to a couple of bored archangels," Vi pointed out, and Mayra chuckled.

"I don't serve them," she said. "I serve a world that may collapse on itself at any moment without someone to believe in it. To choose it."

Vi let Mayra drift into silence, comforted by her thoughts.

"Should I wish you luck?" Vi asked, after a moment. "For victory against a demon king?"

Mayra closed her eyes, half smiling.

"Now that," Mayra said, "would be a miracle, indeed."

— Ω —

"Well," Volos said. "This is a surprise."

Isis grimaced.

"Hello, husband," she said glumly.

"I take it there is something you need?" he prompted.

Better to get it over with. "I wondered if I still held any significance for you."

He didn't look surprised.

(Granted, he didn't look *pleased*, either, but he certainly didn't look surprised.)

"Bargaining for your friends, then, are you?" Volos looked somewhere between skeptical and amused. "Admirable, Isis, but not recommended. You know better than anyone what a deal with me means."

"Yes," Isis said. "And as much as I'd rather not revisit the consequences, unfortunately I think I should probably try to spare them the worst of it if I can."

"Oh, sweetheart," Volos said with a laugh. "You poor thing."

She folded her arms over her chest. It hadn't seemed like a good idea five minutes ago. It seemed like a worse one now.

"You look like him, you know," she remarked. "The ghost."

"Funny that," Volos agreed.

"I can't imagine the mortal is very comfortable in there. If he's even still in there," she amended.

"You know," Volos postured optimistically, "after sacrificing his entire family line, there's not much left of his will to contend with. He's really rather quiet."

"Still," Isis said. "That's a lot of mortal guilt."

"I do sometimes experience a headache sensation," Volos agreed. "Do you suppose that's the guilt?"

"No," Isis said, shaking her head. "Probably dehydration. Guilt is more intestinal, or so I've been led to believe."

"Ah, well, my digestion is perfectly fine," Volos assured her. "But thank you for asking, wife."

"I didn't," Isis said.

"Yes, I'm aware," Volos agreed, and briefly snapped his fingers, abruptly trapping her within her own ornate birdcage of twisted gold bars. "There," he determined, nodding firmly. "Shouldn't take long, love, and then I suppose you can come back to me, if you wish."

"The deal was that you wouldn't control me any longer," Isis said through gritted teeth. "Are you really going to defy your own queen, Volos?"

"That *was* the deal, sweets, but you broke it," Volos reminded her. "You came to find me, didn't you? In the end. So consider it null and void," he declared, snapping his fingers again to produce the thin parchment of the contract before tearing it neatly in two. "To tell you the truth, I suspect I will be wanting companionship once Death's sovereignty is at an end. I anticipate many pressing demands on my time."

He turned to leave then, vanishing the remains of their deal into the span of the air between them. It was over.

It was over, but Isis called out for him anyway.

"Volos!" she shouted, with the force of all the rage inside her, burning like embers on her tongue.

He turned slowly.

"Yes, wife?"

She glared at him.

Then she let the glare melt.

"Did you miss me?" she asked with all her softness, the words falling like petals from her lips.

The mortal's mouth quirked.

"Only a little," the demon king replied, pivoting around and striding away.

# XXII

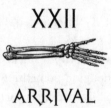

## ARRIVAL

There was a distinct aura of pearl-clutching hysteria around both the archangels, whose heads were bent in muted argument overlooking Death's final table when Fox spotted them and approached.

"Well," Raphael exhaled upon sight of him, "I see you're finally here."

"Yes, finally," Gabriel irritably agreed. "Never mind that we've been circling chaos for nearly four hundred rounds already. By all means, take your time."

Fox gamely chose to overlook that particular commentary. "I brought what you asked," he said, holding up Death's ledger. "And I brought the ghost as well, though I have no idea why he's necessary, and frankly, I'd like some answers of my own—"

"Tom says he also has questions," Cal supplied unnecessarily, and Gabriel flashed them both an impatient glare.

"Hush, hush, yes," Raphael said, snatching the scroll from Fox's hands and holding it up for Gabriel to peer at it over his shoulder. "Yes, it looks as though there is an opportunity to do as we discussed—"

"As we discussed?" Fox cut in.

"He and I we," Gabriel clarified. "Not you and he we."

"Which is?" Fox prompted, suppressing the urge to bang their heads together like a pair of coconuts (unclear whether the thought itself might impact his ledger, but again, that didn't matter and never had). "I certainly hope you've thought of something to get me out of this by now."

"Out of it? Of course not." Raphael looked plainly aghast at the suggestion. "You *must* play, Fox D'Mora, but seeing as you've taken so long, we're going to need to advance you in the tournament—"

"—which we will do," Gabriel added, "by entering the ghost in the tournament in Volos's stead."

Fox glanced at Cal, who abruptly ducked.

"Sorry," Cal said, dodging something they (or at least Fox) couldn't see. "He flails a bit when he's upset."

"How is entering the ghost in the tournament going to fix anything?" Fox demanded, nudging Cal away before he collided defensively with his chest. "Does that mean you get to have two players in the game?"

"No, no, of course not," Raphael corrected impatiently. "There are rules, after all. But his name is Thomas Edward Parker, yes?"

"Yes," Fox said, frowning. "But—"

"And he's called Tom, isn't he?"

"Yes, but—"

Gabriel pointedly held up the ledger, gesturing to the scripted *Thomas Edward Parker* that was scribbled into one of the lines, signifying the original Tom Parker's entrance to the game.

"Damn," Fox muttered, kicking himself.

(It was becoming increasingly clear that, somehow, this might have been his fault after all.)

"Call it a loophole," Gabriel informed him, "but a contract is a contract. Tom Parker may play for Tom Parker, which will at least manage to slow Volos down for a bit. It means he will miss at *least* one round, which is helpful, seeing as he's looked relatively unstoppable so far."

"But isn't that cheating?" Cal asked tentatively. "I think that Mayra would say that it is."

"Oh, really? Is it?" Raphael cut in sarcastically. "Thank goodness you're here to speak for her, then, seeing as we, her supervisors, had absolutely no idea—"

"It was only that it seemed like the stability of the universe was ever so slightly on the line," Gabriel added with an equally droll insouciance. "But forgive us our oversight, you're so right, we shouldn't *cheat*, not *now*, with *so very little* at stake—"

"Just go with them," Fox sighed, aiming at where Cal had ducked a second time. "The faster we get this over with, the faster we get to my godfather and get out of here."

"He says—" Cal broke off, staring. "Sorry, he's just, there's a lot of shouting—ah, okay, he says he doesn't understand why he's being held responsible when he couldn't manage to summon two f— ah, sorry, language . . . Okay, essentially," Cal summarized with a frown, "I think he's trying to say that he opposes the idea, and adds that he doesn't have a personal stake in the matter—"

"Well," Raphael informed the ghost briskly, "as a former mortal, you really should."

"Yes," Gabriel agreed. "To play for mastery of Death is to play for mastery of all mortality, in case it escaped your attention—"

"What's going on?" Vi interrupted, jogging up to them. "I was just with Mayra but she disappeared, so I thought she might have been summoned again—"

"Well, yes and no." Raphael exchanged a glance with Gabriel. "She'll have been extracted for her part in the game, I assume."

"Which is not a summons," Gabriel said, "but sure, close enough."

"The game?" Cal asked, looking slightly stunned. "Why would Mayra play this game?"

"That," Gabriel informed him loftily, "is none of your concern. As it is, we'll have to hurry. Volos is distracted at the moment, so let's take advantage and put the ghost in play for one of his tournament slots. He can play—" He glanced down, humming to himself as he searched the ledger. "Elaine. She's the only other immortal who's won any of the games so far, aside from Volos."

"What?" Vi asked, startled. "But Tom can't play Lainey, he'll—" She glanced over, looking a bit mournful. "I know you don't, Tom, but *still*, I don't think you should—"

"He doesn't have to win," Raphael supplied quickly. "Actually, it's better if he doesn't, seeing as he is now Volos for all intents and purposes. Either way, though, it buys Fox some time to win a few games—"

"If he can," Gabriel challenged roughly, his gaze cutting sideways to Fox. "Which I suppose we'll just have to find out, won't we?"

"For being the people who started this game, you sure have no faith in your ability not to lose it," Fox commented to the archangels. (Vi and Cal were silent, suffering the knowledge of Tom and Mayra's involvement, respectively.)

"Well, *we* wouldn't lose," Raphael said. "First of all, we're not people."

"At best, we're entities," Gabriel added, "but we can't play. We're not in the ledger."

"Rightfully," Raphael contributed. "As this entire game is stupid and reckless."

"Yes," Gabriel confirmed. "Thus its undeniable appeal, unfortunately. It's a cycle of misfortune that begins with boredom and ends with suffering." He paused. "And then shuffles back to boredom again."

"Which is, again, partly your godfather's doing," Raphael reminded Fox. "The suffering part, that is. There's a reason he's the end of the game's ledger. He was the first to play, and thus he'll be the last to win or lose."

"Why not simply trust him?" Fox asked, glancing between them. "He's never lost before. Why would he lose now?"

The two archangels exchanged an uneasy glance.

"It's just best not to underestimate Volos," Raphael eventually said.

"Yes," Gabriel agreed. "Better to stop him before he has a chance."

"Well," Fox sighed, striding ahead to the nearest empty table. "I suppose there's nothing left to do but try to get to my godfather, then."

$$- \Omega -$$

"Are you sure?" Vi whispered to Tom, wishing she could take his hand as she had earlier before immediately registering what Mayra had said; that this—to feel as she did—naturally rendered her unhelpful.

"Whether I'm sure or not, I doubt it matters," Tom muttered back. "And anyway, I'm actually relieved that it's Lainey, seeing as

I have some questions I'd like answered. Namely," he exhaled, "precisely *how* responsible she is for my death, because I no longer have any doubt that she is."

It was a fair point, though not a very helpful one. The game only had one rule, and Tom wasn't in much of a position to win.

"Be careful in there," Vi said, and swallowed. "In the game, I mean. It feels—like nothing else, really." She hadn't noticed that she'd paused until it had been silent for a beat too long, unintentionally leaving room for a larger confession. "I only mean," she blurted hastily, "that it's—it's very, um—"

"I was there, Vi," Tom said, his gaze sliding to hers. "That was really me."

She held her breath; let it out.

"Oh," she managed.

His face warmed with something that might have been a smirk, though she was feeling optimistic. Maybe it was a smile.

"Worried about me, Viola?" Tom asked.

She laced her fingers together, trapping her apprehension somewhere she could still control. Managing, as it were, her condition.

"Well," she replied steadily, "I do still have a house to sell, you know. I'd rather not expend my energy for nothing."

Tom kindly pretended not to hear the underlying gravity of her concern.

"You never fail to disappoint me," he murmured fondly, shaking his head.

— Ω —

"Hello, Tom," Lainey said quietly.

He had always assumed his attraction to her was for obvious, normal reasons. The raven of her hair, the ebony of her skin. Gold winked from her ears, glittering around her neck, her shoulders glistening with a sheen of iridescence. The curve of her hip—he knew its shape in the dark, from afar, as above and so below—it rolled like a wave, or the line of a cove. Maybe she had always reminded him of the ocean.

Or maybe he was weak, and she was hot.

"Hello, Elaine," he replied. "Are you ready?"

"Yes, actually," she said, and if he had been hoping for any semblance of shame or remorse, he didn't receive it. "Do be careful, will you?"

"With what?" He tried to imagine a world where she'd been a threat to him all along. It felt the same, pretty much. She'd always been bad for him. "With you?"

"He'll be very angry," she said simply. "When he discovers what you've done, he'll take it out on you and Fox. Not the archangels. And I," she added with a sigh, "cannot allow you to lose, Tom."

Fair warning. She'd never given him that before. "I can handle you just fine on my own, Lainey."

"I always liked when you called me that," she said. "Elaine is my real name. Did you know that? My true name. You always made me feel so normal when you called me Lainey, but it unnerved me when you called me by my name." She paused, her gaze drifting. "It was almost like you knew, all along, what I really was."

"Did I?" Tom asked, as she tilted her head, exposing the familiar line of her neck.

She didn't answer.

"Come on, Tom," she beckoned with a sigh, letting her palms rest against the table just before she closed her eyes. "Let's play."

# XXIII

## THE IMMORTALS' GAME

*"Tom, you remember Lainey, don't you?" Mrs. Wood asked, setting down a plate of cookies on that sticky-hot day in August. "She's been at St. Cecilia's in Boston, but she'll be starting at University of Chicago this fall."*

*The girl across the table looked up, meeting his eye.*

*"Lainey," Tom repeated, testing her name in his mouth.*

*The Lainey Wood he remembered had been a stiff, colorless girl with almost no interesting features. They'd spent every summer forced together at the Woods' VIP Box at Wrigley listening to their parents discussing business—or else the so-called Curse of the Billy Goat, as if a goat could be more responsible for the Cubs' resounding performance flaws than their lack of talent.*

*The Lainey Wood that Tom Parker had once been forced to accompany in her virgin-white ball gown and equally colorless expression had been a sour, unpleasant girl with no particular thoughts, other than perhaps her hair and the dignity of fulfilling her parents' wishes. She'd been sullen, uninterested (and uninteresting, more importantly) and even Tom, who'd been in the midst of discovering the full scope of what, precisely, his dick was capable of doing, could not have managed an iota of interest, making a point to take her home immediately after her debutante ball ended and ignoring her friend requests from there.*

*The Lainey Wood he remembered had watery blue eyes, indeterminate blond-brown hair, and clear but unremarkable skin. She had the posture of a girl who had been too tall for her age too early, always slumped. She had not been poised, hadn't been beautiful, and she certainly hadn't been breathtaking.*

*And yet here he was now, holding his breath.*

*This girl, whoever she was, held up a finger to her full, berry-tinted lips, locking her dark gaze on his.*

*"Hello, Tom," she said, as if she knew why he was staring. Daring him to look away.*

*"Hello, Elaine," he choked out, wondering why he'd never really looked at her before.*

— Ω —

"I don't understand," Vi said nervously, watching Tom's fingers grip the edge of the table more tightly. "What's happening?"

"Ah," Raphael said, waving a hand. "Sorry. Forgot you can't see everything."

The projection of a young Tom and what appeared to be his introduction to a young Lainey Wood plastered itself onto the glass walls around them, and Vi took a step forward to see more closely, watching a foreign look of wonder fill Tom's eyes.

"How is this a game?" she asked with a frown. "It looks like a memory."

"Well, it is and it isn't," Gabriel replied. "Elaine won the toss, so she chose to start the game with a memory."

"Hers, or his?" Cal asked.

"His, by the look of it," Raphael supplied, displeased. "Which already puts him at a disadvantage."

Vi swallowed. "Disadvantage? How?"

"Well, you tell us," Gabriel postured with a scoff. "How hard is it for *you* to relive your past?"

*Fair point,* she thought. "But how was he supposed to—"

"What, prevent it?" Raphael guessed accurately, and shrugged. "It's certainly possible, but there's a reason some are better than others at this game."

"You mean it's a game for liars and cheats," Cal said to his hands.

"It's a game for *immortals*," Gabriel amended for him.

"Yes," Raphael agreed, "and I said what I said."

— Ω —

*Lainey pulled Tom into her dorm room, signaling for him to be quiet.*

*"My roommate's asleep," she whispered.*

*"Could go to my house," he suggested, fingers greedily dug into the softness of her waist. "Or yours."*

*She made a face.*

*"I don't like it there," she said.*

*"Where, yours or mine?"*

*"Either one," she replied with a shudder. "Your house is creepy. Mine is . . ."*
*She trailed off. "It's just not home. I prefer when we can be in our own space."*

*She gave his arm a tug, leading him inside her dorm, and he felt something;*
*a nameless sensation of what came next, like for a quick hitch of time he could*
*see well into the future. Like he was standing in the frame with two handfuls of*
*futures and pasts, all of it gripped between white-knuckled fists, and it occurred*
*to him that he no longer felt like a natural part of the landscape.*

*He felt, too, a stab of something he was certain hadn't been there before.*

*"Lainey, I—"*

He paused, freezing in the doorframe.

*"Tom?" she prompted.*

He took a step back, testing. Another step. He turned, as if to
leave, and suddenly the vision shifted.

"You're learning," Lainey remarked.

She rematerialized in front of him in the corridor of her dorm,
which dissolved, becoming instead a room with gleaming white walls.
It was lit by nothing and yet, somehow, incandesced from within,
glowing impossibly with light.

"Is this the game?" Tom asked, glancing around them with a
frown. "Is it simply that I can control things now, or—?"

"You could always control things," Lainey pointed out. "You
could have left back then, too, when it happened between us the first
time. But you didn't."

"So say I do it over," Tom suggested. "Say I don't follow you inside. Say I never sleep with you, and you never have any power over
me." It was a distillation of what they'd had, a half-truth at best, but
he'd spent so long fighting for the upper hand it felt unnatural to
concede it now. "What happens then?"

"You can't actually do it over," Lainey told him. "The game
doesn't transcend—"

"Reality?" he guessed.

She considered it, then shook her head. "The past," she corrected.

"What's past is passed, and cannot be altered. But reality is, of course, always subject to your choices. To what you alone believe to be real."

He considered this, frowning.

"What were you going to do from here?" he asked. "If I hadn't turned away, I mean."

"Remind you," Lainey said simply. "I would have reminded you of what we had, and what we were."

"You were bored," Tom said, and then paused, swallowing. "You were always bored, always rebelling for no reason. There were no consequences for you." He paused, blinking. "You used me, actually. Many times, now that I think about it."

"And yet you thought you were in control," Lainey countered, "didn't you?"

Around him, the scene shifted.

*The walls were white, the sheets were white, the sun bore down white-hot onto the pillow beside him, and Lainey's ever-changing raven hair was draped across him, strewn out in braids like rivulets across his chest from where she leaned against him. All of it was gleaming, all of it was fragile; all of it was at once steadying to his constitution, and yet in perilous danger of collapse.*

*"This never happened," he whispered to her, and she shook her head.*

*"No," she agreed. "This is the game."*

*He drew a finger up the side of her arm, watching her shiver.*

*"Funny how real this is," he said, "and still, how real it isn't."*

*She twisted around to look at him.*

*"You think we weren't real?" she asked, her fingers splayed across his chest.*

*"You did contribute to my murder," he reminded her. "A bit difficult to romanticize that, don't you think?"*

*"That," she said, chewing her lip, "was a precondition of knowing you."*

*"What, killing me?"*

*She shrugged. "I had a debt to pay, long before we met. It doesn't mean that you meant nothing. It doesn't mean we weren't real."*

*He wasn't sure he believed her.*

*He certainly wasn't sure he agreed.*

*"That seems like quite a price," he said slowly. "Shouldn't some costs be too high?"*

"Careful," she warned. "That's the sort of attitude that will cost you the game, and Volos will never forgive me if I let you lose."

"How can you possibly force me to win?" Tom demanded.

Lainey looked away, sighing, and glanced back.

"Close your eyes," she said.

"No."

"Tom, don't be stubborn."

"It's called self-preservation, actually, E—"

He broke off. She shook her head.

"Close your eyes," she said, "and I'll show you how you died."

He paused, his mouth opening, and then he snapped his jaw shut.

"You can do that?"

She nodded. "The tables can do that."

He withered.

"Fine," he said, and closed his eyes.

"Now open them," she said.

"This is a stupid game."

"Just do as you're told, Tom."

"I don't see why I have to—"

He broke off, registering the woman in his arms as his eyes snapped open.

"What does reality feel like now?" Lainey asked, wearing Vi's features as her own.

"Stop," Tom said instantly, scrambling away from her in the bed. "Leave Vi out of it, she doesn't—she isn't—"

He stopped, staring at her. At the softness of her eyes, the same shade as Lainey's but indescribably different. Not the color or the shape. More like the crinkles beside them, the mirth she concealed so carefully but still couldn't help but show.

When Lainey smiled, Tom suddenly knew it had never been real.

She may have felt love with him, but it had never been free. It had never been joy.

"You want me to win this game?" he asked, suddenly registering what she'd said.

Vi-Lainey nodded. "You have to," she said. "I can't win it for you, Tom, it has to be you, and you do not want to be a loser in this game. You will never understand the pain of loss until you have lost this game."

*Tom hesitated.*

*"You can't use her against me, then," he said quietly. "If you do—"*

*Lainey had found his weakness. He had known it a long time ago, long be-fore he asked Vi to come with him for no reason other than the one that kept her close. Maybe he'd known it the moment she'd set eyes on him, in some manner of speaking, because it was the first, the only time Tom Parker had been witnessed, and it was easier to be cruel than it was to be seen.*

*"Yes," Lainey agreed. "If I use her, I win. And you lose."*

*"But don't you also lose in some way," he said slowly, "because it's proof that I no longer love you?"*

*"Ah, but the tricky thing about love," Vi-Lainey said, inching toward him, "is that it can save you just as much as it can hurt you. Don't you see?" she asked, Vi's dark eyes lit with pain as she drew her fingertips over his cheek. "Don't you see that this is how I'll win? Because I love you enough to destroy the depths of myself?"*

*She leaned closer, her lips near his ear.*

*"If you defy Volos and lose this game, there will be consequences," she whis-pered. "The king of vice will take her. He is accustomed to taking; he does it easily, and you cannot fight him, not here, in his domain. So to spare the both of you—because I love you, Tom—I will not allow you to lose. But I cannot allow myself to lose either. Not again."*

*The implications were clear: she had moved her piece on the board. She had used his heart against him to the detriment of her own, and for it, she would win.*

*Two choices, then. Do as the archangels asked and lose; confess his heart and thereby admit his selfishness, his vice. Lose, and risk something—someone—that was not, and had never been, a game.*

*So maybe it was only one choice. One rule.*

*"Elaine," Tom sighed. "You're always trapping me, aren't you?"*

*She leaned away.*

*"Do you love me?" she asked, in Vi's voice.*

Don't you see I love you enough to destroy the depths of myself?
*(This is how you save her.)*

*"No," Tom forced out, wrenching the pain of it from his chest.*

*At once Vi sparkled back into Lainey, her features glowing and luminous.*

*"Very good, Tom," Lainey said softly, drawing his lips back to hers.*

— Ω —

"It's only a game, Vi," Cal said, his hand closing around her shoulder.

She couldn't bring herself to shake his touch.

*I know,* she tried to say, but couldn't quite manage it.

— Ω —

Fox climbed down the stadium steps to find Death with his wrists bound to the table, his human mask worn and ragged as he bent his head over the wood, contemplating the grains.

"Papa," Fox opened, tutting with disapproval. "This," he said, gesturing around the gilded coliseum, "isn't by chance the thing you wanted to tell me about earlier, is it?"

Death glanced up, slowly shaking his head. "You shouldn't fucking be here."

"Band," said Fox.

"Don't have it." Death gestured to the shackles around his wrists.

*Fair enough,* thought Fox.

"Want to tell me what all this is about?" he asked instead, forcing his usual air of geniality. "You appear to be in some sort of trouble."

Death's eyes weren't quite right, not as they usually were. The human quality Fox had always abstractly known was false was discolored, disfigured, more spectral. "It shouldn't concern you, Fox."

"It shouldn't," Fox agreed, "and yet it does."

Death said nothing.

"It seems that the past is never really passed for us, is it?" mused Fox.

"I always wondered whether I would have to pay." Death cast a look at his hands. "This is the cost of my arrogance, it seems."

"You know," Fox ventured, "what I don't understand is why everyone's so worried. You've never lost before, have you?" he prompted, and Death shook his head. "Then why would you lose now?"

"I will lose," Death said simply.

"You say that, but—"

"I will lose," Death repeated. "You do not understand the game, Fox."

"You're right about that," Fox agreed. "I have no concept of what this is, or why people are so desperate to play it. The archangels say they're losing on purpose," he added. "The other immortals and creatures." Different than Tom losing, of course, because Tom was playing as a loophole for Volos. The other immortals were forfeiting of their own volition, voluntarily paying the price for their loss. "They're letting Volos win."

"I expect they will," Death said. "Many of them have reasons to oppose me, and the loss of me makes very little difference to them."

"Why?" Fox asked. "Because you're such a tyrant, Papa?"

"Because I cheat," Death said flatly. (Selfishly, Fox was relieved that Brandt was not there to hear it.) "Or so they call it, anyway, when I attach my conditions to their prizes."

"So then simply cheat again," Fox urged him. "Do whatever you have to, Papa, but I don't think you can rely on me to win. I don't see why I would be any better at this than you are."

"Well, of course you don't see it," Death told him. "You're a mortal."

Fox groaned. "Not *this* again—"

"Yes, this again," Death said firmly. "You're not one of us, Fox, and for once, that gives you an advantage. Because for you, there are things worth winning for. It is why a mortal has managed to win this game before, and why you must win again now—because for you, the reward is always greater. It will always be more than anything you could make for yourself, and so your costs will always be less."

"Not for Tom Parker," Fox noted, referencing the man under Volos's command, and Death blanched.

"Well, I underestimated him," he said. "I have a long history of doing so."

"Of underestimating Tom?"

"Of discounting mortality," Death corrected, looking saddened as his gaze met Fox's. "Had I sorted that out long ago, I'd have been far better for it."

Fox politely side-stepped the comment as related to himself.

"How did Tom Parker die?" he asked instead.

"He didn't," Death said. "He's in there still, somewhere inside the host he's currently serving for Volos. He bargained with the king of vice, it seems, after the curse I levied on him. The curse of insatiability," he clarified, "which seemed more humanity's doing than mine at the time. I thought he would succumb to me eventually, like any normal mortal, but I suppose no one is ever the same after playing this game."

"Not him," Fox corrected. "I meant Tom Parker the fourth. The ghost."

"Ah," Death said. "Volos killed him."

Fox frowned. "Not the siren?"

"Water deity," Death corrected. "More mermaid than siren, really, though that's mostly semantics."

"Fine. Not her?"

"She certainly contributed," Death permitted. "But it was Volos who killed him, in the end."

He paused; Fox, meanwhile, wondered if that was really the entire truth.

"Strange, isn't it?" Fox asked, chewing his thoughts. "That all of this would converge so . . . neatly."

"Oh, Fox." Death reached up wearily, pausing when the chains cut off his progress partway. "You misunderstand. This is no coincidental convergence; this is a series of events that is entirely my responsibility. My doing. You—" he exhaled bitterly "—should not be held accountable."

Fox watched Death's shoulders stoop, bowing beneath something weighty and unfulfilled, and suffered a surprising breath of opposition.

"But I'm your son," Fox said, and at the words, Death looked up, startled.

"Papa." It seemed so simple all of a sudden. So obvious. They had never fully reconciled, not really, not in this way. Neither of them had ever really come out and said it; instead, they'd danced around it, pretended otherwise, never acknowledging the bleeding. Never attempting to heal the wound. "I am Fox D'Mora, aren't I?" Fox asked him. "I am *of Death*, Papa, and I have known no other father. So why shouldn't I be the one to absolve you of your wrongs?"

Death flinched.

"Because I will lose," he said softly. "I will lose because I have a regret, a terrible one, and such things are more powerful than you can imagine, Fox. They outlast even me, and the regret I have is no small thing." He looked up, pained. "You will not like what you see, Fox, when you see what I have done."

Fox forced the warning voice in his ear aside.

"I won't let you lose," he said. "Just tell me how to win, Papa," he exhaled, just shy of pleading, "and I promise you, I'll make certain you don't lose."

Death paused for a moment, glancing again at the grains of the table before him.

"Listen very carefully, then," he opened.

Fox leaned forward in communion, as he had done so many times before.

"This," said Death, "is how you win the game."

— Ω —

"Hello, Mayra Kaleka," said the king of vice.

She lifted her chin.

"You will not own me," she informed him. "No man has."

"Yes," Volos agreed. "But I am not a man, am I? Your body does not interest me, and I will not try to take your pride. I know that I cannot," he added spiritedly, "because I am not vain enough to believe it possible, nor do I think it's worth the trouble of finding out." He winked at her, folding his arms over his chest. "A mortal's pride is of little value to me, Mayra Kaleka, unless it earns me what I want."

"Then what will you have from me, Volos?" she demanded, summoning strength to the gaps in her constitution, filling up the holes of doubt. "There is nothing you can take that wasn't stripped from me while I lived."

"Oh, on the contrary," he murmured, chuckling, and cleverly changed his mask.

"I will take your heart," said Calix Sanna in the voice of the king of vice.

— Ω —

"People have secrets, Fox," said Death. "And it's easy enough to tap into them because few can ever truly conceal them. Understand a person's heart, what makes them soft and what makes them hard, and find the source of their materials."

"And then?" Fox asked.

Death shrugged. "Then drive it in them like a knife."

— Ω —

*"I need a reaper," Fox was saying to Cal, a perilously familiar replaying of the moment when Mayra had first seen him; the day she had first seen the dark curls he wore like a crown, and the smile he reserved only for her. "Can we rely on you?"*

*"Who is we?" Cal had asked, his eyes traveling to where Mayra stood. "Are you part of this too, angel?"*

*The curve of his mouth had always been like a caress, an embrace, and she felt it down to her soul, down to the crevices of her heart, buried in the places that only she could touch—*

"Get out," Mayra said stiffly, forcing the memory away. "This isn't for you, Volos."

The scene shifted.

"How long can you hold me off, angel?" Volos asked, materializing at her side to lean with his arms folded, propped against a gleaming white wall. "You can't keep me out forever, you know, and you certainly can't win."

"I can win," Mayra countered, teeth gritted. "I'm far stronger than you think."

"Strength doesn't win," Volos replied, conjuring a white-frothed beverage from nothing and taking a sip, deeming it satisfactory before continuing. "I merely have to outlast your own demons," he clarified, "and being one myself, I should think it well within my pool of talents."

"I have no demons," Mayra lied.

Volos chuckled. "Sure you don't."

— Ω —

"You must hold your own, Fox. Deception will help, if you can manage it. It will be harder or easier depending on the talent of your opponent, but it will be a gamble either way.

"You must know yourself, without reservation, in order to properly defend your weaknesses. More importantly, though, you must know yourself better than your opponent. You must know that they will strike if you give them ammunition; they will reach where they are not invited in; so then give them something that's easy to see, and let them believe it to be more than it is."

— Ω —

*"So, this is it, then," Tom said, circling Lainey where she knelt with her head bent against his chest, her tears slipping into his blood as he lay cold and unmoving on the floor of the Parker mansion. "This is how I died? You killed me?"*

*"Yes," she replied, not looking at him. "And you can see how much it pained me."*

*Tom looked around the room, placing himself in his memories. He recalled the sensations he had already relived so many times; the pattern of the blood splatter on the floor and the emptiness of the room when he awoke.*

*Tom paused his circling, glancing back down at where her fingers wrapped around the bloodied knife.*

*"This isn't how it happened," he said, and watched her stiffen.*

*"Yes, it is."*

*"No, actually, it isn't," he informed her. "You want me to win the game, don't you?"*

*She hesitated. "That doesn't mean—"*

*"You want me to win the game," Tom continued, "but you also have to win, so you want me to feel as if I've beaten you, somehow." He scrutinized the scene again, looking for its imperfections. "This must be a lie. You want me to feel as if I've come out of this with the knowledge that I've caused you pain. But—"*

*He reached out, and the scene shifted.*

*"You didn't cry," he said, glancing down at where she sat frozen beside him. "You never cry. I used to think you couldn't do it."*

*She didn't turn.*

*"I'm a water deity," she said dully, and he watched her posture; watched it give under the pressure of her lies.*

*"You didn't cry," he determined, "and you didn't kill me, either."*

*At once, the knife that had been in her hand reburied itself in his chest.*

*"Someone else was here, weren't they?" he asked. "You didn't do this alone."*

*She didn't move.*

*She didn't breathe.*

*"Tell me the truth, Elaine," Tom said quietly.*

— Ω —

"You can toy with time, with physicality, with memory. The only thing you cannot touch is your opponent; the one thing you cannot alter is what exists for them, what's real. Like a book, you can read the page they show you, and if you're clever enough you can skip ahead, or travel backward, but you cannot change the content of the story. You can only change the way the story is read."

— Ω —

"Maybe this will refresh your memory, Mayra Kaleka," Volos said, and snapped his fingers.

Abruptly, the scene shifted.

*"You were with the reaper again," Raphael said sourly.*

*"I was with Fox," Mayra felt herself say. "I've been assigned to him, as you know."*

*"Mayra," Gabriel sighed, "do you believe us to be idiots?"*

*"I do," she replied. "Is that relevant?"*

*"Fraternization is frowned upon," Raphael reminded her. "And this, whatever it is, is impermissible. Your ledger is at stake."*

*"It's nothing," she said.*

*"Really," Cal breathed in her ear. "Nothing?"*

She balked, startled.

"You're not really here," she told him. "I know you're not."

"So then I'm not," he said, shrugging. "What if I were? What difference does it make?"

She blinked. "Stop."

"Why?" he asked. "Because Cal would stop?"

"He would."

"Fine. I'll stop."

"You're not him."

"You want real?" he asked, and again, her vision spun.

*"We shouldn't see each other," she said. "Don't have Fox summon me anymore."*

*"You don't mean that," Cal begged, and where he'd always worn a smile just for her, the look of pain on his face was just for her, too. "Mayra, you don't mean that—"*

*"I'm costing you more time," she said. "I'm costing both of us more time—"*

"Stop it," she said.

"Stop what?" Cal murmured in her ear.

*"Mayra, it's worth it." His eyes were so lovely, so gentle. So easy to hurt. "A moment with you is worth far more than an eternity of paradise—"*

*"Don't say things like that," she said, vigorously shaking her head. "Don't."*

*"Why, because you can't stand to hear them?"*

*"Because—" she began, and broke off, the weight of her fears settling into her fragments, the depths of her many fractures. "Because, Calix Sanna, I am not worth the cost!"*

All at once the scene evaporated, misting itself to nothing and dissolving Cal's face along with it, his hands still tenderly outstretched for hers.

"And there it is," Volos said in her ear, laughing with utter delight. "There's the truth, Mayra Kaleka. That you do not believe yourself worthy of much at all, do you?"

*"Get out,"* she snarled, pivoting to face him.

He smiled, curling the backs of his fingers against her cheek.

"With pleasure," he crooned, laughing as he disappeared.

— Ω —

"Remember, Fox, you are not playing your opponent. You are playing the game. You must be the victor against the game itself."

"And the game is what, exactly?" Fox asked. "Is it simply to win against myself?"

Death gave a reticent smile.

"It is to win against your demons," he said, "and therefore gain mastery of yourself."

— Ω —

*"How did it really happen?" Tom asked, but Lainey no longer seemed willing to entertain him.*

*"It's over," she said, her voice unfaceted and cold. "We've reached a stalemate, Tom, and there's no point continuing. You no longer love me, and I've lost my one card to play."*

*"I still want an answer," Tom demanded. "Was it the demon king?"*

*The demon wearing his ancestor's skin rippled into being.*

*"Yes," Lainey said.*

*"You're lying," Tom snapped. "Who was it? Who held the knife?"*

*She didn't answer.*

*He began to vigorously pace the floor.*

*"It was somebody's birthday," he said, and Lainey shook her head.*

*"It wasn't."*

*"An anniversary, then," Tom said helplessly. "Something."*

*"Stop torturing yourself, Tom. I told you, I can't let you lose—"*

*"But what was it ever about?" The whole thing was dizzying, meaningless, impossible to win. "Was it really always about this game?"*

*"The mortal had a price," Lainey said through gritted teeth. "He paid in blood, as Volos requested."*

*"Volos requested," Tom echoed with a frown. "But if Volos could have taken me himself, he would have. Clearly he would have, so—"*

*"Stop it, Tom—"*

*"Elaine," he said, reaching for her, and she stiffened at his touch.*

*"Let me go," she said.*

*"No."*

*"Tom—"*

"You think I don't love you because I've come to know your secrets," he murmured, pulling her toward him, "but that's not true, Lainey. Elaine." He sighed. "I knew you were a goddess, and I loved you. I worshipped you. I knew what you were, and I loved you for it."

She flinched.

"If I no longer love you, it's not for knowing what you are, or what you've done." But no, that wasn't right either. He hadn't understood until this moment just how simple the truth really was. "Elaine, I'll always love you. I just don't choose you. And if we're being honest," Tom said quietly, "you never chose me, either. You're not even choosing me now."

She looked away. "I wanted to be human."

"You were never human," he replied. "Not for me. You were only ever a deity for me."

"I—" Her eyes fluttered shut. "Tom, please—"

"Show me, Lainey." This time, he knew she wouldn't refuse. "Show me how it happened."

There was a pause, at that; a tick of withheld breath.

A breeze, like the rush of the sea.

And then a flickering, and a return to the scene of the crime.

"You had better heed our agreement, Volos," said a familiar voice, and the back of a familiar head. "I don't appreciate having to take care of this for you."

"Blood debt," Volos replied, shrugging. "The mortal owes me."

"And yet I'm the one paying," the man grumbled.

"Your fault," Volos said. "Perhaps you should have thought about that before you tied the Parker bloodline to your ledger."

"It's not a ledger, it's a book," the man said, "and it isn't meant for you, so you had better follow through with the terms of our deal."

"I always do," Volos said, holding out an expectant hand.

The man turned his head, his golden hair catching in the light as the scar on his mouth stretched to a thin, grim line.

"Take it, then," said Brandt Solberg, placing the thin leather volume in Volos's hand and cleverly concealing a handful of torn pages behind his back. "I have my own score to settle, starting now."

— Ω —

Vi gasped.

"What?" Cal asked, glancing worriedly at her. "What is it?"

"Fox," she said, turning to the archangels. "Who does he play?"

Gabriel looked down, eyeing the scroll. "The result of this game will be two wins," he said. "Fox will play the water deity. Volos, I'm sure, will take the ghost's place once the game is through. He's already beaten the angel."

"And then?" Vi pressed. "After Lainey. If Fox wins?"

Gabriel's mouth tightened, his finger resting on the scripted name.

"The godling," he said, glancing up at Raphael.

"Well, that's a turn," Raphael replied with a grimace.

Vi didn't wait for them to see what she had already seen.

"It's a trap," she said hoarsely, taking off at a run and yanking Cal along behind her.

— Ω —

"Hello, godling," Persephone sighed, and Brandt dipped playfully into a bow.

"Mrs. Lord of the Dead," he offered grandly. "A pleasure, as ever."

"Shall we just get this over with?" she asked, gesturing to the table with a look of dull indifference. "I'm told I have no choice but to lose this round, so we might as well try to make it relatively painless."

"Not that you wouldn't lose either way," Brandt reminded her. "After all, it wouldn't be your first time losing to me, would it?"

She pursed her lips in distaste.

"Do you really want to destroy Death this badly?" she asked. "Are you truly so set on vengeance that you would subject us all to Volos's reign instead?"

"Ah, but vengeance is so terribly the wrong word," Brandt countered, tutting quietly in disagreement. "And here I thought you of all people would understand, *jenta mi*."

Her expression, which had already been filled with displeasure to begin with, promptly became a scowl.

"You and I are not the same, godling," she accused him. "You serve no purpose. You are aimless."

"Whereas you," Brandt pointed out, "simply fell in love with darkness, didn't you?"

"Do you really mean to tell me this is an act of love?" Persephone prompted, scoffing. "No, godling, I would not believe you capable. You are a thief as surely as I am a queen."

"More so, even," he said, "as I at least manage a full calendar year in my profession."

Her eyes narrowed.

"So if the word isn't vengeance," she said, "then what is it?"

Brandt shrugged.

"Perhaps it is restitution," he suggested. "A reparation for an injury caused, one might say."

"And how would Death pay?"

Brandt met her gaze head-on, unbending.

"Leave that to me," he beckoned, resting his palms against the table, "after I win this game."

— Ω —

"Wait," Cal said, and faltered, something suctioning him frustratingly in place as Vi took off, darting in the direction Fox had last gone. "Vi, wait a minute, I can't—"

"Hold, please," a voice said, a hand closing around his shoulder. "Calix Sanna, is it? A reaper, beloved of an angel," the king of vice murmured in his ear, the threat traveling up Cal's spine in a shuddering wave. "Tell me, what do you know of Fox D'Mora? His weaknesses," he suggested. "His secrets, et cetera, et cetera. I find I could do with knowing what a mere mortal might have done to prompt two archangels to draw him as a weapon, and a trip into Mayra Kaleka's conscience has proven that you might be just the person to know."

"You're wrong about that," Cal retorted, spinning to face the man who looked so much like their friend Tom Parker. "You won't get a word out of me, Volos."

"Not even to save yourself? Or better still, to have Mayra?" Volos asked, batting his lashes. "I could arrange it for you, you know. I find I'm rather inclined to weigh your answer quite favorably." He gave Cal a knowing look. "Your angel's loss in the game need not be a loss to the entire cosmos, as far as I'm concerned."

"She'd never accept that," Cal snapped. "Not if it meant turning on Fox."

To his displeasure, Volos smiled.

"What?" Cal forced out.

"That's not a no," Volos informed him.

He blinked. "Yes it is," he countered stubbornly, and Volos rolled his eyes.

"Listen," Volos said impatiently, "when you've trafficked in these sorts of things as long as I have, you learn to understand the difference between a *no* and a *push me, Volos, until I break,* and for the record, I've done enough breaking to see it coming."

Cal stiffened, saying nothing.

Volos waited expectantly, and then he sighed.

"So be it, then," he said, and snapped his fingers, delivering Cal to darkness.

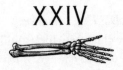

## XXIV

## THE THIEF, THE FOOL,
## AND THE GAMBLE

"This isn't the coincidence it appears to be," Vi was babbling nervously, wringing her hands as she accosted Fox at the top of the atrium's coliseum-style stairs. "Fox, I just—I think you should know—"

"Actually, it turns out that this isn't coincidence at all," Fox supplied with a sigh, Death's words churning in his mind to no productive conclusions. "I've just spoken to my godfather. Evidently," Fox grumbled under his breath, "this was all some kind of inevitable unraveling."

"It's worse than that." Vi reached urgently for his arm. "Fox, I really think you need to know who you can trust, and—"

"I doubt trust has any place in this game, Vi," he told her, placing his hands on her shoulders and gently nudging her aside. "In any case, my opponent is waiting. I've stalled long enough, which I'm sure the two archangels will have words about. Where's Cal?"

Startled, Vi turned, glancing over her shoulder. "He was right here," she said, aghast. "He was *right here,* I swear—"

"Well, I'll find him later, then. In any case—" Fox shrugged. "It's only a game, isn't it?"

He strode forward, heading for the tables, when Vi's hand shot out after him, her icy-chilled fingers closing around his wrist.

"Fox," she said desperately. "Fox, it was Brandt who gave Volos the ledger. He's the one who killed Tom, and they have some sort of deal . . . I don't know what it is. I don't know. All I know is—" She exhaled. "All I know is that he isn't what you think he is, Fox."

Fox paused, letting this information settle across his shoulders like a mantle as one of the many ghosts of Brandt Solberg slipped out to whisper in his ear.

*Lucky you hate me,* Brandt had said.

Fox closed his eyes. *Did I say I hated you?*

*Well.* That same airy chuckle, which, unlike everything else in all of the worlds, never seemed to change. *If you don't hate me by now, Fox, then you're simply not paying attention—*

*The godling,* Death rumbled, *is not a good man.*

Fox's eyes floated open, registering the wrench in current circumstances with a sigh.

It was always so disappointing how little he could manage to be surprised.

"No, Viola," he assured her, gently disentangling himself from her grip. "Unfortunately, he's *exactly* who I think he is."

— Ω —

"You," Lainey ranted, "are a fool. A fool for coming here at all, and doubly so for trying to trick Volos by using Tom. He'll be furious when you face him—*if,*" she added, her dark gaze sliding carefully to his, "you even manage to make it that far."

"Let me worry about that," Fox assured her, painting on the old, familiar mask. It always came easiest in the wake of Brandt Solberg's betrayals. For half a moment he'd nearly been his old self again, like time itself had been reversed, but now, no more. Now the old Fox was dead, and all that was left to do was win.

"You nearly lost your round to the ghost, you know," Fox pointed out with the cheeky look that had always gotten him laid or slapped, depending on his timing. "I wouldn't be so confident about your win."

"I have no choice," Lainey replied stiffly, unamused. "Volos will kill me if I lose. He'll rescind our deal. I'll lose everything, including what Death has granted me. I will lose everything and be delivered back to the sea, as if none of this ever happened."

At that, Fox opened his mouth to speak; then he blinked, registering it.

Blinked again.

And a third time.

"Wait. That's what you *want,* isn't it?" he realized aloud, and Lainey held a steady finger to her lips.

"Let's just play, Fox D'Mora," she suggested, taking her place at the table.

— Ω —

### Five minutes ago

"This round ends in a draw," Gabriel said, pursing his lips. "So both players win—"

"—despite our very clear instructions *not to*," Raphael contributed with obvious displeasure, scowling fiercely at Tom.

"But what does that mean?" Tom demanded. "How do we both win?"

"It means our wins are conditional," Lainey said to him. Then she turned, funneling a breath into a conical twist of mist and sending it toward him, offering it to his ear.

"Be very careful," her voice whispered in warning, like foam washing over the length of his cheek. "This is the true importance of the game: that the reward must be worth the costs."

Tom frowned. "I don't underst—"

"Demand your own safety," her voice insisted, hushed and frantic. "Make the condition of your win that Volos will not take you as punishment, nor Viola. Demand it of me," she said again. "Trust me, Tom. Just do it."

She was showing him how to stack the deck in his favor; it only seemed fair to offer her the same chance. "So then what should I ask of you?"

She touched her palm to his cheek, more girl than ghost this time.

"Curse me with memory," she murmured. "Give me clarity for all that I've done."

Tom frowned.

"But wouldn't that only cause you to—"

"Just do it, Tom," she said again, and they both understood.

It was goodbye.

— Ω —

"You're under Volos's control," Fox noted, circling Lainey in the midst of nothing but airy, self-illuminated white. "You clearly made a deal with him."

"Make your move, mortal," she suggested, not meeting his eye. "The longer you take to play each round, the further along Volos gets, you know."

"Oh, but I *am* playing," Fox informed her. "Only someone desperate would make a deal with a demon king, don't you think?"

"Or," she said warily, "perhaps I'm more clever than you think."

He was already quite certain she was. "Fine. You want to play?" he asked, not waiting for her gaze to slowly shift to meet his. "Show me a memory, then."

She didn't even have to blink.

*"Tom," she whispered, tangled in bed with him, the air sticky-hot and treacle-thick, the room filled with discarded clothes and tempered whispers. She touched her hand to Tom's face, and Fox, seeing the ghost for the first time, was startled to see how much he looked like his ancestor.*

*Thomas Edward Parker IV leaned over to meet Lainey's kiss. From a distance, Fox frowned with bemusement, trying and failing to see the significance of this memory.*

*But then, perhaps seeing was not the issue.*

*"Show me the truth," he said, and something crackled into being.*

*A voice, cutting through static like a stereo.*

*"Do it, Elaine," said the king of vice, the sound of it amplified in Fox's ears. "I don't have much time. Get it over with."*

*Fox watched Lainey flinch.*

*"What's wrong?" Tom murmured, his hand pausing on her skin as he intuited her discomfort.*

*"Nothing," she told him.*

*Elsewhere, Volos chuckled.*

*"Go on," the demon king urged. "I'm not leaving until you do. By the way,"* *his voice added, "it's the anniversary of our deal, did you know that? Let no one call me unsentimental."*

*"Lainey?" Tom asked again.*

*Fox saw her swallow; watched her suffer in a way that Tom could not possibly have known how to read.*

*"I just need something from you," Lainey said, wrapping her fingers slowly around her lover's wrist. "There's something I need you to do for me—"*

"Stop," Fox said, and the scene flickered out, Lainey appearing again before him.

He glanced up, eyeing her. "It was always like that, wasn't it?"

"Yes," she replied.

"You found Tom Parker's descendant on Volos's orders?"

"Yes."

"Why?"

"This isn't the game," she warned him. "I can't tell you."

Right. Of course.

"Then show me," said Fox.

Obligingly, the scene shifted backward, traversing the current of time.

*"Well, well, well," said Volos's voice, only the gold of his crown visible against the dim light of the anchialine cave. "So this is what a creature does when granted humanity, then."*

*Lainey swam up from the depths of the darkened pool, gasping when she broke the surface. She slicked her hair back from her face, resting her chin on a glossy bed of limestone.*

*"It isn't like I thought it would be," she admitted.*

*"What isn't?"*

*"Mortality." She looked away. "Or I suppose humanity, as you call it."*

*"You're not human," he reminded her. "Just because your pieces have been made to fit doesn't mean you contain the same materials. Death knew this," he pointed out. "He knew it, and laid that curse upon you without regard for the consequences. He did it consciously," he added, "purposely, so that your prize from him would never truly be a prize."*

*Fox watched, frowning, as Lainey hesitated, biting her tongue. Clearly she was torn; she'd already deduced as much, and possibly more.*

*"I know who you are," she said to Volos. "I know better than to make a deal with you."*

*He nodded, unsurprised. "You require something else, you know," he said. "Something you neglected to ask for."*

*"Which is?"*

*"Well, my dear, companionship, of course. For what human is truly human without love?"*

*"Love?" she echoed with a scoff. "I don't need your help for that."*

*"Don't you?" Volos countered. "It's been decades since you played against Death and won. What have you gained for it?"*

*She hesitated.*

*Then, with a swallow, "Say I believed you. What exactly would you offer me?"*

*"I can't manufacture love," Volos said at once, so at least he had candor in his favor. "But I can mimic it with surprising skill."*

*Lainey looked away. "Lust, then, I take it?"*

*"A bit more," Volos said. "It will be love, certainly. Not a sweet one, or a tender one. But seeing as you are not capable of it on your own," he said with a shrug, "I don't see why the complexities of its fruition should matter."*

*"But what will you take, then?" she asked uncertainly. "In return, what will you have?"*

*"Your secrets," Volos said. "The eternality you knew in the waves."*

*"Why?" She looked bewildered. "You're already immortal."*

*"Yes," Volos slyly agreed, "but I know when a thing has value, whether I have need for it or not."*

"Change it," Fox said, sensing he knew the rest. "Move forward."

Again, Lainey obliged.

*"This is your family now," Volos said, showing her their faces, their postures, their fears. "You will take the daughter's place."*

*"Why this family?" Lainey asked.*

*"They have all that any mortal would desire. Wealth, status, connections," Volos said. "You will have what every human wants."*

*"But you promised me love," she reminded him warily.*

*"Yes," Volos said, "and you'll have it. You can have the mortal's heart."*

*"Which mortal?"*

This, too, Fox didn't need to see.

"Forward," he said gruffly.

A leap, an instant blur of hysteria.

*"You killed his father! And his uncle!"*

*"I didn't. It was technically part of a deal."*

*"Keep him alive. You must! Please, I'll do anything, just don't take him—"*

*"Will you? Do anything, I mean. Because I find I'm rather in need of a partner. Someone," he mused, "with excellent gamesmanship, in fact."*

*Lainey's eyes widened. "Anything!"*

It was desperation, Fox realized and sighed, recognizing the evidence of her weakness just as it glinted in Volos's eyes. "Forward."

*"Why did you give him to me only to take him away?"*

*Volos shrugged. "I knew I would have need of him, and furthermore, I never promised you forever. No mortal gets to have forever, and you wanted to be mortal, so obviously neither do you. Do you know how long love lasts, on average?" he mused. "Very rarely does it stay. Love is frequent, and often fleeting. But you wouldn't have known that, would you?" he prompted guilefully. "All you understand of love is what I have given you—which, as a reminder, came with a price you've yet to pay."*

So much for candor, then, thought Fox.

*"I won't help you," Lainey protested. "I won't!"*

*"You're already bored," Volos reminded her. "This love isn't enough for you."*

*"Give me my secrets back, then," she begged. "He should be the one to have them. I feel restless without them, like even when I'm with him, I cannot be still—"*

*"One look at them and you would lose him," Volos informed her. "Were he to see you for what you are? No man would ever understand. He pulls away from you already, does he not?"*

*"Only because I can't explain it." Lainey looked stricken with rage and grief. "He thinks I'm . . . he thinks I'm reckless," she exhaled bitterly. "That I'm careless, that I'm incapable of feeling as he feels—"*

*"All of which you are," Volos reminded her. "And if you want this to be over, then either you will play your part in ending it, or I will only make it worse until the terms of our deal are satisfied."*

*She swallowed then, blankly; saddened beyond a blink.*

*"I want it to be over," she conceded hoarsely. "I just want it to be done."*

Another shift.

"I didn't ask for this," Fox called out, pivoting with irritation when the scene began to change. "I wasn't done—"

"It's a game, Fox D'Mora," Lainey replied irritably. "You play, just as I play."

"*The final round is yours to lose,*" said Brandt, *his voice, his face sending a ripple of dismay through Fox's chest. "Whatever Volos says, whatever demands he makes of you, you will lose, but not until then. Do you understand?"*

*Lainey looked at him with a wordless mix of resentment and uncertainty.*

"*There is a man,*" *Brandt said simply.* "*A man who is the godson of Death. He must be compelled to play the game.*"

"*Why?*"

"*It doesn't matter,*" *Brandt replied, listless and blank.* "*Not to you. Your job is to procure the ledger for Volos. My job is to kill the mortal, to make sure the ledger changes hands. After that, it will all be over.*"

"*But—*" *She gaped at him.* "*But I'll be the one killing him, then!*"

"*Only if you believe in technicalities,*" *Brandt countered.*

"*I do,*" *she growled.*

"*Well, more's the pity for it,*" *he said (in what translated very neatly to* bummer*).*

"*Doesn't it burden you at all?*" *Lainey asked him.* "*This man you seek to find, this godson of Death. Does it not pain you, that you will be the one to pain him? Does it not destroy you to destroy him?*"

*The question, Fox knew, was not particularly about Brandt, and Brandt seemed to know as much, too.*

"*I have already,*" *Brandt replied.* "*As have you.*"

*Lainey deflated.*

"*As have I,*" *she agreed.*

*The two of them nodded in concert: commiserators; co-conspirators; comrades in betrayal.*

"*I wanted mortality,*" *Lainey whispered,* "*only to find that I couldn't bear it. There is such vacancy, such longing, such loss.*"

"*Yes,*" *said Brandt.*

"*How do you bear it?*" *she asked him, looking pained.*

*Brandt shrugged.* "*I don't,*" *he said, and before she could argue, he reached into his jacket, digging something out of the lining that Fox had never thought to check before.*

"*Here are your secrets back,*" *Brandt said, slipping what Fox could see was a small silver necklace into her palm. "But be sure that Volos doesn't know you have them or neither of us will get what we want."*

*She looked down at the pendant, curling her fingers gratefully around the tiny shell.*

*"How did you get them?" she asked.*

*To Fox's surprise, Brandt looked up, finding his gaze in the corner.*

*Impossible, Fox thought with a start. Impossible that Brandt could know he would be standing there, and yet—*

*"Stole 'em," Brandt replied, and the scar on his lip stretched upward as he smiled brilliantly, turning away.*

— Ω —

Vi found Isis sitting with her back to one of the golden arches of her cage, staring into space and drumming an impressively recognizable riff from AC/DC.

"What," Vi began with confusion, but the look on Isis's face stopped her, the rest of the sentence faltering on her tongue and embarking instead as a cough.

"I suppose I shouldn't ask," she concluded instead, and to that, Isis gave a low, gravelly chuckle.

"Whereas *I* suppose," Isis countered neutrally, "that I should probably tell you that I sort of know Volos."

Vi stepped closer, opting to lean against one of the bars of Isis's cage.

"Only a little?" she prompted dryly.

"Well, I suppose a bit more than a little," Isis permitted. And then, with a sigh, she added, "I'm his wife."

Vi blinked. Whatever she had been expecting, that decidedly wasn't it.

"You're—what?"

"Well, I'm sort of . . . made from him," Isis explained, though Vi did not feel remotely informed by this apparent clarification. "All demons are made from him, actually, hence his being king. They made me when they felt he needed a counterpart." She cleared her throat. "A, um, companion, I suppose."

"They?" Vi echoed.

Isis gestured around, flapping her hand indeterminately to the floors and ceilings.

"They," she confirmed.

*Balance is king,* Vi heard Mayra say in her mind.

"But if he's the king of vice," Vi pressed slowly, "then that would make *you*—"

"The queen of virtue," Isis agreed, making a face. "Which was not a position I enjoyed. I made a deal with Volos," she added. "As it turned out, the more powerful he got, the more he drained me. The more everyone drained me, in fact. He has it right, you know." She glanced up at that, directing a small shake of her head to nothing. "Using mortals is always preferable to letting them use you."

The statement hung heavily in the air between them and Vi fidgeted, giving an ambiguous nod.

"So what was the deal you made?" she attempted.

"That he would let me go." Isis glanced her way again. "That he would find me a body—" she paused to gesture pointedly to herself "—and I would be allowed to leave, but his terms were that I wouldn't interfere with his business."

"Oh," Vi said quietly, recognizing now the purpose of the cage and shuddering slightly, sensing the cost. "I take it you abandoned your end of the deal, then?"

Isis grimaced. "Just a little," she confirmed.

Vi waited, biting her lip.

"Seems odd," Vi commented. "You all have so much magic, and yet you only use it to trap and trick each other."

"Well, immortality is naturally flawed," Isis reminded her. "Mortals understand this, you know, in some primitive way. That things that last forever are inherently less interesting. Marriage," she said blandly. "Familial obligations. Lifelong careers. There's a sense of dull repetition for a mortal, so why wouldn't there be one for an immortal, too?"

"Well," Vi said uneasily. "I'm not sure that's entirely true. A lot of people mock those things until they find them. The issue is that we only get so much time, you know?" she added wistfully. "All the monotony of being mortal is in the trying-to-live bits before you realize the whole thing is your life."

"Funny, then," Isis sighed. "Is there no good way to exist?"

Vi hesitated.

"Well, there's pizza," she attempted.

Isis brightened. "That's true."

"And, you know, friendship and stuff." It felt silly, so Vi paused after she said it, glancing down at the ground. "And anyway," she added, clearing her throat. "It still seems like we shouldn't let a demon king win, you know?"

"Well, you're not wrong," Isis permitted. "Though I'm really not sure I'd be any help at this point regardless. I'd have to watch the games," she explained. "It's been a while since I've seen Volos, so I have no idea what he's capable of anymore. Not to mention that his abilities are either enhanced or hindered by the mortal he's being housed in," she added as a caveat, and Vi frowned.

"So is it possibly a good thing that in this case, the mortal is a two-hundred-year-old man who's beaten Death once before?"

"Tied," Isis corrected. "Tied with Death once before."

"Right, but—"

"And no," Isis said flatly. "It's a rather unfortunate thing."

"Plus, that's assuming Fox even makes it past Brandt," Vi said with a sigh. "Who, by the way, doesn't appear to have the purest of motives. It turns out he's sort of in league with your husband," she added, and Isis balked.

"Impossible," she said, and paused. "Or is it?"

"Recent revelations suggest not," Vi said glumly. "He's the one who killed Tom. And he gave Volos the ledger from his book."

"Did he give Volos the entire book?" Isis asked.

Vi shrugged. "Does it matter?"

"No way to tell," Isis replied. "It certainly could. *But*," she murmured thoughtfully, "there's no way of knowing without watching."

Vi stepped back, eyeing the cage.

"I assume there's no way out?" Vi asked.

"Well, you know what they say about assumptions," Isis replied. "But in this case, you're correct."

Vi tapped her mouth, thinking.

"Well, in physics, for every action there's an equal and opposite reaction. Newton's third law; sort of like a mortal version of 'balance is king,'" she clarified unnecessarily, as Isis frowned, not yet deriving her conclusion. "What I mean is: if you're made from Volos's magic, then this is made from *your* magic, so can't you simply destroy it the same way he made it?"

Isis blinked.

"Seems like," Vi continued, postulating slowly, "on some philosophical level, maybe you put *yourself* in a cage. Right? So maybe you can just as easily, I don't know—" She shrugged. "Make it disappear."

"Do you really need me, though?" Isis asked, frowning. "You have a very clever angel, you know. And a not-too-stupid reaper."

"Gone," Vi said, shaking her head. "And even if they weren't, and even if there's nothing you can do, you're my friend, Isis. I'd rather have you with me than leave you here."

At that, Isis stared at her for a moment, considering her; and then she rose to her feet, stepping closer to where Vi stood on the other side of the bars.

"I'm sorry," Isis said, giving Vi an unnerving, unreadable look. "About Tom. I know you like him."

Vi swallowed a lump of pain, forcing it out of her mind.

"You said you leave creatures alone," she said gruffly.

"I do," Isis said. "But you're my friend."

Vi sighed.

In a blink, the golden cage was gone, and Isis glanced down at her hands.

"Huh," she said.

"Huh," Vi agreed.

"Well, then," Isis said contentedly. "Let's go try to stop my husband, shall we?"

— Ω —

"What will you take from me if I lose, Fox D'Mora?"

"Information," Fox replied grimly. "I have no need for anything else from you."

Lainey stepped forward, studying the angles of his face as if she could see the facets of his character underneath; sorting him out, deconstructing him. "You are kinder than the man who raised you," she observed.

In return Fox shook his head, considering that perhaps she'd pieced him back together somewhat imperfectly, based on her deduction. "Death is not a man," he reminded her. "And as I've heard it told, kindness is a rather mortal invention."

Lainey considered him, her dark eyes softening slightly.

"I can't help you beat him," she said, shaking her head. "I'm sorry."

"Volos, you mean?" Fox asked.

She nodded. "I don't know how to beat him, or I'd have done it myself by now."

"Ah," Fox said, shrugging. "Well. That's fine."

"But," Lainey continued, "I can help you beat the godling, if you need it."

Fox considered it. He had never beaten Brandt at anything before.

Still—

"No, thank you," he replied. "I think I need to win that round on my own."

Lainey nodded.

"Well, if it helps," she exhaled, "I think that's a good first step."

She turned to leave; elsewhere, he knew, she would simply take her hands off the table and try to wash them clean, wandering away to await her inevitable punishment.

"One thing," he called after her, hesitating. "Did he—"

"Did he betray you?" she asked knowingly, and Fox nodded. "I think it's better if you don't know," she said slowly. "Better, actually, if you know nothing."

"Ah," Fox said again. "Okay."

Lainey nodded, turning over her shoulder and disappearing from view.

"Fox D'Mora wins," he heard Raphael say.

He opened his eyes, finding himself alone at the table.

"What happens next?" Fox exhaled, running the tips of his fingers over the crescent moons his nails had bitten into his palms.

— Ω —

"Come on," Vi whispered, tugging Isis after her. "It's starting."

"He must be tired," Isis remarked, frowning. "Or hungry. Mortals have a rather pitiful tendency toward hunger and exhaustion."

"Probably both," Vi agreed, wishing she would hurry. "But still, these games don't last long."

"True, presumably Volos has a time-sensitive agenda," Isis replied. "He generally functions within the realm of immediacy, so I suppose that's about as sensitive as time-related agendas can get, don't you th—"

"There you are," Tom cut in, swooping down next to Vi. "Listen, Vi, I need to talk to you about what happened back there—"

"Not now," Vi said, her stomach turning slightly. Isis cut her a sidelong glance, but luckily there were plenty of other things to worry about.

"Like what?" Isis prompted, but Vi didn't even bother to oppose the unwelcome invasion of her thoughts.

"It's starting," Vi said again, and watched Fox step up to the next round at the table, resting his hands against the wood.

# XXV

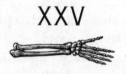

## DECONSTRUCTION

Fox eyed Brandt across the table, watching him coolly take his place. Brandt, meanwhile, took no notice of Fox, instead greeting the table like an old friend. His fingers hovered longingly just above the wood, and Fox couldn't help but wonder, just as he always had, what could possibly be going through Brandt's labyrinthine mind.

The one he thought he'd known, once.

Fox opened his mouth, ready to speak, but Brandt replied without looking up.

"Save it," he said. "For the game, I mean."

Fox's mouth tightened. "Does this game really mean so much to you?"

Brandt's gaze traveled miles of furtive thoughts to find a place to land, settling on Fox's face.

"Save it," he repeated.

Fox grimaced.

"Then let's play," he said, gripping the edge of the table and letting his eyes fall shut.

— Ω —

Aside from the bright white, like staring directly into the sun, the only difference between the real world and the game was how quiet it got. There were no whispering immortals, no sets of eyes following every motion; every twitch of insecurity; every breath of falsehood.

"I take it you start," Fox opened gruffly.

Brandt blinked, and with an instantaneous shift, the blinding white room became the old tavern Fox had once frequented in his village outside of Frankfurt. Brandt gestured to a table and offered Fox a tankard of ale, sliding it toward him. Then Brandt sat down on the bench, adjusted his posture, and took a sip, as unperturbed as if nothing remarkable had happened.

As if they were not currently playing for the fate of mankind, or at the very least, for the ashes of what they'd once been.

"I don't want a drink," Fox told him warily.

This, like most things Fox said to Brandt, was ruled inconsequential. "Have one."

"I said I don't—"

"Don't be a child, Fox," Brandt interrupted, and Fox nearly countered with fury, only he remembered this was a game.

This was a game, and he would have to play it well.

"I assume you think this will be easy," Fox commented, grudgingly taking the empty bench across from Brandt and turning the handle of the tankard toward him. "But you forget, Brandt Solberg, that I am the only soul in any of the worlds who knows what you really are. I will always be the one to find in you what nobody else can see."

Fox waited for Brandt to flinch, but he didn't.

He merely took another sip of his ale, carefully toying with his response.

"You know what they say about assumptions," he eventually replied, and briefly, Fox wondered if strangling him would serve him any points within the game. (Violence was, after all, sometimes the answer.)

"Are you really so angry with Death?" Fox asked him. "I knew you were given to vengeance, Brandt, but—"

"Not vengeance," Brandt corrected him. "Restitution."

"Fine. Restitution, then." Fox paused, tightening his grip on the handle of his tankard. "Did you plan this before you even met me?"

"No," Brandt said. "In fact, I didn't think it would ever be a necessity until I met you."

"But what is it you want from Death?" Fox pressed. "His power? You never wanted that." He felt certain, even if he couldn't explain why, that Brandt had always been many things, but never ambitious. Never spiteful.

Never cruel.

"What makes you think I don't want power?" Brandt asked. "Nobody doesn't want power, Fox."

"Not true," Fox countered. "You never did. You never have." He paused again. "You have to be doing this for another reason."

Brandt lowered his tankard slowly. It left no circle of condensation on the table.

"Do you really believe you still know me so well?" Brandt asked carefully.

Fox considered whether the question might have been a trick.

Decided, ultimately, that it didn't matter.

"Yes," he said. "Yes. I have always known you."

A brief pulse of time passed between them, and then Brandt took a breath, looking up.

"This has nothing to do with Death," he finally admitted. "Only incidentally," he amended, "because I needed his help and he, quite rudely, refused time and time again to give it. But this has never been about him, nor about his power."

Another beat of silence.

"This," said Brandt, "is about you."

Fox blinked.

"There is only one way to show you the truth," Brandt continued, "which is to make you see it for yourself. Because of the mistakes I've made, there is only one place where I can show you the truth of what I've done, and it is here."

Fox blinked again.

"What?" he asked, not altogether wittily.

"Just take a drink, Fox," Brandt advised, gesturing to his tankard.

Fox looked down.

He sighed.

And then he raised the tankard to his lips.

— Ω —

*"Where are we?" Fox asked, glancing around a room identical to the one where his body currently stood with his hands on the table, transporting him into the*

*realm of the game. Unlike the game he was currently playing, however, all the ta-bles within the celestial atrium were presently occupied in full. Fox and Brandt, invisible observers, were leaned privately against the atrium's far wall, facing the table below the dome ceiling farthest away from where they stood.*

"When *are we is,* I think, the question you mean to ask," Brandt said, and gestured to the atrium's entrance from the foyer, where a much younger, slightly rumpled version of Brandt strode dauntlessly through the doors. *The immortals in the room shifted around, eyeing him; some seemed to recognize him, but most did not. He strutted (truly, there was no other word for it) to the table below the apse, nudging aside a waiting opponent to stand opposite what Fox realized with a jolt was his godfather; a spectral, incorporeal version of Death that he'd only seen once before, and then only briefly.*

"Fine," Fox grumbled. "When *are we, then?*"

"The beginning," Brandt said, *just as the younger version of him opened his mouth.*

"I want a turn," young Brandt announced. *He wasn't speaking English, Fox noted, but it was comprehensible enough.*

*(Magic rooms, he supposed.)*

"Fuck off," *replied Death.*

"My father is Odin," *young Brandt announced, unfazed,* "and I demand a turn at the table."

"Perhaps I was unclear," *Death informed him.* "By fuck off, *I meant* no."

"Well, clarity is king," *Brandt replied irreverently, and Death wavered in sight for a moment.*

"I know who you are, godling," *Death said, sounding displeased.* "You're a thief. A cheat."

"Yes, and a swindler," *Brandt said.* "A veritable rook, if it pleases you."

"It doesn't" *was all Death said.*

"Well, easy enough to be rid of me." *Brandt was blinding with arrogance, gleaming with youth.* "One game is all I'm asking."

*Death flickered slightly; the equivalent, Fox intuited, of arching a brow.*

"One game?" *He seemed amused.* "Not many win, you know."

"I will," *Brandt boasted.* "And if I don't, then so be it. I have more to gain than to lose."

"Ah, yes," *Death murmured.* "Cursed with a mortal's lifetime, aren't you?"

"Glad we're on the same page," Brandt agreed.

Fox warily glanced askance at the Brandt who stood at his side, eyeing his feet.

Fox considered that perhaps Brandt had replayed the scene often enough in private to know its contents by now, so he returned his attention to the young man with the scarred mouth; to the boy at the table who would one day change his stars.

"I already know you play the game," Fox murmured quietly, and Brandt looked up with a nod.

"Move forward?" he asked neutrally, and Fox nodded.

The room shifted, the game evidently over.

"I won," young Brandt announced, sparing a cleverly handsome smirk at Death. "So now, I'll have my reward."

"Which is?" Death prompted.

Brandt didn't hesitate. "I want what my father's other children are entitled to. I want to know the secret to Iðunn's loyalty, that I may possess the source of immortality she supplies to the other gods."

"Why not simply wish to live forever?" Death asked dryly, unimpressed.

"It's not about living forever," Brandt replied.

"What's it about, then?"

Brandt shrugged. "Something of a softer vengeance?"

Death rolled his eyes.

"Fine," he said. "Iðunn's secret is not much of a secret."

"Tell me anyway," beckoned Brandt, and Death considered him a moment before answering.

"She longs for the world," he said eventually. "Bring her the world and she will return the favor. She will give you the youth you feel you deserve."

"How am I supposed to bring her the world?" Brandt looked irritated by the task.

Death shrugged.

"If it were so easily accomplished," he said, "then perhaps others might have attempted it."

"Fine," Brandt said again, thinking. "Then perhaps I can give her my world."

"That is no easy task," Death warned.

"As you said," Brandt agreed, "if it were easy, then anyone would have done it."

*Death eyed him closely, as if something inside him had been struck by recognition.*

*"You are not without some virtues," remarked Death.*

*"Well, don't tell anyone," Brandt replied, and Death frowned, considering him again.*

*"You'd be better off living a mortal's birthright than your own," Death noted, or perhaps warned. "Perhaps you would be wiser to live a single lifetime. To fill it with mundanities. You know; companionship and such."*

*"Thanks," Brandt replied. "But no thanks."*

*Death looked unsurprised. "You're not very wise, are you?"*

*"Not even remotely," Brandt confirmed. "But I'm many other things. Resourceful, mostly."*

*"Yes," Death said. "I can see as much."*

*"Funny, you don't look impressed."*

*Death sighed. (As did Fox, who did not understand the purpose of bearing witness to this scene except to see a side of Brandt that he'd already come to understand had always been there.)*

*"You don't have much regard for honesty, do you?" Death guessed. "I can see the cracks in your foundation. You came here thinking yourself invulnerable, but you would not have chosen to come at all if not for suffering of an immensity you will never be able to outlast."*

*"I find the truth overrated," Brandt replied insouciantly. "Few people really want it. Even fewer actually care. What's the point?"*

*"Interesting," Death said, touching his chin. "So could you do without it, then?"*

*"What, truth?" Brandt asked, looking caught off guard.*

*"Your truths," Death corrected.*

*"I have no truths," Brandt said stubbornly, and only then did Fox understand it.*

*Only then did Fox's heart begin to ache.*

*"Then that's what I'll take," said Death, as Fox had been abruptly certain that he would. "For my reward, godling, I will have—"*

"Stop," Fox said, and the scene froze as he turned to Brandt.

For a moment, he stared. He looked, and looked, and looked, and when he had taken in every line of weariness and reticence—when he had all but touched Brandt's cheek with the weight of his hard-fought clarity—he swallowed hard.

"Show me," he managed.

Brandt seemed implicitly to understand. "What would you like to see?"

Fox exhaled.

"Everything," he said.

— Ω —

Finally, Brandt thought. Finally.

(There was eternity, and then there was this.)

*"What do you give the goddess?" a younger version of Fox asked the ghost of Brandt from the usual place in the woods, their old meeting point by the river.* Brandt, the real one, stepped forward, placing his lips near the real Fox's ear as he watched the past version of himself deflect the question, glancing ambiguously—callously, as he could now see through Fox's eyes—away.

"I write the books for her," Brandt confessed to Fox now, the taste of confession sour on his tongue. "I gave her my innermost thoughts, my desires, my wants. She asked for my world and at first, she was happy with trivial stories. But eventually, she could not be satisfied with merely my description of the sky at dusk, or of the way the earth smells when it rains. She asked for my world," he exhaled, "and so I gave her myself."

"And then?" Fox asked, and Brandt took a breath.

He nudged the scene forward.

*"Is it sex?" Fox asked childishly.*

"For a time, yes," Brandt said.

Fox blinked.

"Forward," he said.

*"Why do you offer me the apples?"*

"As I said, it seemed rude not to," Brandt said.

Fox scoffed.

"Also," Brandt permitted, "I'm afraid that I have always felt the inclination to share my possessions with you." *To share everything with you,* he didn't say.

"Is that why you stole my ring?" Fox asked bluntly, gesturing to where it sat upon his finger.

Brandt shook his head.

"I have more talents than theft," he said. "I told you. I made it."

Fox frowned. "Is that true?"

Had he more time, Brandt would have laughed until he cried.

"I didn't bring you here to lie," he said simply, and Fox blinked; tilted his head as though he might answer; then evidently decided better of it.

"Forward," he eventually said.

*"Where do you go when you're not here?"*

"To Iðunn," Brandt supplied, and Fox nodded.

"Why did you always come back?" he asked. "Just . . . boredom?"

Brandt felt a shudder of disappointment take up residency in his chest.

"For you," he said. One of the few truths he had ever managed to tell—by virtue of a silly, conversational loophole that had taken most of Brandt's not-inconsiderable prowess as a gamesman—but evidently, Fox hadn't actually believed him.

Fox seemed to suffer this realization as fully as Brandt had.

"Forward," Fox mumbled.

Brandt nodded.

*"Are you telling me this will end?"*

"I never wanted it to," Brandt said.

Fox flinched.

"Forward."

*"Call me yours—"*

"I was," Brandt said. "I am."

A beat of silence.

A rasp this time. "Forward."

*"Will you still love me, do you think? If we are ever to be old and gray."*

Brandt felt Fox's breath hitch and leaned forward.

"Yes," he said, and Fox's eyes closed.

"Forward," he choked out.

*"So it's a no, then. You won't love me. Do you love me now?"*

"Yes," Brandt said to Fox again, and the other man's mouth tightened.

"How can you possibly put me through this," Fox began tightly, "and not want me to lose?"

Brandt paused the montage of their lives on a gleam of bright, unflinching white.

"I didn't do this because I wanted you to lose," he said, turning to look at Fox. "I did this because I believe you are the only one who can save us both."

Fox scoffed. "We only need to be saved because *you* did this to us—"

"There was no other way to reach you," Brandt insisted. "Death banned me from the tables. I couldn't have found you, even if I tried. And I did," he added miserably. "Believe me, Fox, I tried—you cannot know how hard I tried—"

"But why did you come back to play in the first place?" Fox demanded. "Wasn't the life we had good enough for you?"

Fox turned away out of sadness, or anger, but Brandt had spent long enough allowing silence to live between them. His hand shot out, closing around Fox's arm.

"What life could we have had where I never told you that I loved you?" Brandt begged, and it was wretched, and undignified, and all of it, every breath of it, for Fox. "What kind of life could have ever been enough if I never confessed that I would love you, Fox, for every day that I walked this earth?"

Fox took it like a slap, reverberating from the impact.

"Immortality is empty without you," Brandt told him, hoping for once in his stubborn, impossible life that Fox D'Mora would listen to him. "Eternal youth is *nothing*, Fox, without you—"

"Don't," Fox spat, tearing his arm from Brandt's grip. "Don't. I can't lose this game, Brandt, you know I can't. Thanks to you," he added harshly, "I have a responsibility to my godfather to win this, and to win the game after it, too. I have to beat a fucking *demon king*,

Brandt, and I—" He broke off, flinching. "I have always been weak for you, and how, *how* can you say this now?" he demanded, transitioning so effortlessly to anger, to indignation, to a vindictive, spiteful vision of hurt. "If you've given away your truths, then how can I possibly believe you now?"

"There are no rules in the game," Brandt reminded him. "I told you. This was the only way I could say what I needed to say, because the game has no rules."

"It has one rule," Fox corrected him bluntly.

"Yes," Brandt agreed. "But for you, I will gladly break it."

Fox stared at him.

"Listen to me," Brandt insisted, cutting him off before he could speak. "You can hate me if you need to, Fox, and you can be angry if you want, but listen to me: there's a mortal in there." He paused, making sure Fox was listening, and then carried on briskly, as if his heart did not sit broken in his chest. "There's a conscience living in the king of vice's host, and only *one* being can play at a time. Right now, Volos is the player," Brandt pressed hastily. "The mortal is inactive—for purposes of the game, the mortal's sentience doesn't exist. But to ensure his control over the body, Volos is playing two opponents at once, and the only way to win against him is to force him to lose the battle to his own host."

"How the hell am I supposed to do that?" Fox demanded, and Brandt shook his head.

"I can't answer that for you," Brandt said.

"Helpful," Fox muttered.

"Fox," Brandt attempted, pained. "Listen to me—I wouldn't have done this if I didn't believe you could end it—"

"Why not? I've only ever been just a mortal to you," Fox spat back. "To you and my godfather both."

"You've always been more than that," Brandt pleaded. "Fox, please, you have always been more—"

He lunged forward, curling his fingers in Fox's collar, and pulled Fox into his arms.

"Please," he whispered, and once the word had melted, syrupy, into the spare bit of distance between them, Brandt closed his eyes, pulling Fox's lips to his.

Fox didn't move.

He didn't breathe.

Brandt still remembered what it had once been to kiss Fox. He had lived, haunted, with the memory of it for centuries, knowing the way Fox leaned toward him; knowing the precise degree of closeness that Fox D'Mora preferred. Brandt had traveled all of the worlds carrying nothing but a book and the knowledge of the places Fox liked to touch, and where he liked to *be* touched; of where he'd sought to conquer, and where he'd laid himself adrift in Brandt's so-often shaking hands.

Brandt had told Fox once that he would destroy him. Brandt had been overburdened with ego then, but two centuries of searching does something to a person. It bends a person to the purposes of sorrow, to the whims of memory, to the fears of solitude. Brandt Solberg had spent so long searching every corner of the universe to taste Fox D'Mora on his lips one more time, and now that he had, he was emptied of everything.

Consummately emptied; painfully so, as Fox didn't move.

Didn't breathe.

*Don't go,* Brandt thought, but even before it happened, he knew that for the first time, Fox D'Mora was going to be the one to take the steps away from him.

He waited, feeling the pieces of himself prepare to shatter, and Fox did not let him down.

"I would not have gambled you," Fox said hoarsely, letting the words turn toxic on Brandt's lips.

Slowly, Brandt sank to his knees.

And then, over the sound of his pounding heart—just beneath the dull roar, the current of his blood rushing through his veins— Brandt Solberg heard the archangel Raphael's voice.

"Fox D'Mora wins—"

"Fox," Brandt mumbled, his voice breaking. "Fox, wait, please—"

He stumbled back from the table, wrenching his hands free.

"Fox, WAIT—"

"Well, you certainly betrayed me with gusto, godling," Brandt heard Volos say in his ear. "Luckily I'm accustomed to such things; vice is, as you must know, highly unreliable." Volos hummed something like amusement to himself, convulsing in a chuckle. "Though, you *are* aware the cost of such a stupid, stupid decision, aren't you?"

Brandt withered, registering the absence of Fox at the other end of the table and knowing that this, at last, was the end.

"Yes," he said.

He felt Volos smile against his cheek, the sensation of it chilling the surface of his skin.

"Good," Volos chirped, disappearing behind a series of twisting gold bars that grew up around Brandt from the floor. "But the rest of your payment will have to wait, godling. Now, if you'll excuse me," he pronounced giddily, "I have a mortal to finish off."

— Ω —

"Are you okay?" Vi asked nervously, reaching out for Fox. "Fox, are you—"

"Where's Cal?" Fox demanded, looking around. He couldn't think about what had just happened; couldn't let it weaken him, not with so many games still to be played. "Where'd he go?"

Vi hesitated.

"What?" Fox barked. "What is it?"

"Well, I don't know," Vi said tentatively, glancing at Isis. "But since Mayra lost her game—"

"Volos took him," Isis darkly confirmed. "As punishment for losing, Volos took what mattered most. He has a habit of it," she added. "The thing about vice is that love can be a virtue, but the lines of separation so often blur."

"Can't you do anything, then?" Vi asked, and Isis shook her head.

"Even if I could, your best option is still Fox defeating Volos before he can get to Death," she said, glancing pointedly at Fox. "You have to win this game. For Mayra, for Cal, for Death, for Br—"

"Leave him out of it," Fox said stiffly, glancing over his shoulder. "He's done enough."

Vi blinked in surprise, reaching for him. "Fox, are you—?"

He pulled away without looking.

"I have a game to end," Fox muttered, tearing a path toward Volos.

# XXVI

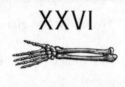

## THE DEMON KING

Volos was staring hungrily at Fox from the moment he entered the game.

"Hello, mortal," he said. "I presume you're familiar with me by now?"

"If you think I'm going to call you *your majesty,* you're wrong," Fox bluntly replied, and Volos shrugged, shifting to circle Fox where he stood.

"So," Volos said. "The archangels lied to me. You're no normal mortal, are you?"

"I'm a mortal," Fox replied, trying not to let his eyes follow the scavenging path that Volos prowled around him. "I don't see why the conditions of my mortality should concern you."

"No, certainly not," chuckled Volos, leaning in briefly and taking a strange, disconcerting sniff near Fox's cheek. "Mortals," he sighed. "Such a peculiar flavor. Nevertheless, I think the godling did me a favor," he mused, watching Fox as he tried not to react, curling his fingers carefully to a fist. "Knowing that you have any relation to Death is hardly much use to me now—and it certainly does you no favors; but knowing Death has a weakness, on the other hand . . ." he purred, trailing off pointedly. "It's rather rewarding information for one such as myself, don't you think?"

Fox shifted his head, leveling his gaze at the demon. "Is this really just a game for you?"

Again, Volos laughed.

"Anything is a game if you play it right," he advised, shrugging again. "But your instincts are correct: this is a war," Volos murmured. "And I'm afraid you're merely one of the pawns, mortal."

Fox said nothing.

"You know something?" Volos mused, tapping blithely at his mouth. "This whole thing has been lacking a certain element of frivolity. A sad dearth of whimsy, if you will," he lamented. "Perhaps we should play a game now, to remind us of all the fun we're going to have? Or, at least, the fun *I'm* going to have," he amended, looking ravenous with delight.

Again, Fox said nothing while Volos continued his deranged soliloquy, unfussed.

"The others you have played in the tournament have clearly let you win," Volos noted, his expression darkening slightly, "but as you might guess, I will not. How about this," he murmured, and extended a hand, clapping it firmly around the back of Fox's neck. "Let's play 'two truths and a lie,' shall we?"

Pain seared from where Volos's nails dug into Fox's neck. He struggled not to speak, biting down hard on the inside of his mouth until it was flooded with a coppery taste; a mix of blood and loathing, a salty brine of desperation.

"Scene one," Volos announced.

An image plastered itself to the forefront of Fox's brain, glazing over his eyelids; he could tell—might have guessed without looking—that it was a moment with Brandt. An early one, at that, the two of them sitting beside the circle of trees by the banks of the river. Fox saw the look on Brandt's face; the familiar trace of his gaze. Brandt always had a way of looking, of quietly searching him with a glance, and no one had ever matched it. No one had ever looked at Fox the way that Brandt had, and now the sensation of it seared against his retinas, temporarily blinding him until he convulsed with an unwilling yelp.

"People have secrets, Fox," Volos said in his ear, a perfect imitation of his godfather's voice. "Understand a person's heart, what makes them soft and what makes them hard, and find the source. Then—" The demon king gave a delicate laugh. "What was it? Ah, yes." His fingers tightened again. "Drive it in them like a knife."

The image changed. This time, Fox saw nothing but darkness.

This time, he heard Brandt's voice; felt it, like a deafening clap of thunder in his ears. He felt Brandt's lips, too, and tasted them, and smelled the tart sweetness on his breath—the inescapable, persistent astringency of *apple* that was so inseverable from having loved the man; the immortal; the godling.

Fox struggled to force it out—the memories were his, after all, and so he tried desperately to shield them—but there was no skirting the inevitability of the truth. Isis had been proof enough of it.

There was no hiding from a demon.

"Let's see," Volos murmured. "And for the last scene?"

Fox opened his eyes to an ornate mirror, brushed and gilded and gold, as he stared down at the hardened version of his own unmistakable reflection.

"I would not have gambled you," mirror-Fox said stonily, and Fox shuddered, realizing this must have been what Brandt had seen in the final moments of the game.

"Now, tell me," Volos invited with a manic chuckle in Fox's ear. "Who is the liar after all?"

His last words to the love of his life. True, but not the truth. Fox understood now what Brandt had meant, that there was no life at all if it meant living with an eternal absence. Because now, forevermore, Brandt would live the rest of his days with the emptiness of a lie, and for that it would be Fox who suffered most. Not Death. Not the demon king. Not even Brandt.

Lose the game, Fox finally understood, and lose everything.

*Why would anyone agree to this?* Fox heard in his mind, an echo of Brandt's voice.

*Because you wanted something else more, of course.*

"No guesses?" Volos prompted, sighing in feigned lamentation. "There are no wrong answers," he urged genially, pairing it with another malicious laugh. "Well, there *are* wrong answers, actually, but let's burn that bridge when we get to it. Sorry," he added, frowning, "is that the correct mortal aphorism?"

*Why would anyone agree to this?*

*Because you wanted something else more, of course.*

"Mm, not up for guessing games, I see. A pity, as I'd so hoped you'd be more fun; nonetheless, I suppose I'll have to just spoil it. I'm afraid you're the liar this time, little fool," he pronounced, looking immensely pleased and not at all remorseful. "Aren't you? You pushed the godling away to win a game, so in the end, you're no different than he is—which is, of course," he mused, moistening his lips, "a delicious turn of events."

*You have to be willing to sacrifice everything,* a ghost of Brandt said again, *to gain one thing that matters most.*

"Should we play some more?" Volos prompted. "Just think of the things we can see . . . the pain we can inflict . . ."

*You're not one of us, Fox,* Death contributed in Fox's mind, *and for once, that gives you an advantage. Because for you, there are things worth winning for.*

*I remember being mortal,* he heard Mayra sigh in his ear. *I remember the feel of it; the doubt, the pain—*

*I wanted mortality,* Lainey whispered, *only to find that I couldn't bear it. There is such vacancy, such longing, such loss—*

*I don't feel anything anymore,* Vi lamented. *And I swear, I used to feel everything.*

"Come along, mortal," Volos called to Fox, venturing gaily through the space and painting the scenes of Fox's memory, filling the bright white room with images from Fox's own destructive head. "As you can see, we have quite a lot to be done, and certainly I'm pressed for time, but a little reconnaissance is never an irresponsible choice—"

*In general,* a past version of Brandt murmured, *mortals have different rules—*

*Different feelings,* Isis contributed, *different matter, really—*

*Volos is playing two opponents at once,* Brandt's voice reminded him, *and the only way to win against him is to force him to lose the battle to his own host.*

"What do you feel?" Fox asked quietly, half to himself.

Volos pivoted away from the collage he was making of Fox's memories, frowning at him with impatience. "What?"

"Sorry. Not you," Fox assured him, shaking his head. "You're a creature. A demon. So obviously you feel nothing."

"I'm an immortal," Volos corrected. "But yes, obviously, true."

"Like I said," Fox repeated with a shrug, "I wasn't asking you. There's one thing you don't understand, Volos, and that is what it is to *feel*. To feel loss, specifically," he amended, and took a few steps closer, bringing himself eye to eye with Volos. "But I suspect the person whose form you currently occupy has known what I have known."

Volos shifted away, his eyes narrowing.

"You play a dangerous game, mortal," he warned, and Fox shook his head.

"Maybe," he conceded, "but then again, perhaps you fail to give me my due."

"And what is that?" Volos barked a laugh. "Who do you think you are, mortal, compared to the king of vice?"

Which is when Fox gladly, joyfully understood.

"I," Fox replied, "am Fox D'Mora, and I am a mortal who was raised by Death. I'm a man who has loved, and been loved, by a god. I have been guided by an angel and protected by a reaper; I have befriended a vampire and a ghost and a demon, too. I have known creatures and mortals and immortals alike. I have no powers, but I have known bliss and grief and suffering, and for two hundred mortal years, I have felt every facet of it all. I may not be the king of anything," he informed the demon king, "but who I am is the one thing that matters more than everything else."

"So?" Volos scoffed, clearly unimpressed.

"So," Fox began quietly, and gave a slow, petulant smile, carefully meeting the eyes of Volos's mortal host. "Now, the only question left remaining is this: who are *you*, Tom Parker?"

# INTERLUDE VII:

## PAST IS PASSED, PART III

### Thomas Edward Parker I
### 1865

"Strange, isn't it?" one of the other soldiers said, turning to Tom. "War's over and we're just supposed to go back home 'n start again." He shook his head, letting out a weary sigh, and turned back to Tom. "Said your name's Palmer, wasn't it? Any relation to the Prairie Avenue Palmers?"

"No, it's Parker," Tom corrected. "We've got a little livestock and corn out near DeKalb."

"Ah," the man acknowledged gruffly. "Well, s'pose life's easy enough out there. Got a girl waitin' for you?"

"Yeah," Tom replied. "Grew up the next house over."

The man arched a brow. "Don't sound too thrilled," he noted, and Tom shrugged.

"Yeah, well, it's all pretty formulaic, isn't it?" Tom prompted.

"For-myoo-lae-ick," the man repeated, chewing the word up and spitting it out. "Son, you'll have to speak English—"

"I just mean it seems pretty planned out," Tom clarified. "I'm supposed to go home, marry Betsy, have some kids and just . . . *struggle*, like my dad did." He kicked at a spare pebble on the ground, tilting his head. "Dunno. Maybe I should go out west."

"Maybe," the man said, shrugging. "I hear they've got plenty of gold out there."

"Ha," Tom coughed up. "Sure. And I've got magic beans." He grimaced. "Betsy would never go for it."

"Hey, nothin' wrong with a little life after something like this," the man said. "It's a lucky thing to die in your own bed, boy. Lord knows we came close to doin' it on the battlefield more'n enough times."

"Never felt bigger than when I was close to death, though," Tom commented, and paused. "Swore I saw him a couple times," he murmured, giving into a moment of whimsical certainty.

"Who, Death?" The man laughed darkly. "A very hospitable gentleman he is. Took plenty of us in out there, didn't he?"

Tom grimaced. "True."

"Well, you're young still," the man assured him. "Got a long life ahead of you. No need to speak to Death anytime soon."

"Wish I could." Tom shaded his eyes from the sun. "I'd like to ask him what any of this was for."

"What, poor men dyin' for rich ones? That's just the world," the man told him. "Doubt even Death himself knows any better."

"Still," Tom said. "I'd like to think there's more."

"More what?"

"I don't know." Tom shrugged. "More *life*, I guess."

"Well, they're sayin' there's some German out in Chicago who can talk to the dead," the man chuckled. "Look him up, maybe. Trade your magic beans for his ghosts, 'cause he seems to be doin' pretty well. Might need a pretty skirt to get him to talk to ya," he added meaningfully, "but hey. Maybe he's got answers."

"Huh," Tom said, curling his tongue around the idea. "Yeah. Sure. Maybe."

— Ω —

"He's got a ring," one of the girls informed him. "Touches it, and that's how he talks to the dead."

"Interesting," Tom mused, glancing over at the man who was clearly well into his second or third round of drinks.

From there, it wasn't especially difficult to get Fox D'Mora wallpapered enough to talk.

Fox had a singular melancholy to him—a dreariness, ennui that was grounded by a sense of unresolved loss—and, as Tom had gambled, he wasn't above a few drinks with a stranger so long as Tom kept them coming without pause. Fox seemed a normal enough man, too, or *would* have seemed that way, if not for the strangeness of his artifacts: the broken watch, the faceless signet ring. The ring, Tom was confident, was the key to it. The girls were all certain of it, and whether or not their accounts were true, enough of them had told the same story that Tom figured it had to be part of it, somehow.

"So," Tom said, once Fox attempted to stumble to his feet and failed, falling drunkenly back to the bench. "Long night, don't you think?"

"Mphmhph," Fox returned incoherently.

"Come on," Tom said, "let's get you out of here." He threw one of Fox's arms over his shoulders, nodding to the other patrons. "Had a bit too much," he explained.

"Don't fuckin' care," said the bartender.

Tom shifted Fox under his arm. "I'll get him home," he said to the largely indifferent bartender, and was thereby forced to support the entirety of Fox's weight as they swayed unsteadily to the door.

"Where do you live?" Tom asked Fox with difficulty, panting already.

"Mphmm," Fox replied, managing something resembling a point.

The walk wasn't far, thankfully, and anticipation spread through Tom's veins, igniting with each step as they struggled to Fox's front door. Tom needed to be getting home to his wife, he knew, but he wasn't in Chicago every day, was he? He'd have to take advantage of his time away from the struggling farm. He was sick to death of corn.

Sick enough to *summon* Death, in fact.

Once they arrived in Fox's room—rented from an innkeeper who, like the bartender, didn't seem much surprised by their stumbled procession—Tom helped Fox down to his uneven bed with a lurch, falling abruptly beside him and pausing to catch his breath. Fox, meanwhile, threw his arm out and gave a loud, incomprehensible grunt, his right hand falling on Tom's chest and leaving his ring to glimmer in the light of the small gas-lit lamp.

"Hey," Tom said, pointing to the ring. "Can I see this?"

He reached for it slowly, carefully; the other man groaned something like a no, about to resist, but it seemed that the moment his head settled in against the bed, a series of snorts that might have been snoring escaped into the pillow instead.

Tom waited.

"Hello?" he asked, waiting to see if Fox was asleep. He was.

"I'll just borrow it," Tom promised (probably a lie, though no guarantees) before slipping the ring from Fox's finger and eyeing it in his palm, frowning around the room momentarily and then tip-toeing into the corridor.

"Hey," he heard, and turned sharply, finding himself face to face with a tall, heavily cloaked man. "Give that ring back."

"It's mine," Tom said quickly, hiding it behind his back.

"No it fucking isn't," the man replied. "It belongs to the mortal inside that room, and he may be an immense little shit, but you still have no claim to his things."

Tom blinked.

"Death?" he asked uncertainly.

The man shrugged. "Among other monikers."

Tom swallowed hard.

"I had some questions for you," he began.

"Well, fuck off," Death replied, and then he sighed, snapping a small band around his wrist. "Sorry. I meant no," he said, and turned away.

"But—wait," Tom protested, lurching after him. "I was just won-dering if there was a way to, you know—"

"There isn't," Death said, and looked up. "What are you doing here?" he demanded, and Tom turned with a jolt, realizing there was someone behind him.

A few feet away, a man with sleek blond hair and an unmissable scar across his upper lip leaned against the wall, biting casually into an apple.

"Oh, you know. The usual," the blond man replied, and Death's eyes narrowed.

"I told you to stay away from him, godling."

"Um," Tom ventured, glancing between them. "Sorry, but—"

"Yes, you did say that," the godling agreed with a drawl, "and I, rather true to form, have elected not to listen. Of course," he added slyly, "if you'd just *let* me see him—"

"No," Death cut in irritably. "He's better off without you."

"Oh, is he?" the godling mused, and though a certain element of insouciance remained in his tone, Tom got the sense the argument had somehow escalated. "Funny, and I thought he'd just had the ring that *I made him* stolen off his finger by some sort of pilfering mortal—"

"Sorry," Tom attempted again. "What's going on?"

"Nothing," Death and the godling snapped in unison.

"And give the ring back," the godling added, turning to glare at Tom. "I don't appreciate the theft."

"Ironically," Death muttered.

"Oh, grow up," the godling retorted. "Your opposition to me is getting old."

"You're the one who lost, godling," Death shot back. "The game is over. Move on."

"Game?" Tom echoed. "What game?"

"There is a game the immortals play," the godling theatrically monologued, "and it has no rules—"

"Save one," Death snapped. "*Don't lose*, and you lost, Brandt Solberg. You shouldn't have gambled something you didn't want to lose."

"You shouldn't have cheated," the godling called Brandt countered. "You took something from me knowing perfectly well the day would come that I would need it back."

"Yes," Death confirmed, "because you annoy me, godling. Immensely."

"No," Brandt countered again, Tom's attention bouncing between them like a tennis match. "You liked me then, I'm sure of it. You only hate me now because you somehow believe I'll hurt your—"

"Don't," Death warned, glancing pointedly at Tom; Brandt, too, appeared to acknowledge the misstep, closing his mouth firmly on whatever he'd been about to say. "And you already *did* hurt him, didn't you?"

"Again, that was entirely your fault," Brandt said impatiently. "And if you would just let me *see him*—"

"No," Death said. "And stop looking for him."

"Never," Brandt said. "And if you don't think I could find traces of him through every time and world, you're wrong."

"Do you really think I'm going to let you pursue another one of your selfish immortal vendettas?" Death snapped. "You collect them, godling, like the thief you are, but I won't let Fox be one of them. And as for you," he continued, turning sharply to Tom, "give the fucking ring back."

"Band," Brandt called after him lazily.

Death glared at him, snapping it once.

And then, before Tom could ask him to stay, Death disappeared, leaving Tom alone with Brandt in the hallway.

Tom found he was disappointed.

He found, too, that he was helplessly confused.

"What's the immortal game?" he asked.

Brandt's mouth tightened, the scar across it more stark than ever.

"The immortals," Brandt said. "They get bored. They gamble. The only way to win is to have nothing to lose," he added, turning his dull gaze on Tom. "Do you have nothing to lose, mortal?"

Tom paused, considering it.

"I have nothing to lose," he confirmed, "and everything to gain."

"Ha," Brandt scoffed, turning to leave. "Well. I know a thing or two about being desperate myself."

"Well, hang on. What if I played it?" Tom asked, stepping hastily toward him. "If I return the ring to Fox," he added, finally revealing it from behind his back, "then will you take me to play the game?"

Brandt paused, but didn't turn. "I'm not allowed at the tables."

Tom deflated slightly. "Oh."

"I didn't say I wouldn't do it." Brandt pivoted sharply, as if he'd made up his mind. "I can take you there, certainly, but Death will be furious."

"Oh," Tom said again, frowning.

"Doesn't matter," Brandt muttered, making a face. "He's always angry, Death. Consequence of, I don't know, morbidness. Moon cycles. The perpetual nature of his existence. In any case," Brandt said, eyes flicking over Tom with hardened resignation, "if I'm going to help you do this, you'll have to be certain you can win."

"I can win," Tom said firmly. "I'm sure of it."

Brandt considered him for a moment.

"Then give the ring back," he said, "and let's go."

Tom nodded, turning to Fox's door, and paused.

"Do you want to see him?" he asked.

Brandt's eyes floated shut for a moment before he ultimately shook his head.

"I can't," he said. "Rules."

"But—"

"I can't," Brandt said again, harsher this time.

Tom nodded.

"Okay," he said, slipping back into the room.

— Ω —

Tom won the game handily. He had no connection to his life, after all; Death tried, Tom could tell, to break into his secrets, to draw out something he could use, but there was nothing there—and anyway, Tom got the feeling that Death didn't really care to play it anymore.

"It's an addiction," Brandt had told Tom in preparation. "He's promised Fox more than once that he won't play it again, but Death is not without his limitations."

"What will he take from me?" Tom asked Brandt, and the godling shrugged.

"Hard to say," he replied. "You're the only mortal who's ever been allowed to play."

"What about Fox?" Tom asked, frowning.

"Fox has never played," Brandt said, "nor would he. It isn't a game for mortals."

A point that Death, too, had been quick to point out.

"You shouldn't be here," Death had said, but Tom had been prepared for that.

"Neither should you," he challenged, and Death grimaced.

"Fine," he permitted, and gestured to the table.

In the end, the game concluded with a tie. Death never lost, Brandt had said, and he didn't that time either. But more importantly, neither did Tom.

"I want success," Tom said, claiming his reward. "I want to have more."

"More what?" Death prompted irritably. "Money? Fame? Prestige?"

Tom thought about it.

"Yes," he replied.

Death sighed.

"Fine," he permitted, and turned to leave, but Tom called out to stop him.

"Wait," he said. "Don't you take something from me?"

Death sighed again, with a grimace this time.

"Spend less time with the godling," Death advised. "He's selfish, you know."

"Fine," Tom said. "What's your cost, then?"

Death considered it for a moment.

"If you want such a mortal reward," he decided eventually, "then you'll have a mortal punishment, too. Let the costs of your success be the same as any mortal would face."

"That's—" Tom blinked. "That's it?"

"Yes," Death said, turning away. "That's it."

— Ω —

For a while, Tom didn't know what, if anything, had actually come to pass; he even began to wonder after some months if he'd merely dreamt the whole thing.

But then, that winter, all of the crops failed except for Tom's.

He took his surplus and began selling it in Chicago, renting a bit of space on State Street and operating his business from there. He rented a room in Chicago, too, spending most of his time in the city, and communed regularly with other burgeoning businessmen, reminiscing with them about the war and sharing some fraction of his wealth wherever he could to gain a foothold of fraternity. Eventually, he convinced other men to join his endeavors, turning the street (with the help of the friends he'd made over time) into something of a retail success.

*Your son was born last week,* his wife Betsy wrote him. *A healthy baby boy with eyes just like yours, so I've named him Thomas Edward, after his father. Will you come home soon?* she wrote hopefully, but Tom could not stomach the thought of it; of returning to his little life. He watched the street's retail flourish and tossed the letter aside.

Meanwhile, Fox D'Mora located himself on the north side of the city, or so Tom heard. Tom, however, didn't seek him out again. He had other things to worry about by then, and he very much doubted that Fox had any idea what he'd done.

Brandt, however, was a semi-frequent visitor.

"Are you happy now?" Brandt asked him. "You have everything you wanted."

In answer, Tom frowned. He had everything he'd ever wanted, yes, but it was still work, wasn't it? It didn't feel quite like the gift he had hoped it would be. It was starting to take its toll on him, too; his hair had sprouted a sprinkle of white, which he wasn't particularly proud of.

"How is it that you never age?" Tom asked Brandt suspiciously, glancing at the apple in his hand. "Is it because you're a god?"

"A demigod," Brandt corrected him. "And no. It's because I won my youth in a game."

"Do you think Death would let me play again?" Tom asked hopefully. "For youth this time."

"Ha," Brandt said. "No. You don't want to play again."

"Seems a waste to have all this wealth and only a small lifetime to fill it," Tom said.

At that, Brandt paused.

"Be careful what you wish for," Brandt warned, and then he turned to leave, vanishing through an invisible door without warning.

A few days later, Tom began hearing voices.

At first he thought they were simply his thoughts. *More,* it seemed to beat percussively, hammering into his head; *more, more, more,* until eventually it became a question.

*Do you want more?* a voice asked in his ear.

"Yes," Tom mumbled deliriously to nothing.

*Well,* the voice said in his ear. *Then suppose we make a deal?*

— Ω —

Tom didn't understand what had happened until his eyes snapped open to find his hands bloodied, his wife's body sprawled motionless before him. He thought, for a moment, to let out a scream, but stopped the moment he registered something cold and slick in his hands: A knife. A bloody knife.

*The* bloody knife, he realized, that was buried in his wife's chest.

He leaned closer, holding his ear to her chest.

No pulse.

Definitely dead.

"No," Tom exhaled.

All at once, her chest expanded, and Tom fell backward, tumbling onto his rear as his dead wife's eyes snapped open, her head turning sharply to face him.

"Well," Betsy said, "I have to say, this is a nice little mask. Your wife has lovely features."

Tom inched forward. "Bets?" he asked cautiously.

Betsy, who was almost certainly not Betsy, laughed.

"Not quite," she said. "Do you really not recognize me?"

Tom shuddered.

"Are you a demon?" he half whispered.

"Not just any demon," not-Betsy told him smartly. "The *king* of demons, actually. Though I can see why you might not be able to process that in full, being a mortal and all that."

Tom stared at her, his heart pounding.

"So then is she . . . dead?" Tom asked, swallowing hard.

"Oh yes, quite," the demon replied, with a laugh that was firmly too harsh to be Betsy's. "That was the deal, you know. You gave me a mortal, and in exchange I've given you youth. Ta-dah!" his dead wife added, for what seemed to be effect.

"I didn't realize it would be my wife that you would take," Tom said slowly. He hadn't been particularly in love with Betsy, true, but still; she wasn't nothing. He'd known her all his life, after all. She was the mother of his son. He hadn't known that she would be the cost.

"Oh, my apologies, I thought that would be obvious," the demon said, batting Betsy's lashes at him. "Well, not to worry. Now you get to be young for the next, oh, forty-odd years. Isn't that a fun trade?"

"What?" Tom said, frowning. "But—but that's—"

"A mortal's lifetime," the demon reminded him, sitting upright and dusting off Betsy's bloodied skirt. "If you want more than that, it'll cost you."

"Cost me what?" Tom asked, but he should have known the answer.

"Oh, you know," the demon said, dabbing on some of Betsy's blood for lipstick and giving him a chilling smile. "I'm sure you'll think of something."

— Ω —

"His name is Volos," Brandt said, looking repulsed. "Did you make a deal with him?"

"No," Tom lied.

"Good," Brandt exhaled with obvious relief, shaking his head. "You don't want to. He's worse than Death, you know."

"I didn't realize you thought anyone was worse than Death," Tom commented, and Brandt shrugged.

"Death's an uppity blowhard," he said, "but he's definitely no Volos."

Tom forced an indifferent shrug. "What's that?" he asked tangentially, gesturing to the book in Brandt's hand.

"Ah, a secret, mostly," Brandt mindlessly replied. "But also, it contains everything I've ever seen or heard."

"Oh," Tom said. "Is Fox in there?"

Brandt flinched. "Yes."

"Sorry," Tom offered.

"It's fine," Brandt muttered, not looking at him. "You just lost your wife."

"I did," Tom agreed.

"How's your son doing?" Brandt asked. "Is he adjusting?"

Tom glanced over to where his son presently stood behind the register, speaking with his usual charismatic warmth to customers. As the customers drifted out the door, though, Ned's lively composure fell away, his gaze sliding to Tom's. His son's remarkably similar eyes landed coldly on his before Ned turned wordlessly away, heading into the stock room.

"He thinks I killed his mother," Tom remarked.

Brandt's brow arched. "Did you?"

"Of course not," Tom lied again, though this time, Brandt seemed less willing to believe him. "Anyway," Tom continued. "Tell me more about the book."

Brandt slid it closer to his chest, tucking it into his jacket pocket.

"Maybe another time," he said, giving Tom a strangely disconcerting look.

— Ω —

Ned was nearly sixteen by the time Tom realized that he was dying.

*Well, you have the organs of a much older man,* Volos's voice in his ear reminded him. *You weren't very specific, you know, and the devil is in the details.*

"The devil is in my head," Tom grumbled.

*Actually, the devil is rather lovely company. I think you misjudge him.*

"I thought you were gone," Tom sighed.

*I was for a bit. You were boring. But I have a few things I need, so I think there's some use you can be to me yet, if you'd like to make another deal.*

Tom paused, considering it.

"You can't have my son," he said gruffly. *He still hates me,* Tom didn't add, *and I'm quite certain he always will.* "He has a bright future. I'm proud of him."

*Oh, he certainly does,* Volos agreed. *It would be a very great pity to take him, but still, I need something.*

"What?"

*A seat at the immortals' game,* Volos said. *Death won't allow me to play, and the two stupid archangels can't be bullied into it for some reason. I need you to do it.*

"Why?"

*You're already in the ledger. You've played once before. And also, no other being would be stupid enough to let me in their head.*

Tom grunted his agreement.

"So all you want to do is play?" he asked. "That's it? You play, and I get—what?"

*Another lifetime,* Volos said. *I wouldn't grant you immortality for this. But sure, one lifetime seems sufficient.*

"I need to be able to travel between worlds," Tom said, thinking of Brandt's invisible doors. "You have to give me that too, plus another lifetime."

*Fine,* Volos said. *But you'll be taking on a hefty debt.*

Tom shoved his doubts aside. "Just give me what I want," he said, "and I swear, I will get you a seat at the tables."

— Ω —

"No," Death said flatly. "Volos will never have a seat at the tables."

*He can't keep me from them forever!*

"You can't keep him from them forever," Tom echoed dutifully.

"Well then, consider the tables permanently closed," Death snapped. "I grow weary of this game anyway. I don't wish to play any longer."

"Let me play, then," Tom suggested wildly, and felt a stab of pain in his mind; as though a nail had been dug into it and curled around, hooked inside it. "Just—*ouch*—"

*You think you can go back on our deal by challenging Death? Oh, mortal. You complete fucking fool. It's too late for you, didn't you realize? You. Are. Mine.*

Tom stifled a cry of pain and Death frowned, his mouth thinning with suspicion.

"You should not have played this game," Death noted, as if he could see behind Tom's eyes.

*Past is passed,* Volos said with a scoff, and Tom swallowed.

"Past is passed," he echoed.

— Ω —

*Time is running out, mortal. I graciously gave you another lifetime, didn't I? But a mortal's existence is like a blink; like an itch, and then it's gone. You've only indebted yourself to me, Tom Parker, and you'll have to pay the cost eventually. Tell me, what do you think will happen to you when you die? How will you be received when Death comes to know the deals you've made? Not everyone is as accepting as I am of vice, you know, and you have some of the worst of them. Pride. Greed. A terrible inclination for deception. You can flee this realm, but you cannot flee your debt to me, nor can you escape your fate.*

*You will not be well received, I assure you. I require a seat at the tables, mortal, and I will not wait patiently to collect.*

— Ω —

"He told me that you would come for me," remarked Ned without looking up.

By then, Tom had searched every world for a solution, to no avail.

*Time's up,* Volos had said. *More payment is due, mortal, unless you're finally ready to call it quits and face your debt.*

He wasn't.

The souls of Tom Parker and his only son belonged to old men by then; his son, of course, looked much older than he did for lack of any immortal pastimes, but still—they were both already so tired, consummately wrung out by their respective lives.

"Who told you that?" Tom asked. "That I would come."

"The blond man," Ned said, staring out of his bedroom window. "The one who used to be your friend."

*Ah,* Volos said in Tom's mind. *The godling.*

"Ah," Tom agreed. "And what did he say?"

"That I needed to keep myself and my family safe," Ned said, turning back to Tom with a frown. "That's why I didn't get married for so long. Why I didn't have children. To protect them, protect everyone, from *you*—"

"But you did have sons," Tom reminded him. "One that you named after me, in fact."

Ned swallowed hard.

"Because I made a mistake," he admitted quietly. "I thought you were gone. I thought I was—"

"Safe?" Tom asked.

Ned gave a devastated nod.

"The blond man gave me something," Ned added. "A book. He said to keep it from you."

"A book?" Tom echoed, surprised.

"He said you would come someday," Ned said, swallowing. "Either for me or for it. So which is it, Father?" he asked neutrally. "What have you come for?"

Tom flinched. "I—"

*Do it,* Volos said firmly. *Do it now.*

"I'm so sorry, my son," Tom said, closing his fingers around the handle of the knife.

— Ω —

The life of Tom Parker's only son bought him another lifetime of youth.

"Why did Ned think I wanted Brandt's book?" Tom mused aloud, staring into nothing.

*The godling did say it contained everything he'd ever seen,* Volos hummed thoughtfully. *Perhaps it contains portions of the game's ledger.*

"What does that matter?" Tom asked.

*Well, it would mean that Death can be made to play the game once more. Whoever possesses the ledger can compel him to the tables.*

"And I suppose I have to get it for you," Tom sighed.

*Well, you do owe me quite a debt.*

"I killed my son for you."

*No. You killed your son for* you. *I only set the price; I don't wield the knife.*

Tom shuddered.

"Can't you torture someone else?" he asked unhappily, and in his head, Volos chuckled.

*Call me sentimental, mortal, but by now I really prefer to torture you.*

— Ω —

"I see you're back," Brandt commented, his gaze fixed to the table before him. (It seemed that increasingly, people were loath to meet Tom's eye.) "How were your travels?"

"I need the ledger," Tom said, not bothering to answer the question. "You have to give it to me."

At that, Brandt's gaze slid silently to Tom's.

"I can't simply give it to you," Brandt returned, looking somehow both smug and cold. "Even if I wanted to—which I don't," he clarified, "I left that book with Ned for safekeeping. It no longer belongs to me."

Tom frowned. "But why Ned?"

"I like the boy," Brandt said, shrugging. "He means well, he works hard; he's the opposite of a thief, and I find it endearing. And besides, I knew he'd never give it to you, which is what I really wanted out of this." He tipped his glass back, setting it heavily on the table. "The goal, Tom Parker, was for you to never gain access to that book, and Ned will be the one to make sure that you never will."

Tom felt his very soul flinch at that.

"He—" Tom attempted, and faltered. "He's dead, Brandt."

Brandt blinked.

"I didn't want to," Tom added slowly, "but—"

"Then the ledger belongs to your bloodline," Brandt interrupted, bending his head with a mix of grief and guilt. "Not to me. If you wish to see your own blood spilt over it, then so be it. Let that be on your head."

He turned away, but Tom reached out for him, grasping his arm. "Please, Brandt—"

"How often is he there, Tom?" Brandt asked, not turning around to face him. "Volos. Is it all the time yet?"

Tom wanted to argue, to persist in the lie that he had never allowed a demon in his head, but there was no point denying it.

"No," he admitted. "No, sometimes he's away, but—"

"Good," Brandt said, his voice clipped. "Then you're not totally gone. Cling to that before it's too late."

"Brandt, please, *wait*—"

The godling walked away.

*"I have a debt,"* Tom shouted after him, stumbling forward, and only then did Brandt pause. "Please, you have to help me—he's expecting another payment and I, I can't—I can't do this again, I have to—" He bent down, his neck weary. "I have to live with the costs, Brandt, *please*—"

"We all do," Brandt cut in coldly. "We all have costs, Tom, and we live with them. That's life."

He turned to leave again and Tom let out a loud cry of anguish and frustration, half choking on it.

"You destroy every mortal life you touch!" Tom shouted after him. "If not for you—if not for that *game*," he spat, "my son would still be alive—"

"Don't you put that on me," Brandt snapped at him. "I'm not responsible for your choices."

"What about Fox D'Mora, then?" Tom threw out wildly. "How did you destroy him?"

Brandt glanced over his shoulder then, and for one brief moment he looked equally like he might choke out a sob, throw a punch, or draw a weapon; he looked, devastatingly, as if he would have preferred to crush Tom underfoot than help him, even as Tom sank slowly to his knees.

But then—

"How did I destroy Fox? Like this," Brandt said firmly, just before he walked away.

— Ω —

"I want more this time," Tom said. "I can't kill my grandson the same way I killed my son and his mother. People already believe there's a curse," *and I can't do it this way anymore,* he didn't say.

*What do you want, then? Magic?*

"Yes," Tom said. "I want power."

*You do realize your debt will increase.*

"Fine," Tom said dully.

What was two debts to him now?

*Granted, then.*

— Ω —

"I told you, I don't want anything to do with this," Brandt snapped. "Stop seeking me out, stop following me. You've already paid with both your grandsons' lives. All you have left is one descendant! How much more can you stand to lose?"

"All I have left is one chance," Tom said mechanically. "One chance, Brandt, and I need the ledger."

"No. The cost is too high, Tom, *much* too high—"

"But what if there was a prize worth winning?" Tom asked.

Brandt scoffed. "There isn't."

Tom shook his head. "Isn't there?" he challenged.

Brandt's eyes narrowed. "If this is a threat—"

"Not a threat. An offer," Tom cut in. "If you'll hear it."

"I told you, there's nothing th—"

"Fox," Tom cut in again. "If Volos challenges Death and wins, he will give you Fox."

He watched Brandt's mouth freeze in place, snagging around the sound of Fox's name.

*He just needs a compelling reason,* Volos had commented, and Tom Parker had known just the one.

"He'll reverse everything Death has done to you," Tom assured him. "If you only give him the ledger, you can see Fox again."

Brandt frowned, suspicious.

"I know better than to make a deal with the demon king," he said.

"*Do* you?" Tom asked dubiously. "Because the tables are closed, Brandt. You cannot earn him back through Death. You cannot play again. Your only choice is to make a deal with Volos if you ever want to see Fox again."

Brandt chewed the thought carefully.

"Does Volos know who Fox is?"

"No," Tom said, shaking his head. "He has no interest in me or you. He only wants Death."

Brandt's mouth tightened, his gaze narrowing with concentration.

"I'd be a fool to trust Volos," he said again.

"A desperate fool," Tom agreed. "As am I."

Brandt paused again.

"I would have to be the one to kill your descendant," he said eventually. "The deal is the ledger *only*, and the only way I can be certain of that is if I'm the one who ends the bloodline. I have to gain access to the book myself." He paused, swallowing. "Volos cannot be permitted to see what else exists in it," he murmured, "until the time is right."

"And when will the time be right?" Tom asked, but he was struggling already.

By then, so few of his thoughts remained his own. Autonomy of his own mind was fleeting and painful, and there was no knowing when Volos would return.

"When it's too late to turn back," Brandt said.

— Ω —

"Do you really feel nothing?" asked the water spirit named Elaine, her voice hushed. "No remorse whatsoever?"

"Me? Of course not," Volos replied from Tom's mouth, chuckling. "My host, on the other hand—"

Tom, by then only a blip in his own consciousness, imagined a world where he could shudder.

"It must be killing him," Lainey murmured, and Tom considered that it was.

"His debt to me is what's killing him, as well you know," Volos replied. "If he had ever truly wanted a life worth living, he would have been more specific about what he asked."

"And you blame the mortal for that? You do realize this is Death's fault, don't you?"

"Ironic, isn't it? Or it would be—but then again, it's not precisely Death's fault. It's Death's *doing*, obviously, but if we're being more specific, it's actually *life's* fault—though that leaves us with so little to blame. In any case, he's withering, and I'll need more."

"And what exactly is 'more'?"

"What I am owed. No more, no less. I'm not unreasonable."

"What has he promised you?"

"The mortal? Never mind what he's promised me. Your debt is unrelated to his."

"Is it, though?"

"Well, I suppose not in the grand scheme of things. But I don't think it worth your time to worry prematurely."

*Help,* Tom thought.

Nobody heard him.

— Ω —

"Fox D'Mora?" Volos mused, circling the tied-up set of archangels. "Now where have I heard that name before?"

Tom, by then long trapped in a corner of his own mind, couldn't have answered even if he'd been the one Volos had asked.

"Ah, well," Volos sighed contentedly, shaking Tom's head. "What does it matter now, I suppose?"

# XXVII

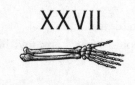

## MORTAL COMBAT

Volos let out a terrible yell, the sound of it vibrating around them both; ricocheting, violently, against the blinding white walls.

"What *is* this?" the demon king seethed through clenched teeth, and Fox, who knew it well, merely shrugged.

"Guilt, most likely," Fox supplied, grabbing the back of Tom Parker's head to wrench it upward, looking directly into the other man's eyes. "Mortals have nothing on the gods or creatures for power, Volos, but we know a thing or two about self-destruction. Pain," he noted, letting a portrait of young Ned Parker flash around the room. "Loss," he added, wallpapering it with Betsy Parker's bloodied smile. "Regret," he finished, watching consciousness flit in and out of Tom Parker's eyes, the strange, inhuman quality of them flickering more violently the more Fox spoke. "What do you regret, Tom Parker?" he asked, and the man dropped to his knees, falling forward to his forearms.

For a moment, he rocked back and forth; crying out in anguish, battling his demons.

His *demon*, which must have raged within his bones.

Then, slowly, he quieted, becoming little more than a tremor of a man at Fox's feet.

"What do you regret?" Fox asked him again, and the man at his feet looked up.

"Everything," Tom Parker rasped hoarsely.

Fox bent down, leveling Tom's gaze with his own.

"Isn't it painful?" he asked quietly. "Persistence. Isn't forever a terrible blessing, and a terribly blissful curse?"

Tom's eyes, red-rimmed, dragged to something above Fox's head.

"I'm afraid," he whispered. "I'm afraid. I'm afraid. I'm afraid—"

Fox sighed, rising to his feet.

"A very mortal impulse, fear," Fox told him, taking two steps away.

— Ω —

Beyond the table, there was a stunned silence.

And then:

"Fox D'Mora wins."

# INTERLUDE VIII:

## INCORPOREAL

The king of vice was without a body.

It wasn't strictly necessary to have a corporeal form (he'd certainly done well enough without one) but it was rather unkingly to fail to possess something when one was in want of it. Volos, having finally been expelled from the mortal Tom Parker by virtue of the game (and, he supposed, the mortal's own damaged state of being) suffered a moment of abject frustration, propelled as he was out of the game's realm and back into the Otherworld, hovering above the table.

Already the immortals he'd rounded up were beginning to discover themselves released from their cages; elsewhere, an angel was turning wide-eyed to a reaper and professing her apologies to him, falling at his feet. The reaper, in turn, was lowering himself to his knees beside her, placing his hand so carefully, so delicately, so reverently atop the bend of her spine that she would not immediately know for certain whether in fact they were actually touching. *You have nothing to be sorry for,* the contact said.

There was no place for the king of vice there.

A water spirit marked for destruction counted her secrets like cards, spreading them out in front of her, reading between them like lines of text. Slowly, she began to transform: her legs sprouted fins, her lips sealed themselves into waves, and her eyes returned to the hollows of the sea. Slowly, slowly, she became again what she'd once been—not a being, but a current, a force, a spirit. She dissolved back into foam, heaving a sigh that salted the earth's shore, driving gracelessly against bigger things; stronger things. With her secrets restored, she became again nothing; became, again, everything; and the king of vice could not touch her there.

A godling looked up slowly, his gaze falling on the man he had fought so long and so hard to love, always returning to him with the force and inevitability of the water spirit's tide. There had been lies there, and deceit, but he was still the son of a god; he possessed a god's divine armor, even while his mortal ribs wrapped around a mortal heart.

Which is when Volos had an idea.

Fox D'Mora stood with his hands on the table, still at war with Tom Parker's fractured soul, and for a moment, Volos licked anticipation from his spectral lips. Imagine, he thought, the possession of the godson of Death; what power, what prospects! He could yet win against Death, and even just a small piece of Volos—even just a breath of him, who had seen the mortal's heart and knew the wanting in it, the yearning, the *longing*—

"Nope," said the queen of virtue, snapping her fingers, and Volos felt something snatch him up with a *whoosh*, dragging him to the center of the table like an anchor. "You're finished now, husband. I think you've done enough damage for one mortal's lifetime, don't you?"

She'd trapped him in gold. Volos thrashed against the metal.

"Will that hold him?" a vampire asked tentatively, and the queen of virtue shrugged.

"Not forever," she said. "He'll find a way out eventually."

"What then?" asked the vampire.

"Well," said the queen of virtue sweetly, "then he'll have me to contend with, of course."

# XXVIII

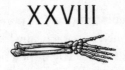

## SINS OF THE FATHER

"Do I have to do this? Everyone's fine now," Fox said, gesturing to Mayra and Cal where they stood quietly beaming at each other, affectionately refracting their respective planes of light. "And the immortals are out of Volos's cages, aren't they? So I really don't see why any further game-playing is necessary."

"First of all, everything is *not* fine," Isis corrected him, with a gesture to where Vi and a vacancy in the air that Fox assumed to be Tom Parker IV were standing purposefully apart from each other. He noted, too, that Isis was currently wearing her husband on her head as a crown; a strange contrast with her mortal athleisure that didn't seem worth pointing out for the moment. "And secondly—"

"Excuse you," Raphael cut in with a seraphic look of indignation. "I rather think it's our job to lay out the details of what the mortal must or mustn't do—"

"Is it?" Isis asked skeptically. "Is it *really*, though?"

"Right, so, secondly," Gabriel continued, attempting to pick up where Isis had left off, and frowned. "Wait. What was the first thing?"

Raphael, helpfully: "That things aren't fine."

Gabriel, bolstered: "Right, things are most certainly not fine."

Raphael: "For one thing, however this ends, we'll all have to face an inquiry."

Gabriel: "Yes. And it won't be pleasant."

Fox, mildly: "Inquiries rarely are."

Raphael: "We won't pretend there weren't some wrongs committed."

Gabriel: "It's crossed our minds that perhaps mistakes were made."

Raphael: "Some minor misconceptions—"

Gabriel: "—totally unintentional, of course—"

Raphael: "—not to mention practically harmless—"

Fox, with a roll of his eyes: "Right, practically harmless. Nearly *didn't* destroy mankind—"

"Did that happen?" Raphael prompted. "Did it?"

"Yes," Gabriel agreed. "Are you currently in service to a demon king?"

"No, but—"

*"No,"* Raphael emphatically confirmed, "so basically, it's fine."

"I don't understand how this all happened," Vi ventured, taking a tentative step forward and looking over at Fox. "Are demons normally this powerful?"

Isis, to Vi: "No, this was a contractually driven exception."

Raphael: "Yes. Supernatural clauses, et cetera."

Fox, with a groan: "No, no *et ceteras*. Explain what you mean."

Gabriel: "Every being who plays the game signs a contract."

Raphael: "A waiver of liability, if you will."

Gabriel: "Yes, which leaves them beholden to the laws of the tables."

Vi, frowning: "So when the tables are in play—"

"The various players are beheld," Raphael confirmed. "And then of course there was the small issue of Volos being particularly powerful where it comes to situations of vice, which certainly didn't help."

"I still don't understand why we can't simply stop now," Fox protested. "The whole Volos situation is taken care of, isn't it? So why can't you just end the game here?"

"We can't end the game," Gabriel said stiffly. "We didn't start it."

"Yes, and we didn't invent it, either," Raphael added. "The tables don't answer to us; we simply operate them."

"Why, again?" Vi asked them.

The two archangels shrugged.

"Bored, mostly," said Gabriel.

"Also, we're very adept at contracts," contributed Raphael.

"Though, again, primarily there's just such a vastness of time," Gabriel lamented, "and so little with which to fill it."

"But I don't want to play my own godfather," Fox cut in, lest they forget the point at hand. (Already the archangels had adopted an air of having spiritually gotten past their grievous, mortality-threatening error.) "Can't I just forfeit?"

"Whosoever masters the table masters the game itself," Raphael replied, so perhaps they hadn't entirely forgotten. "If you play it, and either you or Death win, then the tournament is ended, and the game need never be played again."

"Yes," Gabriel sniffed, "so best to close the cycle now, unless you'd like mankind to suffer this particular threat a second time."

Fox looked up, eyeing where Death stood at the table, no longer shackled in place. Just beyond him, Fox could also see that Brandt sat alone in one of the stadium seats, his fingers quietly steepled at his lips.

Fox tore his gaze away, focusing instead on his current immortal problem—which happened to be the man, or not-a-man, who'd raised him.

He made his way to the final table, taking the coliseum steps one by one.

"Papa," he said when he arrived, the seats beginning to fill around them with the occupants of every world. "I don't want to do this."

"Too bad," Death replied. "You heard the shitty angels."

"Papa," Fox groaned. "Band."

"Don't tell me what to do, mortal," Death retorted. "I raised you, didn't I?"

Inwardly, Fox sighed.

"Do I really have to do this, then?" Fox asked, somewhat sulkily.

Death shrugged. "Only if it matters to you that you never have to play it again."

A fairly convincing argument. Fox paused a moment, grimacing, then nodded.

"Okay, Papa," he sighed. "Let's play."

— Ω —

Vi waited until Fox had wandered unwillingly over to the final table before allowing herself to look up at where Tom was standing, his gaze already on hers.

"Hi," he said, somewhat underwhelmingly.

She ran through her options. She could run away, which was always a good one. The urge to lie somewhere atop a pile of clean linens was also compelling. Neither of which was helpful.

"Hi," she permitted with a sense of braced concession, noting that Isis, still wearing Volos as a crown, had conspicuously wandered away.

"So," Tom continued, floating over to her. "This was a pretty weird way to find out the Parker curse was actually my great-grandfather being in debt to a demon, right? Not to mention that my girlfriend was never really my girlfriend," he added, looking as if he hadn't quite come to grips with that part yet. "But I think it's probably best not to dwell on that."

"Well, at least you got an answer," Vi reminded him. "And maybe now you can, you know. Move on." She paused. "Right?"

Tom tilted his head, considering it. "I hadn't thought about it," he admitted. "But I suppose so, yes."

"And to think, all of this was just a contractual discrepancy the whole time," Vi remarked with a perfunctory sense of pragmatism. (A mystery, then, why it came out of her mouth so glumly.) "If I'd just asked Sly to look at the deed to the house sooner, we might not have had to go through any of it, would we? We might never have had to cross worlds, or save Death." She paused. "Or defeat any demons, for that matter."

"Though we also might never have gotten to know each other," Tom pointed out.

"That's true," Vi said, and then, after a moment, "But maybe that would have been better."

Tom floated very still, not saying anything.

"Well, thank you, anyway," he said after a few moments, his voice unusually brisk and toneless. "For coming, I mean. Even though you clearly didn't need to."

"Well, I had to make sure everything was taken care of," Vi reminded him. "I had a responsibility to the house. And, you know. The sale."

"Right," Tom said. "Yes, of course."

Another pause.

"And," Tom sighed, "I'm sorry about—"

"Don't worry about it," Vi cut in, and if it sounded sad, that was probably just a trick of the inner ear, or some kind of acoustical issue. "It was just a game, right? All of this was just a game for bored immortals, so none of it ever meant anything. Nothing about any of this was ever real."

Especially not the parts that had felt more real than anything, she thought, remembering the way his fingers had laced with hers.

"Right," Tom said quietly, nodding his agreement as they turned to watch Fox's final match. "Right."

$$-\ \Omega\ -$$

"Hello, Papa," Fox said, opening his eyes to the bright white room for what he hoped, desperately, would be the final time.

"Hello, Fox," Death replied, materializing across from Fox in his usual form. The one Fox had known for his whole life, which he realized now was only a fraction of Death's existence.

"You know, I've never given much thought to why you look like this," Fox commented, gesturing to Death's corporeal form. "Do you look this way to everyone?"

"No," Death replied. "I designed this form for you. Hazel eyes," he said, gesturing, "to match yours. Dark hair like your mother's. Your father's height," he added. "I could go on, but I think you get the idea."

"Why?" Fox asked quizzically. He'd never given any thought to it before, but it suddenly seemed relevant. Important, even.

"Why what?" asked Death.

"Why did you make this for me?"

"Well, you were a baby," Death said with a shrug. "I couldn't exactly *not* take the form of something familiar, could I? It would be . . . I don't know, a poor attempt at habitat adaptation. I do have other outfits, though," he added. "The cloak and stuff, you know. But easier this way, I think."

For a moment, Fox remembered what he'd seen in Tom Parker's memories; the conversation between Death and Brandt that meant the two beings Fox trusted most with the fragility of his heart had always been keeping secrets from him. Part of him wanted to be angry—a very great part of him was, indeed, angry, and betrayed, and deeply, irrevocably wounded.

But then again, that hardness of feeling seemed so very burdensome. Some things, reasoned Fox the collector, with his broken watch and his faceless ring, were simply not worth carrying around.

"Impractical, cloaks," Fox remarked in agreement. "Always getting in the way, I find."

"Well, I'm not without some theatricality," Death replied. "I have other forms, too. Feminine on occasion, though gender is already such a flimsy construct—and not," he added, "one of mine. I can also be animals, elements; that vague sensation of having forgotten something at home—"

Fox interrupted, "But you chose this one because . . . ?"

"Because you liked it best," Death replied easily, and after a moment, Fox nodded.

He let a few seconds pass.

"I don't actually have to win, do I?" Fox asked.

"You do, I'm afraid," Death said. "The archangels are correct. If we both lose the game, the whole thing would be ripe for the taking once more, and Volos will not stay contained for long."

Fox shook his head. "But why are you so convinced that you will lose?"

"I told you. Because I have a regret."

"Yes, you've said this, but—"

"I have a regret," Death continued, "which is highly impractical. A mortal sensation. I find it disturbingly weakening, and no other immortal would share it."

"Well, what about me?" Fox asked. "I have regrets."

"Do you?" Death countered. "Were there things you failed to say?"

"I—" Fox paused. "No, not exactly, but—"

"Anything you might have done differently?"

"Well." A very complex question for a spontaneous thought exercise. "I'm not proud of everything I've done, but *differently*? I don't—"

"I have a regret," Death said. "And therefore, I will lose this game."

Fox chewed his lip.

"You kept Brandt from me," he said. "Is that it?"

Death blinked, and the scene around them shifted.

*"Please," a wearied Brandt was pleading. "Please, you have to give it back. You have to give it back, I'm begging you—"*

*"No," Death replied, and it was unclear to Fox whether Death's voice was actually cold or if Death himself remembered it that way. "You gambled him, godling, and you lost. You are selfish; you wish, as you always have, to possess all things. You have always been a thief and a liar, a cheat and a swindler, and now you think to somehow rightfully possess my godson's love? No, godling. You will not."*

*"Take something else from me, then," Brandt begged. "Take whatever you want, just please, please don't take Fox—"*

*"You'll never set eyes on him again," Death curtly replied. "Not so long as I maintain my hold over the mortal world. And you are banned from the tables, godling, as you have always been. You will not compel me here again."*

Fox, who had known so much of Brandt and still so little, could see on Brandt's face that the consequences of this game were far worse than even the darkest of his imaginings.

*"But he is waiting for me." Brandt's voice was a croak of resignation, a broken strain. "Will you tell him what I've done?"*

*"Oh, so tell him you gambled him?" Death scoffed. "Yes, I'm sure he'll fucking love that—"*

*Brandt shook his head. "No, you don't understand." It wasn't his usual recalcitrance but something darker, something harder and more condemning when he looked up to meet Death's eye. "Listen to me, you don't understand him. He's a mortal—he's going to feel pain in my absence whether you think that's what's best for him or not—"*

*"I understand everything,"* Death corrected. *"I'm an immortal being, god-ling, and can certainly match the intellect of a meandering thief. Is that all?"*

*Brandt looked pained, his head dropping in misery.*

*"Will you tell him I love him?"* Brandt asked.

*"No,"* said Death.

*Brandt raised a hand to his face, covering his mouth for a moment, and then he nodded.*

*"Fine,"* Brandt managed wearily. *"Maybe it's better that way."*

Elsewhere, Fox knew, a past version of himself was waking up alone.

"You can stop now," Fox called from inside the vision, swallowing hard as the image of Brandt rose numbly to his feet and turned away, disappearing from the tables. "Papa, I understand that you regret it."

The scene around him flickered, and then Death materialized beside him again.

"No, that's not my regret," Death said. "I simply wanted you to see it." He paused. "I didn't think I was doing such a terrible thing," he said slowly, almost childishly. "I thought I was protecting you."

Again, Fox could have been angry. Was, ultimately, very angry.

But two centuries of anger had not served him nearly as well as one day of honesty. Not as well as one moment, one fleeting breath of peace.

"You were protecting me," Fox said, because he understood that much, and could forgive that much, whether Death asked for it or not. "In a sense. But you also caused me the most terrible pain of my lifetime."

"Yes," Death said, "and that is part of my regret."

Fox frowned. "Only part of it?"

"Yes," Death said.

"But then—"

"I regret," Death explained slowly, "that I spent so long transacting the Ends of mortals that I underestimated their abilities. I might have gone eternity never needing to know," he added, to which Fox nodded his understanding, "but I made myself weak when I took a mortal godson."

He paused.

"When I chose," Death amended, "a mortal son."

The phrase registered first, and Fox's breath suspended.

And then confusion set in.

"You regret raising me?" Fox echoed, blinking, and Death shook his head.

"No, not that. Never that. I regret underestimating you," he corrected. "I regret thinking you were so small and fragile that loving an immortal was something from which you needed my protection. I regret that in my attempt to insulate you from the beings I believed to be far more complex than you, I caused you unimaginable pain—which," Death determined quietly, "is in fact something I should not be capable of feeling, but which I have learned, irrevocably, from you."

"What, pain?" Fox asked, bemused.

"Yes," Death said.

"Because I hurt you?"

"No. Because I hurt," Death clarified shamefully, "when you hurt."

For a moment, after hearing his godfather's darkest confession and knowing that it had been haunting him for so many years, Fox wanted to comfort him.

Instead, though, Fox chuckled.

"What?" Death demanded.

"Papa," Fox sighed, shaking his head. "That pain you feel? That's love."

Death paused.

"Is it?" he asked.

"Yes," Fox said.

"Well," Death grumbled, "then it's fucking stupid."

"It is," Fox agreed. "And a highly mortal impulse."

"I hate it," Death said. "I'd prefer it gone."

"Doesn't really work that way," Fox said with a shrug. "But if it helps, it's very nice to hear."

"Is it?" Death asked again, frowning. "Sounds fake."

"Yes, well, I'd imagine that to most mortals, the godson of Death playing in an immortal gambling tournament also sounds fake, so it is what it is."

"Limited imaginations," Death commented. "Stupid, I think, that mortals could possibly believe that only one world was made for them."

"One world *was* made for them," Fox said. "Isn't that the point?"

"Hush," was Death's predictable reply. "You've always been too clever for your own good."

"Wish I'd been a little cleverer, actually," Fox admitted. "If I'd understood more, maybe we could have hurt a little less."

They paused for a moment.

"So, what if you win?" Fox asked, clearing his throat. "What will you take?"

"I can't win," Death said.

"Well, not with that attitude," replied Fox.

"No, I actually can't," Death repeated. "I'm just waiting for *you* to win."

"And how am I supposed to do that?" Fox asked.

"How should I know?"

"You're Death," Fox reminded him. "You know everything."

Death shrugged.

"If you win, you are entitled to something from me," Death remarked tangentially.

"Am I?" Fox asked.

Death nodded. "That's why most beings play the game to begin with," he clarified. "Should be pretty straightforward. You can have anything you want. Immortality," he suggested. "Wealth, riches. Anything."

Fox thought about it.

"I'd want you to take Tom Parker," he said. "If you could be gentle with him, that would be ideal. I think he's probably suffered enough not to have any continuing debt."

"That's a given," Death agreed. "The end, not the gentleness. In general, though, I'd call that request a personal favor, not a reward."

"The ghost," Fox added. "Help him meet his end, too?"

"Right," Death said. "Yes, that's doable. And the vampire?"

"Why?" Fox asked, surprised. "She's fine, isn't she?"

"Well, she's in love with the ghost," Death said.

"What? How did you know that?"

"I know everything, young man," Death reminded him.

"Oh. Then ask her what she wants, I suppose."

"Well, I'll have Raphael and Gabriel sort that one out," Death said. "Though, who knows what will even happen to them once God and Lucifer find out what's transpired."

"Don't they already know?" Fox asked. "Omnipotence and all that."

"Omniscience," Death corrected, "and sure, they technically might *know*, but who can keep track of everything that one knows when one already knows everything?"

"Dizzying, but fair," said Fox.

"Anything else?" Death asked.

"Mayra," Fox said. "And Cal."

"Ah, yes," Death agreed. "Done. And?"

Fox paused.

"Forgive Brandt," he said.

"What, pardon his ledger?" Death balked. "Easier said than done, Fox—"

"No," Fox said, shaking his head. "Just . . . forgive him."

"Oh. Well, okay, done," Death said blandly. "That's really only difficult for mortals."

"Right," said Fox, thinking that was probably true.

"Do *you* need help with it?" Death countered, arching a brow. "Forgiving him, I mean. For what he's done."

Fox took a moment.

"No," he replied, surprised by how easily it left him. "I love him,

Papa. I forgave him the moment he came back to me. I would love him still, even if he left me again. I would love him through several lifetimes, I think," Fox determined, resigning himself to the truth, "and I would love him in every world, if he asked."

"Oh," said Death. "Oh."

Then he made a face. "Sounds stupid."

"It is," Fox agreed. "Immensely." If he could make another choice he probably would, but that was never within his purview as a mortal, or as the man that a demigod had so foolishly, self-destructively, and—in the end—truthfully chosen to love.

"So do you want eternity, then?" Death asked him kindly. "I could give it to you, if you wanted."

"No," Fox said, shaking his head. "To be honest, I think it might be overrated."

"Huh," Death said. "Interesting take."

"Yeah," Fox sighed. "I actually . . . don't really want anything. I mean—" He shrugged. "Sure, there are things I might want in the future, but I think I can figure those out for myself, so—"

"Well," Death interrupted, looking pleasantly surprised. "Are you ready to win the game, then?"

"What?" Fox asked, startled. "How?"

"Like this," Death said, and stepped toward him. "I love you, Fox."

Fox blinked. That was it? It seemed so abruptly underwhelming, and at the same time, puzzling beyond comprehension. His godfather accepted him, valued him, *loved him*—the only thing Fox had ever really wanted—and for that to be a loss, it rendered the whole game staggeringly convoluted, and also, impenetrably fucked.

Because it seemed, for a moment, that his only option was indifference, with no other alternative to circumvent pain. So, to love was to lose? Was that always true? Was it necessarily resigning yourself to something horrible, so rife with cyclical irony that the only ending you could ever achieve for having opened your heart to another being was one that caused pain so invariably, because no matter what happened, for better or worse, its only plausible outcome was loss? The choice was untenable, then, because it wasn't one. If all of this was written, predestined, like living with your hands tied behind your back, then what was even the point? If the only way to win was not to feel, then it seemed very clear that the only way not to lose was never to play. Never, in fact, to live.

So then it was a curse, existence. Life was a death sentence, after all, and even the sweetest of loves would still always end. Fox, a mortal, had never had any other choice but to accept it.

*Although—*

It occurred to him, absurdly, that perhaps there was a flaw in his deduction after all. Because as his godfather never tired of reminding him, Fox was a mortal. He wasn't a very good one, obviously, but he still was one, and perhaps he'd been misunderstanding everything this entire time. He assumed it made him inferior somehow—he'd assumed this whole time that in routinely pointing out his mortality, Death had always intended to belittle him—but he was wrong about that, wasn't he? Mortality wasn't shameful. And it wasn't weakness, because it was what made him different from the others who'd played at these tables only to lose.

Because maybe, Fox thought with a sudden thunderclap of clarity, maybe it *was* a choice. To love, to forgive, to lose, to live—it was always a choice, and thus, the fact that he was a mortal was finally one worth celebrating. Because it *would* end! Maybe that was the entire secret, and therefore the whole thing was actually astonishingly simple. That over and over, he was presented with the same impossible decision—live and suffer, love and grieve—but still, every time, with all his being, his answer was and would always be yes. It would be difficult and painful, and however it ended, it would end—but still, he could choose it. To live, to love; it was always a choice, and inherently a brave one, to face down certain doom with open arms.

Fox D'Mora would never be more invulnerable than the moment he realized that he could feel it all, no matter the costs, and still say yes.

So he did.

"I love you too, Papa," Fox said.

Death smiled.

And then—

"Fox D'Mora has won the Immortal Game," announced Raphael, and slowly, the bright white walls fell away.

# XXIX

## FOREVER IS A GIFT (. . . AND A CURSE)

"You'll have to stay," Raphael said.

"Yes," Gabriel agreed. "Because balance is king."

"Right," Raphael added. "And yes, Volos may be defeated for now—"

"But there's no ridding the world of him entirely," Gabriel concluded. "He is vice, and he is necessary still."

"And even if he weren't," Raphael lamented, "he'd break free soon enough."

"Right," Gabriel agreed, as he often did. "And we can't have him running around unchecked."

"Yes," Raphael said, "because, again, balance is king."

Isis heaved a sigh, folding her arms over her chest.

"You know that if he were here he'd say that Volos is king," she reminded them.

"Sure," Gabriel permitted, "but Isis is queen, isn't she?"

It was—astoundingly, given the archangels' track record—the correct response.

"True," Isis conceded, grudgingly satisfied. "So. Do I have to give this mortal's body back?" she asked, gesturing lasciviously to her human breasts.

"Yes," Raphael confirmed. "Though I'm sure she'll be very happy with what you've done to it, if that helps."

"It appears to have been considerably augmented," added Gabriel supportively.

"Are you hitting on me?" Isis asked.

"What? No." Raphael blanched. "It's just a compliment."

"A creepy one," said Isis.

"There's no need to be rude," Gabriel muttered, wounded.

"Fine," Isis said.

"Also, you could try to be a bit more virtuous," Raphael suggested, which pleased Isis substantially less.

"I'm not the *personification* of virtue," she reminded him. "I'm just the queen of it."

"Fine," Gabriel sighed. "I think you see our point, though."

"Fine," Isis gamely echoed. "Maybe I do." She paused. "And to be honest, I did miss Volos a little. He's sort of entertaining."

"Oh, vastly," Raphael agreed. "But that's the problem, isn't it?"

"I mean, yes, he's the worst," Isis confirmed. "But, you know. In an endearing way."

"Agree to disagree," Gabriel said.

"And anyway, like we said," Raphael reminded her, "balance is king—"

"Yes," Gabriel agreed. "So keep him in check."

Isis tilted her head in contemplation.

"Well. Can I visit Lupo and the others?" she asked.

"You're the demon queen," Raphael said. "You can do whatever you want."

"What's going to happen to them?" she asked.

"Well, they're living in the Parker house now," Gabriel said. "Since nobody's coming back to claim it, I suppose it's theirs permanently."

"Can't imagine the lawyers are having any fun with that," Isis remarked.

"Yeah, well, we're not too fussed about lawyers," Raphael said.

"Aren't you two basically lawyers?"

"We're more like judges," Gabriel corrected, "and I don't know if you noticed, but we're kind of suspect ourselves."

"I did notice, actually," said Isis, rolling her eyes.

— Ω —

"So," Raphael said, "as to the subject of your ledgers—"

"We were not previously aware of the nature of your good deeds on behalf of the godson of Death," Gabriel said, "but that has now been factored in."

"Your service in the afterlife is complete," Raphael concluded.

"You may go," Gabriel agreed.

"Go," Cal echoed. "Go where?"

"On," Raphael supplied.

"To what?" Mayra asked.

"We don't know," Gabriel said.

"We've never actually been there," Raphael admitted.

"We're told it's lovely, though," Gabriel assured them.

"Yes," Raphael agreed, "but again, no actual confirmation, so take that with a grain of salt."

Mayra and Cal exchanged glances.

"Counteroffer," Mayra suggested. "We keep doing what we're doing now, only I get more miracles a year."

"Yes," Cal said, "and we get each other's relics."

"Oh yes, good idea," Mayra agreed, nodding firmly. "Yes, that."

There was a pause.

"I'm sorry," Gabriel said blankly. "What?"

"We like what we do now," Cal said. "You know, helping mankind and all that."

"Yes," Mayra confirmed. "Also, it's very obvious that you've been bribed."

"Oh, immensely obvious," Cal agreed. "There's no way our ledgers evened out. Did you actually see what we've *done* on behalf of Fox?"

"Not too many good things," Mayra said. "He's sort of a little shit."

"Yes," Cal said. "So, we assume Death got to you."

Raphael and Gabriel exchanged glances.

"Yes, fine," Gabriel grudgingly admitted. "Death bargained for your respective retirements."

"Knew it," Mayra said, snapping her fingers. "He's a real pal, Death."

"That's an outrageous thing to say," said Raphael.

"True," Cal said. "But still, the point stands."

"Besides," Mayra said, "we can't go anywhere yet. We still have to keep an eye on Fox, don't we?"

Raphael and Gabriel exchanged another glance.

"You're going to pass on the offer of paradise," Gabriel clarified slowly, "so that you can 'keep an eye' on the godson of Death?"

"Well, he's the master of Death too, now, isn't he?" Mayra asked. "Also, he gets into a lot of trouble."

"Yes," Cal agreed. "He's kind of a handful."

"And we love him," Mayra said. "Inadvisably."

"Very inadvisably," Cal agreed.

"Yes," Mayra said. "So anyway, this seems like a fine compromise."

Raphael sighed.

"Fine," he said. "You may have each other's relics."

"And seven miracles a year," Gabriel permitted.

"Ten," Mayra countered.

"Eight," said Raphael.

"Twelve," Mayra said.

"Can I have some?" asked Cal.

"Fine," Raphael said. "Twelve miracles between the two of you."

Mayra and Cal glanced at each other, wordlessly conferring.

Raphael and Gabriel waited.

"Fifteen," Mayra eventually said, and Raphael groaned.

"Fine," Gabriel growled. "Are we done here?"

Cal Sanna gave Mayra Kaleka one of his five smiles.

(The one, of course, that he reserved just for her.)

"Yes," Mayra agreed. "Yes, I think we are."

— Ω —

"This," Raphael said slowly, frowning, "is quite a ledger."

"You *murdered* someone?" prompted Gabriel from over Raphael's shoulder. "That's just . . . I won't lie, it's not great."

"Well, I ate his heart," Vi said, somewhat sheepishly. "But in my defense, I was hungry, and not entirely in control of my, um, appetite."

"That is an exceptionally poor defense," Raphael informed her.

"Yes, Viola, hush," Tom cut in. "As her representation in this matter, I will hereby speak on my client's behalf."

Vi considered pointing out that Tom would be doing no such thing, but felt under the circumstances that the effort would be wasted.

"Why are you here again?" Raphael asked Tom.

"I'm clearly defending my client," Tom replied. "Aren't you listening?"

"You aren't a lawyer," Gabriel reminded him. "You have an MBA, not a JD, and Death specifically said that all we had to do with either of you was to help you move on."

"Details," Tom demurred, waving a hand. "Anyway, Vi's obviously in trouble, isn't she? So I'm here. And the point is, Viola Marek is a singularly good human being. She cares about others more than anyone I have ever met. She helped me," he added, glancing reassuringly at her, "when there was nothing in it for her."

"She was trying to sell a house," Raphael said.

"She said that over twenty times," Gabriel added, once again eyeing the paperwork.

*"Details,"* Tom emphatically repeated. "Everyone knows she was lying about that." He glanced at her. "It was me she wanted to help. Wasn't it?"

Vi sighed, no longer seeing the benefits to continuing this particular charade.

"Yes," she finally confessed.

Predictably, Tom was undignified in his triumph.

"I knew it," he said, in a tone more appropriately assigned to the message *I was and have always been right about this and also, everything.*

"Stop," Vi replied.

"Anyway," Tom continued, his uncontainable smugness still dominating the atmosphere of the room, "she did everything in her power *not* to give into her impulses, didn't she? It's not her fault she was turned into a vampire," he informed the archangels, "and she shouldn't be punished for incidental damages."

"I'm not entirely confident that you understand criminal law," Raphael said.

"Nobody understands it," Tom countered. "It's the product of political bias!"

Vi looked at him with astonishment. (Either Tom had been listening to her more closely than she suspected, or . . . no, she couldn't quite imagine the alternative. Best to keep listening until a more reasonable conclusion arrived.)

"Still," Gabriel said. "We can't do anything about her ledger being negative."

"I'm still not sure how mine managed to be positive," Tom admitted. "I mean, I had a lot of premarital sex."

"Plus he's a billionaire," muttered Vi, "and a Republican."

"Actually, he's not," said Raphael.

"Not what?" asked Vi, before remembering. "Oh, right. He's *only* a millionaire—"

"Not a Republican," Gabriel corrected. (Tom looked away, apparently overcome by the shame of being outed.)

"Also, we go easier on the sex thing than you think," Raphael continued to Tom, "plus you did a lot of philanthropic work. Hence not being a billionaire," he added to Vi, who had been shockingly unaware of Tom's apparent social conscience.

"Yes," said Tom, still visibly flustered, "but I did those things because I *had* to. Vi's a good person just because she's, you know. *Good*," he said firmly, turning to look at her. "She's the best person," he said quietly, "and I think she deserves to be happy."

Vi blinked, suddenly registering that she hadn't let out a breath in several seconds.

Then she exhaled, slowly.

"I don't mind if I have to work," she contributed, clearing her throat. "Mayra granted me a wish, so I've already had enough divine favors."

"What did you wish for, by the way?" Tom asked, and Vi's cheeks heated slightly.

"You," she said. "Only I didn't know it at the time."

Tom blinked.

"Oh," he said softly, and then she swallowed, meeting his curious gaze as if somehow, hopefully, that might be answer enough.

"You can work it off as an angel if you want," Gabriel offered, interrupting.

"Or a reaper, more likely," Raphael told her.

"What about the other options?" Vi asked, tearing her eyes from Tom's. "Just out of curiosity."

"Well, you could be reincarnated," Raphael said. "With a ledger like this, you could be, hm hm hmm—" He looked down, eyeing a chart that manifested from nothing. "A parrot."

"Could be fun," Tom said optimistically, "but I'm thinking no, right?"

"Yeah, no," Vi agreed. "Being a cat part of the day was fine, but I'd rather not be a perpetual bird."

"You could join Odin," Gabriel said. "Be one of his warriors."

"Eh," said Vi, who was not especially coordinated. "Maybe not that."

"There's that spot in Hades' underworld," Raphael said, frowning in thought. "Just sort of a nothing-zone where Persephone has a garden?"

"I mean, the souls can be loud at night," Gabriel said. "It's not a great neighborhood."

"Certainly not paradise," Raphael agreed.

"But could she really live there?" Tom said. "And, um. Feel?"

"Aren't those the same thing?" Gabriel asked.

"Not really," said Vi.

"Well, in any case, the answer is no, I think," Raphael said. "Afterlife rules and such. Plus you might have to do some odd jobs from time to time, which might be inconvenient."

"Odd jobs?" Vi asked.

"Yeah," Gabriel confirmed. "Feed Cerberus when Persephone's gone, et cetera—"

"Well, who doesn't like dogs?" Tom said.

"Do you have much experience with three-headed ones?" Raphael asked dubiously.

"Meh," Tom replied, shrugging. "It's fine."

"Hang on," Vi said, turning back to Tom. "This is crazy. I'll just—" She glanced over at the archangels, swallowing hard. "I don't know. I'll just work on my ledger however you want me to, and maybe I'll—maybe I'll move on later. And, I don't know, find you. Right?" she asked Tom, whose eyes suddenly went warm, or wet, or something else she was slightly terrified to be wrong about. "It'll be fine," she exhaled. "You don't have to do this, you know. You don't have to defend me, Tom. I'm going to be fine," she repeated, "and you can just move on, and be, I don't know. Happy, I guess. That's all I want," she mumbled, looking down at her hands. "That's all I want."

Tom stared at her, giving her a strange, unreadable look.

And then—

"Yes, actually, I do have to do this," Tom said firmly. "Don't you understand, Vi? Can't you see that—" He groaned. "Hasn't any of this shown you anything at all?" he demanded, rounding sharply on the archangels. "There has to be a place," Tom insisted furiously, brandishing a finger at them. "There *has* to be. Out of all the worlds, there has to be *one*, at least, where Vi can just—" He grimaced. "Just *live*, right?"

Raphael glanced at Gabriel.

Gabriel made a face.

Raphael countered with a head tilt.

Gabriel shook his head.

Raphael pouted.

"Um," said Vi, bewildered. "Sorry, but—"

Gradually, Gabriel sighed, turning back to them.

"Hold on," he said gruffly, and Vi blinked.

— Ω —

When she opened her eyes again, it was to a groggy vision of a far too familiar ceiling.

"Oh *no*," she muttered. "Not this fucking house again."

At that, Sly's face promptly hovered above her.

"Oh good," he said cheerfully. "You're awake."

Vi sat up unsteadily, her head instantly rushing with nausea.

"God, I'm *starving*," she groaned. "What happened?"

"Juice box?" Sly offered, holding it up, and Vi shoved it away, gagging at the smell of it.

"What the—"

"Sly, you know she's mortal again," Louisa chided him, entering the room with an admonishing shake of her head. "You'll have to get her, I don't know. Nachos? Cheese fries? A bar of soap?"

"Pizza," Vi said, blinking. "Pizza would be ideal. Chicago Classic," she added, "well done."

"Ah yes, we call that the 'Queen of Virtue' now," Lupo said, entering the room just as Louisa exited, dialing into her phone. Lupo perched lightly on the bed at Vi's feet, giving her a kindly smile. "How do you feel?"

"Starving. Achy. Excited? Hungry. Angry," Vi said. "No, wait, confused. No, excited again. No, anxious? Sort of like, burdened? And like nothing will ever be right again? Kind of. But also, I don't know, relieved? Or maybe it's—no, sorry," she finally determined, "never mind, it's mostly hunger—"

"That angel friend of yours said it might be this way for a while," Lupo offered apologetically. "It'll take some time to adjust."

"Mayra was here?" Vi asked, surprised.

"She left you this," Sly confirmed, picking up a small scroll. "Said to give it to you when you woke up. She'll be back soon," he added. "She said she wanted to do something about a hurricane in Puerto Rico, but then she'll be right back."

"Huh," Vi said, unrolling the scroll and reading it aloud. "Be kind to a stranger: five points. Forgive a grudge: fifteen points. Wait five seconds before honking when the light changes: one point. Choose to give rather than receive: thr—"

"Is that a sex thing?" Louisa interrupted hopefully, reappearing in the frame. "Eh, probably not. Pizza's on the way," she added, bounding out of the room again.

"Sounds like a list of good deeds," Lupo mused. "Does your ledger need improving?"

"Yes, actually," Vi said, setting the scroll down. "I guess the archangels gave me another chance."

She paused, something swelling uncomfortably in or around her lungs, and Sly frowned.

"What's wrong?" he asked. "You look like you're having some sort of indigestion."

"I think I'm sad, actually," Vi said, gauging the rupture that lived somewhere in her viscera. "Yes," she thought aloud, feeling the thing that was both pain and light, like confessing a truth or breaking a heart. "Yeah, I'm sad."

"Well," she heard from the doorway and jumped. "That just won't do, will it?"

And all at once the sun rose in her chest, warmth reaching her cheeks, her mouth, and confusingly, her vagina.

"Thomas Edward Parker *the fourth*," Vi exhaled at the sight of him, and Tom grinned, loping in from the doorway and falling down beside her on the bed to take her hand in his.

"Actually, Tom Parker's already famously quite dead, so I needed a new persona. I was thinking I could take your name," he suggested. "Tom Marek?"

"That's very progressive of you," Vi said.

"Yeah, well, I've unfortunately been outed," sighed Tom.

"Unfortunately," Vi agreed, pausing to press her free hand to her chest.

"What?" Tom asked, looking concerned at the motion. "What is it?"

"Nothing," she assured him. "It's just that—" She swallowed. "I don't know. Something is—" She broke off, blinking. "Oh shit," she realized, feeling the moisture at her eyes. "Fuck me, I'm crying, I don't—what the—"

"If it's intestinal, it's guilt," Sly advised.

"No, I just think I'm," she attempted, and swallowed. "I'm just so happy that you're here," she exhaled, sheepishly sighing it out, and Tom took her in his arms with his broad, infuriating smile. His dark hair fell briefly into his eyes and Vi brushed it away, feeling the excellent swelling again in her lungs and suffering the euphoric creak in her chest at the feel of him, close and comfortable and real.

"You'll want to leave, boys," Tom called to Lupo and Sly, not bothering to turn around from where he held her. "It's about to get deeply inappropriate in here."

"Well, don't take too long, there's pizza coming," Lupo reminded them as he and Sly shuffled out the door (Sly somewhat less quickly, as if to catch a glimpse of whatever ensued, so that was a conversation to be had). "And if you're going to live here," Lupo added to Tom before he left, "you're going to have to pay us rent, you know."

At that, Tom turned over his shoulder, glaring at him. "This is *my house*," he reminded them, exasperated.

"Nope," Sly countered. "We bought it for seven dollars. It's ours now."

"You can have it," Vi assured them.

"We know," Sly said, winking at her, and then he and Lupo slipped out the door, leaving Vi and Tom alone together.

"So," Vi said, feeling a little itch along her arms; anticipation, she estimated.

No—

*Arousal,* she amended, suddenly registering the feel of Tom's fingers alighting on her arm.

"So," Tom replied.

"What should we do now?" she asked, rendered a little breathless by his closeness.

Tom smiled.

"Well, are you happy with the way things turned out?" he asked her, and she considered it.

"I only ever wanted to be normal," she said. "So yes, I suppose now I finally am."

To her complete lack of surprise, Tom scoffed his disagreement.

"You've never been normal, Viola Marek," he chided her, shaking his head.

"Why," she asked, "because I'm paranormal?"

"Stop," he groaned, reaching out to shove her away, but she caught his hand and ran her thumb slowly over each of his knuckles; tracing the shape of them, traveling the length of them, glorying in the happy of her ever after. (Or, at the very least, her now.)

"You're not normal, Vi," Tom murmured to her, tangling his fingers with hers. "Not even close, and I mean that."

"What else do you mean?" she prompted, and he smiled again; brilliantly this time.

And this time, when he kissed her, she felt everything at once.

— Ω —

"So," Raphael said. "What's our punishment?"

God and Lucifer exchanged glances.

"Nothing," God said.

"Or everything," Lucifer amended.

"Depends how you look at it," God agreed.

"Wait," Gabriel attempted, coughing. "We're not in trouble, then?"

"Oh, you definitely are," God said. "You were bookies for an illegal gambling ring."

"Not ideal," Lucifer commented.

"Definitely not ideal," God agreed.

"Okay," Raphael said slowly. "Sure, but—"

"You'll just have to continue doing your current jobs for all eternity," God suggested, turning to Lucifer. "Right?"

"Right," agreed Lucifer. "That sounds fair."

"Oh," said Gabriel.

"Oh," agreed Raphael.

God and Lucifer nodded.

"Off you go," they said in unison, sending the two archangels back to their void.

# XXX

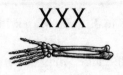

## MASTERS OF DEATH

The moment the game had ended, with Fox and his godfather temporarily parting ways, Fox sought out Brandt where he remained alone in the emptying stadium seats, absently staring into the crowd of newly freed immortals.

"Godling," Fox called to him from down below, lingering only steps away from the table by which he'd won his future.

Brandt blinked at the sound of his summons, then rose slowly to his feet, appearing to briefly hold his breath before descending the coliseum steps toward Fox.

"*Lillegutt*," Brandt returned obligingly, coming to stand beside Fox at the table.

Fox rolled his eyes. "Once again, I'm not a child."

"I know," Brandt agreed. "You're the master of Death now, aren't you?"

They both looked askance at the table.

"I think that's just a technicality," Fox said, "but I appreciate you finally giving me my due."

"Well, you were never just a mortal, Fox," Brandt said, and then blinked, startled.

It was starting, Fox thought.

Again, all over, anew.

Helplessly, his mouth quirked up. "That was a truth, wasn't it?"

Brandt stared at him, confused.

"I shouldn't be able to do that." He touched his hand to his mouth in fear, or awe.

"Well, you can now," Fox informed him with a shrug. "I pulled a few strings."

"Oh," Brandt managed, and swallowed.

They both paused.

"Have you ever noticed how bad the truth tastes?" Brandt asked, soliloquizing as only Brandt could do. "Real truths, I mean. They're so bitter and unpleasant. I'm out of practice, obviously, but still, I think it should be noted somewhere in the minutes that the truth is actually somewhat sour in flavor, and—"

"What do you love more," Fox cut in, having recently realized he didn't have that kind of time. "Me, or vengeance?"

Brandt froze.

Blinked.

Exhaled.

"Well, it's really more like—"

"Restitution, sorry," Fox amended. "Right, careless of me. But still." He swallowed. "I hope it's me," he continued slowly, "because . . ."

He trailed off, raising his wrist, and Brandt blinked.

"The watch," Brandt noted, frowning. "You took it off?"

"Yes," Fox told him. "I don't want forever. I just want—" He stopped. (As Brandt had said, Fox was out of practice. But importantly, he was a quick study.) "I just want one lifetime with you, actually, if I can have it. And if I can't," Fox said, exhaling the hesitations of his past, "then I definitely only want one lifetime, because forever without you seems pretty fucking worthless."

Elsewhere, probably, a twig snapped; a breeze displaced a branch; a bird took flight.

(Life, as it always did, went on.)

Then—

"Band," said Brandt.

Fox blinked.

Then, dutifully, he snapped it.

"Well," Brandt said, clearing his throat. "I take it you agreed to give Time his watch back in exchange for my truths?"

"Yes," Fox said, nodding. "You know how immortals love deals. They're all about their contracts."

"And what if I told you I preferred immortality?" Brandt asked neutrally.

"Then I would still have no regrets," Fox told him. "Which," he added, shrugging, "is what I've recently been assured is the important bit."

Brandt nodded slowly.

"I have been doing this for a long time," he said, after a moment.

"Doing what?" Fox asked.

"Existing," Brandt replied. "Strange to give it up. I'd never considered the prospect of losing my hair," he determined thoughtfully, reaching up to run a hand through it, "or of aging at all, actually."

"Neither had I," Fox agreed. "Not for some time, anyway. But I suppose," he offered genially, "the prospect of it seems acceptable under certain conditions."

"Such as?" asked Brandt.

"Well, if I can do it with you," replied Fox.

Brandt swallowed again, processing this.

And then he reached out, his fingers extending tentatively before they settled around Fox's cheek.

"You will never grow old for me, Fox D'Mora," Brandt promised him, and instantly made a face. "Blech," he coughed up incoherently, extending his tongue. "Tastes *terrible*—"

Fox wanted to laugh; but then he'd gambled so much on one move, he wasn't quite sure he could manage it yet.

"Better make a decision," Fox said, finding his throat suddenly very dry. "I don't have forever anymore, you know."

The scar on Brandt's lip leveled as he smiled.

Then he drew a golden apple from his pocket, eyeing it in his hand.

"Do other apples taste this good, you think?" Brandt asked, drawing it up to his nose and taking a deliberate, careful sniff.

Fox held his breath.

"Well, I suppose I'll find out soon enough," Brandt mused, and shifted to place the apple on the table beside them, centering it right where Fox had defeated Death to win the immortal game.

Fox waited, knowing that whatever Brandt said next could equally bless him or destroy him.

Brandt didn't disappoint him.

"Will you love me, Fox D'Mora," Brandt began, not taking his eyes or his hand from the apple on the table, "for as long as you walk this earth?"

An easy question, much to Fox's relief.

He reached out, catching Brandt's wrist.

"Longer," Fox promised.

And this time, when Brandt kissed him, he didn't pull away.

— Ω —

"Is this really necessary?" Fox asked the archangels. "Neither of us is dead."

"No, you aren't," Raphael said with palpable relief. "So thankfully, you're not currently our problem."

"Still," Gabriel sighed, "we do have to close the inquiries."

"Okay," Brandt charitably allowed. "So then what do you want us to say?"

"That you won't do it again?" Raphael suggested, glancing at Gabriel for confirmation. "Is that right?"

"That's a good start," Gabriel confirmed.

"Hang on," Fox interrupted. "You want us to say we won't get unwillingly dragged into an immortal tournament—*again*?"

"Or is it the whole 'replicating a ledger that ends up getting one or two people killed' thing that's bothering you?" Brandt mused, not looking up from his fingernails.

"Both. Neither," Gabriel said.

"We really don't know," Raphael admitted.

"Though while you're here, we should discuss your ledgers," Gabriel added accusingly. "Do you have any idea how much adultery is on here?"

Fox glanced at Brandt, frowning. "Yours?"

"Yours," Brandt corrected. "Though yes, I had some moments."

"You seduced a married goddess," Raphael reminded him.

"I said I had moments," Brandt replied.

"There's also *unbelievable* amounts of theft—"

"Yours," Fox informed Brandt firmly.

"And yours," Gabriel told Fox.

"Okay, but—less," Fox insisted.

"You're both relatively terrible," Raphael informed them. "Are you sure you want to be mortal? It's going to be a highly questionable life."

"I think we can manage to get it together," Fox assured him.

"And if we don't," Brandt added, "we'll just eventually come here and work for you, won't we?"

Raphael and Gabriel exchanged a grimace.

"Oh," Brandt added. "And by the way, I'm keeping the key."

Gabriel sighed, pinching the bridge of his nose.

"What was your plan, godling?" Raphael demanded. "How did all of this possibly work out so favorably for you?"

"We know for a fact Fortune hates you," Gabriel added.

"Well, in fairness, there were many opportunities for it to go horribly wrong; though, I suppose it was less of a gamble than you might think," Brandt said, glancing at Fox. "I was never going to accept Fox as a prize from Volos, obviously—I'm not stupid."

"There's no point pretending you're innocent, either," Fox informed him, to which Brandt rolled his eyes.

"You," he muttered with a sigh, "don't know the half. Haven't you two figured it out by now?" he prompted, turning to the archangels. "I knew you'd pick a mortal, and I knew that Fox would be the obvious choice to play the game."

"You did no such thing," Raphael scoffed.

"You? Predict our movements? Impossible," Gabriel sniffed.

"Fine," Brandt said, collapsing back in his chair with a shrug. "Then it's a mystery and we'll never know."

"No, don't do that," Fox said with a long-suffering groan. "*I* want answers even if these two don't. You seemed genuinely surprised when you found me at the Parker house," he pointed out, which Brandt acknowledged with a shrug. "Did you know this was going to happen even then?"

Brandt shook his head. "I *was* genuinely surprised to see you so quickly. It had been a possibility, obviously, but I didn't think it would work that fast," he said, before gesturing to the archangels in mock-deference. "I, of course, can't see everything that may or may not come my way, unlike more omniscient present company."

"But then how did you know it would be me they chose?" Fox pressed, as Gabriel and Raphael chose to overlook Brandt's tone of sarcasm in favor of preening beatifically at each other. "Or that I would go with you, after everything? Or that I could even win?"

Brandt sighed. "So many questions, *lillegutt*—"

"Don't," Fox growled, and Brandt laughed; the boundless, limitless laugh of a man who possessed happiness at last.

"Perhaps," Brandt said, turning slowly to face him, "I just had a little faith."

— Ω —

"So that's it, then," Iðunn said sadly, running her fingers across Brandt's final book of everything. "The godson of Death defeated the immortal game, ran away with the son of a god, and now his tale is over?"

"Oh, the story's far from over," Fox assured her, glancing at Brandt, who nodded. "And we can come back to visit you, of course. There doesn't have to be a trade involved."

"That sounds lovely," Iðunn said with a contented sigh. "Well, I'll miss hearing your stories until then, *gudssønn*. I'm afraid I'll be quite lonely without them."

Brandt bent down, brushing his lips gratefully across her cheek.

"I thank you for my youth," he told her, "and for everything you made me see about my world."

"And I," she replied, "thank you for sharing all of it with me." She glanced up, smiling briefly at Fox. "Though I can see now that his world now belongs to you, the master of Death."

"Oh, that's just a story," Fox assured her, managing a smile in return. "I'm just a regular mortal. Nothing special."

"I doubt that very much," Iðunn replied, running her hands over the leather volume. "Is any of it real?" she asked, gesturing to the

worn pages inside before looking up at them, her expression bright
with hope.

"All of the important bits, yes," Brandt said.

"Though some of the dialogue may be misremembered," said
Fox.

Iðunn's lovely smile broadened as she reached out her hand to
Fox, taking his fingers lightly in hers.

"Then go," she told them. "Have your lives together, and may
they be long and full of wonder."

She released his hand, and Fox stepped back to permit Brandt a
more private farewell.

"Was that another of your immortal benedictions?" Brandt asked
quietly, once Fox was out of earshot. "I find those to be something of
a blessing and a curse, you know."

Iðunn laughed her youthful laugh, dousing them both with
beauty.

"No," the goddess replied, her voice warm. "No, *gudssønn,* not
this time. This time," she murmured, "it's just a silly woman's wish."

# XXXI

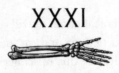

## A WORD FROM OUR SPONSOR

You know something? Fox is right. Only a mortal could have won it.

Not just *any* mortal, obviously, but the game was designed to go on forever by beings who only know how to go on forever, so by extension, only a being who understands how to end could have possibly ended it.

Fucking dizzying, I know.

I won't keep you much longer. I just wanted to say that I started this whole sad episode of mortal tomfoolery with the details of your world, and the Otherworlds, so perhaps now you understand. Or perhaps you don't. It's not your fault. You're not designed to understand everything as I understand it. But still, I thought perhaps you might like to end on a lesson from Fox; though he is not, in any way, an apt role model for anything else. As I've said, I would not recommend him as a friend, or a counselor, or a lover, or basically anything of consequence unless you wish to rob a bank, or commit a heist.

Or, alternatively, win some sort of high-stakes gamble for humanity.

Fox says he's cleaning up his act now, but he's young still (in the scheme of things) and I'm sure he'll slip up again as he continues his wander from world to world. He is, after all, a right little shit, however dearly I may love him, and the godling is no great influence, as I'm sure you've sorted out. I might have chosen someone else for my godson, but as I understand it, that's not my position to undertake, so I suppose I shall simply continue my tasks of undertaking.

(Get it? That's a pun, which I'm told is the height of wordplay.)

While I have you here, though, let me remind you that although Fox D'Mora is technically the master of Death—having bested me, as you know, in an immortal game of wills—that *does not mean* that he keeps a golden lasso tied around my neck, or anything of the sort. Can we rid ourselves of this misconception, please? It's libel. A veritable massacre of my faultless reputation. True, Fox D'Mora is hardly your average mortal; yes, he wears a ring that was made for him by the son of a god, and yes, he *used* to have the relic of an angel and a reaper, and he *once* wore a watch belonging to Time, but that's it. He's gotten very carried away with telling the story; though, again, I attribute that particular flagrance to the godling.

(Writers. They have such an unforgivable tendency for lies.)

In any case, I have a number of things to do, so I'm going to leave you with this: try not to take it personally when I see you again. It's bound to happen, after all, and I'd like to be able to keep it friendly between us, if we can. We're both simply fulfilling our purposes, aren't we? You're a mortal, and I'm Death. It could never have gone any other way.

But, if Fox is to be believed, then it isn't the worst thing to meet an end.

To have lived is, as he tells it, reward enough in itself.

(But, of course, he's full of shit, so—)

(Chances are, he's lying.)

# ACKNOWLEDGMENTS

*January 2018*

The book before you would not exist without a number of people in my life. Special thanks to my mother, for listening to my ramblings about my very, *very* recalcitrant plot; to my godmother, for teaching me about vampires; and to my fathers for endless support, even though I know perfectly well you had no idea what I was talking about. Tine, thank you for helping me craft my Norse godling. Editing credits and eternal love to Aurora (my rant friend and goddess of the dawn), Cynthia (the first person to ever read this book in its entirety), and Sally (my murder pal and bouncy wall): thank you to each of you for helping me clean up my mess.

And, of course, last but not least, a heaping mound of gratitude to my famed illustrator and friend Little Chmura, who is responsible for bringing my characters to life: you are a blessing, and I will never be able to repay you for the beauty you bring to my work.

As for the story, you may have noticed I employed some real locations in Chicago along with some fictional ones. I called the city home for three years, and I found myself attached enough to affectionately alter its history. Some notes on the characters: the Parker family is based on the legacy of Potter Palmer, whose Lake Shore mansion no longer exists, but certainly served as excellent inspiration. The Parker Curse is based loosely on the Kennedy Curse (no demons that I know of, though) while the backstory for Fox is based (also loosely) on the story "Godfather Death" by the Brothers Grimm. (That one doesn't end so well for the godson—just a warning.)

I often say that writing is a lonely process; I am alone right now, actually, drinking a Red Bull (not a sponsored statement, although willing to consider selling out—hit me up, Red Bull) and hoping I didn't make a mess of the characters who swam into my brain and demanded their stories be told. I've been pondering how to put everything I'm feeling into words, and I think it is summed up insufficiently with: thank you. I consider myself a storyteller (an artist, on my good days), and I am nothing without someone to tell the story to. This story means a great deal to me, and I thank you, from the bottom of my heart, for reading it.

If all has gone perfectly to plan, then perhaps I have given you something that stays with you for a while. If everything has gone terribly, then . . . I'll sort that out in the next book.

For now, suffice it to say once more that it has been an honor to put these words down for you. I very much hope you've enjoyed the story.

*September 2022*

As my books continue to be blessed with a second chance at life, I have ever more gratitude to bestow. Enormous thanks to my beloved agent Amelia Appel as well as Dr. Uwe Stender of Triada US. To my incredible team at Tor—my gift of an editor Lindsey Hall and Aislyn Fredsall, my publicists Desirae Friesen and Sarah Reidy, my marketing team Eileen Lawrence, Andrew King, Rachel Taylor, and Emily Mlynek, my production team Jeff LaSala, Rafal Gibek, Jim Kapp, and Michelle Foytek, my publishers Devi Pillai and Lucille Rettino, foreign rights agent Chris Scheina, Christine Jaeger and sales team, audio producer Steve Wagner. On the UK side, thanks to my editor Bella Pagan, to Lucy Hale and Georgia Summers, to my marketing team Ellie Bailey, Claire Evans, Jamie Forrest, Becky Lushey, Lucy Grainger, and Andy Joannou, to my publicity team Hannah Corbett and Jamie-Lee Nardone and Stephen Haskins of Black Crow PR, to my production and editorial team Holly Sheldrake, Sian Chivers, and Rebecca Needes, to sales team Stuart Dwyer, Richard Green, Rory O'Brien, Leanne Williams, Joanna Dawkins, Beth Wentworth, and

Kadie McGinley, the audiobook team Rebecca Lloyd and Molly Robinson.

On the art side of things, huge thanks to cover designer Jamie Stafford-Hill and UK designer Neil Lang, and of course to Little Chmura (@littlechmura) for breathtaking new interior illustrations and to Po (@polarts_) for gorgeous endpapers.

To Garrett and Henry, forever, as many times as I can say it, as profoundly as I can.

And finally, to the bookish social media communities whose love of these books has given me the shot of a lifetime. I won't waste a breath of it. Thank you for letting me tell you a story, and I hope you're enjoying the ride.

xx, Olivie

**Turn the page for a sneak peek**

**of more from Olivie Blake**

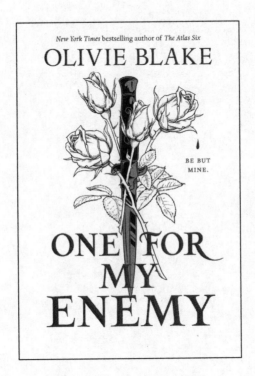

*New York Times* bestselling author of *The Atlas Six*

OLIVIE BLAKE

BE BUT
MINE.

ONE FOR
MY
ENEMY

**Now available from Tor**

# THE PROLOGUE

Many things are not what they appear to be. Some things, though, try harder.

Baba Yaga's Artisan Apothecary was a small store in Lower Manhattan that had excellent (mostly female) Yelp reviews and an appealing, enticing storefront. The sign, itself a bit of a marvel in that it was *not* an elegantly backlit sans serif, carried with it a fanciful sense of whimsy, not unlike the brightly colored bath bombs and luxury serums inside. The words BABA YAGA were written in sprawling script over the carved shape of a mortar and pestle, in an effort to mimic the Old World character herself.

In this case, to say the store was not what it appeared was an understatement.

*I just love it here,* one of the Yelp reviews exclaimed. *The products are all wonderful. The store itself is small and its products change regularly, but all of them are excellent. Duane Reade has more if you're looking for the typical drugstore products, but if you're looking for the perfect handmade scented candle or a unique gift for a friend or coworker, this would be the place to go.*

*The hair and nails supplements made my pitiful strands twice as long in less than a year!* one reviewer crooned. *I swear, this place is magic!*

*Customer service is lovely, which is such a rarity in Manhattan,* one reviewer contributed. *I've never met the owner but her daughters (one or two of which are usually around to answer questions) are just the most beautiful and helpful young women you'll ever meet.*

*The store is never very full,* one reviewer commented blithely, *which is odd, considering it seems to do fairly well . . .*

*This store is an absolute gem,* said another, *and a well-kept secret.*

And it *was* a secret.

A secret within a secret, in fact.

Elsewhere, southeast of Yaga's apothecary on Bowery, there was an antique furniture store called Koschei's. This store, unlike Baba Yaga's, was by appointment only.

*The storefront always looks so cool, but the place is never open,* one reviewer complained, giving the store three stars. *On a whim, I tried calling to arrange a time to see one of the items in the window but couldn't get in touch with anyone for weeks. Finally, a young guy (one of the owner's sons, I believe) brought me in for about twenty minutes, but almost everything in the store was already reserved for private clients. That's fine, obviously, but still, it would have been nice to know in advance. I fell in love with a small vintage chest but was told it wasn't for sale.*

*REALLY EXPENSIVE,* contributed another reviewer. *You're better off going to Ikea or CB2.*

*This store is sort of creepy-looking,* another reviewer added. *There always seem to be weirdos moving things in and out of it, too. All the stuff looks really cool, but the store itself could use a facelift.*

*It's almost like they don't want customers,* groused a more recent review.

And they were right; Koschei did not want customers.

At least, not the kind of customer who was looking for him on Yelp.

# ACT I

## MADNESS MOST DISCREET

*Love is a smoke made with the fume of sighs,*
*Being purg'd, a fire sparkling in lovers' eyes;*
*Being vex'd, a sea nourish'd with loving tears.*
*What is it else? A madness, most discreet,*
*A choking gall, and a preserving sweet.*

Romeo to Benvolio,
*Romeo and Juliet* (Act I, Scene 1)

# I. 1

(Enter the Fedorov Sons.)

The Fedorov sons had a habit of standing like the points of an isosceles triangle.

At the furthest point forward there was Dimitri, the eldest, who was the uncontested heir; the crown prince who'd spent a lifetime serving a dynasty of commerce and fortune. He typically stood with his chin raised, the weight of his invisible crown borne aloft, and had a habit of rolling his shoulders back and baring his chest, unthreatened. After all, who would threaten him? None who wished to live a long life, that was for certain. The line of Dimitri's neck was steady and unflinching, Dimitri himself having never possessed a reason to turn warily over his shoulder. Dimitri Fedorov fixed his gaze on the enemy and let the world carry on at his back.

Behind Dimitri, on his right: the second of the Fedorov brothers, Roman, called Roma. If Dimitri was the Fedorov sun, Roman was the moon in orbit, his dark eyes carving a perimeter of warning around his elder brother. It was enough to make a man step back in hesitation, in disquietude, in fear. Roman had a spine like lightning, footfall like thunder. He was the edge of a sharp, bloodied knife.

Next to Roman stood Lev, the youngest. If his brothers were planetary bodies, Lev was an ocean wave. He was in constant motion, a tide that pulsed and waned. Even now, as he stood behind Dimitri, his fingers curled and uncurled reflexively at his sides, his thumb beating percussively against his thigh. Lev had a keen sense of danger, and he perceived it now, sniffing it out in the air and letting it creep between the sharp blades of his shoulders. It got under his skin, under his bones, and gifted him a shiver.

Lev had a keen sense of danger, and he was certain it had just walked in the room.

"Dimitri Fedorov," the woman said, a name that, from her lips, might have been equally threatening aimed across enemy lines or whispered between silken sheets. "You still know who I am, don't you?"

Lev watched his brother fail to flinch, as always.

"Of course I know you, Marya," Dimitri said. "And you know me, don't you? Even now."

"I certainly thought I did," Marya said.

She was a year older than Dimitri, or so Lev foggily recalled, which would have placed her just over the age of thirty. Flatteringly put, she didn't remotely look it. Up close, Marya Antonova, whom none of the Fedorov brothers had seen since Lev was a child, had retained her set of youthful, pouty lips, as fitting to the Maybelline billboard outside their Tribeca loft as to her expression of measured interest, and the facial geography typically fallen victim to age—lines that might have begun expelling around her eyes or mouth, furrowed valleys that might have emerged along her forehead—had escaped even the subtlest indications of time. Every detail of Marya's appearance, from the tailored lines of her dress to the polished leather of her shoes, had been marked by intention, pressed and spotless and neat, and her dark hair fell in meticulous 1940s waves, landing just below the sharp line of her collarbone.

She removed her coat in yet another episode of deliberation, establishing her dominion over the room and its contents via the simple handing of the garment to the man beside her.

"Ivan," she said to him, "will you hold this while I visit with my old friend Dima?"

"Dima," Dimitri echoed, toying with the endearment as the large man beside Marya Antonova carefully folded her coat over his arm, as fastidious as his employer. "Is this a friendly visit, then, Masha?"

"Depends," Marya replied, unfazed by Dimitri's use of her own diminutive and clearly in no hurry to elaborate. Instead, she indulged a lengthy, scrutinizing glance around the room, her attention skating dismissively over Roman before landing, with some degree of surprise, on Lev.

"My, my," she murmured. "Little Lev has grown, hasn't he?"

There was no doubt that the twist of her coquette's lips, however misleadingly soft, was meant to disparage him.

"I have," Lev warned, but Dimitri held up a hand, calling for silence.

"Sit, Masha." He beckoned, gesturing her to a chair, and she rewarded him with a smile, smoothing down her skirt before settling herself at the chair's edge. Dimitri, meanwhile, took the seat opposite her on the leather sofa, while Roman and Lev, after exchanging a wary glance, each stood behind it, leaving the two heirs to mediate the interests of their respective sides.

Dimitri spoke first. "Can I get you anything?"

"Nothing, thank you," from Marya.

"It's been a while," Dimitri noted.

The brief pause that passed between them was loaded with things neither expressed aloud nor requiring explanation. That time had passed was obvious, even to Lev.

There was a quiet exchange of cleared throats.

"How's Stas?" Dimitri asked casually, or with a tone that might have been casual to some other observer. To Lev, his brother's uneasy small talk was about as ill-fitting as the idea that Marya Antonova would waste her time with the pretense of saccharinity.

"Handsome and well hung, just as he was twelve years ago," Marya replied. She looked up and smiled pointedly at Roman, who slid Lev a discomfiting glance. Stas Maksimov, a Borough witch and apparent subject of discussion, seemed about as out of place in the conversation as the Borough witches ever were. Generally speaking, none of the three Fedorovs ever lent much thought to the Witches' Boroughs at all, considering their father's occupation meant most of them had already been in the family's pocket for decades.

Before Lev could make any sense of it, Marya asked, "How's business, Dima?"

"Ah, come on, Masha," Dimitri sighed, leaning back against the sofa cushions. If she was bothered by the continued use of her childhood name (or by anything at all, really) she didn't show it. "Surely you didn't come all the way here just to talk business, did you?"

She seemed to find the question pleasing, or at least inoffensive. "You're right," she said after a moment. "I didn't come exclusively to *talk* business, no. Ivan." She gestured over her shoulder to her associate. "The package I brought with me, if you would?"

Ivan stepped forward, handing her a slim, neatly packaged rectangle that wouldn't have struck Lev as suspicious in the slightest had it not been handled with such conspicuous care. Marya glanced over it once herself, ascertaining something unknowable, before turning back to Dimitri, extending her slender arm.

Roman twitched forward, about to stop her, but Dimitri held up a hand again, waving Roman away as he leaned forward to accept it.

Dimitri's thumb brushed briefly over Marya's fingers, then retracted.

"What's this?" he asked, eyeing the package, and her smile curled upward.

"A new product," Marya said, as Dimitri slid open the thick parchment to reveal a set of narrow tablets in plastic casing, each one like a vibrantly colored aspirin. "Intended for euphoria. Not unlike our other offerings, but this one is something a bit less delicate; a little sharper than pure delusion. Still, it's a hallucinogen with a hint of . . . *novelty,* if you will. Befitting the nature of our existing products, of course. Branding," she half explained with a shrug. "You know how it goes."

Dimitri eyed the tablet in his hand for a long moment before speaking.

"I don't, actually," he replied, and Lev watched a muscle jump near his brother's jaw; another uncharacteristic twitch of unease, along with the resignation in his tone. "You know Koschei doesn't involve himself in any magical intoxicants unless he's specifically commissioned to do so. This isn't our business."

"Interesting," Marya said softly, "very interesting."

"Is it?"

"Oh, yes, very. In fact, I'm relieved to hear you say that, Dima," Marya said. "You see, I'd heard some things, some very terrible rumors about your family's latest ventures"—Lev blinked, surprised, and glanced at Roman, who replied with a warning head shake—"but if you say this isn't your business, then I'm more than happy to believe you. After all, our two families have so wisely kept to our own lanes in the past, haven't we? Better for everyone that way, I think."

"Yes," Dimitri replied simply, setting the tablets down. "So, is that all, Masha? Just wanted to boast a bit about your mother's latest accomplishments, then?"

"Boast, Dima, really? Never," Marya said. "Though, while I'm here, I'd like you to be the first to try it, of course. Naturally. A show of good faith. I can share my products with you without fear, can't I? If you're to be believed, that is," she mused, daring him to contradict her. "After all, you and I are old friends. Aren't we?"

Dimitri's jaw tightened again; Roman and Lev exchanged another glance. "Masha—"

"*Aren't* we?" Marya repeated, sharper this time, and now, again, Lev saw the look in her eyes he remembered fearing as a young boy; that icy, distant look her gaze had sometimes held on the rare occasions when he'd seen her. She'd clearly learned to conceal her sharper edges with whatever mimicry of innocence she had at her disposal, but that look, unlike her falser faces, could never be disguised. For Lev, it had the same effect as a bird of prey circling overhead.

"Try it, Dima," Marya invited, in a voice that had no exit; no room to refuse. "I presume you know how to consume it?"

"Masha," Dimitri said again, lowering his voice to its most diplomatic iteration. "Masha, be reasonable. Listen to me—"

"Now, Dima," she cut in flatly, the pretense of blithe civility vanishing from the room.

It seemed that, for both of them, the playacting had finally ceased, the consequences of something unsaid dragging the conversation to a sudden détente, and Lev waited impatiently for his brother to refuse. Refusal seemed the preferable choice, and the rational one; Dimitri did not typically partake in intoxicants, after all, and such a thing would have been easy to decline. *Should* have been easy to decline, even, as there was no obvious reason to be afraid.

(No reason, Lev thought grimly, aside from the woman who sat across from them, some invisible threat contained within each of her stiffened hands.)

Eventually, though—to Lev's stifled dismay—Dimitri nodded his assent, taking up a lilac-colored tablet and eyeing it for a moment between his fingers. Beside Lev, Roman twitched forward almost imperceptibly and then forced himself still, dark eyes falling apprehensively on the line of their brother's neck.

"Do it," Marya said, and Dimitri's posture visibly stiffened.

"Masha, give me a chance to explain," he said, voice low with what Lev might have called a plea had he believed his brother capable of pleading. "After everything, don't you owe me that much? I understand you must be angry—"

"Angry? What's to be angry about? Just try it, Dima. What would you possibly have to fear? You already assured me we were friends, didn't you?"

The words, paired with a smile so false it was really more of a grimace, rang with causticity from Marya's tongue. Dimitri's mouth opened, hesitation catching in his throat, and Marya leaned forward. "Didn't you?" she repeated, and this time, Dimitri openly flinched.

"Perhaps you should go," Lev blurted thoughtlessly, stepping forward from his position flanking his brother behind the sofa, and at that, Marya looked up, her gaze falling curiously on him as she proceeded to rapidly morph and change, resuming her sweeter disposition as if just recalling Lev's presence in the room.

"You know, Dima," she said, eyes still inescapably on Lev, "if the Fedorov brothers are anything like the Antonova sisters, then it would be very wrong of me to not reward them equally for our *friendship*. Perhaps we should include Lev and Roma in this," she mused, slowly returning her gaze to Dimitri's, "don't you think?"

"No," Dimitri said, so firmly it halted Lev in place. "No, they have nothing to do with this. Stay back," he said to Lev, turning around to deliver the message clearly. "Stay where you are, Lev. Roma, keep him there," he commanded in his deepened crownprince voice, and Roman nodded, cutting Lev a cautioning glare.

"Dima," Lev said, senses all but flaring with danger now. "Dima, really, you don't have to—"

"Quiet," Marya said, and then, save for her voice, the room fell absent of sound. "You assured me," she said, eyes locked on Dimitri's now. It was clear that, for her, no other person of consequence existed in the room. "Spare me the indignity of recounting the reasons we both know you'll do as I ask."

Dimitri looked at her, and she back at him.

And then, slowly, Dimitri resigned himself to parting his lips, placing the tablet on the center of his tongue, and tilting his head back to swallow as Lev let out a shout no one could hear.

"It's a new product, as I said," Marya informed the room, brushing off her skirt. "Nothing any different from what will eventually come to market. The interesting thing, though, about our intoxicants," she said, observing with quiet indifference as Dimitri shook himself slightly, dazed, "is that there are certain prerequisites for enjoyment. Obviously we have to build in some sort of precautionary measures to be certain who we're dealing with, so there are some possible side effects. Thieves, for example," she murmured softly, her eyes still on Dimitri's face, "will suffer some unsavory reactions. Liars, too. In fact, anyone who touches our products without the exchange of currency from an Antonova witch's hands will find them . . . slightly less pleasant to consume."

Dimitri raised a hand to his mouth, retching sharply into his palm for several seconds. After a moment spent collecting himself, he lifted his head with as much composure as he could muster, shakily dragging the back of his hand across his nose.

A bit of blood leaked out, smearing across the knuckle of his index finger.

"Understandably, our dealers wish to partake at times, so to protect them, we give them a charm they wear in secret. Of course, you likely wouldn't know that," Marya remarked, still narrating something with a relevance Lev failed to grasp. "Trade secret, isn't it? That it's quite dangerous to try to sell our products without our express permission, I mean. Wouldn't want someone to know that in advance, obviously, or our system would very well collapse."

Dimitri coughed again, the reverberation of it still silent. Steadily, blood began to pour freely from his nose, dripping into his hands and coating them in a viscous, muddied scarlet streaked with black. He sputtered without a sound, struggling to keep fluid from dripping into his throat while his chest wrenched with coughs.

"We have a number of informants, you know. They're very clever, and very well concealed. Unfortunately, according to one of them, *someone*," Marya murmured, "has been selling our intoxicants. Buying them from us, actually, and then turning around to sell them at nearly quadruple the price. Who would do that, I wonder, Dima?"

Dimitri choked out a word that might have been Marya's name, falling forward onto his hands and knees and colliding with the floor. He convulsed once, then twice, hitting his head on the corner of the table and stumbling, and Lev called out to his brother with dismay, the sound of it still lost to the effects of Marya's spell. She was the better witch by far—their father had always said so, speaking of Marya Antonova even from her youth as if she were some sort of Old World demon, the kind of villainess children were warned to look for in the dark. Still, Lev rushed forward, panicked, only to feel his brother Roman's iron grip at the back of his collar, pinning him in place as Dimitri struggled to rise and then collapsed forward again, blood pooling beneath his cheek where he'd fallen to the floor.

"This hurts me, Dima, it really does," Marya sighed, expressionless. "I really did think we were friends, you know. I certainly thought you could be trusted. You were always so upstanding when we were children—and yes, true, a lot can happen in a decade, but still, I really never thought we'd be . . . *here*." She sighed again, shaking her head. "It pains me, truly, as much as it pains you. Though perhaps that's insensitive of me," she amended softly, watching Dimitri gasp for air; her gaze never dropped, not even when he began to jerk in violent tremors. "Since it does seem to be paining you a great deal."

Lev felt his brother's name tear from his lungs again, the pain of it raking at his throat until finally, finally, Dimitri fell rigidly still. By then, the whole scene was like a portrait, gruesomely Baroque; from the crumpled malformation of his torso, one of Dimitri's arms was left outstretched, his fingers unfurled toward Marya's feet.

"Well," exhaled Marya, rising from the chair. "I suppose that's that. Ivan, my coat, please?"

At last, with their brother's orders fulfilled, Roman released Lev, who in turn flung himself toward Dimitri. Roman looked on, helpless and tensed, as Lev checked for a pulse, frantically layering spells to keep what was left of his brother's blood unspilled, to compel his princely lungs to motion. Dimitri's breathing was shallow, the effort of his chest rapidly fading, and in a moment of hopelessness, Lev looked blearily up at Marya, who was pulling on a pair of black leather gloves.

"Why?" he choked out, abandoning the effort of forethought.

He hadn't even bothered with surprise that his voice had finally been granted to him, and she, similarly, spared none at the question, carefully removing a smudge from her oversized sunglasses before replacing them on her face.

"Tell Koschei that Baba Yaga sends her love," she said simply.

Translation: *Your move.*

Then Marya Antonova turned, beckoning Ivan along with her, and let the door slam in her wake.